TELL

ME

NO

LIES

ANDREA CONTOS

Published in the UK by Scholastic, 2022
1 London Bridge, London, SE1 9BA
Scholastic Ireland, 89E Lagan Road, Dublin Industrial Estate, Glasnevin,
Dublin, D11 HP5F

SCHOLASTIC and associated logos are trademarks and/or
registered trademarks of Scholastic Inc.

First published in the US by Scholastic Inc, 2022

ISBN 978 0702 32327 0

A CIP catalogue record for this book is available from the British Library.

Printed by CPI Group (UK), Croydon, CR0 4YY
Paper made from wood grown in sustainable forests and
other controlled sources.

1 3 5 7 9 10 8 6 4 2

www.scholastic.co.uk

Book design by Maeve Norton

TO STEPHANIE, ELIZABETH, AND SAMUEL: THE SUNFLOWERS TO MY POTATO.

CHAPTER ONE
NORA

This is my confession.

Or as much of it as I can give. There are moments, and then moments built upon other moments, that no longer exist in my head. Spaces of time I can no longer fill with memories. Instead, I'm left with blank spots that I tell myself are unimportant—small parts unneeded to re-create the whole.

But I know that's not true. I know they're some of the most necessary pieces.

And I suppose, if I intend for this to serve as my full account, I should start at the beginning.

It's not where anyone thinks it is.

It didn't start with Garrett Packard's disappearance. It didn't start with the party he was last seen at. And it didn't start when Garrett began dating my sister.

It started in Mrs. Porter's office with a matching pair of essays.

It started with *my* essay printed with Garrett Packard's name at the top.

Could we explain this? Mrs. Porter asked, as if the explanation wasn't horrifyingly obvious. Garrett didn't even belong in AP classes. He barely deserved to be passing standard-level courses, given his intellect (as verified by *me* in literally every conversation we'd ever had).

And yet, Garrett *was* in AP classes and had done well enough to find his way into the top 5 percent of our class. A mystery.

Even so, had it been anyone else standing shoulder to shoulder with Garrett that day, our identical essays with bold red question marks slashed over their headings, I might've understood Mrs. Porter's need to ask for an explanation.

But it wasn't anyone else. It was me. And never in my life have I had to *cheat*. Certainly, if I *were* to cheat, it wouldn't have been off the likes of Garrett Packard. He once insisted narwhals were mythical creatures (even after being shown proof) and thinks the Oxford comma is—and I quote—"too much extra work."

Perhaps I should've been more deferential. Things may have turned out differently had I apologized to Mrs. Porter, told her I had no earthly clue how *Garrett Packard* and I just so happened to produce the exact same essay.

It's possible that letting the anger that filled my chest and crawled toward my cheeks govern my response was *not*, ultimately, in my best interest.

As best as I can recall, I crossed my arms, and the reply that sprang from my mouth was "I don't have to explain myself to you."

Mrs. Porter was under the impression I did.

Consequently, I found myself in the office of one Wilbur G. Wentville, Birmingdale High's esteemed principal.

I say "esteemed" with extreme sarcasm. And not just because he had a penchant for wearing short-sleeved button-down shirts with ties.

Mr. Wentville could've made the right decision. He could've looked at the pair standing before him—that would be me and Garrett—and known instantaneously who was to blame. Instead, he vacillated.

Why? Likely because this little conundrum placed him in a very difficult position. Should he malign my name? By my junior year, I'd been in contention for admission to Brown—the school I'd set my path toward from the moment I understood college existed.

My record was impeccable. I ran the debate club, served as student body president. I took the highest-level courses and did regular volunteer work in the community.

The girl who appeared on the Birmingdale home page, smiling and organizing mock presidential elections, caring for abandoned animals at the shelter? That was me.

But Garrett Packard was only a sophomore when he became Birmingdale's star quarterback. Honorary son of every alum who never could decipher how to leave their hometown behind. The ones who packed the stands and made generous donations to ensure the sports program never suffered from tragic fates such as: a lack of merch featuring our mascot—the highly-unfortunately-named Stuey Stallion—or players having to *gasp* wear the same helmets as last year.

Praise be to the football gods.

All of this meant Principal Wentville would create an enemy no matter what his decision. And so, as weak men are wont to do, he refused to.

Instead, he ordered us to rewrite our essays.

In detention.

In detention, together.

It wasn't a matter of whether I was capable of such a thing. Of course I was. It was the injustice of it.

Even more than that, it was the inefficiency.

I'd completed that assignment and cleared it from my mental

task list. To redo it would be a duplication of effort for no benefit aside from placation of Principal Wentville's demands, which were born out of Principal Wentville's utter lack of spine, which in turn made my cooperation an act of aiding and abetting an act of cowardice. And the strike on my record? Unacceptable.

I had a *plan*. By age nine, I'd decided what my life would look like, and I *committed* to making it happen. Undergraduate at Brown. Ace the LSAT. Law school at Stanford. Absolutely crush the MPRE—honestly, an ethics exam? I excel in ethics. For instance, I know that stealing someone else's paper is wrong. And then, of course, is the bar exam, which only 60 percent of applicants pass.

I remain unbothered by that statistic. Odds have no better chance of stopping me than anything else.

And aside from one lapse—which I've vowed to never let happen again—there have been no deviations from the plan. And I was not about to let Garrett Packard force me to break my vow.

My fingers ached with the force with which I gripped the arms of the chair, all the words in my head assembling themselves into proper order so that I could put a quick and efficient end to the nonsense of the last twenty minutes, but then.

But then I took the briefest of seconds to survey Garrett. He'd undoubtedly support my rejection of Principal Wentville's ruling. How could he not? Limited intellect or not, Garrett Packard would have to be disgruntled by the implication he may have cheated. Whether I valued it or not, he *did* have a reputation to uphold. College scouts tended to take umbrage with cheating.

But it wasn't anger I saw on Garrett's face. His face, in fact, held no expression at all.

Curious.

More so, a thin veil of sweat graced the edges of his hairline, and when his eyes met mine, it was only fear that lingered there.

I wonder now, knowing what I know, if I should've taken pity on him in that moment.

Obviously, we both knew the truth: Garrett had used his relationship with Sophie to gain access to my essay.

He'd likely showered her with enough compliments to fill her self-esteem to the brim, leave her so drunk on them she wouldn't question when he left the room, disappearing a little too long. So she'd ignore that feeling that told her he wasn't quite as honest as he claimed.

Back when Sophie and I were little—two tiny blondes only a year apart—inseparable, our bond unflappable, wearing matching skinned knees and a history so tightly wound it seemed one had never existed without the other—people used to refer to us as The Linden Sisters.

We weren't Nora and Sophie. What use was it to call to us separately when we always came together?

I don't recall when that changed. When my blond turned dark and my thoughts peeled free. When existing as a single being began to feel like a noose fitted around my neck.

And so I tore at the bonds that joined us, rubbed at the threads until they frayed. When Sophie clung harder, I pulled further away, until we became Nora and Sophie and the world couldn't recall a time we'd ever been simply The Linden Sisters.

For that, I'm not sure she's ever forgiven me. But that was the role I was tasked with filling. From my earliest memories, my mother was there, telling me there was no time for tears. Sophie was the one who cried. I was the one who was strong.

Be strong, Nora. It's my mom's voice I hear whenever emotion grips me. It was her voice I heard then, telling me to let Sophie go.

So I did. Even if Sophie didn't understand why. And I'm not sure she's ever filled the place I used to inhabit.

Ergo, her relationship with Garrett Packard is, at least in part, my fault. Despite everything, I'm the big sister. My job, as my parents used to say, is to look out for Sophie.

But what Sophie will never admit is that I freed her too. All the best parts of her—her infectious joy, her spontaneous spirit, the magnetic draw she holds over every room she enters—I would've drowned them all.

I *did* look out for her. I did the thing she couldn't, and I did it for her, perhaps even more than for myself.

And that's what stopped me from pitying Garrett that day. Because, you see, it would always be my job to look out for Sophie, and if Garrett Packard had something to hide, he was a threat.

Sitting there, eyes locked with Garrett, his so pleading I swore the hammer of his heartbeat pulsed through them—that was the precise moment I vowed to figure out why.

Why Garrett was scared. Why he was suddenly so desperate he'd steal an essay that was sure to get him caught.

That was the precise moment I decided to find all of Garrett Packard's secrets.

CHAPTER TWO
SOPHIE

I miss the girl I used to be.

The one who knew who she was. Sophie Linden. The dancer. Garrett's girlfriend. The popular one. Friend to everyone.

Well. Almost everyone.

But then Garrett disappeared and all those parts of me went with him, the ground beneath me fracturing and splitting wide, forcing me to choose which side to jump to. Now all the pieces that included Garrett are smashed into dust far below, and I'm standing alone, with nothing but emptiness in my sight. Sophie Linden. The dancer. And nothing more.

I know exactly how pathetic that makes me. My whole world demolished by the absence of one person. Hardly a feminist icon. Definitely not something I'll admit to my biographer when they chronicle my dance career one day.

But it's hard to move on when you're constantly reminded of everything you don't know about your boyfriend's disappearance because there's a walking, talking reminder that lives in your house, sleeps in the room next door, and, despite being your *sister*, won't say a word to you about it.

Actually, not true. She says words. She says Nora-words. She says, "Honestly, Sophie, you and your overactive imagination," after I told her I saw her at the Halloween party. And when I told her I *didn't* imagine it and I *recognized* her, she said, "I assume you'd been drinking? You probably wouldn't have recognized *yourself*," and okay, that happened *one time* but there was Jägermeister involved and I never made that mistake again.

I know what I saw. Even if that's not what I told the cops.

Skinny arms wrap around my shoulders and squeeze tight, the momentum of Isa's hug nearly toppling us both to the dance studio's marley flooring.

"You coming to my house to get ready?" Her voice is way too chipper, like forced happiness will make us both forget that Garrett's been missing for a month today.

"Yep. Just need to run home and shower first."

I don't even know why I'm going. Or what I'm going to do once I'm there. The last party I went to ended with me and Garrett fighting. It was the last time I saw him. And our last words were not good ones.

I shouldn't go. But Mom is starting to give me that look. The one that says she's going to start asking questions, and right now my biggest goal is to keep my shit together and keep myself out of trouble. Thanks to a little incident after Garrett left (it involved Jessica Horton and I don't regret it), I am on the shortest of ropes. Mom threatened to not let me go to the summer dance intensive in NYC that I've been planning for nearly a year if I didn't "shape up and fly right."

Those are literal words she used. Like someone's ornery grandpa. And then she stormed out the door to go to work.

Seconds later, she popped her head back in to add that if I breathed a word to Dad about what happened, I wouldn't be going then either.

He knows about the intensive. Of course he does. He's paying for it. All his "I left you all for my secretary" guilt means he writes the checks when he needs to. Mom just doesn't want him knowing the bad stuff because it makes *her* look like she's failing as a parent.

Shape up. Fly right. Go to the intensive, impress Olivia Winstein so I can spend my senior year at the University Arts Conservatory.

All I need to do is be exactly like Nora.

It's like I'm set up for failure.

And if I fail, I'll be exactly like Mom. Stuck in the same city I grew up in, dreaming of the life I could've had while ignoring the one I'm in.

I pull the ribbons from my pointe shoes until they flutter to the floor, and Isa shoves them into my bag. "Charla can't come."

"What? Why?" It's always me, Isa, and Charla. It's not the same without all three of us. Mostly. Far less lately.

"She's sick." Isa stares at me and sighs. "We don't have to go."

"I want to go." I sort of want to go.

"No, you don't."

I yank my hoodie over my head and stand. "I'm going. *We're* going."

Isa glares, her dark eyes narrowed, and she shakes her fist at me. "Sophie Linden. I swear to god."

"Isadora Moreno." I fail to match her level of intimidating.

If we were texting, this would be the point she'd send me the picture of herself where she's holding a slipper next to her face like she's going to throw it at my head.

Because I am *me* and Isa is Isa, she sends me the la chancla picture often.

I jam my hand into my bag and feel for my keys. Nora would keep them in one of the pockets so they'd always be easy to find. "I want to go. I do. It's just . . ."

"The Stans."

"The Stans." Most notably, the aforementioned Jessica Horton.

I didn't think it was possible for people to idolize Garrett more than they did when he was the star quarterback, junior prom king, and all-around sun at the center of Birmingdale High's orbit, but then he vanished and, somehow, their fanaticism multiplied. Exponentially.

And thus emerged The Stans—a group of diehards who worship Garrett's memory and hate me for having any place in it. Some of them are convinced it's my fault.

Because the truth is, no one *really* knows what happened to Garrett. Despite all the police, the private investigators his parents hired, and even The Stans re-creating his every breathing moment, no one can say for sure whether he's missing or exactly where he wants to be.

That hasn't stopped them from trying to bring him back—in the most pathetic ways possible.

Like if only we could mount enough photo collages of him to the school's walls and get #ComeHomeGarrett trending, he'd forget why he ever wanted to leave.

My fingers land on a slip of paper, and I pull it free. It's crinkled, covered in Mom's handwriting—a grocery list she carefully wrote for me that I likely promised to take care of and never did.

I unzip the bag wider and peer inside, shoving aside tights, leos, easily a year's worth of hair ties and bun holders, but no keys.

"Did you lose them?" Isa doesn't say "again," but she means it.

"No." I grab a bundle of bobby pins that have graciously piled themselves together and shove them in a pocket.

"Mm-hmm." She backs away, smiling, but with that look that says she doesn't believe me.

"Where are you going?"

"I'm gonna check your coat pockets."

"They're not in my coat pockets. I put them *in my bag.*" I glance up as she takes another step back. "Isa. Isa!"

She darts through the door, narrowly missing the jazz shoe I fling at her head, and I turn my bag upside down, shaking everything into a pile so I can find my keys. I need to prove I didn't lose them before she gets back so I can make her admit defeat.

I paw through the pile, but my keys are nowhere, even though I know I put them in there. I *know*.

But then all thoughts of keys get sucked from my head. All thoughts of anything. Because I'm staring at a different piece of paper now. Different handwriting too.

The corner pokes against my finger, the paper shaking in my grip. Garrett's handwriting slashes across the page: *I've missed you, babe.*

Sweat blooms over my skin, my leo too tight, too constricting, so I can't suck in a full breath.

My thoughts fight against themselves, each of them pushing to the forefront.

I don't remember him giving me this. I haven't cleaned this bag in forever—maybe I just missed it before.

No, the paper is too new, too crisp. It's been a month.

I want to hope. To convince myself this means something. But it doesn't make sense, the idea that Garrett returned just to put notes in my dance bag. That's not Garrett's way.

But it's not like leaving in the dead of night was Garrett's way either. The way he acted that night—worried, *scared*—that definitely wasn't Garrett's way.

The note shakes in my hand, the words blurring through a veil of tears. I want him here with a desperation that sinks into my bones, stealing all other thoughts in my head. Having him back would be like the world righting itself and the weight of not knowing where Garrett is, whether he's okay, whether I helped drive him from my life or someone left him no choice, all of that would be gone.

I'd be Sophie Linden, and I'd be all the things I'm supposed to be.

I scramble for my phone, but there are no calls from Garrett. No texts.

It's Garrett's handwriting. I know it is. But it's been a *month* and all I get is a note I may not even have found?

My hand fists around the paper, crushing it until it's nothing but a tiny wad, and I gather the note from Mom and race to throw them both in the trash.

It's gone now. Forgotten. Just like Garrett.

I immediately pull it from the trash and try (fail) to smooth the wrinkles against my leg, white paper stark against pink tights. Maybe it's nothing. Or maybe it's everything.

Isa appears in the doorway, and I yelp, which earns me a raised eyebrow.

I rub my arms, breathing deep, letting the familiar scents of the studio comfort me—hairspray and wood barres, perfume and sweat. "I didn't find them."

Isa smiles, mercifully ignoring my jumpiness. "That's because I did."

She holds up the keys that I most definitely did *not* put in my jacket pocket, and I snatch them from her hand. "You win this time."

"Every time. Pick you up in two hours."

And then she's gone, leaving me to sort my shit out all by myself. That never goes well.

Five minutes later, I'm headed to my car, bag swinging behind me and smacking against my hip with each step, but I stop just inside the door and scan the lot.

It's empty. Of course it's empty. Garrett isn't waiting for me, a bouquet of flowers clutched in his hands to show how much he's missed me.

He's not in the bushes either. I check.

Garrett is *gone*. It's better if I believe that.

He's gone because he wants to be. And Garrett doesn't change his mind.

The Stans, his parents, randos who only knew him from two-minute conversations in the hallways, they can have their opinions, but I knew him. And that alone means I know more than anyone. All they have is conjecture.

And I know what he said to me that night. I know that he asked me to leave with him. I didn't think he was serious. Not really. I should've asked more questions. Cared enough to ask more questions. Garrett has never been a dreamer—running away together in the middle of high school was a level of fantasy even I couldn't imagine. But I know he was scared. And I know he wouldn't tell me why.

The only facts no one can dispute are that two days before no one ever saw him again, he withdrew ten grand from his savings, and the note they found in his car was verified by handwriting experts to be from him.

Hey Mom and Dad,
I need to find my own way.
Love,
Garrett

You know who didn't get a note? Or a phone call? Or even a hint that "his own way" did not include his long-term girlfriend?

Me.

He asked me to go, and I said no. He left anyway. He left me to carry the weight of who we once were, and I'm not sure how much longer I can. Some days it feels like I'm not even just Sophie Linden, the dancer, anymore—I'm just a reminder of what's been lost.

And all the people who believe Garrett is actually missing, that some terrible fate found him that night, also believe there's something I'm not saying. Some huge secret I'm hiding that could mean the entire difference in finding him.

And the truth about *that* is, they're right.

CHAPTER THREE
NORA

I found myself alone in Principal Wentville's office. How, I can't quite bring myself to recall.

But I do remember this—the moment he left the room with Garrett, I sprang from my seat.

It's an odd thing, who people choose to place their trust in. None of us deserve it any more than the rest. And yet, I'd been deemed trustworthy.

Should Wentville have left me alone in his office, with full access to whatever systems he may be logged in to? Of course not. Foolish of him.

For me, quite convenient.

A breeze streamed through the open window, ruffling the papers strewn over Wentville's office and driving goose bumps up my arms, infiltrating the stuffy room with the notes of magnolias and rare October rain. On days like today, the ocean seemed to carry inland, lacing every breath with salt water and sand.

But as it usually did, the rain retreated and the emergent sun snuck past the edges of the window shades, glaring against the computer screen, where my answers lay.

I slid into Wentville's chair, still warm from his body.

Very distressing.

I wiggled his mouse to bring the screen to life as his voice, mingled with Garrett's, drifted from the hall. Wentville sounded conciliatory, as if this decision had been forced on him from some higher power. As if this entire disaster wasn't Garrett's fault.

Window after window filled the computer screen. Various documents in various states of revision, an email account with far too many unread, internet browsers I didn't view for fear of what Principal Wentville may be googling, and, lastly, exactly what I needed.

The school's management system stared back at me, Amber Donahue's grades splashed across the screen. Suffice it to say, Amber would not be challenging anyone for valedictorian this year.

The keys clicked beneath my fingers as I typed in Garrett's name, and I held my breath as the voices outside the door grew louder.

Garrett, it seemed, was losing his cool—in plain view of anyone who might walk into the main office.

There are few things one could argue that Garrett and I share, but a desire to protect our reputations may have been the singular exception. And I, for one, would *not* be making a spectacle of myself in the main office, unless I were very, *very* distraught.

As Garrett's file loaded on the screen, things began to make more sense.

He was struggling. Not horribly so. Not anything that would not be reparable for the average student. But Garrett wasn't supposed to be average.

Maybe that was another thing we shared.

Shouts rang out behind me, and I'm embarrassed to admit I jumped. If Wentville reentered the office, not even *I* could concoct an excuse that would spare me immediate expulsion. But it was just kids heading to lunch on the plaza outside the window, where I should be, if not for Garrett Packard. The dishonorable bastard.

I scanned through the other tabs on Garrett's record, but there was nothing of note. What I had was enough though.

Something had happened to Garrett. Something that had caused his grades to slip. Something that led him to cheating.

I typed Amber's name, leaving the system exactly how I found it, because I had no intention of giving Principal Wentville a reason to lose his misplaced faith in me.

The door handle turned, and I sprung from Wentville's chair, slipping into my own just as he lumbered into the room. He wore cuff links with khaki cargo pants. Tragic.

He smoothed his tie and collapsed into his seat. His upper lip glistened, as if he'd run several laps around the track rather than engaged in a simple conversation.

Spineless.

He sighed. "Now, Ms. Linden, I know . . ."

He didn't actually trail off, he just said nothing of note or interest, and since this is my confession, I choose not to waste my time recounting it.

Certainly, he expected me to protest his decision. As defeated as he looked, I may have been able to persuade him, but I had different goals now.

Still, I let him fidget, awaiting my response, dreading the arguments I'd make for which he had no rebuttal.

Instead, I said simply, "You know that was my essay."

He sighed again, louder this time. "I hope you understand the position I've been put in, Ms. Linden."

I understood, perhaps better than he may have imagined.

I gathered my things and stood. "And I hope, Principal Wentville, when I've done what's necessary, that you take responsibility for the one you've put *me* in."

CHAPTER FOUR
NORA

It was very unbecoming, the sweat building on Garrett's temple.

Sophie didn't seem to mind. She placed the back of her hand to his slimy forehead, checking his temperature, ever the doting girlfriend, worried for his well-being.

She smiled up at him and he tried to return it, but his eyes kept drifting to the left. To me.

I stood well down the hall, far enough that Sophie wouldn't notice me. I didn't want Sophie to know about Garrett stealing my paper. I sincerely doubted Garrett wanted her to know either.

I, of course, had no plan to tell him we shared such a preference. I'd never seen Garrett that unmoored, and I doubted it would last long. That meant striking quickly.

I waited several more minutes, while Sophie tried to cajole him into leaving school with her, probably to go sit in a park somewhere before dance practice, naming the clouds as they stretch and morph themselves into identifiable creatures. We used to do that. Once.

But Garrett can't, he said. Team meeting. He's sorry.

A terrible lie. So easily refuted.

Sophie frowned, and genuine regret shone in his eyes. He cared about her, maybe more than he wanted to. Sophie drew that out of people. Blink and your heart is on the outside, cradled in her hands.

It was that ability—more accurately, the entire essence of what made Sophie who she was—that drove us apart. Just as much as it was my essence that did the same.

Sophie never lacked for attention—an endless stream of playdate and birthday party invitations from the moment she entered pre-kindergarten. Piles of crudely drawn stick-figure characters showing Sophie holding hands with this classmate or that, claiming she was their "BFF," stuffed into her tiny backpack each day.

It wasn't until many years later, when I found my parents attempting to disguise her social calendar so as not to upset me (unnecessary) while simultaneously suggesting I keep quiet about my own accomplishments to diminish Sophie's feelings of inferiority, that I realized the truth: We held each other back.

Each in our own separate ways, our bond—an inseparable, indestructible link that we'd both clung to—had kept us still, rooted where we were, each of us pulling in opposite directions but never gaining an inch, unable to chase the versions of ourselves we were meant to be.

I did what she couldn't have—I broke both our hearts and let the rest of the world share her.

I won't admit how many moments I've wished I hadn't.

I hid behind a group of band members as Sophie left Garrett's side to bounce down the hall, arms linked with her friends, and Garrett headed toward me, all alone.

He grasped my elbow, fingers driving into my muscle like all his frustration was directed to that one point, and he steered me around.

I did not appreciate his attempt at dominance.

I locked my legs, dug in my heels, and he stumbled forward, confusion giving way to shock.

How many people did Garrett Packard steer in the direction of his choosing each day? Likely many.

He paused, stared down at me as if trying to study me, an aberration, an annoyance that resisted molding itself to his world, his way.

He dropped my elbow, his narrowed eyes never leaving mine, and offered a conciliatory sweep of his arm, like I was to lead the way.

I did, resisting the need to shake my arm to release the tingles that shot straight to my fingertips.

He scanned the throngs of students milling past us, eyes darting, like he was afraid the wrong person might see us together, before bending low, murmuring in my ear, "You can't tell Sophie."

A demand. How thoroughly expected. "I *can* actually. I—"

"Nora." He grabbed my arm again to stop me and released it just as quickly. Perhaps a quick learner after all. "Nora, please."

Please. My, my. How he doth surprise.

I continued toward the library, where we were to serve day one of our detention sentence, and Garrett followed, all his frightened, trembling energy washing over me.

I let him suffer, drowned his angst with the chorus of slammed lockers, raucous laughter, shoes squeaking against shined tiled flooring, until we entered the hush of the library.

I loved it there—not as much as the actual library, where the soft scent of decades-old paper isn't overlaid with stale coffee left behind by students, but it's still a refuge.

Quiet in the chaos.

It's always been a mystery, why people feel wanting solitude is indicative of a personality flaw. Perhaps those who never want to be alone are simply too afraid of what their own thoughts might reveal to them.

I dropped my bag at a table in the corner, one surrounded by rows of shelving, and Garrett melted into a seat, as if it had taken all his energy to remain upright.

"Don't worry," I whispered. "You're safe here."

It should go without my having to say it, but I was uncertain how much awareness Garrett was capable of at that moment.

He gave me a wan smile and dropped his notebook onto the table.

I understood—loath though I was to admit it—what Sophie saw in him. He was conventionally attractive, charming in an expected sort of way, and he exuded confidence regardless of whether he'd earned it.

Normally, that is.

I settled into a chair across from him so he was forced to look at me. "Why did you steal my paper?"

"I didn't."

"Of course not."

He sighed long-sufferingly, as if I was pestering him with such a trivial matter. "I printed my essay at your house, okay? I must've grabbed yours by accident."

He had the entirety of the walk to the library to ponder a valid excuse, and that's what he presented. "How did your name get at the top?"

He muttered, "Fuck!" and dropped his head into his hands.

"Garrett." I kept my voice soft, comforting even. "We both know the truth. Are you going to be able to write another paper?"

The answer was obviously no—if he were capable of writing that paper, he'd have done it initially, but Garrett said, "Of course," like I'd offended him.

I raised a brow in response, and he swallowed, his face rearranging into something softer, quieter. His voice came out breathy. "Sometimes you look just like her."

I don't enjoy admitting that it shook me a bit, hearing him compare me to Sophie. It was a likeness I thought I'd lost.

Strangers used to ask if we were twins. No one could blame them—our blond hair tangling as our arms roped around each other, green eyes nearly identical except for the slight ring of brown in mine. That was before my hair turned dark. No one mistakes us for twins anymore.

"Nora." The pleading was back in his voice, nearly pathetic and wholly irritating. "Please don't tell Sophie."

The slant of sunlight hit the sharp angle of his cheek, washing him in a hazy glow, highlighting the amber shade of brown in his dark eyes.

I was tempted to feel sorry for him. He seemed so lost, so sad. Just a poor, hapless boy who made a bad choice. I pushed the impulse away. Stealing my paper wasn't some harmless prank, and if my instincts were correct, that was the first of many mistakes for Garrett Packard. Though it was likely one of the first times he'd been held accountable.

It is a largely unacknowledged truth that mistakes are things only white men can make.

"Fine." The second the word left my lips, all the tension seeped from his shoulders, until I added, "On one condition."

"Name it."

"Tell me why you stole my paper."

He sucked in a breath, almost a gasp, and I knew I'd asked the wrong question.

Had I to do it over, I'd have asked why he was so scared.

He was an AP student for as long as I was. He *should've* been able to complete a paper like that with the most basic of effort. Something had happened to throw his world so far out of orbit he could no longer write a simple paper. And it was something he didn't want Sophie to know about.

He tapped his pencil to the glossy table, keeping time with the bounce of his knee. "I just didn't have time to do my own. My folks are having issues—you know, with each other—and it's just really affected the whole family."

Liar.

Garrett's "folks" had been "having issues" for as long as any of us were alive. He'd cheated on her only slightly more than she'd cheated on him, and half the town was convinced Garrett's little sister was the offspring of the neighbor.

A shadow draped over the table, bringing a waft of chemically produced rose-and-gardenia perfume that stuck to every inhale.

Garrett was smiling up at Mrs. Tisler before I had the chance to react.

She stared, arms crossed, wholly disappointed in the both of us, and said, "Can't say I expected to see the two of you here," like there were any possibility I was a factor in me and Garrett being mandated to detention.

I stared back, daring her to accuse me of an act we both knew I'd never commit.

She looked away. "Detention is meant to be quiet, and I'm told you both have papers to write."

She scampered away as quickly as she'd come, leaving me with Garrett and the blaze of the afternoon sun blaring through the windows at my back.

I leaned across the table and whispered, "Let's work together."

His brow furrowed, as I suspected it would. My offer was not logical. I should be angry, pining for his utter failure and intent on watching him suffer.

But hushed conversations under the oppressive eye of Mrs. Tisler wouldn't give me what I needed.

Garrett whispered back, "Work together how?"

"We'll meet—your house of course—and we'll write our papers together." And then I added, "To make sure they're nothing alike," because even though I was certain there was no chance of such a thing, I also knew not even Garrett would be foolish enough to accept my help without some explanation of why I was giving it.

And if I were completely honest with myself, this wasn't just about Sophie. There was a part of me that wasn't willing to let Garrett's misdeed go unpunished. I'd worked too hard, sacrificed too much, to have my integrity maligned by a spoiled adolescent masquerading as a near adult.

If Brown discovered I "cheated," my entire plan would be derailed.

The only way to ensure Garrett was punished and I was exonerated was to find proof of his cheating. That I could do.

He raked his hands through his hair and muttered, "I don't know."

Sophie. This was a risk for him. Letting me into his house. The hours we'd spend together that he'd have to provide a believable excuse for.

But the alternative . . . The future he'd planned for was vanishing, drifting into the air like a plume of feathered smoke.

This too was a test. What was he willing to risk? How scared was Garrett Packard?

His eyes met mine, neither of us blinking.

I knew the answer to my question before it passed my lips. "How bad will it be for you if you fail this class?"

CHAPTER FIVE

SOPHIE

The party is terrible, but I'm too drunk to care.

Music swirls around me, drifting through my thoughts and drowning the bad ones. Cranberry rests sweetly on my tongue, masking the bite of vodka, and my limbs feel barely there.

The numbness spreads to my chest, loosening the grip of Garrett's note, flooding out the thoughts I'm too embarrassed to admit. That I'm secretly hoping to find him here tonight. That I look for him in every person that appears. That every conversation is one where I wait, hoping that person brings up his name and tells me they've seen him, gotten one of his notes too, that life can go back to easy again.

"What's up, Little Linden?"

The deep voice pulls me from my minute of peace, and I drag my eyes open. But I know who it is well before that—no one calls me Little Linden anymore. Not for years and years. Not since Nora and I stopped being each other's best friend. "Hey, Adam."

Adam Russo. Tight end. Backup quarterback. Garrett's best friend and my neighbor. He is the literal last person I want to see when the vision of that note is etched into my memory.

He blocks everything from my vision because Adam was—*is*—Garrett's size. Tall, broad, strong enough to bench-press three of me. He's all dark Italian skin and raven-black hair that he likes to run his hands through to impress the ladies.

He rubs the back of his neck before shouting to be heard among the music and chaos of dozens of mingled voices. "How are you?"

He doesn't care. Not about me anyway. The only time Adam gets all weird like this is when he wants to ask about my sister but doesn't want to admit he wants to ask about my sister.

He's been pining over her since babyhood, when he used to follow her around with his fake lawn mower that blew bubbles out the side. Nora might even like him too; I'm just not sure she'd ever admit it.

That would require an outward display of emotion. Nay. That would require—the horror!—admitting she *has* emotions. But if the past few months have taught me anything, it's that Nora admits nothing—and I don't know anything about her.

I raise my plastic cup. "Doing good, Adam."

I'm really not. A month ago, I wouldn't have been alone for more than twenty seconds at a party like this. It's not that everyone is hostile, or even shunning me. It's me. I'm the problem.

I lost myself.

I used to be part of Sophie and Garrett. Now that's gone and I'm not enough.

Not enough to make Garrett stay, not my dad either, not even enough to hold Mom's attention—at least not when Nora walks into the room.

Adam pauses, just a beat too long, before grasping my elbow and leading me from the kitchen and through the back door. The ocean crashes in the distance, the subtle wind thick with the taste of salt and brine. We could walk to the beach from here, and suddenly that's all I want to do—lie next to Isa and get progressively drunker until we fall asleep in the sand.

My name gets shouted from every corner of the yard, and I yell back a hello, not quite sure who I'm talking to. If it were Garrett next to me, we'd split up now. Each of us making the rounds—smiling, laughing, if there were ever babies at high school parties (not recommended), we'd have kissed them and posed appropriately for our photo op.

There are 1,711 students at Birmingdale High School, and I know every one of their names.

Adam settles against a palm tree, and it's quieter out here but still not *quiet*. The bass thrums through the air and mixes with the squeals and shouts as yet another person gets shoved into the pool. Moonlight bounces off the water, wobbling and stretching beneath the force of the ripples.

He says, "So have you talked with Nora lately?"

See? It's always about Nora. "Umm. Sure. Today I said, 'Nora, your car's blocking mine,' and she said, 'Heading out to eliminate a few more brain cells, Sophie?'"

His lips flatten, because I have clearly not given him what he wants. I can't be mad at him—not really. He's one of the few that have gotten a glimpse of the Nora I know.

It's so easy for people to see her Nora uniform—oxford shoes, fit-and-flare skirts, perfectly fitted tops—and assume she's pretentious. And then there are her grades, her achievements, her general air of knowing more than any single person in the room.

But then there's the thing I've watched countless people try to pinpoint; this *something* about Nora that draws people to her, has them questioning the ferocity of the undertow beneath her calm facade.

I've always known what it is. Nora's superpower is that she just does not give a single fuck.

Not about everything, of course. See: grades, achievements, etc.

Nora doesn't care if people like her. Not in the way I *say* I don't care but really do. She's not searching for anyone's approval.

Nora doesn't *need* anyone. And I swear people can sense it. They're *drawn* to it, like if they could remain in her presence long enough, they could steal some for themselves.

Adam says, "Did she say she might come with tonight or . . . ?"

I'm suddenly far more sober. "Why would Nora come to a party? Did she *say* she was coming to a party? Have *you* ever seen Nora—"

"That's not what I meant to ask."

"Well, what did you mean to ask? Because—"

"Can we just fucking forget I—"

"No. No, we cannot." Because Adam knows Nora better than anyone. Maybe better than me. And she'd never admit it, but I swear they've been hanging out lately. Or they were, for a while. And then Nora started being gone more than she was home. Not just for all her normal stuff. I check her bed in the morning, and I swear she didn't sleep in it. And today Garrett put a note in my dance bag and now Adam thinks Nora's coming to a party—just like she did the night Garrett disappeared.

But I can't say that to Adam. I can't say it to anyone unless I want to go to jail for perjury or whatever. I lied for her. Some stupid, pathetic part of me sealed my lips shut when the cops asked.

I would've done anything for Garrett. Anything.

But some things are sacred.

My cup hits the ground, splashing over my feet, and my finger stabs at Adam's chest. A Sophie Moment if there ever was one. All emotion and action, woefully lacking in control or forethought.

But I have a right to know what Adam knows. It's not like I haven't asked him—about why Garrett was so scared that night, why he was drinking when he never did during the football season. I couldn't even get him to acknowledge there was anything to talk about. But now even Adam is acting weird. Nora is my sister and Garrett was my boyfriend and I deserve the truth.

My body sways, all the alcohol flooding back into my brain in a rush. "Tell me what's going on, Adam, or I swear—"

Isa barrels into me, and it's possible she's even drunker than I am.

She tries to whisper in my ear, but it's too loud and my brain is too fuzzy and I can't put together her words in a way that forms sentences.

By then it's too late.

Jessica Horton leads The Stans in my direction.

I should probably care. Especially since the way Jessica's face is all pinched together, it's clear she's about to accuse me of ruining Garrett's life, or ending Garrett's life. Maybe assassinating JFK too.

Isa mumbles, "Let's get out of here, Soph."

But fuck Jessica Horton, and fuck Melissa Martin, and fuck that other girl whose name I can't remember right now. She's new to the club—I didn't think Jessica knew anyone who isn't white and blond.

Jessica flips her hair, highlights catching in the moonlight, and she glares. "What are you even doing here, Sophie?"

I answer honestly. "Drinking."

She rolls her eyes, and Melissa and What's-Her-Name do too, like it's something they planned. "Am I the only one questioning why

31

you're at a *party* and *drinking* on the one-month anniversary of your boyfriend's disappearance?"

Disappearance.

I hate how people keep saying that.

If I get in my car and drive to the store, I haven't *disappeared*. Garrett *left*. I may not know his reasons; I may not even let myself consider what it means if he left because he had to rather than wanted to, but I know I didn't matter enough for him to tell me.

The yard goes quiet, voices dropping to murmurs as the pool's surface goes calm. Only the rumble and crash of the ocean speaks in the silence.

Isa's voice rings in my ears. Pleading. Because she knows. "Sophie. Come on."

I'm not afraid of Jessica or any of The Stans. That's never been the issue.

I may have lain low the past month. I may have let The Stans say what they want without reprisal because I'm *trying* to be a better person. I'm trying to keep in line so I can salvage my future—dance is the only thing I've ever been better at than Nora. Pathetic. But true. Cheers to me.

But the alcohol has killed all my self-improvement fantasies and I am *tired* of playing living memorial and primary suspect at the same damned time.

I step forward, shaking off Adam's grip, and Jessica's sneer wobbles, because deep down, she knows too.

I don't raise my voice. Everyone is already listening. "Tell me, Jessica. What was the last conversation you had with Garrett?"

Everyone knows the answer—Garrett didn't even know her name at first. Ironically, I did.

I was the one who invited her to sit at my lunch table when people were talking shit about what she did at a party at the beginning of the year. I was the one who told them all to shut the fuck up and what Jessica Horton did with her body was her decision and slut shaming was a tool for those who could never hope to get laid.

Two months later, Jessica decided she was done being grateful.

In short, I *made* the monster standing before me.

She rolls her eyes again. "This is about Garrett, not me."

"Exactly. My boyfriend. Not yours."

Adam pulls at my arm, throwing off my already-tenuous balance, and the world blurs. Mottled blends of blue water and sepia paving stone swirl through my vision, but my voice is steady. "I knew him better than anyone, and if there is a single person here who has the right to be here tonight, it's me."

A voice beckons from behind The Stans, asking if I need help, and then another, because these are my people. They always have been.

I've spent the last month quietly letting Jessica do whatever she wanted, because she clearly needed this more than me. Because she didn't even know Garrett enough to miss him.

"You didn't know everything about him." Jessica holds up her fingers, ticking off all the things I didn't know. "You don't know why he took that money out. You don't know why he was spotted in North Hills the week he disappeared, and you don't even know if he's missing or dead!"

Adam says, "That's enough, Jessica," but she's right. About everything.

I've spent the last month wondering why. Why he left. Why I wasn't enough—not even enough for a hastily scribbled letter.

It's like Dad all over again.

I've spent the last month wondering if I could've found Garrett, if only I would've carved out that part of myself that insisted I protect Nora. But maybe (probably) if not for that, I'd have turned into Jessica, leading The Stans in a quest to find out what really happened to Garrett. Maybe that's what a good person would do.

I've tried to be what everyone needs me to be, and all it took was one note from Garrett and everything I've been trying to hold together is falling apart. He's not here. He isn't coming back for me, and that note feels like the cruelest type of hope.

I look to Jessica and seethe. "You were nothing to him. And if he shows back up tomorrow, you will *still* be nothing to him."

Jessica's cheeks go crimson and I can see it in her eyes, the exact moment she decides this conversation won't end the way she needs it to. She steps back, ready to flip her hair and retreat like she's the one showing mercy, but What's-Her-Name—Zuri Jackson! Ha! Knew I'd remember!

Zuri stops her, fingers curling around Jessica's arm as she whispers something in Jessica's ear. Zuri hangs with Nora's crowd. The early acceptance, honor society, overachiever type. I have no fucking clue what she's doing hanging out with the Basic White Girl club that makes up The Stans.

Also, I don't care.

I shove past the three of them and head toward the house, where at least I can refill my drink. I'm nearly to the edge of the pool when Jessica lets out an angry scream, and before I can turn, my body goes weightless.

I suck in a breath seconds before I hit the water and the cold shocks my skin, my ears popping, until strong arms pull me upright.

I sputter and Del Mason appears in front of me, their green eyes wild with concern. They ask if I'm okay, and I nod but I don't mean it.

I'm not okay. I'm anything but okay. Jessica Horton just threw me in the fucking pool.

Del leads me to the ledge, and I should feel smug. I may be falling apart but Jessica has well and truly cracked, and no one is asking her to live in memoriam of her missing boyfriend. I should look at her and smile and tell her to fuck off forever. But she's crying—sobbing, even—and more than anything, I'm jealous.

Jessica may be borderline obsessed, but she knows what to feel. Her emotions aren't tangled into a knot she can't undo.

Del's mouth opens, closes, opens again, before they finally spit out, "What the fuck was that?"

"Oh, you know, I think she was just trying to . . ."

To what? Start a friendly round of Marco Polo? Del is buying none of this.

Katie rescues me, appearing above me with three beach towels, blotting them all over me. Del heaves me out of the pool and Katie says she's sorry, like she has something to be sorry *for*, and I nod and smile at everyone and reassure them all that it's okay. That Jessica is just super drunk and she probably won't remember any of this tomorrow.

Del whispers my name, and I shake my head.

All it would take is a few words to have everyone hating Jessica by tomorrow morning, and maybe I spare her out of some sense of pity. Maybe it's because I don't need another incident that will derail my future. But it's not just that.

Because I replay her words in my head, my brain now horrifyingly sober. *You don't know why he was spotted in North Hills the week he disappeared.*

I stopped being the girl that had it all the night Garrett disappeared, and until tonight, until that note, I couldn't bring myself to want it all back. I wouldn't chase after Garrett the way Mom did Dad, all her desperation strangling her dignity until she couldn't even look at us anymore.

Everyone asks why I was so sure Garrett left instead of being the victim of some horrible fate. I always tell them it was the ten thousand dollars. It was the note in his handwriting. And truthfully, those are pretty hard to ignore. But really, it's because that's what men like Garrett do.

They say girls marry men who are just like their fathers, right? Well, aren't I a perfect cliché. I fell for the guy who left me. Maybe he even cheated on me too. Maybe all his misdeeds were about to come to light and that's why he wanted to leave.

But that's a sticking point this new Zen Sophie hasn't been able to accept. I don't believe Garrett would cheat on me. We promised. It was the one thing I ever asked of him.

Maybe I'm wrong. Maybe he's a cheater and a leaver and a liar. And I'm not sure I can handle it if that's true. Not just because he cheated, but because of who he had to have been cheating with.

I may not have known Garrett was spotted in North Hills that week, but I *do* know that Nora was.

CHAPTER SIX
NORA

Garrett watched my approach from his tiered porch, heavy stone columns bracing either side of him, stretching to an arch that curved tall above his head.

Even through the stripes of sun that rolled over my window, the strain in his eyes was obvious. The tick of a jaw was a palpable thing. Garrett considered my presence a threat.

As well he should.

I curved around the fountain centered in his driveway, pulling to a stop in a small stone-paved inlet. Palm trees spiked the sky, their thin leaves rustling in the constant breeze, casting trembling shadows over the brick pavers that patterned the drive.

My decade-old Honda Civic had no place here, and I couldn't help but wonder if Sophie felt the way I did. Inadequate. *Small.*

She mustn't have. How could she, and continue to come here day after day. Truly, I wasn't sure Sophie had ever felt small.

I wouldn't let Garrett change that. I wouldn't let him ruin either of us.

He gave me a small wave as I cut the engine and gathered my bag, stepping into the sweet blend of magnolias and roses.

Looking back, I recognize that moment for what it was—a turning point.

Or rather, an apex.

The point at which the only option was to follow the momentum down, down, down until we reached the inevitable.

I traced his footsteps into the house, where stale air greeted me, the clip of my sandals against marble flooring echoing through the open foyer. Twin sets of curved staircases stretched toward a second floor, where Garrett's bedroom was likely to be. The place his secrets were most likely to reside.

Garrett muttered, "Through here" in nearly a whisper, though there wasn't anyone to hear us.

Through a living room, past an expansive kitchen, and down a deep hallway, we finally arrived at a library. A cherry-wood table and only a quartet of domed floor-to-ceiling windows to interrupt the flow of bookshelves. The crash and rumble of the ocean filtered through the glass, filling the silence.

I loved that room immediately. Nearly as much as I hated that it was wasted on the likes of Garrett Packard.

He motioned to a seat across the table and slumped into his own. "So, how do you want to do this?"

How indeed.

How to extricate myself from this room without him following. How to find his room in this behemoth of a home. How to find what Garrett was so intent on hiding.

I wasn't even sure what I meant to look for. Failed tests? Other papers of mine with his name at the top? Maybe Garrett had used his access to my house to steal other papers or projects of mine, and this was simply the first time he was exposed.

"Well, I thought we could both go over what we think our major concepts would be?"

Garrett blanched, lending more credence to my theory that he had no earthly idea of what to write about.

A curious thing, really. Garrett was a cheater; that was made clear the moment he stole my paper. But had he cheated his way through the entirety of school, surely he'd have been caught before this. Surely *someone* would've brought it to light.

And even if every solitary paper he'd ever submitted was stolen, there were tests. Those he had to take on his own.

The next forty-five minutes were far too droll to include in any confession and consisted of me feeding ideas to Garrett while making it seem as if he'd created them on his own. Did he notice? Difficult to say. Likely he was too overcome with relief that I seemed to be writing his paper for him.

Again.

Even more importantly, I pretended to take many sips from my opaque water bottle. This meant it wasn't suspicious when I stated I needed to use the restroom.

What *was* suspicious was his insistence on escorting me to it, which I resolved by telling him I had a shy bladder and needed him to *not* stand next to the door like some sort of prison warden.

Embarrassing? Very. But it wasn't like I cared much for impressing Garrett anyway.

He shuffled away as I grabbed the roll of toilet paper from its gold-plated holder (seriously—the possession of money is in no way related to the level of taste a person is blessed with) and tucked it beneath my shirt.

A terrible hiding spot, to be sure, but I was fairly confident that even if he did see me once I'd left the room, Garrett would not be looking at my boobs. Thank you, Sophie.

I slipped out the door, searching for Garrett around every corner, but he wasn't lurking behind any. The hall beckoned, shadowed along the west wall where the sun couldn't reach.

I stretched around the corner, searching for a hint of Garrett, straining for a creak of floorboard. When there was neither, I scurried down the hall.

Certainly there would be back stairs to match the front. Had this been anyone other than Garrett, had it been like when Sophie and I were The Linden Sisters, I'd have asked her to tell me every detail of Garrett's house. We'd have planned this together—I'd have developed a strategy, accounted for all scenarios, and Sophie would've given me all the perspective I lacked. How others would behave, how to approach their reactions and their probabilities.

But for this, I was alone.

I crept past room after room, until a small staircase appeared. Thick carpet muffled my hurried footsteps as I climbed higher. I didn't slow once I reached the upper level, not even when plush flooring gave way to hardwood and my chances of being discovered grew in magnitudes.

In this, brevity exceeded caution.

Choosing the smaller hall to the left proved to be the wise choice, and soon I found myself inhabiting Garrett's room.

There was no plan for this portion. No way to predict something so unknowable. Secrets came in so many forms.

In the end, Garrett's secret did not come in the form of anything beneath his mattress, in his closet, nor his backpack.

My searches were cursory, to be sure. But there was only so much time I could justify searching for an alternate bathroom after an unfortunate lack of toilet paper in the first.

I nearly ignored the clue that would set me on a path to this confession. It was so innocuous, so blandly innocent, I dismissed it outright when I came upon it in a mess of papers, discarded cords, scattered condoms (grotesque), and lube (I'd rather not consider its purpose).

I plucked the business card from where it had wedged itself along the drawer's left wall, the paper thick and soft beneath the pads of my fingers.

It was hardly the caliber of card you'd find available in packages of one thousand for a price ending in the number 99.

These carried an air of exclusivity. Texture woven through paper that felt more like cloth, edges crisp, corners severe, and the printing. Pressed deep into the paper, an inky black that seemed to shine from its recesses.

No name graced the face of the card, no corporate logo or emblem. Just a single phone number.

Perhaps it was nothing, but a card of this caliber with no stated purpose screamed *secrets* and that was exactly what I was trying to find.

I'd no sooner tucked my evidence into my pocket when a floorboard squeaked down the hall, and I nearly flung myself across the room.

My momentum carried into the hall, where I slid across the hardwood, my hip colliding with the wall.

My body made an audible thump, which Garrett had to have heard, evidenced by the increased speed of his footfalls. And I still hadn't found a place to stash my stolen toilet paper roll. I wedged it beneath the back of my skirt, sparing just a fraction of a second to breathe, regroup, wash the emotion from my features, and bury my fear.

And then I headed toward Garrett.

He turned the corner a heartbeat later, stuttering to a stop at the sight of me. "What the fuck, Nora?"

I laced my fingers behind my back, squeezing, twisting, letting the burn override the flurry in my blood, the tremble in my bones.

"I'm going to need you to elaborate." My voice didn't shake. I wouldn't let it. Weakness invites exploitation.

He made all the requisite facial motions with none of the sounds. Once again, Garrett Packard was at a loss for words.

I'd let him borrow mine. "Should we go downstairs and get back to work?"

I raised a brow, like it was he who was out of line, he who'd committed some social infraction, and he shook his head, but then he turned, heading toward the stairs. "What were you doing up here?"

"You were out of toilet paper in the bath downstairs, so I came up here to look for another."

He tilted his head to avoid the ceiling as he traversed the stairs, his form taking too much space. Men of his size were dangerous. They'd never had anything to fear.

He stopped at the bottom of the stairs, not quite a cage but enough of one to count. "Yeah, but—"

A knock rapped at the door, echoing down the long hall until it faded to whisper. And then, "Bro! Open the door!"

I recognized the voice, perhaps before Garrett did.

I'd known Adam Russo from nearly the moment I'd taken my first breath. He and his family waited in my living room for my maiden journey home. Born a mere thirteen days apart, a photo of our first meeting still graces my mother's wall—our tiny hands linked. I called it a reflex reaction. My mother called it fate.

Since this is a confession, and such a baring of the soul requires honesty, I'll admit the truth. Adam Russo saved me that day.

It wouldn't be the last time.

Maybe, if he'd known what waited in his future, he'd have let me suffer.

CHAPTER SEVEN

SOPHIE

I dab at my dripping hair with Katie's beach towel, fog crawling up my car's windows and blocking out everything that isn't me and Isa.

My words come out scratchy, my throat raw. "Did you hear what she said about Garrett being in North Hills?"

"Don't do this to yourself, Soph."

By "this" she means fall back into a fit of anxious depression where I become trapped in a never-ending, self-destructive spiral of trying to make sense of Garrett leaving.

That *may* have been what the first two weeks looked like—until the anger part of the grief process took over.

The anger was much worse. That's when I ran Jessica Horton over with my car. (Still no regrets.)

I twist the towel, fabric burning against my palms. I should let this go. Questioning Nora about anything is not the right move for me.

It will end with Nora blowing me off, coming up with some genius excuse that Mom will absolutely accept without question, and then Mom will look at me with an expression that says she doesn't trust me, can't rely on me, that I've always been the girl to act before thinking—all emotion, no reason. I'm the anti-Nora, and that makes me all wrong.

Shape up. Fly right. *Let this go.* "Did you know that Garrett was in North Hills though?"

Isa sighs. "Nope. Which means it's probably something Jessica made up."

"Yeah. You're probably right." That's what I say, but it's not what I mean.

Nora was in North Hills. She got a speeding ticket. Nora and Garrett were acting weird around each other for weeks. I wasn't imagining it. And a petty, childish, very Sophie part of me would love nothing more than to see the look on Mom's face when I give her proof that Nora *was* with Garrett that night.

That Nora's just as much a liar as me.

"Soph. Can you turn on the car? I'm freezing."

"Shit. Sorry." I stab at the start button, and the engine rumbles to life. "I shouldn't have let her get to me like that."

"She shouldn't have started anything."

True, but I'm supposed to be better than letting Jessica drag me into a stupid drama fight. And now that Del kicked her and The Stans out of the party—literally walked them to their car and watched them leave—everyone will be talking about what happened, and I'm soggy and sitting in *my* car, too drunk to go anywhere and too irritated to call Nora to come get me.

She'll have the upper hand then, and there are questions she needs to answer. I can't hold an inquisition with mascara smeared all over my cheeks.

I crank on the defroster to clear my windshield, and the haze crawls away, inch by inch. Something glints against the glass, and I have to follow the reflection to the necklace dangling from my rearview mirror.

It's not my necklace, and it wasn't there when I parked the car.

My hand moves without me giving permission, and the charm sits cold against my palm. I lean forward, trying to make out the shape, but it's muddy, dirt caked around the form and obscuring it.

I rub my thumb against it and some of the dirt flakes away.

Flakes away. Paper thin. Leaving behind the faint scent of metal.

It takes my body precious extra seconds to react to what my brain has put together.

That is not dirt.

My scream comes first, and finally, I yank my hand away, leaving the blood-encrusted necklace swaying in the empty air.

Isa plasters herself to the door, her eyes darting everywhere and finding a threat nowhere.

She turns to me, eyes wide, and I point. "Not my necklace. Covered in blood."

Her arm darts forward, and she re-creates my entire reaction—granted, in half the time, but it's important to note I'd already warned her that *it was blood.*

She rockets back into her seat, knees drawn close, and crosses herself while mumbling in Spanish.

My breaths come hard, scraping my throat, and my knuckles glow white around the steering wheel.

Someone left that here for me. Someone left a necklace that is not *my* necklace and is covered in dried blood in my car for me to find. On the one-month anniversary of Garrett's disappearance. Garrett's *not*-disappearance.

Thoughts rumble through my head, spinning uselessly in my stupid, drunk brain.

Jessica could've planted it while I was inside, but if she wanted to send me some kind of message, would she draw suspicion onto herself by arguing with me and pushing me in the fucking pool? And what does this even *mean*?

I don't recognize the charm—music notes. I don't do music. I do dance. I know plenty of music people, but I'm pretty fucking sure I'd remember if I'd fought with someone and drawn enough blood to cake a charm with it.

And the note earlier. The thought of Garrett being back was almost too much to hope for, but now I'm just hoping it's not him. That it really was some slip of paper I'd overlooked. Because if it's Garrett, it feels like too much of a coincidence to have all this bloody-necklace business happen a couple hours later.

And my keys. They were in my bag right outside the studio, and then Isa found them in my pocket in the front lobby.

I locked my car when we got here.

At least I think I did.

"Isa, did I lock the car earlier?"

She turns toward me, slowly, like she's trying to gather all her outrage and stuff it down where I won't see it. "Well, I assume yes, Soph, because otherwise you're an idiot."

So much for sparing me her outrage. "We have to go to the cops."

She flinches, and I immediately feel like such an asshole. "*I* have to go to the cops. Sorry. Privileged white bitch is a never-ending condition."

"Ain't that the truth." Her voice goes soft. "You know I would though. If I could."

I nod because of course I know. And I wouldn't want to risk her dad getting deported because of something I did.

And that's what this feels like—every second I sit in this car with that gold chain dancing in my window—it feels like payback. Punishment even. I didn't tell the truth about Nora when the cops asked, and this is my punishment.

I've questioned that decision every single day since I made it, and I feel like I made the wrong call more often than I do the right. And as much as I really and truly do not feel like sauntering into a police station with a blood alcohol level that's over the legal limit—which for me is a big fat zero—*not* going means repeating the same mistake. Except this time, I can't tell myself I did it to protect Nora.

I grasp the gearshift, and then I remember I'm too drunk to drive just as Isa says, "You're too drunk to drive."

I rub my temples like I can compress the alcohol from my system. I don't *feel* drunk anymore, but that's probably just my panic lying to me. "You're gonna have to drive me."

"Cool. Cool. Except they're probably going to want to *see* the car, and also *I'm too drunk to drive!*"

"Fuck!" My palms slam against the steering wheel and arms throb. "You're supposed to be the DD tonight!"

"The fuck I am! I was it last time."

"No, it was Charla last time, and I was the time before that!"

Isa opens her mouth like she's going to argue, but sinks back into her seat. "Shit. You're right."

We sit in silence until she says, "We could just call them to come here."

"With a party filled with a bunch of underage drinking? They'd all hate me."

48

"No one would hate you, Soph. Everyone still loves you. They're just giving you space to heal on your own timeline."

"I swear to god you sound like that teledoc therapist I called in the third month of quarantine."

"You liked Dr. Lewis and said she helped!"

"I *did* like her and she *did* help, but this is a bit trickier than 'extrovert struggling with solitude'!"

We need Charla. I'm the fun, Isa's the heart, and Charla's the voice of reason. Charla is smart, and one of those problem-solver types. She started her own business dyeing ballet shoes—after years of doing her own—because so few retailers carry models that match Black skin tones. She even has *business cards*.

I need to be Charla. I *need* to be Nora.

I fling open my door and storm toward the house. "We'll drive you home before we head to the station."

"Who's 'we'?"

That, I don't have an answer for. Yet.

We slip back inside the house, my Converse still squishing with every step, and the heavy thump of music feels like an assault.

I scan the room, eyes flitting from Carrie passed out on the sofa— she definitely won't work—the couple making out in the corner—not them either—to the pair doing keg stands. Obviously not them.

"'We' is me and my sober person. There has to be one."

I spot him in the corner, hunched over a guitar he's strumming absently, his dark hair shielding his face. He scrapes it back, the rich brown of muscled forearms peeking from his rolled-back sleeves, and a few tendrils fall right back again in a pile of tousled waves. Definite Oscar Isaac aesthetic.

I have no idea who he is.

"You!" I shout across the room, but he's not paying me the least bit of attention, unlike everyone else, who starts yelling my name like I'm rejoining the party.

Loner Boy looks up when I call out "You!" again, louder this time to combat the bass shaking the walls, and his brows furrow when he sees me staring.

Then he glances behind himself—which is the *wall*, I might add—and points to his chest as he turns back. "Me?"

"Yes, you." I'm standing in front of him now, and I don't think he's impressed. I say, "You look sober."

He leans back, tipping the chair onto its rear legs, and a smile teases at his lips. "Always."

"Awesome. I need you."

His brows raise, and I suppose I can't blame him. My hair keeps dripping onto my neck, my makeup is probably smeared across my face, and my shoes are leaving puddles.

"For?" he says, like he's genuinely curious.

"I need you to drive my car to the police station."

"Yeah." He grimaces. "Gonna need a little more detail."

I glare at him even though it's a perfectly reasonable request. Truth is, I'm not a stranger to having a room full of eyes watching to see what I'll do next, and that's exactly what's going on right now.

But this, now, here, is not the time for witnesses. I motion toward the front door and head the same way, breathing deep when I hit the porch and the cool breeze skips along my wet skin.

I turn, and LB has not followed like I asked, which does not bode well for the ride to the police station.

I poke my head back inside the door, and he's staring right at me, a single brow raised like he's waiting for something.

Jesus H. Christ, he's more of a drama queen than I am.

After a quick roll of my eyes, I mouth a "please," and he responds with a wide grin, easing from his chair and meandering across the room like we're on a stroll with his nana in the back garden rather than a legit crisis.

Bless his heart.

He joins me, finally, and he's much taller than I thought. Not massively broad like Garrett, but definitely not scrawny. A swimmer, maybe. His eyes are so dark I can barely make out the irises. They're pretty. And his eyelashes are longer than mine. His hair looks super soft, like if I touched it—

And that is definitely *not* what I'm focusing on right now.

Blood. Charm. Police. Be like Nora.

"Sorry to drag you out here like this." I pause where his name should be, because I still don't know it. "I'm sorry. Do you go to Birmingdale?"

He doesn't go to Birmingdale.

"I don't."

"Oh, well then, that explains why I don't know your name."

"It does."

What the fuck. He's like the world's worst conversationalist. "What is your name, if you don't mind me asking?"

"I don't, and it's Jude."

"Cool. I'm—"

"Sophie Linden. The dancer."

My cheeks flare hot, and my words stumble all over themselves.

I'm used to people knowing who I am, but I'm not used to them saying it the way he does, with a hint of judgment infused.

I can't hold his gaze because for some stupid reason tears bloom at the corners of my eyes, so I stare into the night sky instead.

It's a deep sort of black, like you'd smudge it if you just could reach high enough, the dark pinpricked with spots of bright stars and the mellow glow of the moon.

It reminds me of the night Garrett left, before the storm came. It reminds me of all the texts I sent that never got returned. The night I stumbled back home after searching, calling every friend I knew, praying I could redo those moments when I didn't push for him to tell me why he wanted to leave, after hours spent consoling his parents and sitting alone in that cold police station, my body trembling so hard I'd be sore the next day, and then I stopped at Nora's door, ready to ask the question I needed answered most, and she slammed it in my face.

I didn't demand answers out of her then, and that was my biggest mistake.

I force my gaze back to his, even though he knows he upset me and didn't even say sorry, especially after I said "please" earlier. "Anyway, I'd really appreciate it if you could just drive me and my car to the station. I'll pay to Uber you back."

His head tilts, and a bit of that judgment seems to ease from his face. "Okay, sure."

He holds out his hand, and I drop the keys into his palm just as a knock at the window behind me nearly leaves me jumping out of my skin.

It's Isa, smiling far too wide, her arm slung around Sadie Masters.

I shake my head and laugh, waving them both away from the window and off to do what they're going to do. I'd much rather Isa have fun here than suffer with me and the police anyway.

Jude's already at my car, and I hurry to catch up, sliding into the passenger side and staring straight ahead where the pendant can't enter my vision. "You said 'always' earlier. Why are you always sober?"

"Does it matter?"

"I mean, there's medical or religious reasons, or just 'it's not my thing' reasons. And there are, like . . . 'hey, check out my awesome ankle tether' reasons."

The motor on the driver's seat hums as Jude moves it back far enough to fit his legs. When he's finally settled, he turns to me, all expression wiped from his face, and lifts the leg of his jeans. All clear.

Though he didn't show me the other leg. Is there a standard tether leg?

"So," I say as he deftly maneuvers us onto the grass and through a maze of cars, "you don't go to Birmingdale, but you're at a party with a bunch of people who do."

"Yes."

Is it possible to hate someone who barely speaks? "Can I ask why?"

"You—"

"I know I *can* ask why, so I'm asking why."

His mouth quirks. "Del is my cousin. They asked if I'd come and hang out. Help keep an eye on things."

"Oh, be still my heart! I think that was three whole sentences and two bits of information volunteered without direct interrogation."

He laughs, low and deep. "People talk too much, about things that don't matter enough. And you ask a lot of questions."

"Do I?" I catch my reflection as we ease down the quiet road, and the smile I'm wearing looks almost foreign. "Most people like it."

"Questions?" His palm shushes over the steering wheel as it brings itself back to center, and he glances to me, thoroughly confused.

"Yeah. People like to talk about themselves." We make another turn, only a few minutes from the station, and my leg jitters, my dress now dried and plastered to my thigh, and I just want him to keep talking so I don't have to think.

"And do they say anything interesting?"

"Not really." A laugh escapes, and I want to stay in this car forever. Well, maybe not *this* car. A car without threatening jewelry instead. "But also yes? I mean, even if *what* people say isn't interesting—their plans for tomorrow, or who they want to take to homecoming, or what their grandson ate for breakfast that morning—it may not matter to me, but it matters to them. I don't know, I like people. I like hearing their stories and it makes people feel good to have someone to listen."

He turns and stares, the slant of moonlight revealing the slightest ring of amber in his dark eyes, and I add, "Present company excluded."

He smiles then, real and full and almost like that judgment I felt earlier is gone, but whatever warm and fuzzies that might give leave me that much colder as we pull into the lot.

I jump from the car, and this time he follows even without my having to beg, but I turn at the top step. "You should go."

"Okay."

But then he doesn't move, just stands there.

"Shit. Your Uber. I'll—"

"It's cool." He drags his hand through his hair. "I could stay, if you needed someone to."

His hair would make most girls jealous. It's good he wears it a little long. It works with his aesthetic.

He says, "Is that a no?" and right, I'm supposed to be talking.

Sophie Linden, always with the laser focus.

I step back, putting more distance between us so I'm not tempted to say yes. "No, get back to the party. This is . . . a little more than I'm willing to ask of a stranger."

He nods, walking backward down the steps like only a sober person can, before he stops. "Is everything okay?"

It feels so genuine the tears return to my eyes, but I make myself smile through them, nodding like this is all no big deal, and I know he doesn't believe me because he reclaims the space he put between us.

He stares at the doors behind me, like he's working up the courage to speak. "You're the only person from the party that I talked to."

"Oh." I don't add "That's sad," but I definitely think it and his half smile tells me he knows.

"That makes us not strangers, so if you did need someone just to be in there with you . . ." He shrugs. "I'm good at not talking."

A laugh bursts out of me. Good hair, pretty eyes, sweet, *and* funny. But even more, it feels like he means what he says, that his offer is genuine and given without expectation of reciprocation. It would be so easy, I think, to be friends with this boy. To just be in his company without an image to uphold and a running ledger in my head of where I add value and where I fall short.

That's why I tell him no, why I send him away, why I watch while he retraces his steps down the stairs, and then the space between the halos of light in the parking lot swallow him up.

I turn and pull my dress from my body where it's dried and stiff, then wipe the mascara from beneath my eyes.

This is doing the right thing. Following the rules so I don't have to explain myself later.

Cicadas chirp from the spots among the trees, a steady rhythm that forms a chorus with the crash of ocean waves.

I reach toward the door, and my hand drops. I could walk away, and no one would know. The beach is only a short walk. The wind would whisk through my hair and the waves would surge deep into the shore, frothing around my ankles before it sinks between the grains of cold sand.

It's the only place I've ever felt more at home than onstage.

The memory of Garrett's note shoves itself to the front of my mind, the feel of that bloody charm brands itself on my palm, and all the anger of a month and zero answers pushes me forward.

My fingers wrap around the thick metal handle, and I step inside to the glare of fluorescents and sterile white walls. It's the first time I've stood here since the night Garrett disappeared, and this time, I'm vowing to tell the truth.

I just haven't decided how much of it.

CHAPTER EIGHT
NORA

I don't recall when things shifted between me and Adam, when our relationship underwent the subtlest of realignments that impacted both of us more than we'd dare admit.

Maybe it was the night we were twelve, when his parents paused when I crawled into his bed to sleep, like I had so many summer nights previous. The flare of heat that worked its way from my belly to my cheeks when his dad said maybe Adam should sleep on the floor from now on.

I recognize it now for what it was. Shame.

The embarrassment for an insinuation I hadn't begun to consider. But maybe Adam had.

I am many things, but a fool is far from one. I'm well aware of the feelings Adam developed for me—the feelings he's harbored for years now. I've never encouraged him. Never given him an opening with which he could express them.

It's not cruelty. It's mercy. Adam Russo wants me the way children want a puppy.

Heads filled with visions crafted from hopes and dreams, from sunshine and the gentle lap of waves. No one thinks about the storms.

But Adam, despite his misguided wants, was still my friend. I couldn't recall a time in my life when that wasn't true. And so, it was Adam I went to when I needed someone I could trust.

I waited for him at his car the next day after school, ocean breeze ruffling my skirt at my thighs. The ocean reached everywhere, no matter how far inland you might try to flee. There was no part of this city that didn't live by its pull, that didn't breathe by its rhythms. And so it seems fitting now that it's where this story would end.

But that wasn't what consumed my mind that day. It was the card in my hand, the imprint of the numbers as I traced my finger over them.

Maybe Adam would know what it was for. Garrett had long since been his best friend. I sincerely doubted there was any portion of their lives they didn't share.

But then, some secrets were too dangerous for even the best of friends. And if Adam didn't know its purpose, that would be an even greater reason to pursue it. A thing Garrett would hide from Adam was a thing I needed to know.

Footsteps stormed through the lot, a herd of students escaping the halls into the sun-soaked air, and I squinted against the punishing brightness as Adam neared.

His companion stopped short, a tiny O appearing from glossed lips. I didn't know her name, and if she knew mine, it was likely through association to some school program she suffered through by force.

"Nora!" Adam knew my name and was also far happier to see me, but he stopped where she stopped, stuck between two incongruous worlds.

There was small talk, Adam stating that I was, in fact, Nora, and she was Mandy and he was just walking Mandy to her car, though it was obvious Mandy's impression of their plans was far different.

Sophie would have insisted Adam call her later, leaving him to fulfill whatever obligations he'd established with Mandy. Sophie would've known Mandy's name.

I, however, nodded as Mandy walked away, her shoulders a bit more slumped than when she'd come. "You owe her an apology."

"Seriously, Nora, we were—"

"Liar."

He let a smile slip. "Okay, yeah, that was a dick move."

"I agree with the sentiment."

"My behavior was highly unbecoming."

"Better." I matched his smile—an involuntary reaction that always accompanied Adam's attempt to speak my language.

He wrapped me in a hug, surrounding me with warmth and velvet skin, with the scent of salted waves that always clung to him. Sometimes it still caught me off guard, how his figure dwarfed mine. There was a time we'd been exactly matched.

His breath tickled my hair as he whispered, "I miss you, Nor."

Truth be told, I missed him too. But something had shifted as of late, even more than when we were twelve. Something that made it harder for him to look me in the eye. I couldn't help but wonder if maybe he'd grown out of his illusions about us. Maybe he was finally moving on to a girl who would fit in his world.

I most certainly did and could not. The one time Adam had tried to drag me to one of his weekend parties, I spent the night on the bumper of his car. It was the last place he'd thought to look, thereby spending his entire night shoving through partygoers, asking if they'd seen me, and fielding incredulous "Nora *Linden*?!" responses.

Sophie finally pitied him and suggested where he'd find me.

I stepped from Adam's arms, pressing myself against the car, and held the card between us. "I need your help."

"Where'd you get that?"

Curious response. "Is that the question?"

The car rumbled to life beneath me as Adam hit the remote start. He took a second to open the driver's door and adjust the air-conditioning so he could avoid stepping into a car that had spent the day baking in the sun. "Well, it's clearly a business card, but for what?"

"That *is* the question."

"Have you called it?"

"You know I haven't." A group walked by, their gaze lingering on us just a beat too long.

It had always been this way—the members of my academic circle mused about what kind of conversation Adam could possibly hold beyond the subject of sports, and those in his could never fathom why he'd choose to associate with someone so boring as myself.

Adam waved, and they all smiled or gave a quiet nod in response.

I simply waited for them to go away. "I didn't want to call from my phone."

"Okay." He grabbed the card and headed toward his open door, forcing me to jump into the passenger side to stop what would inevitably be something incredibly impetuous.

He already had the number half dialed by the time I snatched the card from his hand. "Not *your* phone either!"

"What the hell do you think this number is *for*, Nora?"

I clicked my seat belt into place, the leather seat bleeding heat into my tights. "Deductive reasoning. If they don't want to put their purpose on their business card, I don't want a connection to it on my phone records."

"Fair point." He looked to my locked seat belt and back to me. "Are we headed somewhere?"

"I have a key to the supervisor's office at the shelter. We can use the phone there."

Adam's smile grew full, his eyes lit with the spark of adventure, of promises of rules made to be broken. For a moment, we were those kids I barely remembered us being, promising our mothers we were at each other's homes while sneaking off to the woods to sit high in the trees, our legs scratched and bruised and smudged, the wind whispering against our skin and swaying the branches beneath us.

Using my supervisor's office without permission would be our secret too.

He threw the car in reverse and sped from the lot, the scent of burned rubber dissipating only once we reached the open road.

Adam was one of the few who knew that perhaps I was not so boring after all.

The gates were open, ushering us into the back lot and alongside the administration building. We followed the long length of it, past the dock where deliveries entered, past the bins of garbage piled high, until we reached the employee entrance.

There was no sense in concealing our approach—people inside would undoubtedly see us when we entered. Instead, I planned to hide us in plain sight.

We walked in step through the lot while the clouds rolled

overhead, flying past the sun with enough speed to flicker the rays from light to dark.

The journey inside was uneventful, the usual mix of dusty office and stale coffee greeting us as the door swung open.

It's fortunate that I look so worthy of trust, so utterly incapable of subterfuge. Adam's presence drew several long stares, but there was no way to avoid it. I needed his voice.

We crept along the hallway, our footsteps quiet and our breathing a beat too quick for normal, until Vera's office came into view. Adam blocked me with his body, shielding my hands as they slipped the key into the lock.

A quick twist, the handle cold in my hand, and we slipped inside.

Darkness wrapped around me, still and silent, only a crack of sunlight oozing through the edges of the blinds, Vera's jasmine essential oils still lingering in the air.

I closed the door, pressing it flat until the quiet click echoed into the room, and then the press of a lock sealing us inside.

Adam and I huddled around the phone, the heat of his body pressing against my skin as each beep pounded against my ears.

Adam muttered, "You should be the one who talks."

He wasn't wrong. Words were never Adam's strength. But my words were not like everyone else's. My words were distinctive.

My words could identify us.

I didn't need to say any of that to Adam. He knew as well as I did.

A voice came to life on the second ring, and then a simple "Yes?" and I scribbled a response, my pen scratching against paper. Then Adam, telling them he'd like to use their services, using the words I'd scripted for him as his guide.

That was the moment, I know now, that changed the course of this story. Had I known how it would all end, I don't know that I would've been able to set pen to paper that day.

I glanced toward the door, listening for any sign that we'd been discovered, that the baritone of Adam's voice may have given us away. But the hall remained silent, our presence unknown.

A pause stifled the air, and then the voice again, asking who referred us.

Not acceptable. Anyone we named would be contacted, exposing us as the frauds were. Adam's words mirrored my pen. *What difference does that make? Listen, I'm a very busy man and don't have time for games.*

And then, the voice asked softly, could we have someone call us back?

I am loath to admit I froze, even for half a second. But *where* would they call? Certainly not this number. Not my cell phone or Adam's.

They were clearly suspicious, likely from the moment we'd refused to give our referral name. The voice sounded young, a student perhaps. Someone too afraid to misstep, but who would also likely crumble beneath the slightest application of pressure.

I scribbled out a single word: *Karen.*

It took a moment, but then understanding lit Adam's face as he demanded, in his most entitled voice, the words every customer service representative dreads most.

"Can I speak to your manager?"

It only took a few more minutes—a brief back-and-forth of acceptable days and times—and then we left with a location and a name, and the first step on the journey that would change us all.

CHAPTER NINE

SOPHIE

The detective was less than impressed with my bloody necklace.

Maybe he thought my bloody necklace was just some silly prank that was absolutely a waste of his time to investigate, but his detectivey skills were majorly picking up on my freaking the fuck out about being there.

Every minute in there was a reminder of sitting on my front porch, my mom listening in while pretending not to listen in, my dad nowhere near any of it even though I called him and asked him to come, with the police questioning me about Garrett's disappearance. That was before they took me to the station.

Did we have a fight? What was our relationship like? Had he mentioned wanting to leave? Had I noticed any suspicious behavior? When was the last time I'd seen him?

No. Amazing. Absolutely not. You mean aside from him leaving a party with my sister?

That's what I should've said. Maybe I wouldn't have been sweating and squirming in my seat over nothing but a stupid charm necklace that may or may not have blood on it. With blood that may not even be human.

The detective pointed that out. Right before he asked if I'd been drinking. I know he didn't believe me when I said no.

But that was two days ago, I did what I was supposed to do, and I have no more obligation to that stupid necklace.

I will *not* be the girl who nearly gets killed tracking down some serial murderer, thanks.

I can barely remember what the charm even looked like. And the more I try to recall why I was so upset, about the necklace and Garrett's note, the harder it gets to see—memories lost to a murky Saturday night that didn't feel real by the next morning.

Nora slipped around the house like a whisper, a shadow that faded into the cracks the second I looked its way.

For a moment, I considered telling her. Maybe even asking her opinion. Nora would know what to do. And I still needed to confront her. But all my courage shriveled once I was back home.

That's a lie. It wasn't courage I needed. I needed proof. I needed evidence. I needed a solid thing that I could confront her *with*, otherwise Nora would have me tongue-tied and questioning my own name before the conversation was even over.

I know I need to be like Nora, but it's not like I can borrow her brain. I don't think like she does, from multiple angles and all the places their lines intersect. But I feel like I need to. *Someone* left me that necklace, and *someone* put that note in my bag. Garrett hasn't contacted me since and no one else has seen him. So where does that leave me? Fuck if I know.

"Ms. Linden. Care to join us?"

I'm jolted back into my body, which is very far behind the rest of the girls.

Isa stares at me from ten feet away, where everyone else has grand jetéd themselves clear across the room while I stood there twisted in my own thoughts.

I stumble all over my words, muddling apologies to Mrs. Wilson, who is just as unimpressed with me as the detective was.

She stares me down, and she doesn't even have to say the words before I know what happens next. I'm politely directed to take a break, which is balletspeak for "get the fuck out and think about what you've done."

I nod and slink out of the room, my stomach roiling and sweat slipping down the small of my back.

New York. Summer intensive. Senior year at a school that values me. The training that will decide the rest of my life. Whether I'll be stuck here, with the same old people, marrying the wrong guy, who will eventually find a younger me to leave me for, so I can live the rest of my bitter existence mumbling curses about him under my breath so my kids can't hear them—but loud enough that I know they can.

You know, like my mom.

The crisp air of the hallway greets me, chills my heated skin, and I slide down the wall to drop my head to folded arms.

I will fix this when I go back in there. I will out-jeté them all, and I will generally get my shit together.

I focus on the lively cadence of the music that filters through the studio walls, counting each note in my head, my muscles tensing with each move I deny them.

The thud of pointe shoes rumbles through the floor beneath me, and Mrs. Wilson's voice follows. Someone—several someones from the feel of it—have forgotten landings are supposed to be graceful. Like a feather, not a brick.

I have a short-lived moment of guilt for hoping they keep screwing up so she forgets how mad at me she is.

Something vibrates near my foot, and it takes a second to register that I'm sitting next to my bag and that means it's my phone.

If Mrs. Wilson comes out here, she will fillet me if she finds me with my phone in my hand. But self-control has never really been my thing.

I unzip my bag and paw through warm-ups, leos, hair bands, etc., because I still can't be counted on to put things in the pockets. Finally, my fingertips graze hard plastic.

I turn my body to shield my hands and peek at the screen.

The music muffles and the air goes still, until there's nothing but the rush of the blood thrumming through my veins.

Garrett's name lights my screen, and I'm too afraid to move. My entire body sits locked in place, not even a tremor in my hand.

It's just a text, but it feels like a warning. The note in my bag, the charm on my mirror, and now this.

They never found his cell phone. Why would they? He would've taken it with him. But he never used it either.

Until, apparently, right now.

Lucky me.

Before common sense can override stupid curiosity, I thumb the screen up to reveal the contents.

It's just a string of numbers—nothing that means anything to me—and pressure builds behind my eyes.

I will not cry over him. He left.

Without even a note. At least Dad had the decency to call and say goodbye when he walked out.

But then there's that voice, the one I try so hard to ignore, that asks why he left. Garrett was not himself that night. I've tried to make excuses, but they're all just to justify how little I told the cops. Because of Nora.

Garrett was scared. Scared enough to ask me to leave. Scared enough to turn to alcohol that night. Maybe part of me can only admit that now because I was sure Garrett was in control of everything, that he'd always protect me, that I never had to worry as long as I had him. Now I'm not so sure he could even protect himself.

Because there's a note from him and a bloody necklace on the same night, and the only thing I know is that whatever Garrett was running from or to, he did it with Nora.

I stare at the screen, willing it to make sense, and then it does. The number ends in 803. A phone number with the area code last. Not the cleverest method of encryptions, but Garrett was never going to break any IQ records.

My fingers hover, twitching with the need to reach out, to force some connection. I don't know what I'd say to him if he showed up right this second. I don't know what I'd do. Run into his arms or bludgeon him with my pointe shoe. If it were possible to exist in the exact equilibrium where you both love and hate someone, that's where my feelings for Garrett reside.

I type the one question I want answered more than any other: Why?

No dots appear. No response. Not even when it's been too long of a break and Mrs. Wilson is probably preparing an after-class lecture for me.

Maybe this is my chance at a do-over. My heart goes fluttery over the thought. If this is Garrett, he's giving me a chance to set things right. Reaching out for help and this time I won't let Nora stand in my way.

If Garrett is going to show up after months with cryptic phone numbers, then I'll play.

I waddle toward the dressing room, giving tight smiles to Janie and Moira, who are definitely supposed to be in class right now. Moira asks if I'm okay—tight smiles are Nora's thing, not mine—and I nod, pointing toward my phone.

I'm afraid if I open my mouth, even just a sliver, all the words I'm holding in will come spilling out, a puddle of my soul pooling at my feet.

I duck into the changing room, which is blessedly empty, and dial.

It rings twice, and then a voice calls out, "Yes?"

I blink twice, momentarily stunned by the very unexpected phone greeting. It's not like I rang a bell on the counter. "Oh, sorry. I think maybe I misdialed."

"Okay. Have a pleasant evening."

It takes a second too long, just a single tick of the clock, and the line goes dead. But then I replay the voice and I know. I *know* that was Amber Donahue.

I know everyone at Birmingdale. I used to think it would help me win homecoming queen. Look at me now.

I dial again, and before she can speak, I say, "Amber?"

There's a sharp intake of breath, a pause, and the line goes dead.

I pace the room, pointe shoes thumping against the floor with each step.

Mrs. Wilson is waiting for me. Isa will wonder what in the hell I'm doing if I don't go back soon. Very soon.

I *will not* be the girl who gets killed chasing after some murderer.

But then, this is Garrett, and once, I believed he loved me. Once, I thought there wasn't anything I wouldn't do for him. And between Dad and Nora, I know what it's like to be deserted by the people you thought you could trust.

I look to my phone, my question to Garrett unanswered. And maybe I need the answer more than I thought.

I grab my clothes from the cubby and yank them over my leo before class lets out and Mrs. Wilson—and, even more terrifying, Isa—tracks me down.

I won't be the girl who gets killed, because this will just be a conversation—even if it's one I'm sure Isa would tell me to leave alone. To mind my own business and exorcise Garrett from my life forever.

But I've never been very good at doing what I'm told.

CHAPTER TEN
NORA

There came a point where I considered letting everything go.

It was before I knew too much, before all the details became clear and I could still sleep at night without the presence of nightmares. Sophie would be fine. Perhaps Garrett was a liar. Certainly a cheat. Maybe he would even break her heart.

But heartbreak can be mended, and Sophie was always bound for greater things than Garrett Packard.

These were the arguments I made with myself in the days leading up to the meeting Adam and I had arranged with the mysterious phone number. See, it was still a conundrum, the need to find the purpose of the number, weighed against my having no one who could pose as a parent in order to appear at said meeting.

And my time was limited. There were studies and volunteering and friends—yes, friends . . . most people are surprised to hear I have them, though I can be quite personable and am an excellent team member for all trivia games.

Guaranteed victory.

I am an asset.

But none of those things were what gave me pause, not if I'm being honest. It was the man.

I first saw him outside my house, parked near the end of the block, where he assumed I couldn't see him. Or perhaps he intended me to.

His car was black, a sedan, windows darkened just a shade lighter than legal, his baseball cap pulled low, and as I drove past him, he didn't look up.

But surely there was no reason for a man to spend hours standing vigil on my street corner, unless some of my neighbors had suddenly found themselves with far more interesting lives than they'd had previously.

And though my doubts waned minute by minute, then further when he appeared again the next day, any remaining rationalization vanished the night I hurried from the shelter parking lot to the regular chorus of barking dogs, the chill in the air just cold enough to need the coat I'd left in my car, to find him sitting near the exit.

Even now, I can remember that feeling. The looming threat of his presence, cold and dark against my skin. The speed of my heart and the feel of my blood pulsing against my veins. The bloom of sweat over my back and the kick of adrenaline that blasted through every muscle, screaming at me, *warning* me that this was not safe. That this man, and even more concerning, whoever had sent him, did not wish good things.

I nearly canceled my plans with Adam and the arranged meeting. In my weaker moments, I wish I could go back and let my fear rule me that day so I could go back to when I didn't know what I know now. So my life would remain unchanged, my path certain, so I could keep all the plans I'd spent my whole life constructing and enacting.

But then I think of Sophie, I think of how I failed to protect her so long ago and how that one incident turned into a domino fall of Dad leaving, Mom retreating, and Sophie—the one of us who feels things most deeply—paying for all our sins.

How those days where she wouldn't talk, wouldn't look me in the eye, left me broken.

And so I vowed to myself, I would not regret any of my deeds. I would not apologize for them or explain. Not to Sophie, not to anyone.

I kept my date with Adam. I even recruited my friend Monica* to help with surveillance. (*Names changed to protect the innocent.)

The meeting was scheduled for 9:00 p.m., at a small restaurant on the boardwalk. Pizza, gyros, an ice cream shop inside, an arcade to its east. Only steps from the sand of the beach, yards from the ocean. A small wrought-iron fence sectioned off a cramped seating area, a handful of tables crammed into corners covered by climbing vines and flowers.

I turned the business card over in my hand, pressed the thickness of it between the pads of my fingers, let them run over the embossed numbers. A business card made for tuxedoed waiters and pianos played live, for the delicate clink of silver against fine china.

Not here, where games plinked and chimed next door, where children's shouts echoed into the air before they're swallowed whole by the crash of waves and the snap of flags battered in the wind.

But here, it was easy to get lost in the crowd, so many faces none can hold anyone's attention for long. Here, things are ordinary. Miles of beach to escape to, crowds along the boardwalk to slip into if you no longer wish to be seen.

It may have been exactly the place for a business card such as this.

Monica and I settled into our seats, well ahead of our agreed-upon arrival time. We ordered—dinner was my treat, as payment for Monica's participation—and our food was served shortly. Though sadly, I couldn't even enjoy what is normally an excellent grilled-chicken gyro, nor the perfectly crisped french fries, because the unease in my gut grew with every passing moment.

This area may have been perfect for a clandestine meeting, but it was not comforting for a girl with a man surveilling her every move. A detail I declined to share with Monica or Adam.

It was partly foolish of me to take such a visible role in this operation. It could not be coincidence that a strange man began following me shortly after my phone call to this mysterious number, though to my knowledge, they had no way of knowing it was me.

The one person who had reason to be suspicious of me was the one I needed information on the most—Garrett.

In a rather pathetic attempt at disguise, I had forgone my normal skirts and opted for a pair of Sophie's jeans, as well as one of her sweatshirts. It was woefully inadequate, but then, I did have to call out to Monica on the boardwalk before she recognized me.

She had no trouble recognizing the two girls who slid into the table at the far end of the patio, both of them facing the opposite direction from us, which did nothing to stop Monica from nearly diving beneath the table. She opted to bury her entire head inside the laminated menu instead.

I peeled away the side until her face came into view, and at my raised brows, she whispered, "Jessica Horton and Amber Donahue."

Hmm. Jessica I recognized. I had the unfortunate luck of having to work with her on the yearbook committee. Amber I didn't know at all, aside from having seen her grades on Wentville's computer. But the odds of the two of them appearing at this very spot at this very time for reasons unrelated to the meeting we set up seemed highly improbable.

I shifted my chair slightly, metal scraping concrete, so I could watch them.

Monica said, "Are you going to tell me what this is about?"

I spoke around my french fry. "Not likely."

Her head tilted, genuine concern filling her dark eyes. "You didn't send out an email for student council."

"There wasn't any news."

"When has that ever stopped you?"

To that, I had no argument. Aside from laughter. But any joy Monica had roused suffocated beneath the wash of fear as the man in the baseball cap walked by. Officially, not a coincidence. Officially, he'd been sent to, at best, intimidate me. And clearly, my disguise had not worked.

"Nora. *Nora*."

I snapped back into focus. "It's nothing. Text Adam. Tell him to call."

We'd stationed Adam at one of the few working pay phones, where he could call the number and say he'd been held up in traffic. Idle people tend to reveal things. If given enough time, people like Jessica and Amber certainly would.

Not more than a minute later, Amber's phone rang—a flip phone—and a very one-sided conversation took place, Amber saying no more than a series of "ohs" and "okays." Then she placed her phone in her pocket, and stared straight ahead.

Jessica was not pleased. "Are you seriously not going to tell me what that was about?"

Jessica, it seemed, was unbearably unpleasant no matter who she interacted with.

"He said we should wait."

"*Wait?* How long am I supposed to sit here?"

"He didn't say."

"He didn't *say?* Maybe you don't have plans, but I—"

"If you'd like to call Joseph and tell him you had to leave, I won't mind. Maybe you can make the whole family hate you." Amber put on her best cheerleader smile, but her disdain was obvious.

As was Jessica's fear. She turned and slid into her seat with a huff, arms crossed.

Joseph. It was something. It also happened to be an exceptionally common name that would likely lead nowhere.

My leg bounced beneath the table, all the effort of keeping the nervous energy coursing through me needing to come out *somewhere.*

Monica placed her hand over mine, her tone gentle. "Nora, I'm giving up debate club practice for this."

"That's why you got the free gyro."

She shoved my hand away, smiling. "Talk. Now. Or I'm going to extort an ice cream cone out of this too."

I was tempted. Monica was one of the smartest people I knew, and I knew no shortage of smart people. And she might have other information that could aid me in putting this together. But whatever this was, I sincerely doubted involvement would look good on a person's transcript. "Plausible deniability."

Her eyes went wide, and she leaned close, her voice a whisper. "If you have to present 'plausible deniability' as an argument, *you* shouldn't be involved either!"

There were more words after those. Many more, to be frank.

Monica does not excel at hiding her opinions nor the emotions they provoke.

I couldn't confess the details about the secret club, but I could give her something. "There's a man—maybe a private investigator—and he appears to be following me."

"Holy shit."

Accurate. "He makes me uneasy."

"Obviously. Nora, please don't—"

"She's leaving."

Jessica stormed off—whether it was due to lack of patience or something Amber had said remained unknown.

I'd barely finished motioning to Monica before she was out of her seat to follow, where hopefully Jessica would lead us to a bigger clue than "Joseph." Perhaps even Joseph himself.

I pulled out enough money to cover our bill and tucked it beneath a water cup, just in case Amber left too.

She didn't. Not until I texted Adam to have him cancel and Amber received the phone call notifying her that the meeting had been called off.

Jessica had led nowhere, huffing to her car, where she peeled out of the lot, which meant Amber was our last hope.

She paid, leaving a generous tip, which raised my estimation of her, and slipped out of the wrought-iron fencing area and onto the boardwalk.

I waited, counting to ten before I followed.

Looking back, the moment seems almost surreal. The pings and chimes of the arcade fading as I hurried toward the beach so I could track Amber without being obvious about it, or losing her to the dense crowd that might halt my progress. The roar of waves that stretched higher and higher up the beach, toward the plots of tall grass that sprinkled the side of the boardwalk. Monica's voice in my ear, my phone pressed tight, the tinge that marred her normally straightforward tone with what treaded dangerously close to fear.

She'd doubled back after Jessica drove off, running down the main street and cutting back over to the boulevard. "The PI—he's behind you, Nora. Nora, I don't like this."

Should I say I wasn't scared? I could. This is *my* confession, after all, and there's no one to know the truth of any of it.

I *was* scared. Terrified, even. Of the man behind me, of losing Amber, of never getting to the bottom of something so important it needed a threat to keep me from it.

My dad used to tell me I needed to learn to let things go. That not every problem was mine to solve. And then he walked away, leaving all the problems he'd let go of for me to find answers for.

But then, I was the one trudging through sand, the grains sinking into all the crevices of my shoes, chasing a classmate on little more than a hunch, while a man chased me.

Perhaps I had something to learn from my father after all.

My phone beeped, cutting off Monica's increasingly panicked pleas, until I switched to the deep rumble of Adam.

I said, "She's headed your way, coming around the volleyball courts." I kept my voice low, despite the empty beach surrounding me.

It was too late for swimming and sandcastles, only a few couples and smattering of families searching for shells in the dark, their flashlights sweeping across the packed sand where the moonlight didn't reach.

Wind rushed through the phone, blurring Adam's words, but I didn't get the chance to ask him what he'd said, because thick arms wrapped around me and my phone tumbled loose, dropping into the sand just as my feet left it.

A calloused hand clamped over my mouth, slamming my head back to the PI's chest, pinning me until only my legs could move.

They flailed uselessly, my heels making contact with his shins but only enough to draw out a few grunts.

There were people, so many people, just steps away, but their eyes were on the boardwalk, at the moonlight's reflection, tossed from tip to tip as the waves rolled in.

It took no time at all for him to carry me to the water, for his forearms to jam into my stomach as we both fell forward. It took only seconds for the water to soak me through, salt burning in my eyes, my nose, filling my mouth and ramming its way down my throat.

Sand scraped against my cheek, the man's hand fisted in my hair as he yanked my head up, his body still crushing me, holding me still.

I sucked in air, coughing the ocean from my lungs so hard I retched. My head slammed down again, water filling my ears until the world became only the rush and gurgle below the surface and the panic in my chest, screaming at me to *breathe breathe breathe*.

We were on the shore, the sand below me shifting with each wave, steps from safety where the tide couldn't reach. Babies could drown in fewer than two inches of water. Mom had told me that when Sophie was an infant and I was too young to be responsible for ensuring my little sister didn't die, but there I sat, perched at the edge of her tub, too afraid to move, to shift my focus for even a second.

Be strong, Nora.

The man yanked me up again, cold air pummeling my face and oxygen scraping its way into my battered throat, and I tried, I tried so hard to scream, but there wasn't enough air. Not enough room in my lungs with the weight of him pinning me to the deepening depression in the sand. The waves rose up again, battering the side of my face, muffling the world again in a brutal rhythm.

But then there was his voice, his mouth so close his breath tickled the shell of my ear, cooled the sheen of water on my skin. "Let it go, bitch."

His weight left my body, my scalp tingling where he'd fisted a tangle of my hair, and I'd no sooner gotten my arms unpinned from my sides when another wave sent me tumbling. Not far, the shore had always been so close, right beneath me, slipping away as every wave retreated until I sunk deeper and the water rose higher. Shells scraped over my palms as my head went dizzy from lack of air and the way the world spun.

I rolled to a stop, moonlight streaming bright into my eyes, and my lungs heaved again, exorcising the remnants of salty ocean, filling my mouth and mingling with the sour taste of bile that threatened to come up my throat.

And it was Sophie's voice I heard, from those moments when Mom would decide she needed to spend time with us—around a restaurant table, in the car to go shopping or get mani/pedis—when Sophie would fill the uncomfortable silence with a never-ending deluge of high school happenings, from the ever-changing landscape of friendships to breakups to ridiculous promposal plans. From somewhere deep in that useless nonsense, there was this: Jessica and her sordid breakup with Michael Graham.

Then, today, Amber telling Jessica she could tell Joseph she was leaving and make the whole family hate her. It all connected in my head, piecing itself together as I lay motionless.

If Michael's father was named Joseph, it would all make sense, and Joseph was clearly the leader of whatever that business card was for. Whatever secret society Garrett seemed to be a part of.

Stand. I commanded my legs to work, for my body to roll and my arms to push off from the sand, cold beneath my scraped and bruised palms. I needed to *stand* and run and get far from the water, to get closer to safety.

Instead, I lay there, blinking at the dark sky, sipping at the air like too deep a breath might mean the next would never come.

My wet clothes—*Sophie's* wet clothes—clung to my skin, making every breeze an assault, every second another reason to *move.*

But it wasn't self-preservation that forced me from that spot, crawling my way toward the boardwalk because I couldn't trust my legs to support me. It wasn't even my anger.

No, that came later, when I replayed it over and over, every night since the one it happened, until it was replaced with a memory I wanted even less.

He'd called me a bitch, though I'd done nothing to him. At least not that I was aware of. How exceptionally rude.

But more, it was his lack of specificity. Let *what* go? The questions I had about Garrett? About the phone number? I'd discover later how wrong I was to assume those were one and the same question. Related, yes. The same? Most definitely not. What forced me from that spot was the question I needed answered.

And so I crawled, pawing through the sand as I went, nearly

knocking over a couple scouring for discarded shells, dark and invisible as I was on the empty beach.

Finally, a blink of light drew me closer. My phone, Monica's name lighting my screen. My hand touched metal just as it went silent, revealing the string of calls and texts I'd been too busy being nearly murdered to answer.

The call started again, and my shaking finger slid across the screen. I don't remember what she said to me, her voice barreling through the receiver. I only remember the one thing that mattered: Michael Graham's father's name.

It took a moment for Monica to text Adam and ask. And then I had my answer.

That was when I cried.

Because I had his name.

CHAPTER ELEVEN
SOPHIE

Amber's house is quiet, a single light burning in the dining room, giving me a glimpse into her world. The family photos grouped in clusters along the far wall, the generic art print with swirls of burgundy and yellow surrounding stone-hearth bread. Six chairs tucked into the table.

Mom keeps the curtains closed in our house now. No one stalking outside my dining room window would be able to study anything.

Or maybe those closed curtains would tell them everything they need to know.

Ocean-scented air streams through my cracked windows, flitting over my ankles as I recline in my passenger seat, legs propped against the dashboard while I wait for Amber to come home from wherever she is.

At first, the amount of time it took to track down her address irritated me. I had to avoid any contacts that Isa and Charla share with me, since they would undoubtedly find me and death-stare me into leaving if they knew where to find me. But then I called Del and made them virtual pinkie swear not to tell Isa or Charla who I was looking for, and got all the info I needed.

That was two hours ago.

Since then, I have:

Changed out of my ballet gear in my car.

Pulled out my bun and finger-combed my hair at least three times.

Listened to my entire "Crabby and Grumpy" Spotify playlist twice.

Nearly given up approximately 47 million times.

But then I looked at my unanswered text to Garrett and cranked my earbuds higher.

Nora always tells me I never follow anything through. I'm all enthusiasm and no results.

But Nora is *wrong* and I am here, even though Isa and Charla are going to kill me later for leaving and for ignoring their texts; I will die knowing I made Nora into a liar.

Ha! She already *is* a liar! And she stole my boyfriend. Probably.

Honestly, I'd skip town if Nora made me leave a party to hang out with her too.

I drop my feet to the floorboards and max out the volume on my earbuds, singing along to a particularly angry chorus because it's better than therapy.

Something slams into the window next to me, and all my innards climb to my eyeballs while I scream, throwing myself clear across the center console and into the driver's seat.

My head cracks against the window and my feet hit the headliner, and one of my flip-flops tumbles through the air until it splats onto the dashboard.

I scramble for the steering wheel to yank myself upright because I'm about to be that girl who gets killed because her grand escape involved a turtle impersonation.

When I finally right myself and calm down enough to restore vital functions, the only part of the culprit I can see is a torso. I scramble for the locks, but I know I engaged them earlier.

Except maybe not, because they thunk over when I hit the button.

It's a good thing I can dance because otherwise I'd be very worried about my future.

I rip the remaining earbud free and survey the torso, because while my desire for not-death is telling me to start the car and floor it, there's something about the figure that's familiar. And it appears to be . . . shaking. Vibrating?

I take a deep breath, hold it, and listen.

Laughing. Barely restrained, barely-trying-to-hide-it laughing.

I stretch toward the window, putting myself *closer* to the danger. Great job, Soph. "Jude?"

I don't actually have to ask. I know it's him. I recognize his torso.

He bends until his face comes into view, and he's mostly got the laughing under control but his mouth is still twitching. "I am now getting a better idea of why Del sent me here."

Apparently a pinkie swear doesn't mean what it used to.

I yank on the door handle so I can storm out of the car but it's locked, so I look like an idiot, which makes me even madder.

When I finally free myself from the Houdini-level escape room that is my very own vehicle, I face Jude over the roof. "They promised they wouldn't tell where I was." I hold up my crooked little finger. "Pinkie swore it."

"Hmmm." He rocks on his heels. "I guess a pinkie swear isn't what it used to be."

"Exactly!" I'm smiling, because while he's obviously making fun of me, I don't get that sick feeling like I'm failing him somehow, *embarrassing* him. My breath catches as a thought spears itself into my brain: It's not like with Garrett.

My smile wobbles and I force it wide, but the way his voice drops when he says "You didn't answer your phone. Del got worried" tells me he's not fooled.

"I'm perfectly capable of taking care of myself."

"Yeah, of course." He opens my (unlocked) passenger door and bends into the car. My flip-flop sails over the roof a second later.

I catch it—ha! reflexes!—and stick it on my foot before I check my phone and find a whole screen of texts and missed calls. And okay, fine, I bailed on ballet, which is not my usual MO, but it's so super great to realize everyone in your life thinks you're so incompetent that you'd mess up sitting in your own car.

"Hey." He nods toward the back of my car and a second later jumps onto the trunk, the soft ping of metal telling me he's patting it for me to come sit next to him.

I'm supposed to be watching Amber's house, but I'm sick of staring at it and my head is so messy right now I could use the distraction. I hop next to him, metal cold against the back of my thighs. "This is a pretty terrible way to conduct a stakeout."

His eyes flare, and for a moment, it looks like he might ask for details, but then he shakes his head, a smile flickering over his lips. "You are full of surprises."

I laugh. "On rare occasions, they're actually good ones."

He gives me a small smile. I can't tell if it's understanding or pity, but it's a good smile either way.

He makes sense at night, where the shadows give cover and moonlight gives him a space to come alive. He makes sense in the quiet, probably writes poems or paints.

The wind bends the tall trunks of the palms trees above, sending their long leaves into crisp rustling, and it's nice. The quiet. The calmness.

I never considered myself a nighttime girl, but maybe the sunlight was just where I thought I was supposed to be.

He says, "So. Teach me how to be Sophie Linden."

"Uhhhh."

"How to talk to people. Ask . . . questions."

"You want me to teach you how to hold a conversation?" He shrugs, and I mean, it's not like he couldn't use the lesson. "Okay. I'm much more of a 'learn through doing' kinda girl, so let's just practice. Ask me about myself."

"Yeah, sure." He rubs his palms over his jeans, like he's actually nervous. "So, Sophie, tell me about yourself."

Jesus take the fucking wheel. "Not like that! You—"

"You told me to ask—"

"It's a conversation, not a job interview, Jude!"

"I blame my teacher."

I say, "Shut up!" and shove him, my laughter joining his, and it's nice, feeling like someone who has something to say, something worth knowing. Nora must feel like this all the time. No wonder she's so insufferable.

I say, "New tactic. Let's say we just met. You know I like dance, so maybe you ask what styles of dance I do. And I tell you ballet, jazz, contemporary, and modern—"

"Do you sleep?"

"Not often, but you're losing focus. So once I say what styles I do, maybe you ask which one I like best. *Why* I like it best. Maybe then you ask if I plan to dance in college and then what college I want to go to. Think of it like a tree. Dance is just one big branch, and all of those questions are smaller ones for you to follow."

"Tree. Branches. Got it."

"And you can share parts of yourself too! It doesn't have to be an inquisition."

"Or a job interview." He nudges me, and I laugh, the sound quiet against the chirps of insects that fill the night.

"Or a job interview. But don't be that person who only asks questions as an excuse to bring the conversation back around to themselves. No one likes that. Okay, try again."

He does. He asks about my family. (Wise choice. Most people have them.) Do I have any siblings? (I do!) What is she like? (There are no words.) Parents? (Divorced.) Father (Absent.) Mother? (Generally disappointed in me.)

That's when he grimaces and says, "This topic felt much safer when I started it."

I laugh again, even though those answers should have me feeling way depressed. I glance to Amber's house again, and it's still dark, still closed up tight. The longer I stay here, the more I want to leave. Everything. All my questions about Amber and Garrett and even Nora. I want to get in the car with Jude and drive to the beach and pretend I'm someone else.

I swing my legs, my heels hitting the bumper. "What about you? Any siblings to be disappointed in you?"

His eyes crinkle when he smiles. "Only child."

"You want to hear something just truly wild?" At his murmur of assent, I add, "In a conversation, you can give information about yourself even if you aren't explicitly asked."

He leans back, sliding along my trunk until he can rest against the rear window, his gaze turned toward the smattering of stars that surround the sliver of moon. "I'm an only child, and it's because my dad died when I was five. He was an accountant, and then 9/11 happened and he enlisted. My parents met in the service. Got married. Had one perfect son, and then he left on a tour. Never came back."

I shove myself back toward him, and he gives me a shrug paired with a look that says "you asked" but it feels exactly like when I make myself smile when all I want to do is cry. "That . . . sucks."

It's so far from the right thing to say, but it's the closest I've got to the truth.

He's silent for a second, and then his deep laughter rumbles through the air. "It *does* suck. But my mom is the most amazing person I know. Does lesson two talk about how to extricate yourself when you ask the wrong questions?"

"Truthfully? Most people lie or avoid when the answers are too uncomfortable. If it were anyone besides you, Charla, or Isa asking about my family, I would've."

I'm sitting on hard metal, but somehow the ground beneath me feels unstable, because it's true, what I just said. I *would've* lied. I would've smiled and painted a pretty picture that hid all the ugly parts, and to be honest, I don't know what to do with that realization.

His eyes meet mine, a study in shadows, and his fingertips graze my temple as he brushes my hair back. They're slightly rough, calloused, and I want to know everything about how they got that way.

His voice dips low. "I'm glad you didn't lie."

I whisper, "Me too," and I mean it, so strongly the ground tilts again when I remember I'm here for Garrett. For my do-over. I'm here to save him or maybe just apologize, but I am not here to have deep conversations with Jude I-don't-even-know-his-last-name.

I jump from the car, breaking whatever moment I was drowning myself in. "Anyway! Lesson over! Gold star for tonight!"

I turn before he can respond, heading for Amber's house. Maybe there's someone home. I can talk my way in if there is. I am *not* completely incompetent. I *will* crush this do-over.

Jude falls in step beside me and says, "How'd it go with the cops?" because now I've trained him to ask questions even when I don't want him to.

Jesus. The cops. Maybe I should've stayed on the trunk. Because now it's like it never even happened.

I should tell the cops Garrett texted me, right? Do they even care? The very vast majority of people are convinced Garrett left—he left a note for fuck's sake *and* took out ten thousand dollars—and he's off traveling the world, probably with some chick, having grand adventures.

"That well, huh?" Jude shoves back a loose curl, only for it to defy him yet again. You'd think he'd stop trying.

I pause at the end of Amber's driveway. "It was fine. The officer kind of blew me off to be honest. Said it may not even have been blood."

His eyes go wide. "Blood?"

Oopsies. "You really want to know?" I don't give him the chance to answer because, truth is, I suck at secrets, and I'm pathetically trying to reclaim some of what I felt just a few minutes ago. I'm not smart enough to concoct elaborate lies and actually remember them when I need to. And I don't like the way they make me feel, like there's this darkness festering inside me, and if I let it settle there, let it become a real part of me, I'll never be able to scrape it out.

I say, "I was dating this guy named Garrett, and one day he left a party with my sister and never came back. I've never told anyone that, by the way, also I lied to the police about it. The sister part, not the Garrett part. I'm assuming you've heard about that. She won't tell me why. She won't talk to me about anything, actually, even when she's home, which is less and less, and I'm too much of a coward to force her to answer my questions because, I don't know, maybe I'm really afraid she'll tell me the truth, and maybe the truth will be more than I want to hear."

I take in a breath and keep rambling. "I mean, would *you* want to hear that your sister was secretly hanging out with your boyfriend?"

"Definitely not."

"Right? Anyway, the other day I found a note in my dance bag, from Garrett, except maybe it wasn't recent. I don't know. And then at the party I found this necklace that had dried blood on it hanging from my rearview mirror, and then you took me to the police."

His lips part, just a little. "Wow."

"I just confessed my darkest secret to you and all you can say is 'wow'?" He *really* sucks at the sharing-about-yourself part.

I stomp toward Amber's door and knock hard enough to make my knuckles throb. "Tell Del I'm fine."

I knock again, stepping back to look for a shift of the curtains or a light flaring to life, but there's nothing.

I head around the back. I don't know why, exactly; maybe because I'm too embarrassed to go sit in my car again.

The damp grass tickles my feet—it's overgrown. Not by much, but enough. Maybe Amber is too busy phone banking for secret societies to cut it.

Jude jogs up next to me as I turn into the backyard. "Hey. I wasn't—"

"It's fine. I'm being melodramatic."

"Maybe a little. Can we—"

"Shhh." I hold my arm out, stopping Jude where he stands, and whisper, "Did you hear that?"

He whispers back a no, but his body goes as tense as mine.

My eyes strain to adjust to the darkness. Amber's house has no motion lights, no lights at all, leaving us in a thick blackness that leaves me fumbling for anything to grab on to. Anything solid to help me find left from right, up from down.

I hear it again, the smallest shuffle from just behind me, and I spin in place. But there's nothing there. Only more of the dark. I creep forward, arms outstretched so I don't trip over anything, because now that I'm here I really just want to be *not here* but I don't want to go back the way of the shuffling sound.

"Sophie."

I think I like how he says my name. Quiet. Maybe even gentle. Or maybe I just miss hearing *anyone* say it. I turn, but my gaze skips right over him.

A mass shifts behind him, and I know I should scream, or run, or do anything other than the thing I actually do, which is shove Jude directly into whatever the danger is.

There's the *swoosh* through the air, and none of it makes sense until something connects with my ribs, shocking the air from my lungs. Pain explodes through my side, but I can't cry out because I'm too busy gasping, doubled over, my knees in the wet grass.

And it's so stupid, so selfishly, stupidly, classically *me*, but my first thought is whether I'll be okay enough to dance at the summer intensive.

But then someone grunts, and I remember that I physically threw Jude into the source of danger and it's enough to get me off my knees, to get me scrambling toward the figures wrestling in the dark.

Before I can get there the bad guy is on his feet, running from the yard until he's lost in the darkness, so dark even shadows can't survive.

My hand lands on some part of Jude's body, and I whisper, "Are you okay?"

He says, "Yeah," even though he grimaces as he pulls himself to sit upright. "I think I got a few more shots in than he did."

"Sorry, I . . . you know."

"Nearly got me killed?"

I hiss, "Did not!"

"If he had a knife—"

"Except he didn't."

"Lucky for me." He stands and holds out his hand, which I grab on instinct and immediately regret.

My ribs scream, and I want to melt into a puddle of throbbing death.

Jude mutters something about getting out of there and hurries me around the side of the house, both of us scanning in all directions in case someone pops out from behind a tree.

The yard feels four times the length it was on the way there, and it's only once we're safely inside my car—with the doors definitely locked—and driving down the road, Amber's house shrinking to nothing but a pinprick of that dining room light, that I let my body relax.

I squirm in my seat, the pain pulsing from my ribs flaring higher with every inhale. They can't be broken. *Can't.* I'm not throwing away my chance at a dance career because I trespassed in Amber's backyard.

I press my hand against my side—I want to look, but I really don't want to look. "I probably need to go to the hospital. Or maybe to the cops?"

Jude flinches, knuckles white on the steering wheel until he transforms back into bored and disinterested. "Sure about that?"

"Well, we were assaulted, so—"

"On someone else's property."

I settle back into my seat, letting his words sink into me. We could get in trouble. *I* could get in trouble. No straightening up and flying right here.

I'd have to tell Mom everything—about the note from Garrett, the text that led me to Amber. I'd have to admit I didn't tell Garrett's parents or the police that he contacted me. It won't matter that I *meant* to; it'll just be more *typical Sophie,* so caught up in herself she couldn't even go to the cops when she needed to.

I whisper, "Okay. I'll just say I fell. And . . ." I pause, debating whether I should give him this out, and exactly *why* he might need to take it. "I won't tell them you were with me."

He hesitates, like he wants to argue, but once we get to the hospital, I go in alone.

I get home after Mom, mostly because I drove slowly on purpose, letting the ocean air tunnel through my open windows to chase away the reminder of where I've been—of antiseptic and bleach—that clings to my skin.

I'm okay to drive. My ribs aren't broken, just bruised. From my *fall*.

The doctor spoke with my mom in the hall, and I'm nearly positive he's convinced her I'm hiding something. Which I am, but not like they think.

I can dance, but I'm supposed to take some time off. I won't. I can't. I still have to beg Mrs. Wilson for forgiveness for leaving early today.

I ease into the driveway, Mom's car already safely tucked into the garage, and click the locks—three times—as I head to the back door.

The night is still, a cold wetness that coats the air, like the sky might end its silence and send a rush of rain streaming toward me. I almost wish for it, for a reason to stand here and let the droplets soak into my hair, my clothes, let it leave me shivering until the outside of me matches what's within.

Nora didn't come to the hospital.

Mom said she was studying.

Studying.

I told myself I wouldn't ask. I'd been there over an hour—Isa was there, Charla too—and neither of them yelled at me about ditching practice. Because they knew how scared I was, how afraid I might have messed everything up over another stupid Sophie decision.

Even Mom paced the hallways when she thought I wasn't looking. Both her and Dad may treat dance like it's a hobby I'll grow out of one day when I realize you can't pay bills with audience applause, but I think she knows it's the only thing I'm really good at. Without dance, I'm just a C student, destined to be buried beneath the achievements of everyone smarter than me, more determined, more focused. More *Nora*.

That's why she should've been there. No amount of studying should've been able to keep her away. If I close my eyes, let the rustle of palms drift me into an almost dream, I can still feel her fingers combing through my hair like she did whenever I was sick. The chirp of crickets become her voice, soothing me to sleep, thick with fever dreams, and she'd be there when I woke. Always.

I don't know where that Nora went. The one who cared. The one who thought I was worth her energy.

Worth anything.

The door creaks as I open it, the soft glow of the foyer light drifting over the wood floorboards. Mom's humming floats in from the living room as I kick off my flip-flops. She's happy. Relieved. I don't know whether to be grateful or annoyed.

"Honey?" She only calls me that when she's worried. "You okay?"

I wave her off. "Yeah, totally. Go to bed."

She steps back, pauses, fatigue drawn in the lines on her face, sadness in the darkness beneath her eyes. She wants to say something.

No, that's not right. She feels *obligated* to say something, but work comes early in the morning. It's always work.

It was all she had after Dad left. Maybe she understands me better than I think.

She says, "You know you can talk to me, right?" and yep, the doctor definitely didn't believe my trip-and-fall story.

My lips fall open, all the words poised on my tongue, the past month of outrage and guilt driving themselves up my throat. Why shouldn't I tell Mom what Nora did? I'm protecting her, and she couldn't even come see me in the hospital. It's that original lie that's gotten me in every bit of trouble, and honestly? Fuck Nora.

I suck in a breath large enough to hold my entire confession, and a floorboard upstairs creaks.

It steals all the words from my head. Nora is *home*.

I don't want Mom to fight this for me. I want Nora to admit what she did. To my face.

I nod at Mom, as reassuring as I can make it. "Of course I know. It was just a fall. Really."

She gives me a wan smile, a quiet "okay," and then she's gone, slipping up the stairs and into her room, where there are no daughters to worry over.

I follow behind, waiting until the crack of light beneath her door winks out, and I head to Nora's room.

I used to do this, before, when we were best friends. I'd wait until Mom and Dad went to sleep and I'd sneak across the hall and Nora would be waiting. We'd make a tent out of blankets, and Nora would read to me by flashlight, soft glow fading into the corners of our fort. And then I'd fall asleep, and on the nights she couldn't wake me, she'd roll me onto a blanket and drag me across the hall, tucking my pillow beneath my head. For years, Mom would line my floor with pillows to cushion my fall as I "fell out of bed," while Nora watched on with equal parts amusement and frustration. *Do they never wonder why they don't hear you hitting the floor?*

Smarter than everyone in the room. Even then.

I knock, softly at first, then louder, my heart fluttering and my breaths too thin. This is what we are now.

The door swings open, and Nora stands inside the sliver of doorway, her robe tied tight around her waist. "Yes?"

There's so much I want to say, and everything rushes into my head with the speed of that bat against my ribs. I want to scream at her, ask her why she left with Garrett that night, what she knows and why she can't tell me. I want to ask why she was at North Hills with Garrett.

But even when I try I'm not that girl. I'm just me—too sensitive, too emotional, why-do-you-take-everything-so-personally Sophie, and I say, "You didn't come to the hospital."

My voice breaks at the end, and there's a flicker of the old Nora. The sit-by-my-bedside Nora.

This one can't even look me in the eye.

It's gone as quickly as it came. "I was studying."

"Studying *what*?"

It's too hot in this tiny space between us. Too much tangled in all the words we aren't saying, all the secrets that kept building until we lost sight of each other.

She blinks twice and her checks shade pink, and when she speaks, her voice comes out breathy, totally at odds with her words. "I'm preparing for the SAT, Soph. It's highly critical I do well on them. I wouldn't expect you to understand."

And then she closes the door between us, a wall of wood that can't even begin to cover the distance. The click of the lock signals the end of any hope of what I need.

It's not until I'm turning away, hot tears burning their way down my cheeks, that the picture of her comes back to me. She was clothed beneath her robe, and not in her typical Nora uniform of tights. She was wearing *jeans*. Black jeans.

Nora, my sister, who would never deviate from a norm even if it's one she set herself, was dressed in exactly the type of thing you'd wear to do things you wanted no one else to see.

CHAPTER TWELVE
NORA

Joseph Graham, father of Michael Graham (aforementioned ex-boyfriend of one Jessica Horton), was an attorney. Owner of his own firm, with a loving wife and three sons.

Eric was off at college (Stanford) while Benjamin was the youngest, just a freshman, but then there was Michael. My classmate. Monica had to show me his picture in the yearbook. Adam pointed out that Michael was also on the football team with Garrett—and with him.

He didn't actually point out Michael was on the football team *with him*, hoping, perhaps, that I would forget where he spent the majority of his time, as well as who all of his friends were.

He was particularly on edge that evening, when I'd nearly been murdered, after I'd finally crawled up the beach and answered Monica's fourth call.

I'd only been away from my phone long enough for four calls. The average ring time is only 30 to 45 seconds. Four calls, made consecutively, makes for 120 to 180 seconds. Turns out, it doesn't take very long to die.

The clear evidence that I didn't die—that being my physical body still functioning by the time he made it to me—did not seem to console him much.

He fretted and paced and hugged me too tightly before screaming a curse that drew the entire boardwalk in our direction.

We left immediately after. Attention was not what any of us desired. And then he insisted on sitting in the back seat of his own car with me while Monica drove and he told me countless times how sorry he was—like he'd been the one with his hand twisted in my hair, holding me under.

And then we'd all filed into my house, them waiting downstairs while I showered, wincing at the tender spot of my scalp where my attacker had held tight, shaking at the memory of being so helpless, so utterly separated from control.

I started this because I thought Garrett had something to hide. Because of a copied paper. It seemed silly now. Childish. The kind of worry that retrospect does not view kindly.

But how quickly it had become personal. You don't threaten to murder someone unless you are *very* worried. And it seemed *someone* was, indeed, very worried.

I'd been handed instructions. *Let it go, bitch.* But as always, this wasn't just about me. If this was in any way related to Garrett, it was related to Sophie. If they were willing to kill me, they'd do the same to her.

And *that* was why we stayed up far too late, huddled in Adam's bedroom, learning everything possible about Michael and Joseph Graham. About Eric and even little Benjamin too. Until Monica left and it was just me and Adam. Until all the events of the night siphoned the energy from my bones all at once and even the thought of walking next door to my own home seemed too great a feat.

"Don't go." That's what Adam said to me, his eyes serious, his hands fisting and releasing at his sides. "Don't go home, Nor. I'm serious. Stay here."

He couldn't even meet my eyes as he added, "With me."

I don't need retrospect to tell me doing so was the wrong decision. I knew it that night, the moment the words tumbled from his lips.

They filled the room, pressing against me with all the weight they were due, and when I should've said no, my mouth said yes instead.

He offered, as he should have, to sleep on the floor, but I was so cold—still so cold, my hair only having begun to dry. And when I thought too hard, the ocean, the sand, the weight on my back all rushed in, leaving me shaking. And Adam, he was my touchstone. Had always been, just as I'd been his.

So I crawled into his bed, cold sheets quickly warming with the heat of his body. Always so hot, like his temperature ran a few degrees greater than most. He followed behind, leaving the desk lamp at a low dim, as if he knew what the dark might bring me.

The mattress shifted beneath his weight, and I didn't try to resist the way it pulled me closer to him. I didn't pull away as his hand reached for mine and didn't stop my fingers from curling around his when he intertwined them.

This was not like the sleepovers from before we were twelve. It was clear from the shortness of his breaths, the rush of his heartbeat, too quick for normal, but steady—always so steady. I never gave much thought to the size of him—the breadth of his shoulders or the way his body dwarfed mine. He was Adam, and that was the way he was. But then, so close we breathed the same air, it was impossible to ignore.

He unlinked our hands to run his fingers through my hair, brush it from my temple as he dipped his head closer to mine and whispered, "Maybe you should—"

"No." I knew what he planned to say, likely before the thought had entered his head. I should do what the man said. I should let this go.

"Nora." It was the way he said my name that got me to listen, like he'd infused it with a lifetime of feelings poured into two small syllables. "You could've—"

It wasn't me that stopped him then. It was the thickness in his voice. His fingertip trailed down my temple, over my cheek, igniting a rise of goose bumps over my skin as he said, "I can't lose you."

"I'll be careful."

"No. You'll be Nora. And tomorrow you won't wake up scared like you are now; you'll wake up angry. Because he hurt you, because he told you what to do, because he . . . *dared* to challenge the will of Nora Linden. Stop laughing; I'm being serious."

I let my smile fade and replaced his worries with my palm against his cheek, his stubble little pinpricks to remind me where I was, and where I was not. "Okay."

I don't know why I said it. Letting this go was the last thing I intended to do, but maybe, for those few moments, I wanted to.

I doubt he believed me, but in those few moments, maybe he wanted to too. Maybe he needed to.

His lips brushed mine, tentative, halting, waiting for me to do what we both should have. I threaded my fingers through his hair instead, pulling him closer until his hands spread over my back, trembling at first before they turned insistent.

His tongue slid against mine, my hands finding their way to the plane of his stomach, all of it like this was always meant to be what happened next.

Then some rational part of me took over, and I pulled away, my finger to his lips.

A pause. A rewind, to before we changed seventeen years of everything.

He tucked me into his chest, until I was surrounded by the spice of his soap and the gentle ocean-air breeze, and the world went dark with sleep.

He was gone when my eyes blinked open to the hazy touch of sun that had just begun to wake, the sheets cold where he'd been.

And as with most times where Adam was concerned on the subject of me, he was right.

I woke up angry.

CHAPTER THIRTEEN
NORA

I skipped school the next day. And the day after that.

For most high school seniors, this would not be a cause for great alarm. Skipping school is a rite of passage. An expectation, really.

For me, it meant several emails from teachers and a slew of panicked texts from friends and classmates, who were all sure I'd succumbed to a bout of typhoid or polio, as only something so serious could have kept me from school for two consecutive days.

They weren't completely unfounded fears—well, the concerns about all-but-eradicated diseases were, perhaps, though since a large portion of the population seemed to have written off things like logic and science, maybe they were right to speculate—but I hadn't missed a day of school since second grade, when Tommy Welliver drank out of my juice box without my knowledge and gave me strep throat.

No, that's a lie. And since there will be those who attempt to discredit this confession based on the smallest of details, I'll reveal the details I want to admit least. I missed four days a few years ago. We told everyone it was an impromptu vacation. None of us came back relaxed and tan, we went nowhere, and all I got was a lousy parents' divorce and a sister who wouldn't talk to me. But I renewed my focus and set my vow in place and it hadn't wavered since.

Until yesterday. Until I counted down the seconds of when the bell would have rung had I been sitting in class, when I was sitting in my car, down the street from Joseph Graham's driveway, instead.

That was the point when I began to worry.

Not that I wasn't worried before—nearly dying has that effect on a person. Some might say it gave me perspective. AP Calculus seemed less important than it had even twenty-four hours earlier. I couldn't quite bring myself to care that Alice Mass would likely close the distance on our GPAs with the work I'd miss. Not when my throat still remained raw, when my mouth would still fill with the taste of salt water.

That was what made me worry. The *apathy*. It felt too familiar. Too like those four days after I faltered and everything fell apart.

Oddly, it was Adam who pulled me back together that time. He'd found me, high in the twisted oak at the corner of my yard, holes snagged in three separate places of my tights, so my pale skin glared against the black fabric.

He'd poked at the spot as he said, "What did she say?" because of course it could only be Sophie who would leave me in such a state, and I'd replied, "That it was all my fault."

But now that I'd nearly been killed, Adam was the only person I *hadn't* heard from. Truly, I didn't know how to feel about that. He would've noticed my absence, but maybe he no longer cared. I doubted that was the case. Kiss or no kiss, he'd been my friend since birth, and as long as the rules of space and time remained constant, he would still have to see me. Often. He lived not twenty feet from my bedroom window.

Those were not the things I was angry about though. Those were things I pushed to the recesses of my mind while I took to greater tasks.

Namely, finding out everything I could about Joseph Graham.

Boring: He was still an attorney of his own law firm, he had a stately mansion just steps from the ocean, he drove a Lamborghini (on day one), a Ferrari (day two), and when he wanted to feel like one of the regular folk, perhaps the Land Rover in his garage got taken for a spin. It was rumored he planned to run for office one day (hence his sons attending public school—optics are important) and hosted several annual charity drives, which his wife had made a full-time living off organizing.

Useful: He was cheating on his wife.

I didn't even need Day Two to discover that. How pathetically expected of him.

"Miss?" The receptionist looked at me with big doe eyes, her perfectly lined lips enunciating every word with practiced ease. Beside me, Jessica fidgeted.

I should probably provide context for how I came to be sitting in the lobby of Joseph Graham's office, with Jessica Horton. The truth was, I blackmailed her.

Very unbecoming of me but entirely necessary. Also effective.

While serving on the yearbook committee, Jessica had the unfortunate idea to photoshop herself into a picture with Garrett. Sadly for her, Laney Dalton is an excellent photographer and discovered the deception within minutes of Jessica submitting it for yearbook contention.

Laney, smart girl that she is, notified me immediately. We of course opted not to include the photo, and at the time, I felt no need to embarrass Jessica by confronting her.

That changed when a man tried to kill me.

Under threat of exposure to the entire school, Jessica set up the meeting I was about to attend with one Joseph Graham, father of her ex-boyfriend.

Suffice it to say, Jessica hated me deeply at that point.

The receptionist led us both back, Jessica seething in my ear about how she "couldn't believe I was putting her through this" and I was "such a bitch" and a "fashion disaster."

Perhaps her insults would've wounded me if she weren't the girl who submitted a photo to the yearbook with half her calf missing.

Joseph sat behind a heavy desk, a wall of windows at his back and an assortment of furniture placed just so throughout the room. Diplomas hung on the walls, alongside chummy photos with government leaders and diplomats, his adoring family, and an assortment of celebrities.

There is a certain air about men with a bit of power, an internal framework that holds them standing tall even when they don't deserve to. That was Joseph, from the way he leaned back in his chair to his duplicitous smile. "Please, Ms. Linden, have a seat."

Conventional wisdom might suggest giving your real name to the man you're stalking would not be prudent. But I had no doubt he'd find out anyway, and I was hoping this little meeting could end in a treaty of sorts. And those require honesty.

I settled into the plush chair, mirroring his casual pose. "Thank you for seeing me."

His eyes narrowed, assessing. "Jessica said you wanted to discuss something with me."

Sunlight streamed through the windows, casting him in an ethereal glow, and the scent of mint lingered in the air.

He leaned back farther. "Do your parents know you're here?"

"Does your wife know where you spent lunch yesterday?"

Well. I had intended to take things a bit more slowly, maybe finesse him into admitting what I needed to know.

But as I said, I was angry.

"Jessica, you can wait outside." It was possible his utter dismissal wounded her more than my threats did.

Jessica grumbled the entire way out the door, shooting evil looks at both of us on her way out.

"Who are you, Ms. Linden?"

"Well, I go to school with your son, and I happen to know of your involvement with a certain . . . business venture."

As I've made clear already, I had *no* knowledge of his business venture, but I couldn't risk weakening my position by admitting it.

I added, "And it was me you sent Jessica and Amber to wait for Wednesday."

He nodded, likely as close to an acknowledgment of my being at least a somewhat worthy opponent as I would get. "And you want to make use of my services, but . . ." He scanned over the length of me. "You can't afford it, and you're seeking to blackmail me instead."

I raised an eyebrow because I had no response and hoped he couldn't see the way my hands had started to sweat, or how my knee threatened to jump.

He chuckled. I hate that word; it feels so unrefined, but it's the only one that describes what he did. And then he rose from his seat, disdain seeping from his pores, and headed toward the door. "If a simple indiscretion was all it took for my wife to leave me, she'd have done it long before."

Charming.

The door swished across the thick carpet. Another dismissal. But I wasn't Jessica.

"Now, Ms. Linden, if you'll—"

"Those aren't the indiscretions I'm here to talk about. Well, yes and no." I didn't turn toward him—a confident debater does not need audience feedback. "See, I've done my research, Mr. Graham, and in so doing discovered that you have many a donor who are, shall we say, from groups that would not appreciate a man regularly cheating on his wife. And while I'm sure there are no shortage of men who'd look at you with pity and say unironically, 'There but for the grace of God go I,' *their* wives—and surely their fellow *congregants* might indeed care."

His sharp intake told me he was about to argue, so I held up a single hand. Also a dismissal.

"Perhaps that isn't enough for you. It does seem so many are willing to overlook the complete and utter moral failings of others if it suits their cause, yes? How about we discuss your wife's charities. I must admit I'm only seventeen and certainly not trained in tax law, but I *did* spend some time reviewing the annual report of both her foundations, and I compared them to various promotional materials found on her various social accounts. It raised some rather concerning questions. Namely, discrepancies between the percentage of donor funds promised to go to the actual causes, the marketing tactics around which funds would be awarded, which could be considered dubious at best. And lastly, I couldn't help but notice the rather large purchases that seem to be done annually and shortly after these fundraisers—you really should tell your sons to make their social media private. And while people may be forgiving of men's *indiscretions*, the IRS is not."

I waited, breath held, until the door clicked shut.

Joseph Graham appeared in front of me again, leaning against his desk, arms crossed, clearly not my biggest fan. "You don't seem like the type to need our services."

I couldn't exactly say whether I was or was not, considering I still had no idea what his services were, so I said, "And why is that?"

"If you wanted a job, there would have been far more . . . ladylike ways to go about asking."

"I'm not a lady, Mr. Graham."

His mouth quirked. He probably found himself quite charming. "It's not as simple as writing a good paper, or preparing good test answers—the true talent lies in your ability to do so in the name of another person. Convincingly."

Motherfucker! That was the word that swam through my head at the time, but if my face revealed my emotion, Joseph didn't seem to notice. He wanted me to cheat. To do so to help another student.

He said, "We'll discuss your pay pending performance on your first job. It won't be an easy one, I'm afraid. This particular client has"—he paused, considering his next words carefully—"been a bit of a challenge."

He leaned over, scribbling something on thick white paper with sharp strokes of his fountain pen, and held it out to me, poised between two fingers.

And that was how this story brought me right back into the path of Garrett Packard.

CHAPTER FOURTEEN
SOPHIE

I'd make a terrible spy.

I've glanced over Amber Donahue's way approximately five quadrillion times in this single class period. She can't hang up on me in the hallway after class, so that's where I plan to confront her.

She knows something. Something about Garrett. Maybe something about Nora. She knows whether I should be searching for my missing boyfriend or cycling through rage and betrayal because he was cheating with my own sister.

My eyes wander to Amber again, who stares straight ahead like I'm Medusa and she's afraid of being turned to stone.

Mr. Finnegan taps all over the smartboard, drawing molecular diagrams or something I'm supposed to be paying attention to, and Amber is too but she doesn't even blink when Principal Wentville interrupts class to steal some package off a very confused Mr. Finnegan's desk. Pretty sure Wentville could strip naked and she wouldn't even try to shield her eyes.

Despite her all-black, very suspect attire last night, it couldn't have been Nora at Amber's house. Nora wouldn't *hurt* me.

Only, maybe that's not true. She left with Garrett that night. They were acting so weird around each other, and then there were those rumors. The ones some freshman started about Nora and Garrett arguing in the library. I blew them off. I'm good at ignoring conflicts. Like Mom was good at ignoring Dad's "late-night work dinners."

The bell shatters my thoughts, trilling through the room to bounce off cinder-block walls. Amber moves so fast she's nearly out the door before I can gather my books.

I clutch them to my chest, my backpack hanging from one shoulder, and push through the bottleneck at the door, the other students parting to give me passage.

Zuri—aka What's-Her-Name from The Stans—hovers at the exit door, her eyes locked on mine. She still makes no sense. She's not a part of the Jessica Horton crowd, not even in the "Garrett's disappearance brings people together" way. She's from *Nora's* crowd. She should be reciting the periodic table or whatever smart people do in their free time.

My entire body tenses, but Zuri doesn't stop me—she steps aside to clear my path and her eyes flick away like she was never looking at all.

Amber's halfway down the hall before I pop free from the crowd.

I call her name, and her steps stutter before speeding up. She is absolutely avoiding me.

The nerve.

I chase after her, my bruised ribs throbbing with each step, and I ignore the voices that call my name—loud, exuberant, an acknowledgment that I've come to life again, even if it's in all the wrong ways.

I turn the corner just in time to see her duck through a doorway—a hall that leads to the locker rooms—and I hit it full speed, the metal bar slamming into itself and echoing down to where Amber stands.

She turns, anger bursting from her skin. "No."

"No *what*?" For real, I've never done anything to this girl.

"No to you and whatever questions you have, and no to your entire fucking family!" She's screaming by the end, and she punctuates her sentence by spinning and legit *running* in the other direction like she's afraid I'm going to chase her down and tackle her from behind.

"Amber!" I keep my jog slow, my voice calming. "I just—"

Adam appears at the end of the hall, clearly cutting through to the B wing, and Amber barrels right into him, nearly knocking the backpack from his shoulder. He must be severely under Nora's influence if he's started actually bringing books to class.

He has to catch Amber to keep her from landing on her ass, and when she recovers, she shifts herself to stand behind him, only her head peeking from around his arm. "Just leave me alone."

Her anger is gone, only fear left in its place, her eyes rimmed with tears, and I don't even know where to start. "Please. I—"

I just need answers. That's what I want to say. I'm desperate for them. Every cell in my body straining against the confines of my skin, begging her to please quiet all the fears in my head. The thoughts and theories that destroy me, bit by bit, chip away at the center of me until I'm nothing but hollow.

But that's not what Amber needs.

I breathe deep, let my bag and books drop right where I stand, and step forward. "I'm sorry. I shouldn't have chased you—it would totally freak me out too if some psycho bitch hunted me down."

A slight smile wobbles on Amber's lips, and that's when I know I've got her. My best play would be to tell her everything. Confide in her so she can confide in me. But I can't exactly tell her my missing ex-boyfriend texted me the number I called her on. And then there's Adam, standing there, too quiet, too still.

I inch closer. "Someone sent me that number, and I don't know why. And to be honest it's kind of fucking with my head, so I was hoping . . . You know what? Never mind. I'm—"

I'm only half turned when Amber calls, "Sophie, wait," just like I knew she would.

She says, "I can't get in trouble again or I'm out," and I have no earthly idea what she's talking about, but she seems to think I do. I can't disguise the shock on my face when she continues with "But that was your sister's fault—not yours."

I've moved closer on instinct, every hair standing on end, like I'm so close to understanding something that's only been visible through shadow, a figure in my peripheral that blinks away when I turn toward it. "What did Nora do to you?"

Amber wrings her hands, and I'm afraid I'm pushing too hard, so I let the moment hang, the rush of air-conditioning through the exposed vents filling the quiet, the hustle of students rushing to class a distant backdrop.

She sucks in a breath, and Adam says, "I don't think she wants to talk, Soph."

Just like that. He ruins all my progress in the rumble of his deep baritone, and Amber nods, claiming she "has to go" and scurrying away, taking my answers with her.

I stare at him, his eyes harder than I've ever seen them. The door slams shut far down the hall, and I manage to choke out, "Adam, what the fuck?"

He waits a beat too long, like he's weighing his first response

115

against whatever lurks inside him, holding him back from the truth. "You're not the only person he left, Sophie."

I blink at him, because I know. Of course I know. I saw it in Garrett's parents' eyes that night, and in Adam's the next day and the day after. I felt it as his presence slipped from all our grasps—memories fading with each rise of the sun, until recollection feels too slick to hold, until his voice is only a whisper in my head.

Tears threaten as I rasp out, "Do you wonder, Adam? Do you worry that he's really dead?"

It's the first time I've spoken that word out loud. Dead. Not that he left. Not passed away or gone or any of those substitutes covered in softness, gentle syllables to cover the truth's sharp edges.

"No." He holds my gaze, unwavering. "It's not too late, Soph."

I stomp forward, barely holding back the scream in my throat. "Is this a fucking thing now? Everyone speaks in riddles? What does that even *mean*?"

His mouth quirks at the corner, like he might reach out and ruffle my hair like he used to. And then he does—folding me into him until I'm surrounded by the heat of his body, his heavy arms hugging me tight as he tickles the top of my head with his breath, chest rumbling with every word. "It means it's not too late, Little Linden, to decide if what you want is worth what you'll have to give up."

Then he's gone, leaving me alone, standing in the empty hall as he heads back the way he came.

CHAPTER FIFTEEN
NORA

I'm getting a bit ahead of myself, with the talk of Garrett and exactly how, in the end, everything led back to him. Likely because this next part is the portion I want to confess the least.

The day had started badly, my time spent with Monica* the night before reaching far longer than either of us had intended. Huddled around the soft stretch of lighting that poured over the mottled wood of the library desk. The sun had dipped low in the sky, leaving the windows like mirrors, as we whispered the implications of what I'd discovered in my meeting with Joseph Graham.

Garrett Packard, and plenty others just like him, were vile, pathetic cheaters.

That was the only explanation that fit what Joseph had said, and I had unwittingly placed myself in his employ. The injustice of having *already* written Garrett's paper for him—without any sort of payment, I might add—had me so enraged, the idea of sleep seemed an impossibility.

And now I'd have to continue to service Garrett and allow him to keep his imposter GPA through *my* hard work.

I've always had a deep and abiding hatred for cheaters. But more than that, I cannot stand a liar. I suppose that's why I've never been able to sustain a relationship with my father. No number of guilt-motivated gifts could make up for a lack of honor.

And men like my father, boys like Garrett, they had none.

It was rage that kept me up late into the night, finishing the school-work that I'd fallen behind on while investigating Garrett. Also while nearly being murdered. And then I'd stumbled out of bed far later than normal, which meant Sophie found me in the kitchen that morning when I should have left long ago to volunteer at the shelter.

She stuttered to a stop, her hair pulled into a sleek bun atop her head, the top of her leotard peeking out from the warm-up jacket that bore her name in cursive along the left side. "What are you doing here?"

I mumbled, "I live here" as I spooned another bit of oatmeal into my mouth.

"You *sleep* here."

This had long been a topic of contention between us—how seldom we saw each other. It had never been good, but before the divorce, things *had* been different. Not that Dad ever shared in his portion of the housework. He may have cut the lawn on Sunday, driven us to activities when Mom couldn't, but—as is custom in our patriarchal society—Mom carried the burden of parenthood. It was her who purchased the groceries and made the meals, who made the appointments—nay, remembered we *needed* appointments, who read the teacher emails and set up playdates, who counseled us (Sophie) on friend drama and tucked us in at night.

Still, his absence seemed to shift something, to throw off the orbit of our family until we each found our own space in the solar system. Sophie had friends and dance, I had my life plan, and Mom had work.

He made a fool of me. That's what she said to me, when her initial shock overrode the knowledge that those types of discussions were meant for friends and not daughters.

I think of it often. How much vulnerability marriage must take. It's not *difficult* to love a person. But to trust them, that seemed like a venture not worth undertaking.

I swirled my squiggle of honey in my bowl, keeping my voice gentle. "Sophie, you—"

"It's fine." She yanked open the refrigerator, clearly not fine. "You have school. I get it. You're *very busy*."

"You're at practice every night."

"Maybe if I had a reason to be home, I wouldn't."

"Yes, you would." We stared across the island, the years of hurt like the width of the ocean between us.

She slammed her orange juice onto the counter so hard it splashed over the rim, pooling around the edge of the cup. "Okay, yes, I love dance, and it's what I want to do forever. But it's never been the most important thing to me. Ever."

This too had been a point of contention—perhaps *the* point of contention.

I placed my hands in front of me, pressed my fingertips into the quartz of the countertop until they went white. This is what they mean, when they say love is blind. Not that you don't see the faults in the other person, but that you see them so clearly you turn away from them.

Sophie's greatest fault had always been believing in me. Believing that I was the type of person you could ever be completely vulnerable with. She needed someone soft, someone who could reassure her when she stumbled. Not only could I not be that person, I couldn't stop being the person I was.

I solved her problems. I made her decisions. I gave her the opposite of what she needed, just as she did me. She understood my stony silence, the walls I built around myself. She allowed me them and flowed through the cracks like water. If I had Sophie, I'd never need to open myself to anyone else.

I said, "Do you remember when Dad attempted to plant a garden?"

She blinked away the threat of tears and rolled her eyes. "The one the mice completely fucked up the second the fruits and veggies started to grow."

"I doubt the strawberries got bigger than a marble." I laughed, and she followed because that was Sophie—if I was happy, she was happy. "It wasn't just the mice though. Remember he planted sunflowers right next to the potatoes?"

"No." She stuffed the remaining half of her muffin into her mouth and slid into the stool next to me.

"Well, he did. Only, sunflowers have allelopathic properties—"

"Sure. Do I need to know what that means for this little fable to make sense?"

I jammed her with my elbow, and she giggled, almost like the days we spent as The Linden Sisters. "It *means* they have biological traits that can influence surrounding plants, and they happen to be particularly toxic to potatoes."

Sophie was smarter than she ever gave herself credit for. I didn't have to explain my point. I knew she understood when her silence filled the air, weighing it down until it became hard to breathe.

And then the quick inhale that always preceded her tears. "Cool, cool. So I'm the toxic sunflower then, right? I'm—"

"Would you rather be the potato?"

"You know I don't want to be the fucking potato, Nora."

"Good."

"Not *good*." She shoved away from the island. "I hate this story, and I hate this stupid idea that you have that it's a bad thing for us to be close. We're—"

"Sophie." I waited until she looked to me, her eyes glassy and her bottom lip trembling, and I said the words I knew she'd hate the most. "You don't need me."

It happened so quickly I barely had time to react. My bowl flew across the expanse of the island, taking flight at the edge, where it tumbled to the floor.

It shattered into chunks and shards, splinters of itself strewn across the wood and settling between the planks.

She waited for *me* that time, until our eyes met, and she whispered, "Fuck you, Nora."

Then she was gone, taking the sunlight with her.

I should've stopped her. Explained what I really meant in ways she'd understand. It had always been nearly my greatest weakness— taking the things I felt and forming them into words, into a language that made sense to those around me.

But of course I didn't stop her.

Partly because I was a coward. I can admit that now. So afraid to disrupt anything because people were not things you could plan for. People did the thing you least expected when you most needed them not to. Sophie perhaps more than anyone I'd known. Wild. Unpredictable. Golden petals blossoming toward the sky on a thin stalk that followed the will of the wind.

The other reason, I can admit that now too. I was selfish.

Since I've been so transparent—much to my detriment—you know it's true when I say Sophie did not need me. That her reliance on me would only serve to keep her from reaching farther, standing taller, a perfect target for the sun's rays.

But as they say, secure your oxygen mask before those next to you. What Sophie couldn't see was that I was wilting, caught up in something that very well may disrupt everything all on its own.

As if to underscore this point, no sooner had Sophie stomped up the stairs, most assuredly with her phone in hand, frantically texting Isa and Charla to tell them of my betrayal, than my phone rang.

I recognized the area code and prefix—had it memorized for years, still felt the jolt of energy burst through me at the sight of it.

I answered with a quick hello, and a familiar voice asking to speak with me.

Ms. Kohler had become a friend of sorts, forged through my unwavering interest in Brown and my—even by my own standards—somewhat annoying insistence on involving myself in any and all of their programs that might endear me to the school.

But there was a formality to her tone now.

It was that very moment I knew I'd passed the point of disruption long ago, every spoken syllable driving that certainty further home as she said, "I'm sorry to say, Ms. Linden, that we've received a very concerning report about your academic dishonesty."

CHAPTER SIXTEEN

SOPHIE

Clearly, Adam is dealing with some shit.

Clearly, that shit involves Nora.

I suspect we're dealing with the same shit, just in very different ways and for very different reasons.

Or maybe the exact same reasons. How the hell should I know. Maybe it's hypocritical of me to be all angry with everyone for keeping secrets when I've got several of my own lurking about my brain, but at least I'm not skulking about giving grave warnings about "deciding what to sacrifice" or whatever bullshit Adam bestowed upon me today.

But everyone's secrets are only so safe, because there are things that I know, little pieces of their hidden lives, and it sure seems like Garrett is trying to lead me to them—and, if I'm lucky, lead me back to him.

He gave me a number that led to Amber, who landed in some kind of trouble after an interaction with Nora. And then there's the bloody necklace in my car.

Garrett could've left that too. It would just mean he's sending me notes that say he misses me while simultaneously threatening me with some other girl's necklace.

I didn't look for him. I didn't stand vigil outside his house, hoping he'd return. I didn't call him after that first night. I didn't light candles for him or leave teddy bears to rot by his picture beneath his favorite tree in the quad. And I lied. Not for him. I lied for Nora.

I chose her, and maybe Garrett thinks I chose wrong. Maybe this isn't a do-over at all. Maybe Garrett is very, very angry.

A shudder works through me, the spike of cold fear enough motivation to cross the threshold I've been standing in.

Nora's room is neat. Of course it is. She doesn't have a cup overflowing with pencils missing their erasers or the sand from her mini Zen garden settling into the grooves of her wood desk. That all belongs to me. Nora has file folders, in alpha order, and a pencil drawer with plastic dividers that keep her supplies just where she wants them. That *should* make this easy.

I pull open the drawer, rows of carefully labeled tabs standing sentry over their army-green folders.

All of it is blah blah blah school stuff, volunteering stuff. *Nora* stuff. But none of it says "ticket" or "first time I've ever done anything wrong in my life." I need to find it—the proof she was in North Hills that night at the same date and time as Garrett. That speeding ticket is undeniable proof.

I try the other side of her desk, all the smaller drawers. Then I move to her dresser drawers and even the shelf of her closet, all while waiting for her to pick *now* as the time she finally comes home. It would be exactly as always—never on my terms. Always just the way Nora wants it.

I shove aside her clothes, harder than necessary. She could've shredded the ticket. Destroyed any evidence of fallibility. I only know it exists because I found it on Mom's dresser. Dad pays for the insurance, so clearly he could never know about the ticket, which meant Mom had to get it down to something that carried no points. Can't have him seeing the cracks he left behind.

Nora's armoire looms large. My last hope. Skirts fill the rod, grouped by color, their fabrics nearly reaching the shelf below them, fanning over a camera I've never seen before.

I power it on, popping open the preview to view the photos. It takes me a second, my Birmingdale High Rolodex flitting through a thousand entries. It's not as simple as recognizing a face—this isn't a student. The man is older. White guy, salt-and-pepper hair, nice clothes. *Really* nice clothes. Tailored to his tall, slender frame. But there's something familiar, the cut of his jaw, the slope of his nose.

Michael Graham! The guy in the picture looks like Michael Graham. Michael's in Nora's grade. One of the expected-to-get-into-college-by-early-decision types but not like Nora and her friends. He's the vacation-home-in-Aspen, invite-only-parties, already-has-his-future-fraternity breed.

And in this pic, his dad is kissing a woman who is definitely not his wife.

I mumble, "What the actual fuck, Nora" to the air.

Nora wouldn't get involved in shit like this. She'd call it trivial, uninteresting. She'd say, "He isn't *your* husband, Sophie. What business is it of yours?" while silently judging the hell out of him for the dishonesty. Nora has never been interested in gossip, and now she's stalking classmates' fathers and photographing them?

I scroll back but it's the first photo, so I thumb the right arrow. There are several more pictures, none more interesting than the makeout sesh.

My finger freezes over the button on the next shot. To avoid getting too far past PG-13, I'll just say I'd recognize any part of Garrett's body within an instant. That's how I know I'm looking at Garrett's hand in this photo. An accidental shot, for sure, but there is no damn good reason for Nora to be taking pictures of my boyfriend—ex-boyfriend . . . maybe boyfriend. Maybe the boy who wants revenge for abandoning him.

I miss you, babe.

I never thought those words could sound so threatening.

I click to the next shot, and Nora's face fills the tiny screen, a scowl molded deep into the lines of her face. It's the same date. The time stamp only a few minutes after Garrett's hand.

Garrett took this picture of Nora.

Garrett took this picture of Nora on the twenty-third of October, the same day Nora got that ticket.

And no, she doesn't look happy to see him, but Nora doesn't look happy to see anyone lately. I don't even know *who* she sees lately.

Normally we'd have suffered through Thanksgiving—Dad's family in the morning and Mom's at night—together. But she invented some bullshit excuse about volunteering and sent me to Dad's alone, then slipped away after an hour at Aunt Kelly's, leaving me to face the inquisition, courtesy of our cousins, who all wanted to hear more about what happened to Garrett than even Jessica Horton.

She knew what she was doing, knew without her there to balance Dad's attention, it would be even more obvious all the ways I fall short in his eyes. He may never forgive Nora for humiliating him, for taking all his actions and placing them on stark display. Every mistake, every failing, laid bare. But they share a language—syntax built on achievement, success, a holy order built on rising above the lessers.

I don't speak their language. The only thing I'm good at is talking to people and dance. And Dad only sees the latter as a drain on his finances. An unsure future with minimal monetary reward. *Who will you come to when you need to pay rent, Sophie? When you need food? Your mother? We both know it will be me. The only time I hear from you is when you want money.*

That last part isn't true, but it isn't *not* true either. Maybe I'd see him more if I didn't have to hear what a failure I am. How I'll never be Nora. How even though Nora ruined his life he'd still pick her over me. Maybe I'd try if he would've tried for me. If he wouldn't have given up, packed his bags, and left without even a goodbye. Maybe if I were enough, he wouldn't have wanted to.

I slam my finger on the camera to see what other glorious surprises might await me in the next pics, but there are none.

I may not be as smart as Nora. I may be too trusting and naive and the word Dad says when he thinks I'm not listening—*gullible*. But not today.

Nora deleted whatever came after those pictures, and not a week later, she was sneaking off with Garrett, the last person to see him that night.

And I covered for her.

It was me who made it possible for her to keep all those secrets she's tucked away, taken with her as she slips through life without question or consequence. And she let me.

She used me while she snuck around with my boyfriend and lied to me, boldly, brazenly, without a sliver of guilt.

And now I'm going to pay her back.

CHAPTER SEVENTEEN
NORA

I did not beg Ms. Kohler to let me explain my innocence. Nor did I plead. I remain proud of that reaction to this day. The guilty grovel, and I was not guilty.

Not yet anyway.

I calmly explained to Ms. Kohler that there had been a mixup, and surely, whatever report she'd received about my *academic dishonesty* was patently false. I assured her I would talk to the principal on Monday and we could all resolve this soon enough.

None of that was true of course. Principal Wentville remained as spineless as ever, and the only way free from this rather monumental setback was to expose Garrett Packard once and for all. Which I had planned to do anyway, so this was fine.

I was not, by any stretch, threatening to come undone as my entire life began to unravel only a few days after I was nearly drowned by a psychopathic private investigator.

I was also undisturbed by how my best friend since childhood had staunchly refused to acknowledge my existence for over forty-eight hours.

All of these very small things that were completely manageable and *not at all* making me want to launch into a primal sort of scream right there above my shattered bowl of cold oatmeal did not contribute to the thing I want to confess least.

So it was in that moment I decided to storm over to Adam Russo's house and search for answers. Maybe a business card of his own, and then I would know Adam was as much a liar as Garrett.

I burst out our side door, letting it slam behind me as I marched across the sun-warmed lawn, blades tickling my feet as the breeze rustled my skirt and tossed my hair about my neck.

It was the type of day where Sophie, Adam, and I would head to the beach, letting the water froth over our ankles and daring the others to go deeper even as goose bumps sprung over our skin. Where the sun would seep into our pores as the sand shifted beneath our feet, white-tipped waves barreling toward land, where they'd land softly, reaching, *reaching* until they melted into the shore, leaving behind bits of broken shells and rocks unearthed from the ocean's depths.

Then we'd lie shoulder to shoulder, our heads propped by molded sand pillows, and watch the clouds crawl overhead, marking the passage of time we'd forgotten to keep.

Always Sophie to my left, Adam to my right. Always me as a link between them.

At least, that's what I assumed. But it seemed lately, life had become determined to show me all the things I didn't know.

I have never been particularly good with surprises.

History may look more kindly on my entering the Russo home if I were to lie and say I had no idea it would be empty. But again, confession . . . honesty . . . full disclosure—I've covered this previously.

I knew it would be empty. I knew the Russos habitually left their doors unlocked, and even if they hadn't, I knew the garage code was 26-14 for Adam's and his sister's birthdays, and I knew where the spare key was hidden and I even had one of my own linked onto my key chain.

Perhaps we can view my trespassing as an open invitation.

I knocked, softly, only once, and let myself inside.

Jasmine and vanilla swirled through the entranceway, and behind it, the sweetness of chocolate.

Brownies. Never a shortage of baked goods in the Russo house.

I shut—and locked—the door behind me before scurrying through the kitchen, grabbing a still-warm chunk of brownie along the way. A corner piece—the edges are the best part.

While the chunks of chocolate melted deliriously on my tongue, I peeked into the living room, ensuring I was as alone as I'd hoped to be.

Not that Adam's parents or sister would have so much as blinked at me wandering into his room, but considering I planned to snoop through all of his things to see if he too had a business card that matched Garrett's—they were the closest of friends, in case the reminder is necessary—I'd rather be able to conduct my business in peace.

Carpet squished beneath my feet as I bounded up the stairs, two at a time, and then three, until I had to force down an oversize brownie lump so I wouldn't choke on my own labored breathing.

Then I stood in the doorway to Adam's room, licking smudges of melted chocolate from my fingers, and I paused.

I'm not heartless. Not even ruthless—at least where friends were concerned, and Adam had always been my greatest. And yet, there was something I couldn't quite place. Something in the way he looked at me, that night after the *incident*—i.e., my near murder.

Something haunted in his voice as he whispered, over and over, that he was sorry.

There was something—always *had been* something—about who he became with Garrett.

Everyone knows the world was designed for a white, straight, cis, able-bodied man, but there are those who know it and those who expect it. In Garrett's presence, Adam strayed too close to the latter.

I crossed the threshold, every part of me aware I'd done so literally and figuratively. This was a betrayal, no matter how pure my motives. I hadn't even tried to ask him. Not directly.

But I couldn't have, because he shunned me.

So I started with the desk. Sliding open drawers, pawing through them as their contents skittered into now-empty spaces. Then to the dresser, separating each folded shirt from the one below it to ensure nothing had been tucked between. I squeezed each bundle of socks and even shook out every pair of underwear. (I turned my head while doing so, which was as close to providing him privacy as I could offer.)

I yanked bedding from the mattress until it bundled around my ankles, Adam's warm, smoky scent rising from the fabric as quickly as the memories of us lying here just days ago, his hand pressed to my back, his lips insistent.

I stomped on the pool of sheets beneath me and heaved the mattress to the wall, revealing nothing but an expanse of emptiness across the plane of the box spring.

The mattress thumped back down, blowing the hair from my face and chilling the hint of sweat on my skin, rattling the frames on his shelves.

Fitting, since I appeared in several of them, my arm locked around Adam, our suntanned cheeks pressed against each other's.

I jumbled the bedding back onto the bed in the closest approximation of its original position as I could muster, throwing the pillows back into place with a bit more vehemence than I'd like to admit.

Every movement stoked my anger, swelled the building waves of frustration inside me. I wasn't supposed to be here, investigating my friend. I was supposed to be at work, earning volunteer points and placing yet another brick in the staircase that would lead to the rest of my life.

I tore open the closet, hinges creaking with the sudden movement, and riffled through his clothes, jamming my hands into pockets, letting the fabric slip through my pressed hands, searching for a hint of thick card stock that would prove all of this worthwhile.

The flaw in this plan was, of course, that business cards are small. Also flat. In summary, difficult to find.

The top of the closet proved more difficult, if only because of its height, for which I had to wheel over his desk chair, which I may or may not have fallen from at least twice as the seat swiveled beneath my feet.

Not all details need be confessed.

I don't know how long I spent searching through his things, the sheen of sweat transforming into a droplet that trickled down my back. Until my hair turned wild, sticking to the back of my neck, while my fingers became every clumsier with each failure.

I want it clear: I did not hope to find anything that might incriminate Adam.

I wanted nothing more than to leave there ashamed. But it was the not knowing that kept me there, heaving boxes of trophies from his closet shelf, dust tickling my nose, my heart beating faster as time wore on.

I think, looking back on it now, that it was my reluctance to find anything that kept me from finding it sooner. From looking in the one place that Adam would hide something he held most dear.

When we were still little but old enough to fend for ourselves, in the days before Adam had to sleep on the floor when I stayed the night, we'd started a war.

We'd drag a sleep-deprived parent out to the ocean, before dawn had begun to touch the sky, when the crash of waves had no one to reach for and the sand lay flat and smooth, chilled by the depths of the midnight ocean, and we'd search for shells.

Not on the beaches where tourists gathered from their hotels, but where the locals frequented, tucked away from the bustle of tourism, the shores of Pawley's or Cherry Grove, with piers sunk deep into the surf.

The biggest shell won. I held the title for years, and by ritual, all our names and the date of discovery were inked inside its smooth underside. For years I displayed it proudly, pointing it out at every opportunity, until one day, when some abnormally oversize whelk had decided to abandon its home, leaving behind a trophy that neither Sophie nor I were quick enough to run to.

And now it sat between two pictures of us, but untouched by the dust that dulled our likenesses, its tapered end tucked behind the frame, creams and golds highlighting its hard ridges.

My hand shook as I reached out, let the texture press into the pads of my fingers, and as I flipped it to its back, the black ink of our memory still scripted inside, something inside it rattled, slid deeper into its whorls.

I twisted my wrist, let the object slip down the swirl of the shell's body, until it tumbled free, settling to rest on my palm.

The chain dangled from the tips of my fingers, the charm anchoring it to my hand.

Music notes.

Once silver. Now covered in blood.

CHAPTER EIGHTEEN
NORA

A stair creaked, and I barely stifled a yelp, nearly dropping the shell square onto Adam's desk. I'd no sooner placed it back, slipping from my hands to land with a small clunk, before Adam appeared in the doorway.

His brow knit, lips parted, cheeks a deep red as his shirt clung to every plane of his chest. Sweat glistened in his hair, his football helmet clenched in his fist, and once again I became very aware of just how big his body was in comparison to mine.

He said simply, "The door was locked."

"I locked it." I tucked my hand into my skirt pocket, letting the necklace drop to the bottom. "What time is it?"

He took a step into the room, dropping his helmet to the floor. He smelled like sweat and sunshine. "How long have you been here?"

I blinked, and the vision of the necklace swam before my eyes. "Not long."

My voice shook, my heart stuttering in my chest, the weight of that necklace too heavy. There was no reason for him to have that. No reason for him to have hidden it. None that made sense. None that I wanted to envision.

He came closer, his hand reaching out to trail down the length of my arm. "The corner brownie was missing."

My thoughts tripped over one another, tumbling into new orders until they made sense. *The door was locked.* He'd known he hadn't left it that way, but he didn't call out, didn't make his presence known. He knew it was me in the house, and he'd waited until the stair creaked beneath his feet.

I know how I must've looked. My feet bare, while no shoes waited for me downstairs, my hair disheveled, my skin sticky with sweat. But more than that, I looked like I'd woken from a nightmare, that the world had upended and everything I thought I understood about the boy next door, the man I'd lain here with, protections stripped bare.

The words pressed against my lips, the tears against my eyes, while the necklace sat quietly in my pocket. *What is this? What does it mean?*

My body vibrated with the pleas I kept hostage. *Please let this not be true. Please let there be some explanation.*

Because it was a necklace I'd never seen and it was covered with blood. Dried, the thick crimson caked into the deep grooves of the charm, coating the delicate links surrounding it.

I wanted, so much, to convince myself it wasn't blood. But the metallic scent still clung to every breath, lingering like it might never leave.

He'd hidden it for it a reason, in a place no one would look.

Except me.

He said my name again, harder this time, all affection ripped free, and a realization rose up so strongly it took my breath away. I'd never seen Adam angry. Not truly. Certainly not with me.

Annoyed. Exasperated even. But never angry.

It was an entire facet of him that I'd never seen, and that necklace, its presence still so heavy in my pocket, maybe that was a side of him too.

Once I left here—*if* I left here—I couldn't let him know to check for it. Some desperate part of me argued it was nothing. That it belonged to some girlfriend and the blood was just some completely strange misunderstanding.

But I am, and always will be, the sort who is more practical than sanguine, and every bit of my intuition screamed to find a way out. *Any* way out.

I forced tears into my eyes. It wasn't hard, not when he stood just feet from me, a different person than I thought. "I'm sure you're wondering why I'm—"

"Yes."

"I'm here because it's been two days, Adam, and you—" I kept my head down, scanning the room for something I may have missed. Something that would tell him I hadn't been here to confront him for abandoning me after our kiss.

One of the hats from his closet sat there, mocking me. Tumbled out of the closet when I'd been searching. I thought I'd been careful, but there were so many. More hats than any one person could possibly wear.

He grabbed my hand, so small in his, and whispered, "I'm so sorry, Nor. I just—"

I ripped my arm free, forcing him into eye contact, which I held until the moment I stomped away, praying his focus remained on the top of me rather than the bottom as I spun, kicking the hat beneath his bed as I did so.

When I turned, his eyes met mine, and I could barely speak around the way my lungs had seized. "You're my first friend, Adam. My *best* friend."

My voice broke on the end, not an act at all, but not for the reasons he thought.

Tears glistened in his eyes, and I didn't stop him when he smothered me in a hug, his shirt damp beneath my fingers where I fisted the fabric of it.

His fingers threaded through my hair, and he tilted my head just enough to plant the lightest of kisses atop it, his lips brushing my hairline as he said, "I'm such an asshole."

"Why?" The word launched itself free before I could stop it, and I wanted desperately for him to answer it. To explain this all away so I could release this pressure in my chest, so I could hug him back without shaking, so everything didn't feel so upside down and ripped apart.

"I never wanted to hurt you. I just didn't know where we stood and"—he scrubbed his hand over his face, blinking away tears—"I was scared, Nora, that we broke something the other night that we wouldn't be able to fix."

I nodded, let my own tears fall. "Do you trust me, Adam?"

"Jesus, yes, of course!"

"Then be honest." Please be honest. Please tell me the truth.

His face flushed, his hands trembling as they framed my face. He blew out a breath, like he wasn't any more ready than I. "I love you, Nora. You know that, and I have waited *so long* for what happened the other night. But maybe—"

He sucked in a breath, and the indecision in his eyes gutted me.

He whispered, "But maybe it was a good thing you stopped us, before things went too far to take back."

I pulled free, watched his hands drop to his sides, and forced myself from his room, down the stairs, even across our yards without running, his gaze following me as I passed the line that divided our homes.

I ran the second the door closed behind me, my feet pounding against the cold flooring, racing to my room with the window that would always face his, until I could yank the necklace from my pocket so I wouldn't have to feel it anymore.

I dropped it onto my desk, the chain snaked like a river from the blood-laden charm, and it shattered everything I thought I knew.

CHAPTER NINETEEN
SOPHIE

"I have to pee." Isa pops her head between the front seats, nearly scaring Charla directly out of hers and making me jump so hard I put an even bigger hole in the sleeve of the sweatshirt I don't recall *putting* a hole in.

Charla turns to glare at her. "Maybe if you hadn't gotten a slushy at every gas station we've—"

"Two, Charla. I have purchased and consumed exactly *two* slushies out of the fifty-fucking-seven gas stations we've been to so far."

I fling the volume dial on Charla's car so it blasts from the speakers, loud enough to drown them both out. It hasn't been fifty-seven gas stations, but it sure as hell feels like it.

North Hills isn't that big, and yet its gas stations are plenty. All my fiery "I will make Nora pay" rage is quickly reducing to a tiny pile of embers that can't seem to stay lit.

Typical Sophie. Can never focus on one thing for longer than it takes to consume exactly two slushies. "C'mon, Isa, we'll go in together."

Charla rolls her eyes and mutters, "Well, I'm not staying out here *alone*," and then we're all trudging toward the fifty-fucking-seventh gas station of the night.

This would've been much easier if Nora had just left her ticket out for me to see. Then I could go in with authority, confident that Nora and Garrett were here. I just need someone who remembers them, someone who can place them at this location on that night. Together. Because right now even my friends think I'm losing it. So desperate to get Garrett back and reclaim my old life that I'm following conspiracy theories in every direction. And the truth is, sometimes I think they're right. But if it *is* Garrett texting me, if there's any chance he needs my help, or—

I almost can't even think it. If someone *has* him and is using his phone while he's out there suffering, I can't just walk away. Not this time.

But we've been to so many stations with zero success that I'm worried I've missed the only one they happened to stop at, or that it's just a different clerk than the one working that night.

I am, as I've said before, shit at planning things.

I approach the counter, watching in the big convex mirror as Charla drags Isa away from the slushy machine and toward the bathrooms. The clerk eyes me from behind her protective glass, her hair piled into a messy bun above her smudged eyeliner, like I might have a gun rather than my cell phone, queued up with pictures of Garrett and Nora.

Not together. They usually can't stand to be around each other, which was maybe all just because they didn't want me to know what was really going on between them.

I press my phone screen and hold it up to the plexiglass barrier. "Do you recognize this girl"—I flip to the next pic—"or this guy? They would've been in here on a Sunday night?"

"I don't work Sundays." She stares at the magazine in front of her, flipping the page like I'm not standing with my phone pressed against the glass.

"Could you just— Never mind."

This is stupid. I could be practicing. Or eating pizza. Organizing my socks or literally *anything* because it would all be smarter than this.

"What's going on?" Charla appears, using her calm voice. I asked her once how she perfected it, and she said it was all the practice from my white-girl nonsense.

I had no argument. Other than to point out that Isa was filled with just as much nonsense as me and she's brown.

Charla had no argument for that.

"She didn't work Sunday night." I point to the highly disinterested clerk. "What am I even doing, Charla? It's not my job to figure this shit out. I tried. I failed. Let's go home."

"Sophie." She calls to my back because I'm already walking toward the door.

This is so typical of me. Diving into something, then giving up when it gets hard. Nora's voice is 100 percent in my head telling me so.

My phone buzzes, and it's probably her. Like I've conjured her through criticism. But it's not Nora's name that lights my screen.

The door slams in my face because I'm too stunned to move.

Garrett's text glares from my screen, reflecting against the glass.

You didn't look for me.

My fingers fly over the screen even as I step backward, away from the glass door and the way it leaves me exposed. Garrett could be out there, right now, watching.

You LEFT. Your note said so.

Not the note he left for me, because I didn't get one.

Charla's arms wrap around me, bathing me in the scent of her coconut lotion, like she knows my muscles have all gone limp, the phone shaking in my hand.

They're just words. Innocuous. Statement of fact. I *didn't* look for him.

But it all feels wrong. His words don't sound like him. At least, not the Garrett I had most of the time. The Garrett I had until it got closer to the end, when his tone went colder, his temper shorter. Until the night before Halloween, when I finally asked the questions that had been building—about how he'd changed, about him and Nora—and his voice rose as steadily as mine. I flinched when he stepped toward me.

I don't know why. He'd never hit me. Despite the size of him, the strength of him, I'd never been *afraid* of Garrett. Not really.

He blinked, his eyes glassy, and then he left. Left me in *his* bedroom without a word. We didn't talk about it the next day. We just went to the party, where he drank too much—when he normally didn't drink at all—and he asked me to run away with him and I said no. And then he was gone.

"What's her deal?" The clerk has finally bothered to acknowledge my existence. Isn't she just precious.

Charla says, "Her *deal* is that she asked you a simple question and you didn't even try to help."

That's not true, and Charla knows it. I guarantee she read the texts over my shoulder and understands my *deal* has nothing to do with the clerk not helping me—but it seems to be an effective strategy because the clerk sighs, beckoning my phone back to her.

I have to swipe away from my unanswered text to show her the picture again, and Charla takes the phone from me. Her hand isn't shaking like mine when she holds it to the glass.

The clerk shakes her head. "Never seen them. But—"

She scribbles something on an open spot in her magazine, then tears the section free before sliding it into the well beneath the security glass. "Dude named Jimmy works Sunday nights. He's an asshole, and here's where you can usually find him. He doesn't have his own place, so that's the best I can do. Fucking loser."

She pauses, her eyes flickering to the phone screen Charla still holds against the glass. "Your mom is calling."

The phone buzzes a second later, rattling the glass, and Charla holds it out to me.

Call it intuition or a sixth sense or just plain old dumb fucking luck, but I knew it was bad before the phone hit my hand.

I didn't even get the chance to say hello before Mom's voice filled the speaker. "Sophie, you need to get home immediately. The police are here for you."

CHAPTER TWENTY
NORA

I went to school on Monday.

My sister may have been dating a disgusting cheater, and I may have been nearly killed investigating him, and my best friend may have killed someone, but there was no way I could miss more than two days of school.

People would talk. Rumors would start. Undoubtedly, Sophie had noticed, or heard through one of her never-ending social connections, but she was still too angry with me for not making her the potato, so we weren't currently on speaking terms.

I can recount this so plainly, so devoid of emotion, only because time has worn the edges of it, given me the distance from the pain of it.

Or maybe, it's because I know it was only a forewarning to the way this story ends.

But this was before that, when sitting there with Monica*, explaining just how awful Garrett Packard was, and that he was most definitely a disgusting cheater, felt important. (*Still not her real name.)

I did not tell her about the necklace.

She whispered, "So what are you going to do?" and several heads swiveled her way.

Yes, it was the library. Yes, we should not have been talking. But there were clearly a multitude of other tables they could've chosen with absolutely no one surrounding them and yet they'd placed themselves directly beside us.

I glared at them and hissed, "Move or I'll tell Mrs. Tisler you're all chewing gum."

There was no greater sin in the eyes of Mrs. Tisler, head librarian, than gum in the library. And predictably, they packed up their books—a flurry of ruffled papers and slammed covers—and scurried across the room.

Monica stared at me, eyes wide. "What's gotten into you?"

"Oh, you mean aside from my sister's boyfriend being involved in a cheating ring? Or perhaps it was being nearly murdered in the ocean? By a man who is likely still following me but just far better at it now, I presume."

She stared at me, her face blank. Much like that little emoji with the horizontal lines for eyes and a mouth that oozed disdain. Sophie was quite fond of him.

Monica said, "Fair enough."

"What am I going to do? First, I am going to see what I can get out of Garrett when he shows up for detention in three minutes. Second, I am going to investigate how Garrett continues to excel on tests even though my instincts were absolutely exemplary when I opined that he was barely intelligent enough to pass standard-level courses."

Lastly, and I did not say this to Monica—tracking down why Adam was hiding a bloody necklace.

I might have—the desire to have someone tell me my worst fears weren't true was almost too much—but then Garrett shuffled into view.

He mumbled a "Hey" in Monica's direction, clearly having no idea what her actual name was, and she rolled her eyes, mouthing a "Have fun" as she whisked herself away.

Lucky.

There was no sun that day to bathe him in a golden halo. No light bleeding through the windows to warm the table beneath my palms. It was a rare day of gray clouds that moved across a muted sky. The air heavy with unshed rain, the world a little quieter, solemn.

Garrett dropped into the seat, leaning far back enough I expected the chair to break. He barely tried to keep his voice down. "Why are we back here?"

"I didn't have time to drive to your house and make it to volunteer later."

That was a lie. I didn't want him to be able to throw me out, I didn't want the PI to see me at his house, and I didn't want to risk Adam interrupting again.

Actually, that's a lie too. I just wasn't ready to face Adam. Not until I knew more.

He sighed. Loudly. "Okay, well, I did some work on my paper."

He'd done no work on his paper.

It was obvious as he turned his screen toward me that he'd barely progressed past what I'd essentially dictated to him at our last meeting.

"Hmm." I made a show of perusing his "work," pulling his laptop toward me while pretending to read my own words as I propped up the business card I'd found in his room against the screen. "You know what I think you need, Garrett?"

He barely extended the effort to produce a "hmm?" sound.

"Someone to write this for you." I spun the laptop toward him and shoved it in the empty space between his arms.

I waited, until the exact moment his eyes landed on the card, until his skin went sallow and his lips parted in a silent curse.

His eyes dragged from the card and up to mine, then to the card Joseph had given me, which I held between two fingers. "Congratulations, Garrett. Today you get to meet your new tutor."

I smiled at him, and he paled even more, slamming his computer shut and stuffing it deep into his bag. By his twentieth mumbled curse, he'd managed to secure all his belongings and jump from his seat.

He was, quite plainly, losing his shit.

He pointed at me. "No. Not you."

And then he turned and stomped away.

This would obviously not do.

I threw all my things together in the most haphazard way, until my bag looked exactly like Sophie's does on a normal day, which caused me no small amount of anxiety, and hurried after him.

It took me at least two strides for every one of his, so I latched on to his elbow to slow him down, my voice seething through my whisper. "You're a coward, Garrett."

He ripped his arm free. "Fuck you, Nora."

He'd nearly made it to the library doors, where he'd likely sprint to his car. Which left me no choice but to use the biggest weapon I had, even if it was the furthest from the most dignified.

I called out, "I'll tell Sophie."

The group of freshman I'd relocated all spun toward me at once, more than a single gasp emanating from their lips. It was very likely I'd just started a very salacious rumor.

Garrett turned, so slowly it was as if time stood still. "She won't believe you."

Poor, stupid boy.

Sophie may not be speaking to me, we may never be The Linden Sisters again, not like we were before, but about this? She *would* believe me. Some bonds don't break.

I smiled again. "Yes, she will."

CHAPTER TWENTY-ONE
NORA

Sulking is an unattractive trait in anyone, but it was especially so in a boy like Garrett Packard.

We sat in his oversize SUV outside the school, his windows fogging against the wet chill and shielding us from the outside world. From the potential investigator that may or may not be following me. There was no way to tell in an area this size, rows of cars lined to the end of the lot.

He could be anywhere. In any one of them. I'd peeked beneath my car this morning, just in case. I'd taken to locking my doors and sleeping with both sets of keys for the same reason.

"Tell me everything." I turned to face Garrett. He'd chosen this location, but he surely regretted it now. He couldn't run, at least not without shoving me out the door first.

He threw his hands into the air. "It's not like you don't already know."

"I want to hear it from you."

"Whatever."

Sulking. Still unattractive.

I studied him, the sharp line of his jaw, the dark swoop of his hair, the breadth of his shoulders. Conventionally attractive for certain. It was just his entire *being* that repelled me. "You're not good enough for her."

He breathed out, "I know."

"Well. At least there's that. So, why not try, for once, to stop being such a spoiled, self-absorbed, whiny little *piece of shit* and answer the question?!"

Some may say that it was the point I almost drowned that led me to yelling in Garrett Packard's car. Others could argue it was from the moment that necklace dropped into my palm. In truth, I think it was the progression of the two. Or rather, the compounding of them. Every day felt like a part of me had been washed away. Tiny grains of sand being pulled from the shore and tossed into the chaos of waves and currents.

It wouldn't be accurate to say I didn't like it. Hated? Loathed? Detested? All were true. But more, I was terrified. If I didn't have school, work, Brown—if I no longer had my plan, I wasn't sure who I was.

"Okay. I mean. It's basically tutoring." Then, upon seeing the rage in my eyes, he amended to: "It's not tutoring."

"No. It's not. You have one person?"

He looked away, mouth pressed in the flattest of lines, fingers white around the steering wheel. "Yeah. To keep it as secretive as possible."

"How many people?"

"No clue."

"Try again."

"Honestly, Nora, I don't fucking know!"

"Names?"

He listed some. There's no need to recount them here. They're all included in the supporting documentation at the end of this confession. Sub-document B. But that is a topic for later in the tale.

I held my breath while he spoke, letting it go only when he got to the end without listing Adam. But then, he very well could've simply left him out.

My need to know things warred with my need to make the smart decision—to give Garrett not even a single thing to use as leverage.

And truly, did it matter if Adam was a cheater when I was already worried he was a kidnapper? A murderer? I said, "Adam?"

Garrett scoffed. "Oh, *now* you care about Adam?"

"I've always cared about Adam."

"Not the way he cares about you."

"Ah. I didn't realize it was a great moral failing to not reciprocate romantic feelings."

"You wouldn't have asked if you didn't"—he air-quoted—"'reciprocate romantic feelings.'"

"You're an infant. Did he or did he not cheat too?"

"He did not."

I blew out a breath. Pathetic, I know. It shouldn't have mattered, but it did. "Thank you."

I didn't mean it, and like the universe knew it, a torrent of rain opened the sky. Fat droplets spattered against the windshield, battering the roof and echoing against the windows.

I let it fill the silence for a moment, a reprieve from all the outside world, and closed my eyes.

I could've tried to convince him to confess. Walk straight into Wentville's office and tell him the great Garrett Packard was a liar and a thief, and the essay belonged to the brilliant Nora Linden and could we please, immediately, call the advisory board at Brown.

Then my world would be right again. My path solid again. Sure, he'd lose his reputation, his football career, probably his parents' love.

Wait. Of course his parents knew. Garrett didn't pay for this on his own. They'd never let him confess. Even if he did, they'd find a way to bury it, cover it all up. They'd never stand for the scandal.

So it was up to me then. And I'd need proof. I needed to clear my name, and I'd have to do it by destroying Garrett's. And his parents'. And anyone else who participated.

I could live with that.

I said, "What about the tests?"

"We take our own tests."

"And fail them?"

"You're such a bitch."

"Is that a yes?"

"It's a no."

"How is that possible?"

"I'm not answering any more of your questions." He cranked the engine, and chilled air blasted from the vents, carrying hints of ocean-laced rain and thick exhaust.

We rocketed backward, then forward, speeding toward the front of the school. His tires squealed as we rounded the corner, then skidded to a stop at the main entrance.

He clicked the locks and looked at me expectantly.

I said, "Who was your previous tutor?"

Maybe she was like me. Or maybe she was nothing like me, but if I could get her to talk, it might be all I needed.

"Get out."

"Garrett—"

"No. Tell Sophie if that's what you need to do. But we're done here."

I believed him, liar though he was.

Rain spattered against my skin the second I stepped outside, soaking me through in seconds, and I watched as Garrett drove off, a trail of white blooming from his exhaust.

Any naive dreams of letting this go vanished just like that cloud of smoke in the rain.

A secret Garrett was willing to risk Sophie for was a secret he'd die for.

CHAPTER TWENTY-TWO

SOPHIE

I should've gone home.

Of course I should've gone home.

When your mom calls and says get home immediately, the cops are here to talk to you, the smart thing is to get the fuck home immediately.

When you take into account my recent pledge to shape up and fly right, it would have been especially smart.

Not that smart decisions have ever been my thing. Like I said, set up for failure.

But there's actually a *very* good reason why we're headed to the address the clerk gave me. One that I'm sure I'll be explaining to the cops at some point. Right after they apologize for blowing me off when I was clearly right about the blood on the necklace. I have to have been. There's no other reason they'd be sitting at my house.

It's not exactly a subject I want to think about too intently right now.

Instead, I turn over all the thoughts crashing around in my head. If the texts are from Garrett, he's fine and severely pissed off that I've been such a shit girlfriend. If I stop looking for him now that I have an actual lead, my do-over will be done. If it's *not* Garrett, then I'd be walking away from my only actual lead and maybe the only chance to save him.

So, Mom and the cops can wait. I'll make up some excuse about getting lost on the way home or needing to drop Isa off or maybe I'll just give them no excuses at all. I'm not under arrest. You can't charge someone with "failure to return home immediately." If I find something that unravels this whole case, they'll be *thanking* me for ignoring them.

"Are you okay?" Charla glances over to me, which is a strong indicator that I am majorly freaking the fuck out because Charla is driving and she does *not* take her eyes off the road when she's driving.

I'm sure there's plenty of psychological data to be mined from how I chose a Nora 2.0 to be my best friend.

Isa's hand snakes between the seats to grasp mine, squeezing it tight, and Jesus take the wheel, I must be even worse than I thought because Charla doesn't yell at her for getting out of her seat belt.

Charla has *a thing* about seat belts after an accident that left her out of school for six months. Nora tutored her so Charla wouldn't have to repeat the grade.

I manage a whispered "Yeah, I'm fine," but we all know I'm a big, ugly liar.

The cops are at my house. Garrett may or may not be around but has revealed himself only to me and in the most ominous way possible. My dance career and summer intensive and the only plan for my life may be caught in the ocean's riptide, pulled deep into oblivion with every mile we drive away from my house.

But more than that—there's Nora.

"I think Nora's in trouble." The words snap from my throat, shoving themselves into the rhythmic hum of tires against the dark road. There and gone just like the columns of trees that blur past

156

my window and the brightness of the moon that disappears behind the forest's canopy.

It's not just that she was hanging out with my boyfriend. It's Michael Graham's dad too.

I don't want to voice the thoughts in my head. What if they were in some sick kind of relationship? What if a pervy old man took advantage of her and those pictures of him with another woman were because of jealousy? None of that feels like Nora, but if there's one place she's just as susceptible to idiocy as the rest of us, it's romantic relationships.

Not that statutory rape is a relationship. Definitely not. That's jail time. A mug shot and an address that pops up when prospective homebuyers search the national database in your neighborhood.

At least that's the way it's supposed to work. But things have a way of ending in the favor of powerful men like Joseph Graham.

Charla glances to me again before clearing her throat. "Isa, put your seat belt back on."

Isa's hand leaves mine, and a second later her belt clicks into place. *"Nora?"*

I feel stupid the second she questions it. Maybe even before that. "I know how ridiculous it sounds. She probably has the entire penal code memorized for fuck's sake. But . . ."

But what? She's been gone a lot? Nora's always had some project that pulled her away. She's been distant? Nora was *born* distant. An hour ago, I was furious with her for all the secrets she's been keeping. I'm *still* mad at her. I want to punish her and hug her all at once.

It's just this *feeling*. This pull I can't explain. A sickness that keeps building and turning, invading each of my cells until they all carry the same program and it's screaming that something's wrong. That for the first time, *Nora* needs *me*, and I'm failing her.

I'm not smart enough. Not determined enough or brave enough or even motivated enough to put together all the clues. I'm not *enough*.

Not for Garrett. Not for Dad. Not for Nora either.

"Should be just up the road." Charla's voice breaks the silence, replaced only moments later by a muted thump, pulsing stronger as we turn onto a gravel drive. A crumbling sign marks the entrance, the face of it tilted and speared into the grass where heavy stone once held it upright.

A warehouse stands tall across the pitted lot, an amber glow leaking from the rows of windows that aren't boarded by graying plywood. There are no swaying palms planted artfully to frame paved entrances and ocean-side paths. Only skeletal oaks dot the landscape here. Twisted branches black against the moon's glow. They seem to vibrate with the bass of the music, sway with the notes of guitar that grow stronger the closer we get.

"Are we at a rave?" The sound of a zipper punctuates Isa's words, and I'd bet everything she's trying to turn her outfit into something club worthy. "Because I did not come prepared."

I almost ask if we have the right address, but Charla doesn't make mistakes. Isa's hand appears, holding out an eyeliner, and I grab it but my heart's not in it.

Two months ago, I'd have been the first in the door—now I just want to find this clerk and get out of here. Or maybe find Garrett.

I flick open my text screen to Garrett's last message, the one he sent only moments after Mom's phone call:

Are you looking for me now?

I sent back a simple "Yes" to which he responded immediately.

Liar

Liar.

He's right. That's the worst part of it. And I swear he knows. He knows I lied for Nora. I don't know how he can be pissed at me when *he's* the one who left—without a note to me, in case I haven't been clear enough on that point.

But now he's back. Maybe. Or maybe he's just content to ruin my life from a million miles away. Or maybe I'm so racked with guilt, I'm trying to turn myself into a hero who saves Garrett from an evil captor.

But that feels less likely every moment since that text message. Whoever is sending these messages, they know *exactly* what happened between us. If it's not Garrett, it's someone he trusted enough to share things with. There's only one person who that could be, and the idea of Adam sending me weird text messages is the only thing more ludicrous than them coming from Garrett.

So Garrett is back, and he's mad. At me. If he tells anyone I lied, I'll be hated by everyone and an even bigger disappointment to my parents and it's hard to dance from a jail cell, which is undoubtedly where I'll be when the cops find out I withheld vital information.

"Withheld" sounds better than "lied." I need to remember to use that when I'm in handcuffs.

I jam my phone into the waistband of my leggings so there's no chance of someone slipping it from my sweatshirt pocket.

I may not be the sharpest tool, but I know I don't want to be left alone here with no phone.

We enter the building with hands linked—me first, leading the way, Charla at the end so she can keep watch over us, and Isa tucked safely in the middle. Just like always.

This isn't some Birmingdale house party though.

Rusted pillars stagger through the cavernous space, reaching toward the raftered ceilings, the music stretching to fill every inch of the open room. For a Thursday night, it's more crowded than I would've expected, a press of bodies writhing near a makeshift stage along the far wall.

Cold seeps through the walls, the open windows, the cement floor, until goose bumps cover all my exposed skin. Isa made us rave presentable, but it all feels wrong. Like I'm stumbling straight toward something terrible. Fumbling in the dark for a threat I can't see. And if only I could be who I needed to, I could turn on the lights.

I'm not made for this. There's no part of me that is up to this task.

I'm not the girl you trust to follow things through. I'm not even the girl you trust to start them.

I'm the girl who would bring home my report card, still unopened because sometimes it's better not to know, and I'd slip upstairs while Nora presented hers proudly. It was second grade when I tip-toed down the stairs as Mom and Dad read mine, my feet light and silent, my breath held, fingers wrapped so tight around the stair spindle my knuckles matched the whiteness of the paint.

Then, a long sigh, and Dad mumbled, "At least she can dance."

But after tonight, after being here instead of with the policemen in my kitchen, maybe I can't even do that.

Lights strobe overhead, mingling with hundreds of glow sticks that send trails of neon after the mass of moving bodies they circle. Vibrations ring through the floor, tingling up my legs as we move deeper into the mob, the heavy bass drowning my words as I ask the nearest stranger if they know where Jimmy is. They do not.

Neither does the next one, the one after that, or the five others I ask.

My throat's already raw from screaming, and I lost track of Isa and Charla somewhere around stranger three. Of course none of these people know Jimmy. They're here for a show, not because they live here like Jimmy does, which is how the clerk made it sound when she handed us this address.

I inch closer to the stage—where I'm hoping some sort of helper person might know more than half the high-as-fuck glow-stick groupies in the crowd—and every step earns me another crush of a body against mine, another elbow speared into my ribs, until each breath feels like I might not get another.

The crowd parts for someone. Someone big enough to push through the immovable mass, someone who walks in a way I'd recognize anywhere. Even here. Even among all these people.

I blink, then again, as the form slips away, as I lose sight of him in the bodies jumping in time with the music. Garrett. Adam. They're both large enough to force themselves through a crowd like that. They both carry themselves the same way—like they have a greater right to space than everyone else.

I try to follow, but I'm fighting against the pull of the stage, each new layer formed tighter, harder to break through. And maybe it makes me a coward, but I stop fighting. Because the truth is, if it was Garrett or Adam, I'm not sure I want to know.

I scan the stage and surrounding area, searching for someone who might help with what I came here for—to find Jimmy. My gaze gets stuck. It's not just the strong hands, deftly, expertly sliding down the neck of the guitar—though I'll admit they caught my attention—it's the hair.

A little long, tousled black waves that shine off the glare of lights surrounding the stage. His hands are busy so he can't brush it from his forehead like usual. Instead, he flicks his head back, timing it perfectly as the heavy guitar solo fades to its end, and then his voice fills the room. Deep, bold, just a touch of air in the lowest notes. He slides into one just as his eyes meet mine, and they don't leave. Holding me in this exact space even as the bodies around me fight for more room.

I'm mad.

I don't have an actual right to be mad. It's not like Jude owed me a history of all his current hobbies. But I still feel betrayed somehow. He knew who I was. *Sophie. The dancer.* He said it like an insult. But he didn't say: I'm Jude. The singer and guitarist or whatever. He had a perfect opportunity to share during our conversation lesson. And why is he here anyway? Is this a coincidence that he's playing at the same place I came to investigate?

Garrett would say I'm being irrational. That was his favorite word whenever I said something he didn't like. Sometimes he was right. Sometimes it seemed like it didn't matter if he was or not.

I shove sideways through the crowd. It was a dumb idea to assume some sound guy in an illegal rave in a shitty, run-down warehouse would be . . . I don't know . . . manning the speakers or something. But maybe there's a bouncer at the door. And the doors are far from the stage, so *even better*.

The crowd is wider than it is long though, and I'm sweating by the time I break free, sucking in the cool air like I was drowning. That's when Jude's voice comes over the speaker—sans music this time—and says they're going to take five.

"Take five" sounds like my mom saying "shape up." How embarrassing for him.

I shuffle over to some guy standing in the shadows like a serial killer, the tip of his blunt flaring red as I draw near.

He tips it toward me. "You want?"

"I don't. Hey, do you know a guy named Jimmy?"

"You mean Peacock?"

"I guess?"

He nods toward a sketchy door. "I can take you to him."

"Cool." I follow after him, like an idiot. This is absolutely the part where the dumb blonde gets murdered. But it's the closest I've gotten to why I came here, and I can't let it slip free.

Liar.

Every time I blink, the word flashes behind my eyes. He wasn't just talking about whether I was looking for him. He knows. He knows I lied to the police.

Stoner guy leads me through the door, and there's only darkness ahead as it thumps shut behind me, sealing us off from the rumble of the crowd, the flash of lights. It smells like piss and mold, and I have to thumb my phone's flashlight on before I can see where to step next.

163

The screen glares back at me, Garrett's accusation like a razor blade to my skin. The note in my bag, the cryptic texts, each one of them the smallest slice until I'm ready to bleed out onto the filthy floor.

My thumbs slam against the screen.

We need to talk. In person.

I hit send before I can convince myself not to. I don't make demands of Garrett. That's not how we work.

I hate myself a little more the second that thought pops into my head because it's true. He led, I followed. Garrett loves me, I know he does, but he loved me most when I stayed in the spaces he wanted me. When I was the person he wanted me to be, even though it wasn't always the person I *was*.

So I keep walking when Stoner guides me up the stairs, his phone light bouncing ahead to reveal dirt-caked corners and smeared walls, empty bottles and plastic baggies.

I keep to the middle, my skin begging to be scrubbed clean, my breath held for as long as I'm able, and even then, my lungs barely sip at the air.

The door at the top clacks open, and a burst of cold greets me, followed by the sharp tang of kerosene that emanates from the spattering of lanterns across the floor. Old couches are scattered over the space, competing with mattresses topped with bundles of blankets that seem to ebb as my light floods over them.

Candles flicker, flames stretching toward the vast ceiling, casting shadows that writhe against the cracked cement flooring. Gone is the hum of voices, the soft shush of fabrics from a thousand bodies on the main floor. It's quiet. Soft breaths, the scrape of a lighter, the clink of a glass.

I don't like it here.

My lungs feel too tight, phone threatening to slip from my sweaty hand. I shouldn't be here.

It's an uneasy calm, the eye of the storm that lulls you into complacency before the wind, the rain, the full hurricane force comes barreling back onto land, leveling everything in its path.

"Sophie!"

I jump as a voice breaks the quiet, and Stoner mumbles a "fuck" as Jude jogs into the beam of light. He's next to me in a few quick strides, his hand wrapping around my elbow and tucking me next to him.

I'm still mad, but also thank sweet baby Jesus I'm not alone anymore. Also it feels like Jude "took five" just for me—literally stepped out of the spotlight for my benefit—and it makes my throat go tight, my eyes glassy, but when he glances to me, his expression is too closed off to read. I hate it. I can read everyone.

He leans into me and murmurs, "Not really a good place for you."

I have zero chance to respond because in the next second he's saying, "Hey, man," to Stoner, like they're friends when they're clearly not. "I just need to borrow her a sec."

He doesn't wait for permission, steering me back toward the exit we came through. But instead of moving down toward the rave, we head up. Back and forth as the stairway twists until we reach the top.

The door opens to wide-open sky, to the tops of trees and only a sliver missing from the glow of a full moon.

Jude props the door with a heavy stone. "How are your ribs?"

My ribs? This dude is a master of mixed signals, and I was minutes from finding something out. From actually accomplishing what I started for once, and he dragged me away and he wants to ask about minor injuries? I'm a dancer—I'm used to pain.

I answer the way he would. Giving nothing more than what was asked. "Fine."

"Good."

Good. Okay, sure.

He stares like he's waiting for me to fill the silence, which I would totally normally do—but not this time.

I quirk an eyebrow. And I wait.

Ha! I can be different. I can be Not-Sophie. "I wasn't just screwing around down there, you know. I was investigating . . . or something. And you just interrupted me. By the way—you're in a band? That's a thing you could've shared. I'm a dancer; you're a musician. Creative field. Common ground. It would've been a good conversation piece. Along with how you play in creepy buildings or whatever."

He pauses. "Okay."

That's it.

I give him a chance for a few follow-up words. Even an intake of breath like he *might* say something. But no. *"Okay?"*

He shrugs. "Show me some of your dancing."

I swear to the heavens, this boy is trying to make me think I've lost my mind. "Why?"

"You've seen me play. Do my . . . *creative field*. So now you show me yours."

There's a timbre in his voice that makes me feel *some kind of way*, and I don't know if I like it or love it. But then there's Garrett's text in my head again, sucking everything out of me until I'm too hollowed out to feel anything at all.

I bounce in one spot, then the next, because I'm pretty sure I shouldn't be doing jumps on the roof of a building that looks like it's on the brink of collapse.

Something shifts in his expression the moment he realizes what I'm doing, the closest I've seen to the Jude beneath the wall of one-word answers. "I wouldn't—"

He clears his throat, gaze dropping to the rooftop, his voice quiet. "I wouldn't have suggested it if it wasn't safe."

Oh, awesome. Now I feel bad. Nora would tell me I'm being emotionally manipulated, but Nora doesn't understand human emotion, so there's that. "I wasn't suggesting you were *trying* to—"

He holds up a hand to cut me off, but he looks repentant about it rather than like a giant douchebag, so I don't take offense.

He whispers, "Close your eyes," and I do—puppet on a string just like always—but then his hands slip around my wrists, calluses rough against my skin, the heat of him in stark contrast to the sharp bite of wind.

His breath tickles the top of my head as he says, "I play in a band. In creepy buildings or whatever."

I don't open my eyes, but somehow I know he's smiling too.

He shifts closer. "I shouldn't have made you feel bad about looking out for yourself. I'm sorry."

My lips fall open and I finally manage to mumble, "It's okay," but his words nearly overlap mine when he says, "It's not."

I don't know what to do with this—with his apology, with the way I want to excuse it all away even though he's not asking me to. "You're right. It's not."

I look to him for agreement. No, that's not right. For *permission*.

To be mad. To expect things. To use my voice. To demand honesty. Respect.

Except, I don't need permission for any of those things, and it's a realization that leaves me unsteady, my view of the world shifting shape, old pieces creating a new image. I thought I always believed those things to be true, but maybe I only believed them for everyone else.

He nods, his eyes falling shut, and I follow as he says, "Times where I have too much going on in my head, I sit down with my guitar and I lose myself in music because music is who I am. I don't talk much because every time I play a note, or get onstage to sing, you can see my entire soul. But I think you know that. I think you saw me downstairs. And I think that's what dance is for you. So . . ."

His hands leave my wrists, the warmth bleeding from them in seconds, and his lips brush the shell of my ear when he says, "Show me."

His footsteps retreat, and I don't dare open my eyes. Like if I can't see him he'll be blinded to the flush in my cheeks, the way my breaths come too short.

I unzip my sweatshirt so I'm wearing only a tank beneath it, so I can move the way I need to, even as the cold numbs my arms.

I don't look as I take my first few steps. I forget that I'm on the roof of a creepy building and I'm wearing Converse instead of pointe shoes. I let my hair whip around me as I spin rather than tying it up tight.

For a moment, I forget about competitions and intensives and timing every move to music because there is none. It's just me and the moon and open sky. The stretch and pull of each muscle in my body doing exactly what it wants with no one to answer to. No one to judge. No one to say I'm not quite who I should be.

For once, I put my soul on display. And I don't hate what I see.

It takes me a full twenty seconds to look at him once my body stills—my muscles burning and lungs heaving—because I'm a coward. I don't trust that I'm strong enough to love my soul if someone else doesn't.

He doesn't say anything. Garrett would tell me it was great or awesome, even though I'd know he spent half the time glancing at his phone. Maybe I wish he'd have said nothing instead.

Jude's eyes don't leave mine as he covers the space between us in a few long strides. He doesn't speak as his hand threads through my hair, calloused thumb skimming my cheek as his gaze drops to my lips.

His eyes are even darker in the moonlight, and they raise back up to meet mine. I know what he's asking, and I should say no but I rise up on my tiptoes instead, kissing him before either of us can remember all the reasons we shouldn't.

He's so gentle it hurts, the smallest amount of pressure where his fingertips meet my scalp, the softness, the hesitancy, of his lips, like he's afraid to break me. Like I'm a thing to be cherished.

I pull him to me, palms scraping against the stubble of his jaw, bodies pressed so tight I can feel just how much he wants this and just how much he's holding back.

He says my name in that deep rumble and I'm lost to the world, but then he pulls away, leaving too much space between us as he says, "What's wrong?"

I blink because the answer is *nothing*, but then he wipes a tear from my cheek, and then another from the other, and oh my sweet Jesus, I'm that girl who cries during sex. Or not even sex. This is infinitely worse.

I mumble a "sorry" and ignore his pleas to wait and I know I should be running to grab the sweatshirt I left lying on the ground but I need to put an end to this humiliation as soon as possible. So I leave it there, crumpled in a pile on the dirty roof, and I run to the door, flinging it open and throwing myself inside and down as many steps as I can in complete darkness before he follows.

My stomach buzzes, and I barely stifle a scream before I remember I stuck my phone in my waistband. I don't want to look at it.

I want to find Charla and Isa and unload my stupidity on them and eat ice cream. But I'm standing right in front of the door Stoner led me to and my phone has a new text and, while I've never been a spiritual girl, I *do* believe in signs.

My screen casts a muted glow through the empty stairwell, the text in the center of it stealing what little breath I have left.

You'll pay for what you did to me, babe.

CHAPTER TWENTY-THREE
NORA

I found myself at a crossroads.

Three enormous questions to be answered, all for different reasons. I needed to find proof of Garrett's cheating, something indisputable. Something I could confront him with or provide to Brown to prove that I was not the cheater in this situation. That led me to Principal Wentville. See, my theory was thus: Someone at a high level was changing the grades.

There was no way every one of Garrett's teachers throughout all of school had doctored his test scores. Surely *one* of them would have had enough honor to say no, no matter what was offered. That meant I needed to start with the top.

And lastly, I needed to confront what I'd found in Adam's room. I barely slept anymore, with that necklace so close. In my nightmares, I was the girl, Adam holding me down, choking me, blood trickling from lips to snake into the crevices of that charm. And then I'd blink away, bolting upright into the thick darkness of my room, and I'd taste the salt of the ocean, feel that man's knee at my back, the waves pummeling my skin, and I'd lie there until the hint of sun crept past the barrier of my curtains.

But what was I to do? Simply ask him? If he *had* harmed someone, would he launch into a full confession? Not likely. I'd prided myself on being strong for so long, I'd lost track of the times I'd forced a deep breath, reeled it all back in, squared my shoulders, and pressed on, but this felt too big to hold, like I was bound to drop it all at my feet no matter how desperately I held on.

I had no leads, not even a hint of a clue, and I was not going back to his room to look for another. Not after last time. Adding to that particular issue was the private investigator.

I recognize I've restated this point several times, but he quite literally tried to drown me. Somehow, it didn't seem cheating—even a potential scandal like this—would elicit that extreme a response. And Joseph didn't even know who I was until I confronted him in his office.

The attempted murder *had* to have been tied to something else, and when I let myself think about it too much, in those hazy spaces between sleep and wakefulness, when the world existed in a different plane, where everything seemed possible and none of it real, it seemed most likely that it was *Adam's* secret that was worth killing me for. And it was only he and Monica who knew where I'd be.

But that was not possible. Adam wouldn't have me killed. There was no part of me that could accept that.

So, following the Wentville angle it was.

I supposed I could've broken into his office late one night, hidden by the cloak of darkness, armed with the set of lock picks I'd purchased off Amazon and managed to master in under two hours like any proper mystery heroine.

But I hadn't purchased any lock picks and I certainly didn't have even two free hours to master them, and most important, that would be reckless.

What was I to do if someone found me there, clothed in all black, hunched behind Wentville's desk with a stack of his files in my hand? Claim to be the new janitor?

Brown may be suspicious of me now, but certainly a breaking and entering charge would place me firmly in the "banned forever" category.

Therefore, I had to be smart.

And lucky for me, I was.

It took a few days, and a bit of planning, including a trip to the office when I knew Principal Wentville was off-site for a district meeting (according to the receptionist's office calendar that I scanned while waiting for her to retrieve me a Band-Aid I didn't need), so I could request a meeting with him. That way, even *if* they found me in his office, I could say I was merely attempting to catch him after my first failed attempt.

They may not completely believe me, but they'd have no evidence proving my guilt either.

And so, when the pep rally drew nigh and the school all filed down the hallways in a rush of bodies, a writhing mass of shuffled feet and random cheers all moved by the holy school spirit (Praise be!) I tucked myself into an open classroom, waiting for the herd to pass me by.

And when the voices faded to faint echoes and there was only the faint breeze through an open window to keep me company, I inched into the hall, peeking from my hiding spot to scan for teachers.

Finding none, I breathed deep and walked calmly to the front office, my ballet flats quiet on the tile floor.

Music filtered through the hall, meshed with the cheers of hundreds of Birmingdale's most dedicated. Right this moment, Garrett

Packard was likely running through a tunnel of smiling cheerleaders, their pom-poms glinting in the fluorescent gym lights, while *I* was doing my level best to take it all away from him.

I strolled through the front office, my footsteps masked by the incessant bleating ring of the main phone line, past the nurse's station, past the assistant principal's office, and directly to Principal Wentville's.

I knocked first—again, keeping with appearances—and got no answer.

No one skipped the Birmingdale pep rally. It would be akin to telling your ailing grandmother that you planned to skip Thanksgiving dinner.

I grasped the handle, metal cool against my hand, and turned.

Well, tried to turn. It was locked. Perhaps I'd been too hasty in my dismissal of lock picks.

I let out a long breath to calm my nerves. Small setback. Easily fixable.

Hopefully.

I scampered back to the front office, ducking into the hallway to see if any staff were headed my way. Nothing but empty space greeted me.

Using the toe of my shoe, I flipped up the doorstop and let the door swing shut, locking me in the office, all alone.

If anyone did show, it may give me a few precious seconds.

Where to start.

The pencil drawer seemed the most obvious place to keep a ring of keys. They'd have to keep a spare set somewhere, but it came up empty. As did the side drawers, all the coffee cups—both used to hold pencils and for decorative purposes—behind the computer and even at the bottom of the file drawer.

Instead, I found them hanging from a large pushpin stabbed into the cubicle wall. Clearly, Secretary Tammy was never going to qualify for a position in security.

I yanked them free and hurried back to the office, using the one with a purple polka-dotted key grip to open Wentville's door.

I'd wasted far too much time already and had little to spare. There was no guarantee Wentville, or the others, would stay for the entire pep rally. I placed my phone on his desk. Monica* was stationed at the corner of the gym, high in the bleachers, with a view of any movement. If any office staff left the gymnasium, she'd text me.

I wiggled Wentville's mouse, and his screen came to life. A tiny box expected a password, which of course I didn't have, but I did have the knowledge that men of Wentville's age tended to treat cyber security with the same caution Tammy did the office keys.

I slid his keyboard forward and found several Post-its, but none bearing passwords.

A quick scan of his desk revealed a planner—a fat leather-bound monstrosity with worn edges and a zipper whose paint had chipped in most places. A planner. As if smartphones didn't exist.

I yanked it toward me, flipping through pages until the very back, where I came upon a section entitled "Passwords."

My shoulders slumped. When I became wealthy (that was in the plan too), I would send a security consultant to Birmingdale. Not for Wentville—he was still a coward—but for all the students whose data he left so completely unsecured.

I took a picture of it, since I assumed access to his email may come in handy, and flipped the planner closed.

I typed in "Patty16" (his wife? his dog? I didn't know any more than I cared), and the computer whirred as it opened its screen to me.

I'd like to say I knew exactly where I was headed, that I had some idea of what I was looking for, but I was really stumbling my way through, on alert for something that might give me answers.

When they came, I didn't recognize them. It was an unread email from Mrs. Porter—the same teacher who'd originally started all of this with the matching research papers—that caught my eye. Or, more accurately, the attachment.

I clicked on it, waiting for the computer to process before a new screen blinked open. It took a moment before I registered what I was staring at: a copy of the test we had scheduled for next week.

It wasn't the test itself that was alarming. Maybe teachers regularly sent tests prior to administering them. I'd spent less than zero minutes of my life pondering what sort of duties a principal undertook.

That led me to Wentville's download folder, where I scanned through his files. It was that list that gave me pause. There was no shortage of random downloads—board meetings and safety procedures and, apparently, Wentville had a penchant for pictures of possums wearing hats?

But the teacher names, they seemed significant, mostly because they were only from teachers *I* had. That is to say, teachers in AP-level courses.

Most definitely curious.

Unless, of course, Joseph and his Cheaters Incorporated only catered to the students at the highest levels. It would be logical to focus their efforts on those with something to lose. Perhaps a parent would be willing to pay to save their failing student from a lifetime of putting "GED" on their applications, but what would stop them from telling the world about it later? They'd have nothing holding them to secrecy. But if you gained admission to one of the best colleges? If it led you to an illustrious career? You'd kill to keep anyone from knowing.

The thought sucked the air from my lungs. Adam. The bloody necklace. Would cheating be something he'd kill for? This was the boy who'd safely escort spiders from his home rather than squish them. It was more likely he'd cut himself trying to save someone than while harming another person.

Maybe he'd found her, after someone else had harmed her. Maybe his guilt led him to keeping the necklace. Maybe he was holding it for the same reason I was—evidence.

Joseph Graham had very good reason to want me dead. I knew about his cheating ring. I knew about his wife's rather inventive approach to taxes and fundraising. He knew I was willing to set up fake meetings in order to discover information. Someone of his standing would undoubtedly see me as a threat. Perhaps he only granted me the job to keep an eye on me and now he planned to kill me.

Focus, Nora.

Wentville. The tests.

I needed someone else. Someone who'd be more willing to talk than Garrett. Which was to say, anyone.

Only, something rumbled far down the hall, and my gaze flew to the clock. It had been thirty-five minutes already, and I'd barely found anything. Certainly nothing definitive. No smoking gun that would tie Wentville to anything in Joseph Graham's world.

The drumbeats got louder, the blast of brass instruments now accompanying, and my palms went slick with sweat. I had only a handful of minutes.

And then my memory snapped into focus. Amber Donahue, and her dismal grades that I'd seen on Wentville's screen during my last visit.

I logged in—Wentville had his passwords autosaved—and hurriedly typed in her name, scanning through her records.

I found nothing like what I'd seen the last time. No one could've made that sort of improvement in such a short time frame.

Voices reached me, off-key renditions of the Birmingdale fight song echoing against the walls and filtering past the closed door. I needed to leave. Immediately.

But I needed to know more. I needed answers.

A system like this, it would have to keep record of changes to grades. This wasn't Twitter—it should have an edit button.

It took five clicks before I found it. Amber's *true* grade history. She'd started the year off strong. Papers completed. Tests passed.

But then a month passed and she became a different student. Assignments missing, tests completed but certainly not well. And then, the miraculous recovery. Grades overwritten by one WWentvi.

Wilbur Wentville. What an unfortunate name.

A note linked to each subject, and a quick click drew a small box to the screen.

STUDENT ALLOWED TO SUBMIT REVISED WORK/TESTS READMINISTERED

I gasped. Loudly. *Revised work? Readministered tests?!* Those did not exist.

I'd once asked my pre-K teacher if I could redo my leaf rubbing, and she'd given me an emphatic no. She'd told me it was perfect, which was a lie, but she did *not* let me resubmit.

I shoved the keyboard so hard it slammed into the base of the monitor, and for the moments I stomped out the door and to the wall of files in the main room, I wasn't even concerned about the growing bellow of teachers and students returning.

The drawers were blessedly labeled, and I yanked open the Da–Fe drawer, the files sliding on their metal hangers, and plucked Amber's free.

Her ID photo smiled up at me, and I scowled back, even fiercer when I discovered the confidential reason for her readministred tests.

She cited stress from being moved from fourth chair to fifth in band, which was just embarrassing. There was no doctor's note, no actual documentation of why moving from mediocre to more mediocre might impact all her other grades.

Anxiety. Depression. Both far too prevalent in high school society. But this—

This was not that. This was a pathetic excuse for which she'd co-opted legitimate medical conditions so she could *cheat*. And Wentville, it seemed, was a more-than-willing participant.

I took a pic of that too—feeling no small twinge of guilt at the

179

confidential warning—and slammed the file back into place.

That was the exact moment heels clipped down the hall, accompanied by the tinkle of keys, and I am not too ashamed to admit I sprinted back to Wentville's office.

Without pausing to think, I logged out of his computer, slipping it into sleep mode until the screen went black, and slid his chair where he'd left it.

I scanned the room, searching for anything out of place, just when the sun pressed from beneath the clouds, brightening the surface of his desk.

The keys. It would be impossible for Tammy to ignore their absence since they hung just in front of her face. But then the office door swung open, ushering in the general ruckus of the hallway, and it was too late to put them back.

Instead, I tucked them into the pocket of my skirt, my ballet flats slipping on the flat Berber carpet as I sprung toward the door, swinging it all the way open.

Then I tumbled into one of the seats in front of Wentville's desk, smoothing my hair and trying not to make the sweat trickling down my spine obvious.

Wentville's clumsy shuffles trudged down the hall, giving me precious seconds to think. He'd been changing Amber's grades, which had fallen right near the time Garrett's had.

But Amber had already started her ascent, while Garrett had just been assigned to me.

But Garrett, he'd been "a bit of a challenge." That's what Joseph had said to me. I knew firsthand how difficult he was to work with, or maybe his toxic masculinity had prevented him from claiming any personal difficulties that would allow Wentville to alter his grades.

Amber and Garrett were tied together in this. I was sure of it. Wentville as well. But *why*? If I couldn't prove his motive, it would never be enough to convince Brown of my innocence.

"Ahhhhhsfljakdj." That was the strangled sound Wentville made when he schlepped into his office and found me sitting there, my best smile in place.

He pressed his hand to his heart—pretending he had one—and said, "Nora. You nearly gave me a heart attack!"

"Heart attacks occur when an artery that supplies your heart with blood and oxygen becomes blocked, Mr. Wentville. I don't believe I have the ability to cause that."

He started to say something unimportant, which I didn't let him finish, because even though I'd just committed any number of acts that would get me immediately expelled, it occurred to me there *was* something I needed to discuss with him.

I looked him in the eye, no trace of guilt to be had in mine, and said, "I'd like to know who notified Brown University that I was suspected of cheating."

CHAPTER TWENTY-FOUR
SOPHIE

For what *I* did to him?

He fucking *left me* without a single fucking word for an entire *month* without even a single "Hey, babe, I'm traveling the East Coast on a personal journey to learn to live, laugh, and love," and now *I'm* supposed to feel guilty?

I yank open the metal door, sending a blast of kerosene air to flood the space around me, and stomp into the room, phone flashlight held high.

Mind you, this is the same Garrett who used to call over and over when I didn't pick up the phone when he thought I should. The *same* Garrett who showed up to my dance studio more than once when I stayed late without telling him first. And then. Then! I'd ask him wtf he was doing, standing in the parking lot like some kind of stalker freak, and somehow by the end of the conversation, it would be *me* who was apologizing.

I scream out, "Jimmy! Who knows where Jimmy is?"

Garrett would give me his long-suffering sigh, his disappointed voice. "I was worried about you, babe. You know you aren't always the most reliable and then you didn't call and what was I supposed to think? Are you seriously going to be mad at me for worrying about you? You're acting like *I'm* doing something wrong. I can't believe you'd think I'm the kind of guy who'd get mad over nothing."

And then I'd say sorry and he'd say he forgave me. *Forgave me.* Like

I'd done something wrong by practicing a little later. I'd sit there feeling so small. So *empty*. Like I'd never figure it out—how to be who I needed to be for each person I loved. How to be smart enough for Dad, less trouble for Mom. How to be a sister who was worth keeping. A daughter worth keeping. A girlfriend worth keeping.

But that was just one more example of how wrong I was about everything, how no matter what I chose I was always lacking. And so I said I was sorry. Because there's nothing else to say when you're not enough and never will be.

"Jimmy!" My shout echoes through the open space as I stomp through makeshift beds and old couches, past empty bottles and emptier needles. "Jimmy who works at the BP gas station on Sunday nights! Either get your ass out here or I'm telling your boss you watch porn on your phone while you're—"

"Jesus! What the fuck, you psycho bitch!" A scrawny white dude with his hair in greasy purple clumps appears, and I shine my light in his eyes, which makes him cuss even louder.

"You kiss your mother with that mouth, Jimmy from BP?" Jimmy is right. I *am* a psycho bitch.

"What the fuck do you want? *Bitch*." He runs his hand through his hair clumps, and they're not all purple. They're blue and purple and black, and parts of his head are shaved. With a healthy helping of hair gel, I'd bet they stick straight out. Peacock, indeed.

Someone coughs behind me, and my entire body shudders. I don't know how many people are back there. I just charged into their home and drew the most possible amount of attention to myself, and as two more people shuffle in behind Jimmy, all the fear I should have been feeling rushes out from my gut in a wave that leaves me dizzy.

I squeeze the phone harder so it won't shake—so they won't see how close I am to screaming. "My friends are waiting outside that door."

He smiles then, like he knows I'm a liar, just like Garrett's text said I was. "Sure they are, sweetheart."

"Look." I don't dare drop my phone to search for the pictures, too afraid even an ounce more darkness will break whatever's keeping me here untouched. "I just need to know if you remember seeing these two people a few Sundays back. They would've been together."

Saying those words is like acid on my tongue. Garrett and Nora. Together. Maybe Nora's not in trouble. Maybe she's just feeling guilty too. "It's possible the girl got pulled over?"

That's when he remembers. I can see it in the subtlest widening of his glassy eyes, but he says he doesn't. At least until I fish the forty dollars that's supposed to be for jazz shoes I desperately need from my waistband.

I hold it out to him. "This is all I have. That girl is my sister, and that's my boyfriend. My *ex*-boyfriend. And I think you might understand exes, considering yours told me where to find you."

The clerk didn't say that, but I'd bet my life I'm right. I *am* betting it, matter of fact.

He tugs the bills from my hand. "Didn't see her. He was just another douchebag. Only reason I remember him is because of the crazy fucker who came in looking for them."

My irrational compulsion to defend Garrett gets swept from my tongue by the end of his statement. "Who came in looking for him? What did he look like?"

He shrugs. "Big white dude. Don't think he was happy about his girl being with your boyfriend."

184

"She's not his girl."

"Coulda fooled me. Fucker punched the safety glass when I told him they left."

My mouth goes dry, ribs squeezing so hard my heart can't beat right. I flip through the pictures on my phone until I get to the last person I want it to be: Adam. "Is this him?"

"Yeah, that's him!" Jimmy smiles and I feel sick. "Threatened to kill your *ex*-boyfriend. Thought I was gonna have to get the shotgun from underneath the counter, know what I'm sayin'?"

I pull back my phone, all the crucial light now pointed to the scratched and pitted floor, Adam's smiling face centered on the screen.

I've never seen Adam angry like that, but if there's one thing—one *person*—who could elicit that kind of response from him, it would be Nora.

And Jimmy has no reason to lie, and he wouldn't even know Adam existed unless he really was there that night.

I stumble back a step, and I don't even notice how close I am to the person behind me until she says, "Thought your friends were right outside."

Jude is the last person I want to see but I'm also begging him to burst through the doors right now, but then the world crashes in and the floor beneath my feet rumbles and Jude isn't coming because he's downstairs, baring his soul, and I'm up here trying to lose mine.

I mumble that I have to go, but I only make it two steps before someone steps into my path. He holds his arms out, blocking me in. "Hey, hey, hey. You just got here."

I text a 911 to Isa and Charla, but they don't even know how to get to where I am and my fingers are shaking so hard "911 2nd floor" becomes "011 end dloor." Also thanks for fucking nothing, autocorrect.

The guy wraps his arm around my waist when I try to move past him and my entire body screams to run, kick, fight, but I don't.

I giggle. Like it's all some big joke. Haha, scared for my life right now but do you think I'm pretty?

My palm presses flat to his chest, pushing to make more room between us, but then his heart hammers against my skin and that's worse. So is the way his fingers press into my flesh so hard I'll have bruises before he pulls them away.

A girl says, "Leave her alone, Bennie," but he doesn't, and no one else seems to care.

My stomach rolls, sweat blooming all over my skin, and then lights blare through the broken windows. Red and blue swirls that flicker and dance over the cinder-block walls. Someone shouts, "Cops!" and the group scatters, but Bennie pulls me tighter, dragging me with him.

I go limp, every muscle liquid, and it throws off his balance, his reactions just a bit too slow to respond when I drop low and tumble out of his grasp, rolling onto the floor and back up in a move I've been doing since third-grade contemporary class.

He's too slow to catch me before I make it to the door, slamming it open with the most precious clunk of metal I've ever heard.

I cling to the rail to guide me in the dark, bursting into the main room, where everyone's scrambling for an exit. Jude is gone. So is all the band's equipment. They clearly had more notice than the second floor.

My phone buzzes, and I press it to my ear while I follow the herd toward what I only hope is a back exit because the cops are literally right outside the door.

Charla yells, "Where *are* you?" and I scream back, "Still inside!"

An engine revs, and she says she'll meet me behind the building just as the crowd reverses in my direction, shouts that the cops are in the back too, drowning whatever Charla says next.

I can't let her get caught here. Not Isa either.

I scream for her to leave without me, then send a text to do the same, and this time, I make sure autocorrect doesn't screw me over.

Then I do the last thing I should.

I run toward the cops.

CHAPTER TWENTY-FIVE

NORA

"I don't want to be here." Those were the words that came from Monica's mouth, but considering it was also stuffed with a soft pretzel and a bit of popcorn, the statement rang false.

I raised a brow in her direction, for a half second, until yet another person shouldered me out of the way en route to the bleachers. "Yes. You seem traumatized. You have cheese on your face."

She grinned and wiped it away with one of the five hundred scratchy brown napkins she'd pulled, one at a time, from the concession stand's dispenser. "You look weird."

I wanted to argue, but she was right. I'd "borrowed" yet another of Sophie's outfits—mine wouldn't have blended well at a sporting event.

The stadium's lights blinked on, bathing the field in a wash of white that glinted off the band's windwoods. The bleachers rattled beneath a million footsteps, the mesh of hundreds of voices a constant white noise to fill in the moments of pause from the instruments.

The salty scent of french fries and hot dogs warred with the sweetness of cotton candy and elephant ears, all of them overlaid by the subtle current of ocean air, and my stomach rumbled.

So I stole some of Monica's pretzel even though I declined to order any food because I said I was too focused on tracking Amber Donahue so I could surprise her at halftime.

It wasn't the most perfect of plans, but Amber was so caught up with the festivities at school there was no time to confront her. As Monica explained it, Amber and her fellow cheerleaders would perform at the halftime show, and then she'd be milling about while we waited for the second half to start.

I never understood the draw of football games. Or any sport for that matter. I certainly understood the desire to win, and even the feeling of hard work coming to fruition. But *fans*, I didn't understand them. It wasn't *their* victory on the field—it belonged to those who made it happen.

But then Adam had explained it to me. How the beginning of every game felt like those moments before a final. Your body filled with the buzz of possibility, of *potential*. It was the thrill of discovering, through the unforgiving truth of numbers—whether at the top of a page or the scoreboard—who was truly the best.

That I understood.

I shivered, not from the chill brought by the wind, but from the knowledge that Adam was close, that the investigator may be closer. My only hope was that the crowd would shield me, blend me into any number of faces, each less distinct than the next.

I still had plenty to fear from him. There was nowhere for him to drown me here, with Birmingdale far enough inland to make that impossible. But surely there were many ways to kill a person that did not require large bodies of water. Maybe he'd crush me with one of those enormous, padded metal things the football players tackled across the field in practice. Or he'd yell that there was a fire and have me trampled under the feet of my own fellow students. Perhaps he'd lure me to some remote part of the field and bludgeon me with that oversize Gatorade cooler the players all lined up to—

"Nora!" Monica shoved me, leveling me with a look that said she knew I'd been caught up in my murder musings again. "Where do you want to sit?"

There were several minutes not worth recounting for the purposes of this confession, during which I weighed the risk of my back to a crowd where someone who wanted to murder me might be, against being able to access Amber. There was the small matter of Layla being near the top of the crowd, our eyes meeting and mine being the first to break free, which is a story not meant for this confession aside from giving explanation for my motivation to sit at the bottom.

There was a pause while waiting for the national anthem, and finally, we found our seats, our conversation drifting toward what I'd discovered during my conversation with Wentville.

Spineless though he may be, he claimed neither he nor someone from the school called Brown about my record. And for as much as he stammered and blustered through his initial response, his weaselly eyes bugging in response to my inquiry, I tended to believe him.

Monica said, "So that's bad?"

The crowd roared, everyone on our sideline jumping to their feet and blowing obnoxious airhorns, Amber and the rest of the cheerleaders bouncing and bobbling about while all the players advanced far down the field to where Adam had, apparently, caught the ball.

I didn't need to see his name, block letters stark against the black jersey, to know it was him. I knew everything about Adam. I recognized his walk, his stance, and most certainly I knew exactly what his expression changed to when he noticed me in the stands.

The front row. I should've considered the Adam variable when factoring the costs and benefits of choosing this seat.

The crowd settled again as the announcer crackled over the speakers. First down. Seven-yard line.

Go Stallions.

Monica nudged me with her elbow. "Sooooo. Something you want to tell me about you and Russo?"

"He's my neighbor."

"He's your boyfriend."

"Don't be a child."

She gasped. "Oh my god! He *is* your boyfriend!"

"He's my neigh—"

"Boyfriend!" Then she proceeded to poke me while repeating "boyfriend" until I poked her back and it devolved into the most embarrassing sort of slappy girl fight until we laughed too hard to continue.

But somehow, not even that could shake the sense of dread every time I looked at Adam.

"For real, Linden," Monica said, her brown eyes soft, "is everything okay with you two?"

I couldn't offer more than a head shake, not when we were surrounded by listening ears, and she said, "Later, then?"

I nodded. Later.

But then I pictured having to give voice to my suspicions. Having to *show* her what I'd found, and I wasn't sure I could do it. It wouldn't be fair to him, to speak words I couldn't take back. To birth them into the world when I didn't know how fully they'd take root.

There was more though, namely my feelings for Adam, the ones that sometimes strayed beyond the bounds of friendship. I'd kissed him because I wanted to. I was vulnerable that night, tired, in need of something to tether me, and that had always been Adam. But he'd always been more too. A promise. An inevitability.

I kissed him because I wanted to. Because deep in some part of me, it felt as if I'd never be presented with the opportunity again.

I'd been a coward, avoiding the entirety of the subject of Adam rather than confronting it, but that rendered me no better than Garrett.

The referee's whistle blew, and the air went electric, every soul in the vicinity rapt, the excitement like a living thing, pulsating against my skin as the ball flew from the line and into Garrett's hands.

He jogged back two steps. Then three, and I said, "It's bad that Wentville didn't call Brown, because someone did."

"You think . . ."

I nodded, and the ball spiraled from Garrett's fingertips, rocketing through the air while time stood still. "Maybe they're afraid to actually kill me, so they'll settle for ruining my life instead."

Adam leapt into the air, arms outstretched, until his fingertips grazed the ball, and then, impossibly, they closed around it as he fell down down down, his body taut, stretching past the goal line.

His body slammed into the turf, his opponent tumbling down with him, and for the shortest of breaths, my mind went numb, my body cold, as if every cell was dependent on seeing him rise from the ground. Safe, whole, alive.

Obviously he lived. Had he died by football tackle, the entire world—let alone those reading this confession—would've heard of it.

But those moments, I can remember them as vividly as when I thought I might die on that beach, where everything felt stripped down and laid bare.

I couldn't bear to see him hurt, not any more than I could hurt him.

That's what I thought then anyway. I know differently now.

It's hard to capture what the result of a touchdown just prior to halftime does to a frenzied crowd.

An absolute onslaught of noise, the torrent of vibrations through the bleachers, the jostling as spectators celebrated.

But not me. I was frozen. My body locked tight and unable to move as Adam broke free from the pile of teammates and jogged over to me, the ball still clutched in his hand. He broke through the line of cheerleaders and hopped the fence dividing them from the stands, and then he smiled. Like everything we'd said in his bedroom was a figment of our imaginations, like nothing between us had ever changed and never would.

The ball rolled through the air, sailing toward me, landing right in my hands. Monica mumbled, "Boyfriend," and some stranger whom I certainly did not give permission to slapped my shoulder like I'd done something worthy of congratulations.

I'd literally just sat here and let the ball drop into my arms.

Adam's teammates carried him off in a stampede of padded bodies, and I stared down at the ball, leather rough beneath my palms, still warm from Adam's hands. "What am I supposed to do with this?"

No one answered.

But Amber and her cheerleaders trickled off the field, trailing behind the last of the football team, and even though it was against the plan, I jumped to my feet.

The walkway sat thick with people, all of them shoving toward the bathrooms or concessions, blocking my access to Amber.

I pulled free, jumping down the way Adam had come up, the ball tucked firmly in the crook of my arm, until my shoes hit the hard cement at field level. The last of the cheerleaders ducked into the small tunnel leading to the locker rooms, and Amber's blond pony-tail bobbed somewhere in the middle.

I called out her name, and her head swiveled, sweeping over me in favor of someone she actually recognized.

It took two more tries before she realized I was addressing her, a hefty amount of confusion, and, finally, me mentioning I wanted to talk to her about fifth chair in band.

I hadn't gone in with intentions of letting her know I'd seen her file, but her very emphatic reluctance to follow me beneath the bleachers for a talk left me no choice.

After a quick wave to her teammates, we ducked out the side, dirt pluming beneath our shoes as we traversed the area beneath the bleachers. It was far from private—children squealing as they ran in circles at the far side of the field, a few pinpricks of red that gave way to a stream of white smoke from a couple in the far corner—but it was as close as I was likely to get at an event such as this.

She crossed her arms tight, an attitude only entitled white girls could emulate. "What the fuck is this?"

Charming.

"I know about your cheating ring." I recognized the brazen

stupidity in this approach. She could easily complain to Joseph Graham if she had a direct communication path, or to her parents, and that would immediately destroy the very tentative job I'd just been granted. And with it, my power over Garrett.

But my time with Amber was limited. They'd surely notice if she failed to appear at the halftime show.

Her face went pale, blue eyes watery in the glare of the moon. "I don't know what you're talking about."

I sighed and pulled out the card Joseph had given me. "I need information, and I need you to promise not to tell anyone. If you do, I promise you'll regret it."

Shadows crisscrossed her face, highlighting the tremble in her lip, but then it took over—that assuredness that this was most definitely not her problem to carry. "I'm not telling you anything."

She spun on her heel and stormed away, headed in the wrong direction but not lacking for confidence because of it.

I tried to call out to her, to tell her I only needed a name and she could go back to her team. But she did not stop, didn't even pause aside from the quick second it took to raise her hand in the air, elbow bent, middle finger prominently displayed.

Under normal circumstances, I would have found another way. A safer, better, smarter way. Sophie would've charmed her into confessing.

But none of those were what I needed. I needed *quicker*.

And so I took the only avenue remaining.

I tackled her to the ground.

She didn't hear me coming, clearly didn't anticipate even a hint of danger, because she squealed as my arm wrapped around her, both our bodies flying toward the hard earth. The air fled my lungs in a rush, my elbows crashed into the dirt, and the stupid ball popped free.

Amber scrambled, legs kicking and arms flailing, trying to pull herself to standing, but I dragged her closer, our limbs battling until I pinned her wrists, my knees straddling her hips.

The more she squirmed the harder I squeezed, curses flying from her mouth at a rather alarming rate, with only the band belting out their rendition of "Seven Nation Army" to drown her out.

It took four tries, but eventually, when I screamed, "Shut up!" she listened.

I loomed over her, both of us panting, her face smudged and dirty. "I just need the name of your old tutor. That's it. And I'll let you go."

"You fucking bitch. I will—"

I tilted my head, widened my eyes, and whispered, "You will *what*."

Her lips pressed together, her wrists straining. She would hate me forever, perhaps for good reason. And I'd undoubtedly added another person to the list of the current ones attempting to destroy my life. But I'd come too far now.

"Her name, Amber." The band hit their explosive finish, the crowd applause raining down on us from above. "Hurry. They're waiting."

She spat out, "Maddie Armstrong. And fuck you."

I extended my sincere thanks and stood, rolling the wayward football to her with the toe of my shoe. She did not look pleased when I asked her to return it.

I may have tackled one of the head cheerleaders under the

bleachers, but I would not risk expulsion for theft of school property.

She stood and said, "It won't do you any good to know her name."

I waited, the two of us standing across from each other, both of us bruised and dirty.

And she spoke the words that would alter the course of everything. "She's dead."

CHAPTER TWENTY-SIX
SOPHIE

I clutch the paper cup in my hands, warmth spreading beneath my skin but doing nothing to loosen the muscles that remained clenched the entire ride to the police station.

In the back of a police car.

Not even the magic of coffee can fix this.

Mom sits next to me, her spine straighter than mine when I'm standing at the barre, anger pulsing off her so fervently it hurts to sit near her.

We're waiting, for Detective Tickner. This isn't his precinct. Not even his city. They're just kind enough to let him use one of their interview rooms. I'm guessing this might be more interrogation.

Mom's lower lip trembles because of course she's about to start crying. I can have our whole future conversation in my head. *How could you do this to me? I was so embarrassed. You only think of yourself. The world doesn't revolve around you and your problems, Sophie.*

"Ms. Linden?" Detective Tickner is exactly what I'd expect a guy named Tickner to look like. Small, eyes too big for his face, definitely has a complex about his height and acts like an asshole to make up for it. "Follow me."

I trudge down the hall, Mom a half step behind, trying to breathe in the coffee and not the mix of bleach and vomit from the kid they dragged through here ten minutes ago.

We cram into a room, heavy table bolted to the floor and

fluorescent lighting that buzzes and flickers, stark white walls that show the history of every person who's been in this room through their scrapes and scratches.

The chair screeches when he pulls it out, spinning it to lower into a straddle. "My colleague says you brought him a necklace."

"He blew me off." Excellent, Soph. Way to antagonize the guy with handcuffs.

I should be better at this, but I can't think straight because if he's here about the necklace, then it really was blood. A person's. Someone they can't ask directly. For . . . reasons.

"Who were you with tonight?"

I'm stunned into silence. "No one."

"No one? How did you get there, then?"

I am so very dumb. "Why does this matter? I bring your colleague a necklace, with *blood* on it, and he completely blows me off. And then you show up at my house like I'm some kind of criminal. Whose necklace was it? Why was it in my car?"

Tickner ignores all my questions and hits me with "How well do you know Jude Vargas?"

Mom's been making all sorts of gasps—probably because I didn't tell her about the whole bloody-necklace thing, but now she's mumbling questions about who Jude is and "Sophie, what is going on?"

I really wish she weren't here. "Why?"

"I ask the questions."

"Doesn't mean I'll answer them."

"Sophie!" Mom is big mad now, and I'm probably about to get arrested. I should be minding my words. Shaping up. Flying right. But I'm too *angry*. Too confused. I'm tired of everyone else knowing more than me. All these pieces keep drifting through my head, but none of them fit.

I hate puzzles. I hate brain teasers and escape rooms and even sudoku. Frustrating yourself on purpose is absurd.

But here I am, trying to figure out how my sister and my boyfriend hooking up relates to Adam being super jealous and acting wildly weird, along with a bloody necklace, a random dude attacking me, pictures of someone's dad with his mistress, and Amber keeping secrets.

And now there's Jude.

He was there that night when I found the necklace. And sober enough to plant it in my car while I was in the backyard, arguing with The Stans. Then he was there tonight too, and sure, he couldn't have possibly predicted *I* would be there. I got the address from a gas station clerk for heaven's sake.

But Garrett knew. At least he seemed to. His text messages seem to say he knows everything. If he's out there, watching, he could've seen me at the gas station, knew where I was heading, so that Jude could be there, just like at the party.

It sounds ridiculous, that Jude and Garrett could have some secret friendship, but then, Jude knew who I was. Sophie Linden. The dancer.

Tickner stares at me, and I should tell him that Garrett is back but now I'm just too pissed off to give him anything. And I can't exactly show him text messages that say I'm going to pay for what I did to Garrett, now can I? I should've gone to them when it was just "miss you, babe." I could tell them about the note, but it's in the trash. In short, I am fucked.

Tickner leans across the table, fingers steepled. "This is serious,

Sophie. You didn't hear this from me, but Jude Vargas was involved in a young girl dying, and we know he drove you to my precinct the night you brought the necklace. We know he was there tonight, doing more illegal activities. What did he have to do with that necklace?"

My throat goes dry, and my wild theories feel more real. Like Jude could be part of this, part of Garrett trying to make me pay for what I did to him.

Maybe Garrett met Jude through Del, just like me. Or—my stomach flips—the necklace with the musical notes. Jude is a musician. A connection. Maybe not a strong one, but a link directly between Jude and a girl with a lost necklace.

But then I picture Jude on the roof, the feel of his calloused fingers skating over my bare skin, and I can't reconcile it. I can't get the gentleness of him to match with someone who could be involved in a girl dying.

Dying.

The word barrels me over like the force of a wave, turning me so I don't know up from down, so I can't find my footing no matter how much my limbs scramble and reach. It threatens to drag me out to the bottomless ocean, where I disappear, too small to survive in something so vast.

I barely know him, and maybe I'm defending him the way I always did Garrett—automatic, compulsory, without stopping to consider if I even believed what I was saying. He wouldn't go to the hospital with me. He didn't want to go to the police after Amber's.

My legs shake as I stand, and Mom yanks at my hand but I shake her off. "I already told you what happened. I found it in my car.

Someone put it there, and it wasn't Jude. I sought *him* out that night because I needed a ride to see *you*. So maybe you're just looking to scapegoat the first Brown person you could find."

"Sophie Eloise, that is *enough*!" Mom grabs my arm, shoving me forward and out the door, and while she middle-named me, so I will likely pay for this for years, I'm also eternally grateful that she's steering me away from the Bad Man.

I'm nearly to the door when Tickner calls out, "Ms. Linden!" and Mom and I both turn. "I hope you understand the danger you're in."

CHAPTER TWENTY-SEVEN
NORA

I know what you're thinking. This would be the part where police involvement may become necessary.

Garrett's old tutor was dead (if I believed Amber). I had a bloody necklace, which I'd found in Adam's room. Garrett and Adam were friends, and though I didn't have evidence Adam had participated in the cheating ring, I didn't have any proof he *hadn't* either.

These were loose connections at best. A thread so tenuous I doubted any officer would even consider it. That doesn't mean I didn't try.

Monica and I waited for the entirety of seventy-eight minutes outside the police station. Apparently we did not rank exceptionally high on their importance scale.

It took approximately fifteen minutes for him to dismiss me.

Did I know anything other than a name? Was Maddie a nickname or her official name? Had I ever met Maddie Armstrong? Did I know where she lived? Did we know the manner in which she died? Was the necklace even Maddie's? Was I just a jealous girlfriend who'd found another girl's jewelry and wanted revenge?

You see, I had no chance. He'd pegged me as a lovesick teen before I'd sat down.

I'd stormed from the precinct with such anger, Monica could barely muster more than a mumbled "Oh boy."

She didn't quite understand my insistence on going, but then, I hadn't quite shared the existence of the bloody necklace either.

I paced beneath the precinct lights, dropping in and out of the pockets of shadows, palms rustling with the bluster of winds sweeping off the ocean. It was the clearest of nights. The kind I used to spend nestled in the cold sand, watching the stars blaze overhead, the rhythmic roar of waves crashing to the shore.

The sky always felt as infinite as the horizon, filled with possibility, wonder beyond imagination. That's where I always thought I belonged—beside the depth of the waves, a neighbor to the stars. There was nothing out of reach.

I'd planned, worked, achieved, and that was endless too. I didn't believe in finish lines. What was there to do then? Die?

Now everything had been derailed, complicated. I still had to write my paper again, as well as Garrett's since I was his "tutor" now. He also had two assignments due by Wednesday, which I was now responsible for. As well as my own for those same classes. I had several clubs all waiting on responses from me, tests to study for, volunteering to complete. I was in a place I'd never been: behind.

I'd come close once. The days after I ruined everything. It didn't matter that it was Dad's fault, not any more than it mattered that I'd done the right thing. No one cared about why. They only considered the end result. Broken family. Facade ruined. If only they'd recognized how broken things had to have been in the beginning.

But I'd learned from that. For some, ignorance was preferable.

Sometimes the cost of knowledge was too great.

And this seemed to be no exception. I'd nearly been killed. And now there was a girl out there who was.

Of course, we didn't know that for sure. Even after all our googling. But Garrett's reaction made far more sense now. He was willing to let me tell Sophie he was a cheater because there was something with Maddie that was worse.

Murder was worse.

But as my police friend so kindly pointed out—I had no actual idea if she'd been murdered. And no, he would not look anything up for me.

We scanned through far too many obituaries—Armstrong is not a unique name—searched for news reports in even the smallest local papers, and nothing.

"Aha!" Monica jumped from the parking curb, doing a little dance as her phone highlighted her face.

I let her continue for ten more seconds before I snatched the phone from her hands.

Two girls smiled up at me, their cheeks pressed together, beach towels scattered behind them, and a caption that may have been rather moving if I hadn't skimmed it in search of confirmation.

But there, at the end, were the closest we'd gotten to a connection. #BFFs #RIPMaddie #JusticeForMaddie

The hashtags led us to others, all photos of the same girl, and even links to her obituary. But none of them including any information about how or why she died. Still, she had to be the girl I was looking for.

I clicked on the profile for Maddie's BFF and sent a message:

I have something to tell you about Maddie.

I shoved my hands in the pocket of Sophie's hoodie and scanned the forest. Jasmine Contreras had responded to my message within thirty minutes, and she was very willing to convene with me.

Well, with Monica. Since I'd used her profile.

Getting her to come with me had come at the price of a double-quarter-pounder-with-cheese meal and an upgraded milkshake.

She shoved a handful of fries in her mouth. "Which trail?"

I pointed in the direction of the third—had Jasmine not taken such care to describe the tree that graced its entrance I'd likely have missed it completely. Its branches twisted toward the sky, gnarled trunk splitting in two directions like a fork in the road.

I twisted the fabric of Sophie's sweatshirt in my hand. She had no idea how close she was to danger. Garrett, the private investigator, Adam—living right next door.

Maddie was dead, and I could've been. Still *could* be.

I nabbed a bundle of Monica's french fries and shoved them in my mouth. The salt drew water to my tongue, the heat spreading out to warm my limbs. But my stomach twisted and turned with the knowledge I feared this night may bring us.

I didn't have time for sentimentality. Not for any emotion. Those never served me well.

We trudged through the woods for nearly half a mile, our phones glowing over raised roots and fallen branches, sending critters scurrying toward safer spaces, until voices carried on the flutter of leaves.

A fire spit and danced in the distance, flickering through the tree trunks and spiraling smoke into the blackened sky. It smelled of ash and the deep earth of the forest, of alcohol's sweetness and the sharpness of flame. The trees opened into a clearing, a firepit clearly meant for campers rather than high school party attendees.

A small folding table held piles of plastic cups, as well as an assortment of liquor bottles that reflected the glow of the moon. Music played from just beyond the fire—loud enough to make conversation more challenging, but without the threat of drawing authorities.

Laughter tumbled through the treetops, clusters of people huddled at logs around the fire or dancing in the packed grass, bodies swaying against the heavy drumbeat.

There were positively too many people here—finding Jasmine would be nearly impossible.

I had Monica send her a message to notify her of our arrival while I scanned the crowd, but there were too many unfamiliar faces, all of them morphing as they moved in and away from the shadows.

A not-altogether-unattractive boy stumbled my way, grinning in a lopsided sort of way, as he pushed a plastic cup into my hand. "Hey."

I said, "I'm looking for Jasmine" as I eyed the swirl of liquid in the cup he'd given me.

"If you come with me, I bet I can find her." He grabbed my arm, and Monica slapped his hand free before returning her attention back to her messages.

I nodded toward her. "I should probably stay with my friend." For his sake more than mine. Monica took karate.

He stepped closer, until the yeasty scent of beer coated every inhale. "Maybe later?"

Is this what people truly did at parties? I'd sooner have found the nearest twig and driven it though my eyeball.

But I was here for information, for clues. For evidence. I was here to clear my name, right my future, destroy Garrett's, and discover Adam's past. And I was here for Sophie. To keep her safe.

And that was who I channeled when I finally responded, my words laced with venom and sugar and my smile wide. "Maybe. But it will cost you."

He sidled closer. "Oh yeah. What can I give you?"

Gross. "Information?"

His eyes flicked down to my cup. "Don't you trust me?"

The stupidest of questions, surely. "Of course!" I smiled my Sophie smile and touched the drink to my lips, taking the smallest of sips.

The cup jerked from my hands, and Monica glared at me. "Have you never been to a party before?"

"Well, to be truthful—"

"No drinks from strangers. This way." She shoved me forward, pointing me in the direction of a small path on the other side of the fire.

We weaved through the crowd, Monica handing off my drink to a girl who clearly did not heed the "no drinks from strangers" rule, until we found Jasmine, alone in the woods.

She was pretty, even more so than her picture revealed. Persian, with dark wavy hair and soft brown eyes.

She rubbed her arms, her gaze bouncing between me and the forest behind us. "So how did you know Maddie?"

Monica nudged me, and I nearly stumbled forward, like the grass had tilted. I said, "I didn't. Neither of us did."

Jasmine's eyes narrowed. "So why are you here?"

I didn't like the way she seemed to want to shrink into the trees, her body tensed to run at the slightest shift in breeze.

I tried to relax my posture, gentle my voice. If Sophie were here she'd have put her at ease immediately. A quiet smile, her presence like the mist from the ocean on sweat-baked skin. "I know Maddie was part of a cheating ring."

"*She* wasn't cheating."

I snapped my mouth shut before I could point out the very obvious point that helping someone cheat was, in fact, cheating. "But she was helping other people cheat, right? And getting paid for it?"

"Why are you here again?"

I slapped at a mosquito biting at my ankle, and my head swirled as I stood straight again. This entire conversation felt like it was slipping away. Grains of sand between my fingertips just when I need to grasp them tightest. "I've just been offered a job there, which I got after one of their clients stole my paper and got me in trouble. I think . . ."

My stomach rolled, and my eyes glanced to the forest behind her. "Someone tried to drown me. No, that's not right. Someone *could've* drowned me, but he let me live just so he could tell me to stop looking into . . . whatever this is."

She whispered, "Fuck," and stepped back farther into the woods, beckoning us to come too. "The official ruling in Maddie's death was suicide, but—"

She blinked back tears, her voice going thick. "Maddie was working to save money for college. She wanted to go to Columbia. She was smart and happy, and she was so fucking talented—"

"In what?"

Sophie would not have interrupted. But Sophie wasn't here. I was. And this sick sort of dread had bloomed in my stomach, crawling through my veins to bulge against my skin, and all my thoughts felt muddled.

Her lips parted, stunned by the change of subjects. "She was a cellist."

Music.

My mouth went dry, tongue to the roof of my mouth like the cling of salt water on skin. "Did she—did she wear a necklace?"

Jasmine's eyes darted to mine; then, wordlessly, she raised her phone, scrolling until she found what she was looking for.

The music swelled behind us, to cheers and shouts from the crowd. This area was secluded but not enough, and neither I nor Monica would do well with having a police record.

Jasmine turned the phone toward me, and I flinched against the brightness, and then again, harder, as the photo came into focus.

My lungs seized, sweat blooming over my skin, sweet sickness roiling in my gut. There was no way to deny what was right before my eyes.

I could still feel the weight of it in my hands, smell the copper of blood dried into its grooves.

I pressed my hands to my stomach, trying to quell the waves rising inside me. "How did she die?"

My eyes closed, pressed tight, bracing for the words that confirm the worst of my fears.

She said, "She drowned. In the ocean. They think she jumped from a pier."

Monica's hand appeared at my back, like she was afraid I'd fall without the support. "Did she leave a note?"

Jasmine shook her head. "You don't understand. I know—I *knew* my friend, even if you never truly understand what another person is going through, but do you want to know what she did the night she disappeared? She did her precalc homework, and she wrote half her AP English paper, and she texted me to ask if I wanted to plan Halloween costumes. Those aren't things you do if you're planning on not being around the next morning. There was no note. Not a real one."

I rubbed at my forehead, like I could force my thoughts to coalesce through the force of my fingertips. "Then why—"

"Why suicide? She was found not far from the shore, and there was a head injury." She shuddered as she spoke the words. "So they say she jumped from the pier and hit her head on the way down or something. And they found this letter, from Columbia."

My head went dizzy. "What did it say?"

I already knew. The certainty of it driving like a spike through my brain.

Jasmine said, "They rescinded their offer," and I was back in my kitchen, Ms. Kohler's voice telling me they were concerned about my academic dishonesty.

They did the same to her. They took away her future, and then she died.

Jasmine's gaze darted around the forest, her voice a scratch against the cold air. "She couldn't fucking swim. Not well anyway. So why else would she be out on a pier in the ocean in the middle of the night? Especially after getting a letter like that. They found her car there. Parked. With her purse and phone inside. She had the Notes app open, and it said 'I'm done. I'm sorry.' Except Maddie had her own stationery. She thought it made her look professional. *Fake it until you make it, Jas.* That's what she always said to me."

Tears trickled down her cheeks, reflecting the sway of the trees, rolling faster as new ones joined. "She wouldn't have left a fucking 'I'm sorry' in her goddamned Notes app."

My skin went hot and cold, a flame erupting to a frost, my breathing shallow. "Have you ever heard the name Garrett Packard?"

Her lips flatlined, and she shook her head. "No, but if he was a client, she never used their real names."

I unlocked my own phone, fumbling the password three times because I was shaking too much for face ID, my fingers refusing to work quite right.

I pulled up Garrett's Insta, flicking past pictures of him and Sophie. I couldn't stomach bringing her into this, not even in the smallest way.

I stopped at a picture of Garrett and Adam, and to this day, I don't know whether it was intentional. They were both smiling, lounging in pool chairs while the blue water in front of them sparkled in the sun. "The one on the left. Do you recognize him?"

Jasmine's head titled. "On the left? No. But—"

She grabbed the phone, zooming closer onto Adam's likeness. "I know that guy. Nobody knew it but me, but he and Maddie were kind of dating."

My head went dizzy, the trees around me spinning until my stomach lurched. I stumbled to the trees, landing on my knees where sticks jammed into my skin, the soil cold and wet beneath my hands, and my stomach heaved.

I retched until my muscles ached, until there was no part of me not covered in sticky sweat and my hair plastered to my cheeks.

Monica's voice sounded in my ear, panicked, shouting from worlds away. I wanted to stand. I needed to stand and leave here before I learned anything else, but my limbs felt too heavy, wooden.

A scream cut through the quiet of the forest, through the haze of my thoughts, through the blare of music until even that was silent.

And then, a thousand voices shouting, crying, and I forced myself to move, Monica shouldering the bulk of my weight. We made it to the clearing, where those who remained either stood with phones pressed tight to their ears or huddled near the ground.

We stumbled deeper until a crack in the wall of bodies showed what I feared most.

A girl, lying still, her arms and legs splayed from her body, her mouth tipped open to the sky.

My thoughts assembled themselves only seconds before Monica spoke them aloud, her voice barely a whisper. "I gave that girl your drink."

CHAPTER TWENTY-EIGHT
NORA

We drove home in a daze, the stars blurring from beyond my window, trees passing too quick to count. We drove in silence, the weight of our thoughts too heavy to release into the air.

I pressed my forehead to the cold glass, let the residual waves of sickness roll through me, leaving my skin clammy. The rhythmic thump of tires against the road rang like a lullaby to sleep I'd never wake from.

We'd fled the forest miles ago, left behind but not forgotten, the reminder of it like a siren call from the waves.

The screams, the heat of the fire, and the press of smoke against my heaving lungs. The gray of her skin, open eyes turned to the sky like a prayer.

The sirens, the flash of lights illuminating the dark sky—red and blue challengers to the stars.

We watched them through the windshield, tucked down the street, my body still racked with shivers. We watched as they rushed into the woods, their heavy footsteps fading until only the chirp of crickets remained, until the woods went quiet and still.

They ran on the way back, a blur of movement as they loaded her into the ambulance and it sped away, those same lights splaying over the road that held us.

Ainsley. Her name was Ainsley. *Is* Ainsley. And what happened to her is my fault.

I sucked in the cool night air, breathed in the hint of bark and soil and the smoke from the fire, reaching for us, even here.

We could not run from this night.

I wanted to. I wanted to pretend the things I'd heard were a fantasy, a chapter in the life of someone who was not me. I wanted to rewind.

I'm not a coward. I never have been. Challenges were meant to be met. They were meant to be conquered.

But there had never been a cost such as this.

I never had guilt for ruining my parents' marriage—they'd done the hard work well before I made myself the catalyst. Dad had cheated and lied and stolen from the account that was designed to save for all our futures. He had a girlfriend to impress—a terribly difficult thing to do when your wife sees your credit card statements.

I'd watched as he left early, stayed late, as business meetings turned to overnight trips, and my mother, she nodded, believing. Or maybe not.

I found the necklace in his luggage—a string of emeralds that threw rainbows onto the ceiling as the sun darted through the window. The weight of it pressed against my fingertips, cold gems heavy in my hand. The weight of college tuition, and Mom's retirement, and yes, even Sophie's dreams for dance. I rubbed the pad of my thumb over that string of gems, felt every cut and angle, every sharp edge like a blade against my skin.

I tucked it back into its velvet home, safe and secure from the harsh world, just waiting for her soft skin to rest against.

You see, this part is a confession too.

How I waited, planned. How I carefully orchestrated a distraction here, a request there, when Dad's unlocked phone would be in reach. Until I could program my likeness into his facial ID alongside his.

Then his world stood open to me. His lies on full display, all his misdeeds waiting for me to expose.

And so I did. Printing his text messages and his emails, the account statements that he'd nearly bled dry. The accounts that belonged only to him that remained untouched.

He'd planned for a future without us and without planning for ours. And that would not stand.

He was supposed to be home that night, what with Mom at a late meeting. Instead, he did like he had so often before, leaving me to watch over Sophie. She was plenty old enough to watch out for herself, but it had always been that way. A girl too sensitive to survive in this world, too naive to make her own decisions—a delicate porcelain doll, smooth skin so susceptible to damage. Better to be admired if she remained unmarred, if the damage never showed.

Only, Sophie was never so delicate as they assumed, and when she crawled from her bedroom window to the ground below, I lay impossibly still, my breathing even and true.

I waited twenty minutes more, until she was sure to relax into her freedom, and then I called Dad. My voice frantic and my tears plentiful and no I didn't know where Sophie was, and yes, I had promised to watch her but she was *gone*.

There was another call to Mom, my voice innocent when she asked where my father was, as I lied as I sobbed that I didn't know.

They made it home within moments of each other, the police

only seconds behind. In the interest of honesty, I hadn't accounted for that element.

It changed nothing save for one more witness to the evidence I'd laid out.

I know what they saw that night—me, perched on the edge of the couch with a tapestry of paperwork before me. Me, different than they'd ever seen.

I know my mother saw a girl she did not recognize. A girl to be feared.

I know my father saw the same.

Only one of them was right.

It wasn't enough, I realized, for my mother to find out what he'd done. It wasn't enough to witness the fallout.

I designed it all so I could see *him*. To watch the moment understanding settled in, his mind churning through the outcomes and potential excuses and finding there were none that benefited him and none that could save him.

I needed to see it, the *tick tick tick* of the grandfather clock like each consequence falling into place, all coming due at the same moment.

We teach children that life isn't fair, but it's always been more true for some. Like it isn't some part of the world's structure, bent toward the ones who deserve it the least.

But that night, I bent it back, just a fraction, and I watched my father's world collapse around him.

It collapsed mine too, as I knew it would. But no part of me could have lived under the weight of his lies.

The police found Sophie out with her friends, safe, as I always knew she would be. Though I had no idea she'd try to run from them, spraining her ankle in the process.

She came home to our father ripping the clothes from his closet, his shoes jutting from a duffel bag too small to fit them all. She came home to tears and tension and all of us strung tight, a taut sort of buzz crowding through the house like a living thing. Like a single word, the wrong movement might spark an explosion.

He left that night and never returned, not even to collect the rest of his things. They're in boxes now, put there by my hands, buried deep in the attic's corners, where they'll sit beneath building layers of dust, every year more forgotten.

I kept the necklace. Sophie couldn't dance for a month. She lost the lead in the year's biggest performance.

She blamed me—Mom did too—for far longer.

I didn't regret it then, and I don't now.

Be strong, Nora.

But watching those lights fade down the twisting road, the image of that girl on the trampled grass, I wonder if there's a lesson I failed to learn.

Some broken part of me that has always been so focused on the end, I blinded myself to the means.

I don't know where the line is, not where Sophie is concerned. I'm four years old again, perched on the edge of that tub while she plays, where she could drown in only two inches of water. Tucked into the corner of my room with a haphazard fort of blankets, the lights off, pillows stuffed beneath the crack in the door and a flashlight that makes the world only for the two of us while I read to her, and then some more, to muffle the sounds of our parents, until her tears turn to light snores that block the sounds of their shouts.

There was no room for fear then, no space for my own tears, and there isn't now.

Garrett is caught up with the kind of people who will kill for my silence, and Adam . . .

He was dating Maddie, and then Maddie died.

The ambulance disappeared around the bend, until it was only the ghost of its sirens I heard in my head, the specter of its lights splashing over the black road. We wouldn't be following. Wouldn't be heading toward the police station either. Monica handed her that drink, and she wouldn't be safe with them.

She'd looked at me as we stood over that girl, everything coming together in a blink, her eyes wild and shimmering with tears, and I'd yanked her into the woods, deep into the heart of them where the trails don't trespass. Through too-close trees and unyielding branches that clawed at our skin, fallen limbs and stones that sent us sprawling into the mud.

We were scraped and bloody, battered and dirty, but we were free. We were alive.

I didn't know if Ainsley was.

I'd find a way to discover her fate in the morning. It was the least I could do—to face what I'd done.

Monica stopped a whole house down from mine, so no one would wake when the car door slammed. She bit her lip, staring straight forward, hands gripped so tightly to the wheel I expected the bones to burst through her skin.

Sophie would've hugged her. Talked to her in the quietest of voices. She'd have squeezed her hand reassuringly and told her it would be okay, and Monica would've believed her.

I couldn't do any of those things—not the way Sophie could—so I gave her the best of what I was able.

I whispered into the night, "I will find them, and I will make them pay."

I barely felt the coldness of the handle, my fingers still too numb, but I forced them to work, to turn it slowly, cringing as the hinge squeaked when I cracked open the front door.

I had chosen the front because it's farthest from Mom's bedroom, but as with everything else that night, it was the wrong choice.

Mom's face was set in light and shadows, the glare of her phone blaring up from her lap as she sat tucked into the corner of the couch. "Where have you been?"

I blinked, so caught off guard by this attempt to parent. She had never spoken those words to me had never taken that tone either. I said, "Out," like it's the most natural thing in the world, like nothing of the last few hours was real.

"Out? You've been *out*?" She threw her phone to the couch, and it splayed light against the ceiling, until she was just a blackened figure as she rose from the couch. "Do you know how long I've been waiting up for you?"

I glanced at my watch. "Roughly four hours?"

There was a pause, filled only by her ragged breathing. "That was rhetorical."

"Well, you didn't phrase it as such so—"

"I got two emails from your teachers today. You missed school last week? And you didn't turn in an assignment in AP English? You missed debate practice?"

"Are these rhetorical as well? Because you're phrasing them as questions." An edge had crept into my voice, a sharp and angry thing slicing its way to the surface.

"I don't need this shit from you, Nora!" The light on her phone dimmed, just before it blinked out entirely, but I tracked her voice as she moved across the room.

Exasperation melded with her anger, dripping from every word. "You're supposed to be the one I don't have to worry about. I am *trying* to work and raise two kids—and god knows your dad doesn't help anything besides sending his child support—and trying to keep Sophie on track is hard enough. I can't do this with both—"

Whatever she planned to say next withered and died on her tongue as she flicked on the lamp, seeing me—perhaps truly seeing me—for the first time.

I watched her expression morph as her gaze traveled to the angry scratches on my face, the mud caked to my hands, coating my shoes. Whatever she saw in my eyes brought tears to her own, carried her toward me until my entire body stiffened.

She stopped short, held by an invisible barrier.

There were things I could say, responses rising up my throat and begging to be set free. I could've told her that maybe I wasn't the person she thought I was. That I wasn't the person *I* thought I was. Or maybe I was the person she feared I've always been, buried deep beneath the layers of propriety and obedience. I could've let the tears pressing at my eyes fall, and I could've said maybe I was not that strong. Not like she always told me to be. That once—just *once*—I wanted to be the one she worried about.

I didn't do any of those things.

I gathered my emotions and spun them tight. I removed my shoes, carefully, to reduce the mess I'd have to clean later, and then I placed them quietly on the porch.

She didn't reach out when I passed her. I'd frozen her somehow, left her mute.

I flicked the light off as I went, staying to the edge of the stairs where it was quieter, stripping in the bathroom while steam floated around me, clinging to the walls and mirrors. I swiped it away, staring at my reflection. I would not run from what I'd done.

The water scalded my skin, leaving it pink and tender, but the dirt broke free, swirling the drain before disappearing forever.

The house remained dark as I crept to my room, climbing into whatever clothes my hands landed on first, my hair still tangled and dripping.

I'd barely crawled into bed, my knees tucked to my chest, when the gentlest of knocks rapped against my door. Sophie didn't wait for me to answer, simply poked her head inside and whispered my name.

I didn't respond. Perhaps I'd struck myself mute too.

I'd lost count of the number of nights Sophie had spent in my bed. It was me she ran to when she had nightmares, when shadows danced over her walls and became monsters. I never told her no. She'd climb in, her arms circling her legs as if to protect the softest parts of her and I'd tell her stories until her body relaxed, clasped hands falling free.

The bed shifted as she sat, and I forced myself not to flinch when her hand settled on my shoulder. "Nora?"

Fear. That's what I heard in her voice. Compassion. Tenderness. Those too. But her fear, that's what forced words from my lips.

"It's okay, Soph. Go back to bed."

"I—" She sucked in a breath, like she needed a moment before telling me I'd uprooted her again, changed the dynamics of our home before she'd truly adjusted to the last.

She sighed, my scalp tingling where she pulled the sodden strands back from my cheek.

Cold air skimmed over my back as she lifted the covers, settling in beside me, her hand reaching for mine, clasping tight.

She didn't tell me stories, but I drifted into dreamless sleep just the same.

CHAPTER TWENTY-NINE

SOPHIE

Joseph Graham is having a shindig. That's what Mom would call it, because she's an old.

It seems like a stupid place to continue my stupid puzzle/ investigation/death wish, because on my list of important things, Nora taking pictures of a classmate's dad is pretty low.

That is, until you consider that Nora does nothing without reason, and if she took creepy pictures, they mean something. Plus, Amber Donahue and her parents will be there. Garrett's parents will be there too, though I'm hoping to avoid them.

Awkward won't begin to cover it.

We may have gotten invited to a party like this back before Nora torpedoed my parents' marriage, when Dad was free to charm his way into the upper level of the social echelon. But now we are children of a broken home, with a single mother and a father who's created a new life with a new woman, and while Mom works very hard, she does not charm.

So it's left to me.

Fortunately, charm happens to be one of my strengths, and freshman boys make for easy marks.

Tonight, I am Benjamin Graham's date.

All it took was a single lunch hour. He blushed through 80 percent of it, the other 20 was him telling his friends to shut up. He already has more decency than his father.

He obviously doesn't drive, so Isa and Charla are chauffeuring me there. Well, Charla is. Isa is in the back seat with me, putting last-minute touch-ups on my makeup.

I unblock my seat belt to face her, and Charla mumbles, "Sophie, I swear to god," because not even our two-mile-per-hour pace is enough to convince her I'd be fine if we crashed into the car before us. I click it back in and let the belt strangle me while Isa touches up my eyeshadow.

A line forms at the gated entrance, Charla's ten-year-old Honda completely out of place among the smattering of Porsches and Rolls-Royces. Even the normal cars are shiny and new.

The guard at the door leans in as Charla recites my name, and I hold my breath.

It's not like I'm crashing the party. I was invited. By a fourteen-year-old.

He waves us through and we follow the stream of cars toward the front entrance, and not for the first time, I scan the yard for where Nora must've been standing when she took those pictures. And then I scan again, to figure out how in the hell she got past the wrought-iron gates. But then, she's Nora. Of course she did. She can't even be bad at stalking.

Isa squeezes my hand. "We'll be waiting just down the road if it gets too weird." She means with Garrett's parents but doesn't say it because she's the best sort of friend.

I give her a hug and plant a kiss on Charla's cheek even though she acts like she doesn't want me to but really does, and then I climb out of the back seat and onto Joseph Graham's cobblestone walkway.

The house is a study in glass and angles, every corner sharp and slick. A massive window bends around the left corner, where party-goers mingle, bright lighting clear against the dark sky, gowns swooshing around stilettoed ankles, silver trays with sparkling champagne floating through the empty spaces.

Music drifts from the open double doors, a piano rendition of Tchaikovsky's "Waltz of the Flowers" from *The Nutcracker*.

And they say ballet doesn't teach you anything.

I pull my shawl tighter against the wind, but it does nothing to shield the abundance of bare skin that accompanies this dress. Strapless, backless, fitted to my waist and all the way to my knees, where it flairs in soft folds. It's not new. Obviously. If I had money to buy new dresses for some stupid old people party I wouldn't have to beg my parents to go to a single intensive.

Mom says I'm on probation. Which isn't an absolute no. It's that scary place where she's just *dreaming* of saying no, plotting the entire speech she'll give me about what a failure I am and how I did this to myself and if I'd learn to make better choices then I could end up just like my perfect big sister, Nora.

Only, Nora isn't so perfect after all. And she's not home either. She hasn't *been* home. Every night I sneak into her room and bunch some small part of her comforter, and every morning it's exactly as I left it. Every morning, Mom looks a little more tired, the lines around her eyes a little deeper. Nora's absence may be my only saving grace.

"Sophie!" Ben's voice cracks on the second syllable, and his cheeks flame in the wash of light from overhead.

I smile, and he rushes toward me, holding his bent arm for me

226

to fit mine through, and he's trying so hard, I lean down to give a quick kiss on his cheek.

His smile is sweet and shy and instantaneous, and I immediately feel bad for completely using him tonight. If only I could trust every boy this much—instead, I have Garrett and Jude—and I don't know the truth about either.

Warmth rushes over my shoulders as we step inside, the crystal chandelier that floats high above the foyer sending shards of light to flicker over the marble tile. Voices dance beneath the piano's notes (Beethoven now) mingling with stilted laughter and the rough baritones of men who've already had a bit too much to drink.

My heels clip against the tile as we ascend the stairs and ease into the window room, the scents of chocolates and roasted meats and warm breads hanging in the air amid floral perfumes. My head goes light, my heart fluttering. Not because I'm nervous, but because of the *possibility*.

Here's the sad, selfish truth: I live for applause. For attention. For that indescribable feeling of hundreds of eyes taking in every move of your body. Staring in awe at the things you can do that they will never be able to master. I *want* that adoration. I crave it.

And tonight feels like a stage.

A waiter lowers a tray of champagne flutes in front of me and I pluck one free, and after a brief hesitation, Benjamin does too. The waiter opens his mouth—obviously moments from pointing out Ben is an infant—but it takes only a single look before he closes it. Perhaps Benjamin has some of his father in him after all.

I clink my glass to his with a "Cheers!" and sip slowly. Ben does what every freshman discovering alcohol does and chugs it. I definitely have guilt for getting a child drunk, so much so I even suggest he slow down, but if Tickner is right and I *am* in danger, whether it be from Jude, Garrett, Adam, or some other dude (it's always dudes), tonight is vital.

It takes twenty minutes and another flute of champagne for Ben's eyes to go glassy, his tongue loose. His dad's office is on the third floor. No one goes up there during parties. No, there's no key because there's a fingerprint scanner for that floor, but yes, Ben does have access. Obviously, I'll need him somewhat functional—at least enough to walk.

I make several hints about being hungry before Ben catches on and scampers off to get some hors d'oeuvres and I stalk the room.

No fewer than three grown-ass men try to hit on me—in that creepy way where they pretend to be fatherly but spend the whole time staring at your tits—but Amber finally appears.

She's all wrong. Huddled in the corner when she should be at the center of the room, her nail polish chipped and her hair limp. Her eyes dart from person to person, and she chews on her bottom lip until a bloom of red appears. She wipes at it before her hand drops, leaving a smudge of crimson on her white dress.

I can't stop staring. This is not Head Cheerleader Amber. Not even obnoxiously-campaigning-for-homecoming-queen Amber. This Amber looks like someone carved out her soul.

Her eyes lock on mine and her mouth drops open, but before she can run like she clearly wants to, a man steps in front of her.

"Sophie? Is that you?"

Oh fuck.

Garrett's mom appears in front of me, her eyes watery and her steps wobbly. "Oh, look at you!"

She runs her hands down my cheeks, over my shoulders, like she's assuring herself I'm still real.

I give her a strained smile and try to make meaningful eye contact while also peering over her shoulder and between the ebbing crowd to see who has Amber locked in the corner.

"Hi, Mrs. Packard!" I give her a hug that's really an excuse to watch Amber, and when her captor turns, whispering in her ear, I recognize his face from Nora's picture.

My face probably matches Garrett's mom's—pale, sallow, sick. I pull free from our hug and give her a genuine smile. "I hope you're doing okay."

What a ridiculously trivial platitude to give a woman who thinks her son is missing, even if all the evidence suggests otherwise.

Her mouth flatlines, her hands still clasped around mine, so tight my fingers feel tingly. "Have you heard from him?"

I'm gonna be sick. I can't tell her about the texts, and even if I did, is that more cruel than saying nothing at all? I can't be sure it's him. The handwriting on the note looked like his but so did the letter he said goodbye to his parents with (and not me) and she didn't believe that was real either.

It feels like false hope. And I'm not sure she can take it. "No. Not really. I mean, there was this note in my dance bag but—"

Her nails dig into my palms, threatening to pierce straight through my skin, and I have to pull them away. "What kind of note? When? Sophie, *please*. What—"

She claws at me, leaving scratches down my arms as Mr. Packard appears and wraps her up, smothering her in the size and breadth of him. It takes my breath away, how much Garrett looks just like him.

He forces a glass into her hand—a deep amber liquid that looks nothing like anyone else has—and watches as she gulps it in one swallow. He towers over as he leans in, voice low. "I'm very sorry, Sophie. She's not been well."

"Yes, of course." I give my best sympathetic smile. "I can't imagine how hard the last month has been for you both."

Mrs. Packard is nearly limp in his arms, only her white knuckles across his suited forearm a sign that whatever was in that glass hasn't make her completely comatose.

She slurs, "You can't understand," and I want to hug her, tell her I know I can't, but Mr. Packard interrupts us both to apologize again as he moves them both back into the crowd, the tips of her shoes dragging against the floor as she mumbles that it didn't have to be this way.

I'm not the only one who notices. Their retreat is followed by long stares and surreptitious glances, murmurs and whispers, and then, pitying glances sent my way, like they're all so sorry I had to endure her grief. Her anguish. Her . . . guilt.

I swallow against the roiling in my stomach because, beneath it all, that's what I felt from her, but no one else seems to notice. They all just stare as I say it's okay, and she's understandably upset, and no, she didn't mean to leave those marks down my arms; she just startled me and I pulled away.

They tell me how sweet I am, how lovely I look, they squeeze my shoulder and say Garrett was lucky to have me, and for once, the

230

spotlight feels cold, their attention tainted. All their praise leaving me empty and uglier than I was before.

The crowd parts to reveal an empty corner where Amber once stood, and I leave gentle parting words in my wake as I slip through bodies in search of a white dress.

They disappear down a long hall just as I spot them, and by the time I run-walk through the room, the door at the end of it slams shut.

Ben. I need poor, drunk, baby-faced Ben.

I drag him from the chair he's slumped in and prop him up as we move through the room. I make sure to tell several people I'm helping him find a bathroom, just in case someone sees us creeping through hallways.

I have to stop halfway to the door to ditch my heels because Ben can't stop stumbling and I'm not risking a broken ankle and the end of my dance career for this.

We make it through the first scanner, up the flight of stairs, and down yet another hallway only by a show of extreme patience on my part, and a whole lot of talking about Ben's video game stats.

At the scanner for the third floor, he asks if I'll be his girlfriend and I tell him I'll think about it if he can remain silent for the next twenty minutes. He's so committed he only points when I whisper for directions to his dad's office.

I'm as silent as I can be while schlepping a barely teenager through the halls, but the plush carpeting muffles our footsteps, the soft hum of the furnace sending warm blasts of air through the registers to swirl over my bare feet. Scents of cigars and furniture polish battle with the alcohol on Ben's breath, and I strain for the sounds of voices and whispered secrets.

But it's only the two of us, and I nearly collapse in relief when Ben's fingerprint draws a green light from the keypad and a quiet click that frees the lock.

I drop him into a tufted leather chaise and yank up my dress—strapless was not made for hauling around other humans—and try to catch my breath.

Now what?

This would've worked out much better if I could just eavesdrop on a conversation that answered all my questions. Where's a cliché movie plot point when you need one?

I click the door shut and lock it before heading to Joseph Graham's desk, tugging on a small desk lamp that sprays shadows over the dark room. This room doesn't match any of the others. Floral wallpaper coats the walls, cherry-wood shelves spanning from floor to ceiling, a carved-wood desk set before a tall leather chair, and a sitting area with matching chaises.

"Hey, Ben?" I keep my voice low, and he grunts in response, oblivious to me pawing through his dad's drawers. "Do you know Amber Donahue?"

"She's hot."

"Right. Sure. But does she ever, I don't know, come around?"

"You're hot."

Jesus take the wheel. There's nothing that looks not-boring in Joseph's desk, so I move on to his computer, but of course, you need a fingerprint for that. "Does your fingerprint work on your dad's computer?"

232

"Nope." He slumps back into the cushion, and his eyes drift shut.

Awesome. I go back to the files because there has to be *something*, and that's when I see it. Nora's handwriting.

I tug the file free, and it falls open to printouts of pictures Nora took, even more than were saved on her camera, along with what look like financial records to a charity. Which is all still boring.

But behind that are more pictures. Of Nora this time. Leaving school. Walking into the shelter where she volunteers. Along the boardwalk and I swear to baby Jesus it looks like she's wearing my hoodie?

What the actual fuck, Nora?

The floor creaks and I pop my head above the desk but Ben is still passed out and the door is still closed and I'm still snooping through a powerful man's desk.

Goose bumps rise over my neck, the feeling of being watched snaking over my skin, and I spin to the black window, but we're on the third floor, so I'm being stupid. But there, strolling through the garden, are forms that look awfully like Amber and Joseph.

I crack open the window, letting in the salty scent of the ocean, and press my ear to the screen. I'm still three floors up and can't hear a damned thing. Amber's upset though. Her arms flailing to accentuate every word. Something something dry. Or die.

Oh shit.

Joseph is clearly trying to calm her, with a tone I can't even hope to catch any of, so I'm just standing up here like a moron waiting to get caught.

I slam the window shut and eye the folder on the floor. I clearly have no pockets to stash it in, and there is *nowhere* to hide a business card in this dress, let alone an entire file.

Ben! Poor, drunk, passed-out Ben has a suit coat. Even if I can't wear it, I can drape it over my arm. I'll make it work.

He's much heavier when he's passed out, and I'm sweating by the time I drag him upward enough to get one arm free. I have to straddle him while I shove the coat behind his back, his head lolling to the side while drool leaks down his chin. Poor guy. Definitely going to need to tell someone he wandered off so he doesn't spend the whole night like *this*.

A light flashes, and I freeze. I've had plenty of pictures taken of me—I know exactly what that flash means.

"This doesn't look good for you, Sophie Linden." Michael Graham holds up his phone, in case I couldn't figure out he just took a pic that makes it look like I'm assaulting his baby brother.

I motion to the door he appeared from. "That is not a closet."

"Afraid not."

"Fuck."

"Very much so, yes."

"I can explain."

"I very much doubt that." He slides into the room, with that same rich-dude confidence his dad possesses, and I jump away from Ben and yank up my dress once again while racking my brain for all things Michael Graham.

Middle son. Senior. Lacrosse team. Dated Jessica Horton for a minute. Ugh. Jessica.

He slides into the chaise opposite his brother. "What are you doing up here, Sophie?"

I shove a pillow behind Ben's head so he doesn't wake up with a stiff neck, and flop down next to him. "Listen. I'm normally great at small talk, but I think we can just skip to the point where you call your dad and have me arrested or whatever."

Gonna bring a "Home Sweet Home" sign to the police station next time. Maybe a nice bowl of potpourri. Spruce the place up a bit.

He leans back, crossing an ankle over his knee. "Level with me."

"Okay, sure. Amber Donahue is hiding something—and not well might I add. And your dad is involved. He's also got pictures of my sister in that file over there, and she's not exactly my favorite person right now but that's kind of a red flag for a grown-ass man, no?"

I stand and smooth my dress, because if I'm going to jail I'm not going in wrinkled. "In short, your dad is a creep, Michael, and I'm spying on him."

His smile starts small but quickly blooms full, followed by laughter so deep he has to wipe tears from his eyes. When he finally calms himself, he says, "You really don't know anything, do you?"

My cheeks flush hot because being called stupid never ceases to feel like a dagger between my rib cage. "Why don't you educate me, then."

"What did Garrett's mom say to you down there?"

"What does Garrett have to do with your dad?"

"What *doesn't* Garrett have to do with my dad?"

I hate him. Tons. "She asked if I'd heard from him, and something about how it didn't have to be this way? She was already drunk and then Mr. Packard made her drunker. Now, what aren't you telling me?"

"That's a long list." He sighs, like he's annoyed we're having this conversation when he's the one who started it. "You leveled with me, in a rather dangerously honest and ill-advised rant, but I like your spirit, so I'll do the same. I turn eighteen very soon, and with that comes some financial benefits that ensure I'm no longer dependent on my father. Who is, as you say, a creep. In addition, I have some personal scores I'd like to settle."

I raise a brow. "Let's see . . . daddy issues and"—I tap my finger to my lips, smirking at the way his eyes follow—"personal scores. Did someone break your heart, Michael?"

He stands and strides over to me, his arms caging me against the desk. He'd be sort of cute if he wasn't such a pompous asshole. "I guess we have some things in common."

I go stock-still because it's the only thing I *can* do without admitting I really don't know anything, and he steps back, taking the heady scents of cedar and vanilla with him.

He holds up a flip phone, bedazzled with pink gems. It's ugly. "Do you know whose phone this is?"

"Your grandma's?" It's a flip phone, for fuck's sake.

He smiles and reaches for my hand, pulling it to place the phone against my palm. "I like you, Sophie. Maybe one day, after you do what I need you to do—because I'd hate to see this picture get out if you don't—we can reconnect."

Then he's gone, strolling toward the door like he's answered anything.

"Wait. What do you need me to do?" Bits and pieces clang together in my head, another puzzle I don't want to solve.

"Plausible deniability, Sophie," he says, not bothering to turn around. "Some things you'll just have to figure out."

236

It comes together in a rush. The broken heart. The godawful design aesthetic on this phone. "Did you just give me Jessica Horton's phone?"

The door swooshes open, and he turns just inside it. "I'll get someone to take care of Ben. You can leave out the back. Down the hall, turn left, follow the back stairs."

Then he nods at the phone. "Go and get us both a little revenge."

CHAPTER THIRTY
NORA

"What happened to your face?" Garrett fidgeted in my passenger seat, clearly not used to relying on someone else driving. Also clearly too big to fit in my small sedan. He'd tried to move the seat farther back four times.

Again. Not exceptionally mentally gifted.

"I fell." Truth.

"What the fuck are we doing, Nora?"

"We're engaging in a mission."

Also truth.

Though I should likely go back a bit and explain how I came to have Garrett Packard in my car.

See, I woke the morning after someone tried to kill me the second time, and called the hospitals nearest that spot in the woods. They'd tell me nothing, obviously, but social media filled in the gaps. Ainsley Barber was not dead, but she wasn't quite alive either. She'd slipped into a coma, from which she may never return.

I could have let this frighten me into submission, but it fueled me instead. I'd barely sipped that drink, and it had left me on my knees, retching and cramped. Ainsley deserved retribution. And I'd promised it to Monica.

Garrett served two purposes in this. He was perhaps the only person who knew Adam better than I did. And if Adam had been dating, and possibly harmed, Maddie, it was very likely Garrett knew. His second purpose was that though it was quite possible Garrett might prefer me dead to alive at this moment in his life, I didn't think him capable of standing by while I was murdered.

Ergo, Garrett would serve as my bodyguard while spying on Principal Wentville.

He didn't need to know his role in order to perform it, so I simply threatened him. The cheating service may fire me for not adequately completing Garrett's homework for him, but how many assignments would pass before they did so? Certainly, a prolonged period of subpar grades when he'd already been caught stealing my paper would not do.

That made him no less insufferable as he carried out his duties.

He tried moving the seat back for the fifth time. "I didn't sign up for a mission. Why is the heat on two hundred fucking degrees?"

There were other complaints. I'm sparing you from having to hear them all. For a football player he was awfully delicate.

"Don't you want to know how this whole thing works, Garrett?"

"Not really."

Of course not. "Allow me to rephrase. Close your eyes."

There was more complaining and grumbling while I eased my car into a parking space along the south end of the boardwalk. It would only take a few minutes' walk to get to Wentville's meeting place.

I said, "Imagine you're graduated from high school, from college even. From there you have a nice job, fancy apartment, lots of girlfriends—"

"I'm not a player. Sophie—"

"Sure. You have Sophie." I'd die before allowing that. Perhaps the wrong choice of words.

I tamped down the shudder that emanated from my bones, shoving open the door so I could suck in saltwater air, calm the heaving in my stomach. "My point, Garrett, is that you have the life you want. The life that I and every other one of your *tutors* will have laid the foundation for. But Principal Wentville will still be the principal of a high school, and he has proof of what you've done, and maybe one day he'll decide it's worth more to him to *tell someone* than it is to keep quiet. So perhaps it's in your best interest to find proof of something equally damaging for him. Now open your eyes."

I tossed a camera into his lap, and he caught it before it could inflict damage.

Such a pity.

He stared at it, then nodded. "Yeah, okay. I'm in."

Of course. What I would not admit to Garrett was that I still didn't know how Wentville fit into this scheme. Certainly he over-rode previous grades. Egregious enough on its own. But there was the test element I hadn't figured out. How had Garrett and all the others managed to pass them? My theory was that Wentville collected the tests from the teachers in advance, under the guise of review or approval, and then provided them to the students.

It would require *some* level of actual work—imagine that—but a trained parrot could memorize multiple-choice answers. Likely they didn't even memorize the questions themselves, just simply the correct order of A, C, E, B . . .

A rudimentary mnemonic would make it easy. Essay questions would be a bit harder, but still eminently doable, even for some-one like Garrett.

But why? Wentville was risking his job, and there had to be a reason. I suspected it was money, because wasn't it always?

Access to his bank account, courtesy of his planner page of passwords, showed no regular influx of deposits outside the norm. His PayPal showed no activity and he had no Venmo or similar that I could find. Cash would be smarter, and far less traceable.

And an email bearing only an address and time scheduled him only a few hundred feet from my parked car.

I tossed a ball cap to Garrett, instructing him to put it on, and slid one over my own head, and motioned for him to follow.

The sun had nearly disappeared from the horizon, barely a trail of pink and orange left floating above the surface. The ocean churned, waves tumbling to shore with foamy white peaks, rolling from the depths to break the surface with a roar.

Sunday evenings were always some of the quietest—Sunday evenings in October more so—but the greasy, salty scents of the restaurants that lined the strip still hung thick in the air.

Goose bumps prickled my skin as wind whipped from the ocean, so much colder than normal, like a message. Like a warning.

Garrett walked to my left, glancing down to my clothing. "Is that Sophie's sweatshirt?"

Yes. Also her leggings. I'd nearly forgotten what it was like to wear my own clothes. If she didn't have so many, perhaps she would've noticed. "I'll record him with my phone. You take photos. It's point and shoot, so—"

I glanced to him, the camera held to his face, and sighed, pausing us briefly to remove the lens cap. "We stay together."

So I don't get killed.

He held the camera up again and snapped a photo of me scowling. "You look weird in real clothes."

"I always wear real clothes."

"No you don't. You wear prissy clothes."

"*Prissy* clothes?"

"Yeah. Clothes that show you think you're better than everyone else."

"Not everyone." Maybe most people. "But at least I'm not a cheater."

He slammed to a stop, his face pinched. "Are you ever going to let that go?"

"Let it *go*? No, and you know why? Because you were born with more privilege than ninety-nine percent of the population and you *still* couldn't resist using other people to get even further ahead."

I needed to stop there, before my anger burst through the surface and I admitted I knew about Maddie. That I knew about Maddie and Adam. I wasn't ready for that yet. I needed more information before I confronted him so I could look him in the eye and see all the things he didn't say.

I stomped down the boardwalk, faded wood slats reverberating beneath my feet. "Did you ever stop to think of what it's like to be the person on the other end? Doing twice the work for half the credit and—"

"They're not all angels. You know that, right?" A vein throbbed in his forehead, pulsing against the skin that had shaded red. "Sometimes those people you're talking about try to use you right back."

His chest heaved, broad shoulders stretching his shirt with every heavy breath, and our gazes locked.

It was like I was back in Adam's room again, breath trapped in my lungs, every fiber of my being attuned to the slightest of his movements. A sick sort of awareness that could save or doom me.

Something deep inside me yearned to ask the next question, draw forth the next response. He was so close to revealing something he shouldn't. So near to handing me something I desperately needed.

He only needed the smallest push, and I'd escaped death twice now. We were in public—maybe a third would not be as impossible as it seemed.

Be patient, Nora.

It slipped into my thoughts with as much insistence as the command to be strong. I was just on the edge of something, but I needed to remember who I was. I was a planner. I made sound decisions based on thoughtful analysis. This was no time to rush in.

Movement flickered in the corner of my eye, and I grabbed hold of Garrett's arm, yanking him against the side of the building just as Wentville strode by.

We pressed ourselves against the brick, but being this close to him, with the spicy, musky cloud of his body spray surrounding me, filled my nose with the burning need to sneeze.

I slapped at his arm, pointing to the camera, while I pinched the bridge of my nose tight, eyes watering. We couldn't risk Wentville turning around, but my body didn't seem to care.

I couldn't hold it anymore, and when I finally looked up, my nose still hot with my failed attempt, Wentville was gone. "Where—"

"Don't know. I turned around when you sneezed."

Not good. I looped my arm through Garrett's and ran down the boardwalk, scanning every face we passed.

"There!" Garrett pointed down the boardwalk to a small section that expanded toward the ocean, a trio of benches lining the area. That night a break-dance artist filled the space just before it, his music blaring from a speaker aside his cardboard square.

A few onlookers held out their phones—just as I was but for a very different performer—and an idea bloomed.

Maybe there was video of the pier Maddie supposedly jumped from. It's one of the longest on the coast, so I doubted any cameras reached to its end, but she would've had to pass the restaurant that sits just off the shore.

Wentville pulled a phone—a *flip phone*, like Amber had—from his pocket, and I snapped back into focus. "Odd."

"Not really." Garrett sucked in a breath, clearly not intending to have spoken those words aloud. I glared at him, and he said, "We all get them."

"I didn't."

"Guess they don't trust you yet."

Nor should they.

I resumed my filming, hiding behind Garrett's large body so at least if one of us were to be caught it wouldn't be me.

Garrett owed me that.

But Wentville didn't turn. He strode on purposefully, his gait long and hurried.

We followed, keeping distance but remaining close enough to stay in camera range, watching as he traversed the boardwalk until nearly the end.

I spotted his target well before Garrett and whispered, "He's going for the bag."

It was as innocuous as it was obvious. To a general bystander, it looked like a nondescript brown bag from any number of gift shops along the strip, its handles stretched toward the sky, easy for Wentville to scoop as he strolled by.

He did so, not even pausing to check the contents.

We followed him, all the way down to Main Street and doubling back to his car, and only then did he pull the stacks of bills from their hiding place.

Garrett mumbled, "Holy shit," like he was genuinely surprised Wentville didn't feed him the answers to every test he'd ever taken out of the goodness of his heart.

I snatched the camera from his hands before he could react, leveling him with a stare when he began to protest. "My camera, my evidence."

"I took the pictures!"

"And *if* the day comes when you need them, you just let me know."

Obviously I had no intention of giving him anything, but as dangling carrots went, it was a good one.

As evidence went, it truly *proved* nothing. But it did raise suspicion. What reason would Wentville have for picking up large bags of money? I wasn't sure it solved my problems. If I tried to blackmail Wentville and he held strong, he'd be sure to pass on my attempted coercion and stalking to Brown. Too much risk. Too reckless. And it would give too much away. But it was an option, which was more than I had before.

And this evening had already given me so much: Garrett's near admittance to having more information on Maddie than he wanted to share, the possibility of video the night Maddie died, and lastly, if everyone got a flip phone, then Maddie did too.

And I had every intention of finding it.

I was so focused on my plans for uncovering the last remaining layers of this mystery, so determined to correct the errant course my life had taken and put my plans for the future back into place, so oddly driven to find the truth about the death of a girl I didn't know, that I paid no attention to the police car tucked alongside the road on the way home. Apparently, I paid even less attention to the speed limit.

A strobe of red and blue stippled the car, the bright glare of headlights blinding me in the rearview mirror just as I'd asked Garrett if he wanted to stop for something to drink.

He was quite possibly even less thrilled than I about the possibility of the police interaction, though I was quite certain he would not have been calculating the cost of a citation or the increase in driver's insurance. Those concerns were not things boys like Garrett Packard spared time for.

The entire ordeal lasted fewer than ten minutes, my car pulled awkwardly into the nearest gas station, where customers stood at their pumps, happily entertained for at least a few moments while the officer completed his process.

Perhaps I would have gotten off with a warning—I was not in the habit of speeding, or otherwise engaging with law enforcement— but I believe if you spend enough time with humanity, you learn to trust fewer people than you would've hoped. I believe this particular police officer was able to sense that Garrett was a cheat and a liar, and thus, requested his driver's license as well.

Garrett was not pleased. He may have mentioned his family attorney and stammered the predictable diatribe about "knowing his rights," but ultimately complied, but then, he wasn't the one who left with a ticket for fifteen miles per hour above the speed limit.

A shameful mark on an otherwise-pristine record for which I will never forgive him.

I wish I could say things ended there. Instead, I waited while Garrett huffed himself out of the car, hitting his head on the "too fucking low" doorjamb in his quest to head inside the gas station.

By the time he returned, my tire was flat.

He made me pull into a small spot beside the building, where the air pump stood cold and lonely, shrouded in darkness save for the glowing haze of the moon. An empty field lay just beyond us, tall grass swaying in the bursts of wind.

Cars rushed by, headlights spearing the darkness, their tires a constant backdrop against the road. Any one of them could've held the man who tried to kill me twice. Every car that turned into the station could've been the last one I saw.

It's a funny thing, facing death. One would think it would create more fear, that every slam of a car door would travel straight to my heart, that every shout would leave me fleeing for cover.

Fear would have been a normal response. But then, I had never been normal.

Maybe I'd never been as strong as I thought. Or my strength lay in the wrong places.

For all my planning, my goals, my stubborn resistance to deviate from the life I'd mapped for myself, it was death that cleared a new road for me. One without the burdens I'd carried so long, the weight of expectations and the narrow binds of my own mind.

Death, with its looming threat, its nebulous deadline, it shapes so many of our hopes and fears, leaves us racing to beat a clock we cannot possibly outrun. It comes for us all someday, and if my day were to be today, what would I see when my life flashed before me? Sophie, of course. Just a few short weeks ago, I'd have said Adam, but now my new sight had shifted my view. I'd be left with things undone, plans unfulfilled. I'd rushed through this life in hopes for what came next, but now I knew better. I knew "next" was a whisper against a thousand drumbeats, a ripple against the crashing waves of the ocean.

It was those waves I'd been caught up in now, the ones that pulled my feet from beneath me, tossed me into their depths, where up became down and the world ceased to exist outside the quiet gurgle of the water surrounding me. And now I lay on the sand where it left me, my breaths hard and my limbs shaking, blinking to see what had been there all along.

This new path, calling to me, begging me to take just one more step, until I became caught up in that too. Until the answers waiting for me at the end revealed themselves.

A girl had died, another lay in a coma, Monica may be scarred for life over the simplest act—because she saved me, someone else may die. For that, someone needed to pay.

Garrett shrugged off his coat, tossing it inside, the sheen of sweat on his temple catching the wash of moonlight, before he returned for the third lug nut.

I studied him, trying to see what Sophie did. Trying to find some bit of redemption in him. "How well did you know her? Your last tutor."

"I didn't."

Liar. "Was she like me?"

His arms strained under the stubborn resistance of the tire. "You mean like did she ask too many fucking questions?"

"Ha. What did she do to you, Garrett? Or . . ." My throat closed around the words, like it fought against my speaking them.

The last lug nut came free, and Garrett turned his eyes to me. "Or what?"

I tried to hold his gaze, to summon the necessary indifference that would shield me from Garrett knowing anything about where my feelings might lie. But there was no hiding what he likely already knew. "What did she do to Adam?"

It was as close as I'd come to broaching the subject with the one person who might know more than anyone else.

Garrett ripped the flattened tire from the rim, letting it thump to the pockmarked cement. "I know you think I'm an asshole. That I'm fucking privileged and spoiled and never have to work for anything, and maybe that's all true."

He sucked in a breath, his hands shaky as they lifted the spare into place. "But it's not fucking easy either. People see my house or my car or whatever, and suddenly they're a little nicer. Maybe *now* they want to be my fucking friend. And they'll take any route they can to make that happen."

He spun the jack, tightening the new wheel into place, the flash of metal so fast it left a blurred circle in the air.

I clutched my bottled water tighter, let the plastic crinkle beneath my palms. "Are you insinuating she used Adam to get close to you?"

I wasn't certain how that fit in my theories. Whether it meant Adam felt betrayed when he discovered Maddie was only interested in him to get closer to Garrett and then . . . Then what? Adam may have had his heart broken by her, but to kill her for it? I couldn't believe that.

But maybe he *had* truly cared for her, and then Joseph Graham had her killed and he was just as determined as I was to seek justice for her. That felt far more like the Adam I knew.

Garrett shook his head. "I'm *insinuating* that she was a messed-up girl, and maybe if you're worried about Adam, you could fucking show it."

"Adam knows—"

"Adam knows trying to fit into your life is a game he can't win, Nora." He stood, brushing the dirt from his hands. "But keeps fucking trying anyway."

We didn't talk again while he finished the spare, not when he secured the flat tire into my trunk, nor when he came back from washing his hands and we had settled into the car again.

Not even when we exited from the lot, and we both watched as Adam's car pulled in.

CHAPTER THIRTY-ONE

SOPHIE

Of course Jessica would be involved in this somehow. Really, I should've seen it coming. Her obsession with Garrett is weird and beyond even the most pathetic of crushes.

But to be honest, I'm bitter about it. This mystery was already too complicated for me, and now there's another person involved.

Even worse, I don't know what Michael thinks he handed me, but this phone tells me fucking nothing. It's clearly not her regular phone. I've seen her with her basic-bitch glitter case enough times to know.

This one has only three numbers saved. One is just a bunch of dates and times and locations. *Confirming your appointment time at blah blah at blah blah blah.*

The second is more interesting. Someone texts Jessica on September 17 and says they need help. Jessica desperately responds that she's always there for the person.

That was the point I started feeling sick. Maybe it was Michael's comment about us both getting revenge. Maybe it was because I've come to associate Jessica with acting grossly pathetic around Garrett. But I couldn't stop feeling as if it was a conversation between the two of them I clearly wasn't meant to see. Because the number in this conversation isn't Garrett's.

I spent the entire three hours of dance practice trying to mine the recesses of my brain for information on what happened the night of

September 17 at 8:46 p.m. I even checked the planner Mom bought for me to help "organize my thoughts," but it was blank because my thoughts aren't organized.

Mrs. Wilson gave me more disapproving looks than I could possibly count while threatening to pull me from the lead role as Odette in our *Swan Lake* production and screaming, "Focus, Sophie!" at regular intervals. I tried. I really did. I was just focusing on the wrong things.

That's why I'm pacing the parking lot right now, the moon slowly rising in the sky, stars blinking beneath the clouds, breeze gently rolling through the blades of palm trees. I'm waiting for Mrs. Wilson to summon me. She wants to "have a little chat."

Which, honestly, is even more terrifying than the threat of Michael releasing that picture of me to the world.

Jessica's third set of messages isn't a set at all. It's just her, and it says: *We need to talk.*

She sent it on September 18. On the nineteenth, she sent: *You cannot ignore me.*

She seems to be wrong about that though, because no one responded.

My dance slipper scuffs the ground as I turn, marching back toward the studio, and as clouds smother the moon, the only light comes from a single streetlamp and the glow of Jessica's phone.

I need your help.

I try to picture Garrett texting her that. Of him reaching out to her and not me.

Sweat beads on my skin, a sick feeling worming its way through my veins. This whole time, she was right. She *does* know more about him than I do.

I found Mom crying once, after Dad left, and I told her we'd be okay even though we both knew it wasn't true. She said she wasn't crying because she was worried, not even because she was sad or hurt. She was furious.

He'd embarrassed her. Even worse, he'd insulted her by thinking she didn't know. That she'd never find out.

I pitied her. I thought about how Garrett would never.

But I'm holding this tacky bejeweled phone in my hand, and I can *feel* it, how stupid I've been. So focused on dance and the summer intensive, and he was making a fool of me the whole time. Jessica. Maybe even Nora.

I'm the girl whose boyfriend cheated on her with her own sister while she stood there smiling, looking pretty but adding nothing to the conversation. Nora always has something to add to the conversation.

And maybe I'm being played even now. Jude with pretty hair and his gentle kisses and his soft words that make me feel listened to. Garrett would know exactly what to do to get to me—and then he could watch while I betrayed him again.

Gravel crunches, and I spin toward the door, tears blurring my vision, but even when I blink, Mrs. Wilson isn't there.

A hand slams over my mouth, arms wrap across my middle, pinning mine to my sides as I crash into the person behind me. I scream, but it's muffled, quieted by thick gloves that smell sweet, like nail polish remover mixed with gasoline. My head goes light when I suck in air, my legs flailing as I kick but go nowhere.

He's dragging me, like Mr. Packard did to his wife at the party, my feet barely scraping the ground. My leg slams against the corner of the building, rough brick shredding my tights and my skin beneath, but I can't break free, his grip tightening the more I fight.

The sickly stench of rotted food cuts through the sweetness on his gloves as he crams us behind the dumpster, far from the light and any view of the road, and then, finally, his grip loosens and my feet hit the ground and my muscles flex to run but my entire body rebels, going so still I don't even breathe.

My brain catches up a second later. The cold edge against my throat, the glint of light thrown against the brick wall in front of me. A long, slim line with a fractured square to its right.

He has a knife to my throat.

Saliva pools in my mouth, sickly sweet, and I don't dare swallow and press the blade closer.

His hand shakes, and heat zips across my skin, his voice a dark, rough whisper against my ear. "Stop asking questions."

I can't talk, can't nod, can't risk any movement that might send his shaking hand slicing into my flesh again.

He jostles me, like he's just trying to shake some sense into me rather than ready to slice open my throat. "I will fucking kill you and your sister if—"

A scream freezes us both, and before I can even find where it came from, the man is gone and his knife clatters to the ground at my feet. I jump away just in time, and Mrs. Wilson runs toward me, and I hear her asking if I'm okay but I can't answer. She turns my head to see my neck better and gasps, tears filling her eyes before she gathers me up and squeezes me tight.

I don't hug her back even though my brain says I should, and then she's calling 911 and the sirens are in the distance and now that I'm not dead the only thought in my head is that there will be no avoiding Detective Tickner this time.

CHAPTER THIRTY-TWO
NORA

It's a long story, how I came to be in Madeline Armstrong's room in the dead of night.

But not one I'm willing to tell with any detail.

I had help, from an interested party, who informed us that Maddie's highly religious parents would not be home (Monday-night church) and, at any other time, would not welcome our company.

That Maddie had died by suicide was a matter they could not comprehend—not because they were so devastated by her loss, though I suspect that too, but because they truly believed they'd lost her soul forever.

Perhaps someone should have informed them that a god that heartless, that punitive, was not worth following.

But that is a digression not meant for this confession.

It did, however, rather complicate my plan to avoid activities that could jeopardize my future. I still planned on having one, after all, and this was a necessary step to securing it.

Proof. Undeniable, incontrovertible truth, that Garrett was the cheater, not me, that I could send to Brown. But more than that—it was clearing Maddie's name too. It was justice for her and Ainsley. It was showing Sophie who Garrett truly was.

Garrett painted Maddie to be an opportunist, a manipulative sort who tried to use him for his money, who used Adam to get closer to him.

A night's sleep had left me no more convinced that Adam could have killed over something so inconsequential. But then, seeing him drive into the lot last night left me with a chill I couldn't warm no matter how long I spent snuggled beneath the covers.

Garrett hadn't called him. I asked. That meant he'd been following me. Possibly tracking me. And *that* was not the Adam I knew.

I needed the truth—before I left for college. Before I left Sophie only steps across the yard from a boy who could kill over nothing.

My phone buzzed against my hip, and I pulled it free. We'd purchased a wig and makeup, and Monica was now moonlighting as one Nora Linden, who'd gone to the very public library to study from the corner table, where she could see anyone who entered the room.

It was a risk, one she fully understood and took anyway. Not many friends would volunteer to lure a potential killer from you so you could break into a dead girl's house. But Monica knew all too well how the world treated the less than fortunate, and she wanted answers for Maddie too. For Ainsley.

Black car followed me. Safely at corner table.

That was, I supposed, the best we could expect. Though the idea of Monica paying the ultimate price for actions that were not her own sent a deep, sickening sort of dread through me.

Time was exceptionally limited tonight, for both Monica and me.

I tiptoed through the expansive yard, the grass dried and brittle, bare in patches and thick with weeds in others. The farmhouse loomed large in the distance, surrounded by a copse of trees with twisted branches creeping toward the dark sky, splitting the moon into halves.

Smoke from a nearby fire lingered on the breeze, sinking into my clothes, and tendrils of white spiraled in the distance while crickets chirped from the taller of the grasses.

I wore all black, fitting of the type of work I set out to do, for the line I was ready to cross. But death had brought me this far. Who was I to turn back?

I reached the house, the vinyl siding cool to the touch, its surface weathered by the force of the wind, and I kept close to it, searching the darkness for movement, for witnesses.

I slipped the key I'd been given into the lock, letting it click over in a sound that echoed through the night, and gripped tight to the handle.

The door swung inward easily, opening to a small kitchen, the table still scattered with dishes, others bobbing in the soapy depths of the sink. Garlic and parsley stuffed the air, the soft bleed of light from the living room drizzling into the kitchen.

I hurried through them both, not pausing to look at the rows of family pictures lining the walls and crowding the shelves.

The staircase stood at the center of the house, the glass-paned door giving little privacy as I hurried up the steps.

Second bedroom on the left, I'd been told. I didn't need the instruction—it was the only door on the floor that remained closed.

Stale air greeted me as I inched open the door, peering into a darkened room where, at one point, Maddie Armstrong had slept. Had lived.

I slid inside, flipping the light on my phone to scan over the room. The bed remained unmade, items strewn across her desk, clothing draped over the chair—like she'd simply left for mere moments, scheduled to return.

A room frozen in time, waiting for a life that would never come back.

Moonlight trickled through the small slit in the curtain, muting colors to shades of gray, the endless quiet like another presence.

The room had been searched—I'd been told that too. Her belongings scrutinized, her privacy violated as the police tore into her life, item by item, trying to construct a puzzle they refused to examine every piece of.

Her corkboard floated above her bed, pictures of smiling friends with arms slung around one another. Token movie tickets, concert stubs, her acceptance letter from Columbia, each of them a clue to who she was before the day there was nothing left of her.

Sophie had a board just like it. It could have been her smiling face in those pictures as easily as Maddie's.

I couldn't imagine a world without Sophie—it would be a darker place, emptier, lesser than it once was. Is that how Maddie's friends felt? Like some place inside them had been carved free, a crater of shifting sands that would never quite fill again.

Nothing I did here would bring her back. No evidence could change what had already been done. But if she hadn't chosen her end, she'd never received justice either.

I hurried to her bookshelf, the hiding spot I'd been told about, pulling the thickest books from the shelf.

Maddie, it seemed, had created a hiding space in the spot she thought most people would assume the most boring—books. She'd made several for her friends, carving out the insides for a safe place to hide the things most important to them.

If the police hadn't found Maddie's cheater-scheme flip phone, it would almost certainly be there. Unless she'd had it on her that night. Lost it to the tides of the ocean, or to something far more dangerous.

I found it in a Bible, the wispy pages feathering against my fingertips as they fluttered open to reveal the gaping wound in the middle.

The phone dropped into my hand, cold, heavy, weighted down by a thousand secrets.

I blinked at it, turning it over in my palm while I battled my indecision. The police had missed it, but what if this changed their entire case? What if I was spoiling the very thing that would give answers to her family, her friends?

But they'd dismissed her, ignored her friends, who argued the facts that did not fit the girl they knew. The police had taken the simplest answer and transcribed it, filed it. Closed and forgotten. Just another girl. Just another day.

I flicked it open, screen flaring to life.

There were no new messages. No new calls. Only the thinnest of red lines at the top that told me I wouldn't have long to discover whatever secrets Maddie may have hidden in this phone.

I clicked on the only message string listed—a number I didn't recognize.

The first did not come from her.

I'm not coming.

Followed by Maddie's response:

We've been over this. We agreed to the terms.

My breath caught, my finger poised to scroll to the next message, when the screen blinked to black.

My curse died on my lips as a beam of light streamed through the curtains, headlights beamed through the window, tires crunching over the gravel driveway.

I froze, locked in place in a room where I didn't belong. A trespasser in this family's life. I sincerely doubted either they or law enforcement would stand for my reasonings.

I could not be caught here. Death may have changed me, but I had not changed my desire to plan the life I wanted, on my terms, in the ways that mattered to me.

I hadn't come this far to be stopped by the people who should have rectified this initially.

Voices rose from the front porch, muted mumbles that couldn't quite breach the walls, and then the scent of roaring fireplaces and crisp night air slipped through the cracked door.

I shoved the phone in my pocket, the Bible back onto the shelf, cramming it in all wrong, completely suspiciously should anyone enter this room to look.

I slipped through the door, clicking it shut behind me and stood at the top of the stairs, my back pressed to the wall as sweat bloomed over every inch of skin.

Maddie's parents entered silently, only the thud of their shoes to break the unbearable quiet. And then even that disappeared, sock-clad feet a whisper, sadness so thick it crammed itself into all the open spaces, the only true presence left.

I waited until they passed, until only that glass-paneled door loomed at the bottom of the stairs, and I sprinted down them, praying their grief muffled their hearing and their minds.

Clouds had covered the moon in my absence, dulling the sky in a smoky gray that drowned the light, and I receded into the darkness that shielded me.

I went left, far from the view of that glass door, just in time to see it swing open, Maddie's father searching the night for something he didn't know was there.

I ran, my shoes sinking into soft earth, tearing bits of mud from where it lay, tracking it over the same downtrodden grass I'd passed on the way in.

It wasn't until I was tucked safely in my car, my breathing still labored and my heart still ricocheting against my ribs, that I allowed myself to think.

We agreed to the terms.

Maddie had sought to make a deal with someone. She hadn't planned on paying with her life.

I returned home that evening, showering away the bits of mud that had clung to my bare calves, erasing any evidence—any memory— that might be stuck tight to my skin.

I'd broken into someone's home. I'd invaded Maddie's privacy. I'd already written two of Garrett's papers. I'd become a person I barely recognized. A liar. A cheat.

I'd always viewed my father with disdain. I knew the truth behind the charm, saw the dark points he covered with his wide smile and honey-sweet words.

No one suspected him of any of his wrongdoings. Not even Mom's family—not even his own. Most of my mom's friends had chosen him, entirely convinced she was to blame. Too demanding. Too critical.

Poor Matthew Linden, they'd whispered as word of their divorce spread. He'd cheated and lied and stolen—stolen from his wife and even his own children, threatened their futures—and it was him that received all the sympathy.

On days when the anger of it all threatened to erupt through my skin, I'd take out the necklace I'd found in his suitcase, run my finger over the gems, let it rise and fall over the sharp edges, and I'd remember exactly how his face looked when he realized how much I knew. When he understood that I'd set him up, that all those accounts he thought were his alone were now known to all. When the certainty of who we both were became clear.

But that night I was grateful for him. Rather, I was grateful for his tendency to hoard useless objects. Namely a cord that was compatible with Maddie's phone.

Monica had made it home safely. I knew, because I'd driven to the library to watch her walk to her car, and then I'd followed her home and walked her to her door.

If the black car made the journey with us, they'd done it well.

And now it was just me.

I'd just taken the fourth box down from the garage's shelving unit, dropping it onto the floor with the others, when the door shuddered to life.

I had no actual excuse for pawing through boxes of items so useless they hadn't been touched in years, but Sophie would believe whatever I told her and my mother wouldn't care enough to question the excuse I gave her.

It was fine. Nothing I couldn't handle.

The door crept higher, and I rummaged back through the box, trying to relax my muscles, to act *normal*.

"What are you looking for?"

The voice was not one I was expecting. It was the last one I had interest in hearing.

Garrett stood next to Sophie, both of them eyeing me, and my cheeks went hot.

I gestured to the tangle of cords in front of me. "The cord from my laptop wasn't functioning properly. I'm searching for a replacement."

Sophie's eyes narrowed, like she could see my lie for what it was but couldn't puzzle the *why*. "Where did you get that scratch?"

"She fell," Garrett answered far too quickly, far too adamantly. He wasn't aware of how I'd gotten the scratches, but from the way he shifted his weight from foot to foot, from the way his fingers clenched and released, it was obvious he was afraid even one question might be the thread that would unravel his world.

Sophie blinked, her lips parting like a million words wanted to rush forth. "How do you know—"

"I told the class about it," I said. "Mrs. Campbell asked and I told them all, so that's how he knows."

She mouthed an "oh" that she didn't truly mean, a mix of hurt

264

and confusion evident in her eyes as Garrett said, "I could look at your computer cord."

Absolutely not.

And I had no illusions of why Garrett wanted to look at my computer cord. It wasn't kindness, and it certainly wasn't genuine.

Garrett Packard did not trust me.

Under normal circumstances, I'd have applauded his intuition. I was not the sort of person it was wise to trust.

But then I looked at the size of his hands, and I remembered my head held underwater, the sight of a girl who was supposed to be me lying prone on the ground. I remembered that feeling of standing in Adam's room with a blood-soaked necklace in my pocket.

Whatever Garrett's faults, a lack of loyalty was not one. I wasn't sure there was a line he would not cross for Adam. Neither of them had ever wanted for much. The world had never denied them anything. Animals backed into a corner were at their most dangerous.

I waved them both off, attempting a smile that surely seemed more of a grimace. "Mom will be home soon, Soph."

Mom was not overly fond of Garrett being in Sophie's room—too close a reminder of how her life had gone. How I became a reality.

Sophie's gaze bounced between Garrett and me, to the awkward tension building in the open garage, rising until it felt hard to breathe.

I could only imagine the theories that must be hatching inside her head, all the worst thoughts about us both that might try to explain away all the unspoken words littering the air.

Sophie had always been perceptive. She had a disturbingly keen ability to sense others' emotions and mold herself around them.

In that moment, it served neither me nor Garrett well.

But there was no way to tell her the truth—that I was in search of truth about a girl that had likely been murdered. That her boyfriend quite likely knew. That the boy who lived next door may have done it, or may be seeking justice for it, and I still wasn't certain which was more plausible.

Instead, I pleaded with her, trying to communicate without words like we used to. *Send him home, Soph. Go to your room, where it's safe.*

I couldn't watch her at the edge of the bathtub anymore. Couldn't track her every move and protect her from the world. It had always been my most important job—I was strong so Sophie had space to grow.

But now she was surrounded by a danger I couldn't prove and couldn't end.

"Nora?"

The quiver in her voice gutted me. Filled with all the questions she wanted to ask but couldn't find the courage to.

I smiled, forcing all my apprehensions aside so she could only see what I needed her to. "I was thinking, if you're free, we could do movie night soon?"

The smile that lit her face was a knife to my heart, and she blinked back tears. She looked just like the girl who used to sit next to me on the flat section of roof above the back porch, snuggled in her sleeping bag while the movie streamed beneath the stars.

It was enough.

Soon after, she and Garrett were inside, leaving me with the pile of cords and Maddie's cell phone.

I found one, eventually, wrapping it into a tight ball I could hide beneath my shirt. Only I didn't need to. Sophie and Garrett were both in her room, the door closed.

As was mine. I hadn't closed it. I was nearly sure, and I tiptoed into the room, checking all corners and the closet just to be sure I was alone. And there, on my desk, was my laptop, plugged in and charging with the cord that was most certainly not malfunctioning.

I yanked the cord free, sweeping the laptop into a desk drawer and slamming it shut, like I could block out everything I knew with it.

Be strong, Nora.

The mattress creaked as I eased onto it, wrapping myself in a huddle of thick blankets, and I plugged in the phone, waiting for the screen to flare to life again.

The remaining text was as important as it was vague:

Fine. But you come to me.

Maddie was blackmailing someone. That was the only explanation. She'd have no other reason to use her Cheater Inc. phone if it weren't related.

She threatened someone—or *posed* a threat to someone—and it had ended with her admission to Columbia being revoked. And when she still refused to back down, it ended with her body floating in the ocean.

Maddie was me. Maddie was an omen, a promise of where this would end.

You come to me.

My hand shook as I held the phone, thumb poised over the send key.

I pressed the phone to my ear, struggling to take in a full breath as it rang twice, three times, and then a fourth.

I'd nearly given up, nearly lost my courage, when the door to Sophie's room clicked open and Garrett's voice filled my ear with a rasped whisper: "Who is this?"

CHAPTER THIRTY-THREE

SOPHIE

A regular boring kitchen knife. The kind you'd find in the home of any number of suburbanites.

I almost got murdered by a basic Costco asshole who fell for a sales pitch from a dude wearing a headset.

The police came. Took my description. Shaky hands. Gloves. Taller than me. Smelled like nail polish remover.

They took one from Mrs. Wilson too. Five foot eleven. Wearing a ski mask.

I'm sure they'll catch him any minute now.

With that, I'm back to déjà-vuing with Mom and Detective Tickner, who's still giving me no info about the bloody charm necklace, and no indication he has any idea why someone attacked me in the parking lot.

So I told him, about Garrett and the threatening messages, and when he asked to see my phone, I told him I'd deleted them all. I should've thought of that before. He doesn't need to know I lied the night Garrett disappeared; he just needs to know he's back. And now he does. I even cried a little while I talked about how afraid I was to say anything before.

It wasn't Garrett earlier. I know the shape of his body. Of course, that doesn't mean Garrett didn't *hire* someone to threaten me, which is why Tickner knows what he knows.

The cut on my neck isn't deep—I catch glimpses in the trim on the two-way mirror—but I wouldn't let them clean it. Truth is, I can't stand the idea of someone touching me right now.

I'm balanced on the edge. Dirt shifting beneath my feet, head spinning from the sheer emptiness of the space below. I'm trying not to move, not even an inch. I'm trying not to fall.

I'm still sitting in the room, paper cup untouched and coffee gone cold, when they parade Jude by.

I'm shocked into stillness. They can't think he did this.

I don't know him, not really, and I don't know whatever secrets Tickner does, but *why* would Jude care about me investigating any of this? Let alone enough to threaten me?

But then there's that little voice that whispers I thought I knew Garrett too. And Nora. Better than anyone. Maybe Jude is making a fool of me as much as anyone else.

Jude's eyes lock on mine, and they're unreadable.

No. He wasn't there tonight. I may not know much, but I know this. They're using him like they're using me, and it's my fault.

I brought him into this mess, and he's here because of me.

I jump to my feet, but Tickner's there, blocking my path, grabbing hold of my arms, my feet leaving the floor, and I'm Garrett's mom with her glassy eyes, being fed a drink so she'll just calm down, stop talking, play the role, shape up, fly right.

I'm me, behind a dumpster, knife to my throat so I'll stand still, stop asking questions, let it be, look pretty, be who they all want me to be. It all gathers inside me, a wave building beneath the ocean's surface, ripples growing until it breaks free and bursts into the night sky. I don't know the words I say, don't know how many blows I land, but it's not enough.

He threatened to kill Nora. He threatened to kill me. Jude is here and all of this is my fault because I wasn't enough. I wasn't enough to make Garrett stay, and when he left, I wasn't strong enough to admit the truth. When he came back, I wasn't smart enough to piece the whole thing together, and now everything is broken. Even Nora is gone, the house too quiet, the rooms too empty. It was like that for weeks and months after Dad left. Before we got used to the emptiness and it just felt normal.

But not even that normal exists anymore. I'm not Garrett's girlfriend, and I'm not half of the most popular couple at school. I'm barely Nora's sister, and the only thing keeping me safe from the end of dance is Mrs. Wilson finding me with a knife to my throat.

I need to salvage some part of who I am. Sophie Linden. The dancer. Those were Jude's words, and now he's locked in a room just like this, a prisoner just like me.

I'm pulled from the room, down the hall and out the front door, where a cop I've never met waits with me while Mom gets the car, and they shove me in it. Same prisoner, different cell.

We don't speak the whole way home, streetlamps like strobe lights that flash over the dashboard, the soft hum of the heater and steady thump of tires, until we turn into the driveway and the doors stay locked.

She grips the steering wheel, her breaths heavy, like she's struggling with the right words when she's been planning them for weeks.

"Just say it." If she's going to take the one thing I have left, the least she could do is kill me quickly.

"I have tried—" Her voice breaks, and I don't feel guilt like normal.

I feel anger. A spark that flares bright, flooding my veins with heat until I have to press my lips shut to stop from screaming.

She wipes a tear. "I have tried so hard to be patient with you. Let you find your own way. And it hasn't been easy for me to take care of you and Nora all by myself. You have *no* idea how hard it is, how much I worry. You *embarrassed* me in there. Your behavior was unacceptable. I had to tell that detective—"

She drops to a whisper. "That you were clearly not in a mentally stable place to answer questions."

"How terrible for you."

Her fingers flex around the steering wheel, no doubt imagining my neck. "Sophie, I know dance is the only—"

I can't even look at her. "No no. Don't stop. What were you going to say? The only thing I have? The only thing I'm good at? The only thing I'm good *for.*"

"I know it's important to you, Sophie. That's what I meant to say."

I whisper, "No, it isn't."

"Are you calling me a liar?"

"Yes."

"Excuse me?"

"I said fucking *yes!*"

"Sophie Eloise, you are *not* going to that intensive this summer. And I—"

I'm out of the car before she can finish the rest because we've said all the things we need to say.

I can't go in that house, not with only the two of us, so I trudge along the outside, until the unmistakable scent of burning wood curls in wisps through the air. I clutch the strap of my bag because

272

no one is supposed to be here, and I tiptoe around the corner, my dance slippers soaking in the grass's moisture.

Nora tosses something into the fire and the flames flare higher, and through peaks her eyes lock on mine.

She holds out her hand, and it takes everything in me not to run to her as Mom slams the front door. To not cling to this shred of reassurance the way I always have, so desperate for any sliver of approval I'd hold it desperately, even as it pierced straight through my flesh.

The wood cracks and snaps, sending sparks sailing into the darkened sky as I walk to her, my tights ripped, my heart bruised, my neck bloody.

Our hands clasp, and we stare, too many things to say, too far to reach even when separated by inches, and she uses her free hand to sweep the hair from my cheek as she whispers, "I'm so sorry, Sophie."

If I were strong like Nora, I'd demand a thousand answers. I'd stand here stoic and poised, and I'd refuse to react.

Instead, I collapse into her, the tears I've been caging setting loose. I cling to her, her jacket fisted in my hands while I sob, and she's too thin, her body frailer than it's ever been, even as she holds me up until I can't cry anymore and my body feels hollow.

She hands me a tissue, because of course she has tissues. "Better?"

A laugh bursts out of me because I'm not sure what better means anymore. "I'm not going to the intensive."

"Hmm." She drops my hand and steps away, grabbing the pile of papers from her chair and feeding them to the fire. "Hmm" is what Nora says when she has many things to say but doesn't plan on saying any of them.

And this is what no one understands about Nora. Why Charla

and Isa don't understand when they want to know why I just won't *ask* her what happened between her and Garrett, or why she has pictures of Joseph Graham or where the fuck she *goes* every night that isn't here.

Nora doesn't answer anything she doesn't want to. She does not subscribe to the mores of conversation. She doesn't care about social customs or expectations. Nora has rules the rest of the world does not, and there is nothing in existence that could make her conform to ours.

"Nora? Why would a private investigator have pictures of you?"

She shudders, and it chills me in a way I can't describe. Nora does not shudder. "Do you know who?"

"Who the PI is? Or who hired him?"

"The former." She says it in a way that makes it clear she knows the latter.

"Yes."

She tosses the last of the pages into the fire, and it rushes toward the sky, sparks flaring high before they dim and the ashes float back down to earth. Once she's settled on the chair beside me, she says, "I would very much appreciate if you could send me his contact information."

There's *so* much more I want to ask about that, but I'm too afraid to break this tenuous information exchange. "Where do you go every night? And don't say here because I know it sounds creepy but I kind of mess with your comforter and it never changes so I know you're *not* here."

She glances to me, her mouth twitching into a smile. "That doesn't simply *sound* creepy, Sophie, it *is*."

Through my laughter, I say, "Okay, but still."

"I've been taking care of some things."

And that's that. The best answer I'll get. I should ask her about Garrett, but sitting here beside her, looking into her eyes, I know she never would've cheated with him. I'm embarrassed I ever considered it. But there's so much more than that. So many things I can't put together, and I know, more than I've ever known anything, that she already has. "Where did you go with Garrett on Halloween night?"

She pauses, her eyes trained on the fire, but her gaze somewhere endlessly far away. "Do you remember when you first began attempting a double pirouette? You were barely eight. Likely too young. And Amelia Barns was sixteen and decided to help you by giving you absolutely horrid advice."

"It wasn't *horrid*."

"It was. And you nearly injured yourself—multiple times."

"Okay that's true." I reach my hands out to the fire, let the heat spread through my palms and fill the empty places this day has left inside me.

"Do you know one of the things I've always found most frustrating about you, but also the most admirable?"

I blink at her, studying her profile like I must have misunderstood her words. Frustrating, yes. Admirable? As if there was a thing someone like Nora could admire about me.

"You refused to let anyone else help you. Not your instructors or other students. Not even your very knowledgeable older sister, who spent many hours compiling a sizable collection of technique tips and accompanying YouTube tutorials." She rolls her eyes, and things almost feel normal again. "But what I saw that no one else did were the hours you spent in our basement, practicing until you were so exhausted you could barely move, until a double pirouette was no more difficult than a single. I attended your next class. Watching through the window—not creepy though. You executed every turn flawlessly. Better even than Amelia Barns. And then you helped every other girl in that class, teaching them what you'd taught yourself."

I blink away tears, trying to swipe at the ones trailing over my cheeks without it being obvious how much I needed to hear that. How badly I needed to know I hadn't spent my life chasing her without her ever looking back. And I swear Nora is on the edge of saying something else. Something that will connect the dots between my questions and her words, when a shadow moves over the window in Adam's room.

Nora goes still, her gaze never leaving the window, like Adam is standing right before us. The fire spits a flurry of sparks, like it's fueled by the energies around us, like it's drawing from flame that burns even brighter inside her.

Whatever this is. Whatever has brought us both into this place. Adam is involved. And I'm not sure even Nora knows exactly how.

His shadow moves, the window blank and quiet once again, and we sit in silence while the fire drifts low, ebbing flames clinging to the remnants of what it's yet to destroy.

We sit in silence so long my body settles into fatigue, the weight of the day too heavy to hold, so it slips away until it's just the breeze through the trees and the soft glow of the moon. And me. And Nora. "What are you thinking?"

She laughs, the sound bursting out in a rush, like I surprised her.

We used to do this too, back when we were close. Nora's mind always seemed so mysterious—filled with bits of the world I could never see, much less form opinions on. And sometimes I'd catch her, staring into nothing, lost in a place I couldn't follow. I'd stare, convinced if I studied hard enough I could be like her. That some of the pieces that made her Nora could be replicated.

It never worked. And so I'd ask.

I'd ask her to give me a glimpse, to let me in, just a little. And she'd smile like she knew I'd been watching and knew that eventually I'd ask.

And because she was Nora, she always answered.

This time was no different.

The smile drifts from her face, just like the smoke tendrils floating toward the stars, and she stares into the square of light that glows from Adam's bedroom.

She stands, her shadow stretching long into the darkness of the yard, and pulls one last piece of paper from her pocket.

Her pen scratches against the paper, all the anger from earlier bleeding into every stroke until she tears that piece free and holds it out to me.

She waits until my fingers close around it before she says, "I'm thinking, Little Linden, that the worst thing you can do to a man is force him to admit the things he's done."

CHAPTER THIRTY-FOUR

NORA

We've nearly reached the end of this confession. The final culmination of all the events I've laid out thus far. And I find myself struggling to finish. My words immortalized, the many details of my thoughts and decisions laid bare for strangers to see, to analyze, to critique and criticize.

More than that, there is no returning from the finality of what I've started. No reclaiming the plans I'd made for myself. No stopping the wreckage I will bring to many lives.

I won't delude myself on that point. I understand the consequences of what I've put into these words. I know the hurt they will cause, and I know the hurt that has already been inflicted.

It's perhaps the world's great moral dilemma, whether the ends are justified by the means. Whether the pursuit of justice, of retribution, had a line that strained the conscience. Whether an eye for an eye truly meant one life could pay for another, or if when faced with the reality, we could bring ourselves to step beyond that boundary.

In truth, I didn't know if I could. I didn't know if I could let myself not.

Maddie blackmailed Garrett. It was the only explanation that made sense. Garrett had stated she was a bad person. He'd talked about those who tried to use him for his money, for his position. In his twisted view, Maddie blackmailing him fit that narrative.

She was a "messed-up girl" according to Garrett. Maybe that meant nothing more than bold enough to test him.

I had her phone. I could take it to the police. Only, it didn't belong to Maddie any more than the number she'd been messaging belonged to Garrett.

I had video of Mr. Wentville picking up a bag. I had a business card from Joseph Graham.

In short, I had nothing. No proof. No evidence. Nothing but the testimony of a girl who'd been accused of cheating. And that's why I didn't go to the police.

I didn't even know who to accuse. She'd blackmailed Garrett, but it was Adam who had her necklace, covered in blood.

Adam. I'd gone to my window the other day to find him staring from his, an expression I couldn't decipher painted on his face. At one point, I thought I'd memorized them all. But now. Now I wasn't sure I knew him at all.

Which is why I had to follow the last lead I had, if it could be called a lead at all. It was more a passing hope, born out of desperation more than fact.

It was the mission to follow Wentville that led me to it—the people videotaping the street performer.

I theorized that the bar that sat at the shoreline of the pier Maddie was alleged to have jumped from may have surveillance video of that night.

And that was how I found myself at a booth at Wild Mickey's, pretending to survey the menu while I waited for my server to arrive.

I'd missed debate to be here, which my mother already knew about according to the text messages she'd sent me.

I was no longer her strong daughter, the one she could count on. I was no longer the girl who made no trouble, who made smart decisions. I was a source of worry in a life that could take no more, and she wasn't afraid to tell me so.

Dim lighting spilled over the room, shadows pooling in the cracks and crevices, between bodies bent toward one another to combat the force of the music blaring from the speakers.

Layla rounded the corner, still happily unaware of my presence in her section, plastering on a smile I knew she didn't mean as she greeted her next table. It wasn't that she hated her job. It was that being a Black girl in anything approaching a southern state came with a host of challenges I'd never understand.

I dragged my fingertips through the condensation on my water glass, swirling nothings into a looped pattern, when Layla said, "What are you doing here?"

The reaction I expected, but not the one I'd hoped for. "I need a favor."

I could've lied, but Layla would've known. She always did.

She laughed, a deep, infectious rumble that immediately endeared people to her. "And you thought I'd give it to you? You went *out of your way* to avoid me at the football game, and now you show up asking for favors?"

Layla and I had met in the library. Her mother—a high-ranking accountant at a global firm—had arranged tutoring for her.

She didn't need it. It wasn't lack of ability. It was entirely lack of desire. She didn't want to be an accountant. Or a doctor or professor or lawyer. Layla wanted to travel the world. She wanted to *live*. We were, in many ways, polar opposites.

It took me three sessions to decipher that she'd been faking her diminished aptitude with the five tutors before me, convincing them all she was just incapable.

I'd managed to catch her by purposely solving a problem wrong, then irritating her enough with irrational arguments about unrelated matters that she grew frustrated enough to point out my mathematical error just to silence me.

Her mouth snapped shut the second the correct answer left her lips, and then the corner had turned up as she whispered, "You bitch."

Our relationship was born in that moment.

She passed math.

She did not carry that same half smile while she waited for my response from her place at the end of my restaurant booth. I hated it, how we were now, how different things had been before.

That was my fault. I couldn't find my way to being the person she needed, couldn't see my way free from the life I'd planned, so that I might fit into hers. She said she'd wait for me, in soft whispers, her palm gentle across my cheek, to find what I really wanted. What I really loved most. She said to let go. To free myself.

But there are no stronger chains than the ones we fasten for ourselves, and freedom wasn't a thing I could promise. I wouldn't let her wait forever.

That's how we found ourselves here, only inches apart with the weight of those chains between us.

I was not entirely accustomed to asking people for things, and as such, it ranked close to lowest on my skill set. "I know you're angry with—"

"What do you want, Nora?"

I flinched at the anger in her voice. It wasn't undeserved. But it wasn't fair either. There was no world where the two of us belonged together. "Can we talk? It's not about me."

Of course, that wasn't quite true. It also happened to be Layla's most cutting critique of my general personhood—that everything in my world was always about me.

She crossed her arms, narrowed her eyes, raised a single eyebrow, as if to say she did not believe a single word I'd said. And then she sighed. "Order something. I'm on break in ten."

I didn't see her again until she motioned me over with a jerk of her head toward the side door. My food was very likely going to sit out, becoming more lukewarm by the minute. I had no illusions about whether it was intentional.

Layla waited for me next to the dumpsters, a pair of milk crates upended to serve as chairs, and she watched with disinterest as I paced, trying to focus on the ocean-scented breeze rather than the expired food rotting in the trash.

I'd planned multiple ways to start, but standing across from her, wind rustling her curls, the rainfall glow of the security light casting shadows beneath the sharpness of her cheekbones, nothing sounded quite right. And I was forced to admit, if only to myself, that perhaps the idea of coming here hadn't *only* been on account of the street performer.

"I need to see your security cameras."

"Come again?"

"I need to review the video from the security cameras."

"Yeah, I heard that. I'm just over here trying to figure out how you think, even if I *did* have access to those, that you can just come here and ask for a favor like that, *knowing—*"

"It's not for me!" I sucked in a breath. "That's a lie."

I buried my face in my hands so she couldn't see all the things I managed to keep hidden from everyone else. Layla had that way about her. "I just need one night. Maybe two."

Maddie may have died the night she sent those texts—that doesn't mean she was dropped into the ocean then.

I shuddered at the possibility, at the idea of Adam carrying her body to the pier. Pictured his hands throwing her over the edge, watching her lifeless body. She could've been alive, unconscious, her necklace already stained with blood.

"Nora." Layla's hands framed my face, her brown eyes the color of amber bathed in flames, no trace of anger left. "Tell me what happened."

CHAPTER THIRTY-FIVE
SOPHIE

Maddie Armstrong.

That's what Nora's note said. What it did *not* say is who that is or what I'm supposed to do with this information.

I googled her. There are tons, and it's not even like I know the person I'm looking for. A small part of me is terrified this is all somehow connected to the bloody necklace, but Nora doesn't even know about that. Not to mention, I found a friend of a friend of a friend's page that referenced a Maddie A. with a suicide hotline, which is a tragedy for sure, but not the type of thing the cops would be looking for a suspect for. And Tickner is *clearly* trying to pin this on Jude.

Or I'm an idiot and Jude is really involved and I just can't see all the ways how.

Aside from all that, and to be completely honest, I was too tired and feeling too sorry for myself and too angry at Mom and too weirded out by whatever's going on with Nora and Adam to do any serious digging, so I went to bed. I trudged up to my room and found my pillows lining the floor next to my bed. Mom didn't do it, which means Nora did, which means I promptly burst into laughter through tears because Nora may not be very good at *talking* about emotions but I knew exactly what she was saying. She cares about me. She remembers who we used to be. Maybe that a tiny part of her misses The Linden Sisters too.

So I went to bed, but I did not sleep.

Being nearly murdered tends to make a girl a little jumpy.

And now I'm at school—sitting in the last row as usual—watching the back of Jessica Horton's head while I type on her bedazzled flip phone.

Do you recognize this number?

Obviously she'll recognize the number—it's hers. The question is how much it'll freak her the fuck out. As someone who's been on the recent receiving end of creepy texts messages, I imagine it'll be a lot.

Jessica glances to the Apple Watch on her wrist as the text comes through, and she's the exact opposite of Amber Donahue and her statue impersonation. Jessica is practically flailing.

She whips out her phone, fingers flying over the keys even though Mrs. Devlin is staring right at her.

Three . . . two . . . one . . .

"Ms. Horton," Mrs. Devlin says, "care to explain what's so important?"

Whatever color Jessica used to have in her pasty white face is gone, as is her ability to speak. She stammers through a handful of "uhhs" and "umms," and that's the point she's directed to both hand over her phone and take a stroll to Wentville's office.

I wait thirty seconds after she leaves to raise my hand. Obviously, I need to go to the bathroom.

Mrs. Devlin doesn't believe me because, let's be honest, it's not the first time I've used this excuse and it's usually for far less noble reasons, but I play the old girl-problems card and I'm shuffling down the hall a moment later.

I jog to catch up, until I turn the corner to see Jessica's ponytail swaying as she stumbles down the hall.

We pass a #ComeHomeGarrett shrine that The Stans erected around the bottle-filling stations, and even though I'm supposed to be chasing her, my gaze gets stuck on a single photo of Garrett with his arm around Jessica. Not because I'm surprised Garrett has his arm around Jessica, but because he had his arm around *me* in that picture and someone (Jessica) has . . .

I almost can't even say it. "Did you *photoshop* yourself into this picture?!"

I mean, she obviously did because she practically trips over her own feet when I ask—and because she's literally missing part of her left calf in the pic.

But then Jessica recovers and she's storming down the hall again, until I call out her name and she stops dead, turning to face me.

I hold the phone out. "Surprise."

"You fucking bitch."

Wow. Kind of an extreme reaction, even for Jessica. "I'd suggest you start explaining."

What? I don't know. Because Michael Graham is an asshole who's more concerned with his plausible deniability and the impacts on his trust fund than he is making my life simple.

"Give it back." Her lip quivers, and I almost feel guilty.

But then a different response takes over: intrigue.

I planned to make her so angry she'd give up information just to prove she knew something I didn't—just like her telling me about Garrett being in North Hills that night.

Whatever she's afraid I know though, it's enough to draw tears. In front of me. She'd rather die.

I toss it from hand to hand. "I figured since you were headed to Wentville's office, I could maybe tag along."

She barks out a laugh. "*God* you're so pathetic." She steps toward me, just beyond strangling distance, and whispers, "Go ahead."

Okay, wrong tack. "But then I figured, why waste time with Wentville? He's always been spineless. There are tons of incriminating dates in this phone, and who does incriminating evidence better than the police, right? There's this detective I've gotten to know recently. We're good friends."

That one hits.

Jessica's voice breaks, her entire body shaking. "You can't even prove that's my phone."

"You literally have the same gems glued to your other phone, Jessica. Circumstantial for sure, but witnesses who are really holding *quite* a grudge are not. Take a second and think about who might've given this to me."

Angry does not look good on her. She's rabid, spittle flying from lips, fists clenched. "Those dates mean nothing. So I cheated. So what. So does half this school. You think the cops care about fucking biology tests?"

Cheated. On . . . tests? Assignments? Is this some privileged-white-people-paying-to-get-into-the-Ivies bullshit? But seriously— why did no one ask me to get in on this shit?

Jessica's glare turns vicious. "But go ahead. Tell everyone. Be the girl who exposes Garrett as a fraud. Be the girl who ruins her sister's future."

I keep my face empty, void of all emotion. There is no way Nora cheated. Not a single fucking way. "My sister isn't a cheater, and Garrett isn't even here to be exposed."

She shoves her finger in my face, and I really want to bite it off. "And you don't even care. You pretended to love him, but you were just using him!"

Her voice bounces off the metal lockers, the cinder-block walls, and if not for all the teachers being mandated to keep their doors shut (thanks, mass shooters and nonexistent gun control), we'd be surrounded by teachers.

It's better this way, because all the thoughts that have been churning through my head since the day Garrett left and all my emotions—worried for his safety, hurt by his non-acknowledgment, confused by the changes it meant for my life—the one I felt the most strongly was relief.

No more explaining where I was or where I'd been. That first day, when I practiced late and didn't see fifteen calls from him on my phone, when I made plans with Charla and Isa for that weekend and didn't do so with this buzz of worry over having to tell him, hoping he hadn't made others for us, when I could get ready without worrying whether he'd approve of what I wore or what I said, I felt relief.

I felt freedom. Light. Like I'd shed a skin that had slowly begun to cover mine, *squeezing squeezing squeezing* until every breath became shallower. And the worst part is that I let it happen. I let him consume me, bit by bit, let him siphon the parts he wanted and mold the ones he didn't until I wasn't Sophie anymore. I was whatever Garrett needed.

I didn't look for him because I didn't want him back.

And it took Jessica fucking Horton to get me to admit it.

I step within inches of her. "I didn't pretend to love him, but I wish I did because Garrett is a fucking asshole. And if you're right and the cops won't care about you cheating on a biology test, why are you so worried about me going to see them?"

She lets out a garbled scream and charges, shoving me so hard I slam straight back, my skull thunking against the tile so hard my stomach rolls and my eyes water.

Jessica claws up my body, and she's nearly over me when my fingers clench around nothing.

The phone.

I flip and grab at her ankle, yanking until her knee goes out from under her and her chin clacks the flooring and she screams again. A door down the hall clicks open. Then another. And the phone skitters across the tile as her fingertips brush over it.

I shove off as hard as I can, landing straight on top of her, my hand slipping in the puddle of blood at her chin, but if there's one thing I can fucking excel in, it's stretching.

My fingers close around the stubby antenna, and I barely hang on as at least two sets of arms yank me upright, three other teachers barely holding Jessica back as she lunges for me again and again.

And I guess we're both headed to Wentville's office after all.

CHAPTER THIRTY-SIX
SOPHIE

I hold the ice pack to the back of my throbbing head while Jessica glares at me from over the top of the one she holds to her chin.

And once again I say: Fuck Jessica Horton.

She's a cheater, and Garrett was too, and I'd bet the summer intensive (ha! don't have that to bet anymore!) that Nora knew about it. So that's fun. Half the school just breezing through their AP classes while I'm busting my ass and getting disappointed sighs from my parents just because I can't pay the entrance fee to the social strata where the rules don't apply.

I can't fathom what it would be like, to know you can't fail. To be so buffered from the world that there's no fear in what it holds, no constant worry tearing at your chest, reminding you all the things that could go wrong, the rock bottoms just waiting for you to hit them.

But that's where they are—where they've always been—all wrapped up and protected, shielded, elevated in a plane the rest of us can't hope to reach while they stare beneath them, marveling at our struggles, telling themselves if they were there, stripped of all privileges and advantages, that they would find a way. They would find a way to not be like us.

"If I need stitches, I'm suing you."

"Cool. I'll countersue for my traumatic brain injury."

"Ladies!" Wentville enters the office, tugging the sleeves of his suit coat over his ugly-ass cuff links. He likes to pretend he has taste.

He leans against his desk, and when he says, "I don't think I need to explain how much trouble you're both in," he's only looking at me.

He keeps talking, about how he's going to call our parents (go ahead—she's already done the worst she can possibly do to me), we could face suspension (yes please), and this is not conduct becoming of a young lady (absolutely fuck off), but I tune him out because my head won't stop sifting through thoughts.

Jessica didn't care if I told Wentville about the cheating. Either she figured he wouldn't believe me or she knew he wouldn't care— because he already knew.

Half the school. That's what she said. No doubt an exaggeration, but would it be possible for an entire portion of the richest, most powerful members of the student body to cheat their way through school without *someone* talking about it?

But then, I didn't know. And I thought I knew everything.

I'm convinced Wentville is building to the crescendo of his little lecture, where he expels me and gives Jessica a commendation for her bravery, but instead he dismisses us with a warning.

I'm so stunned, I nearly argue. We literally tackled each other in the hallway. I still have her blood smeared across my hand.

He grabs a notepad from his desk, scribbling out a hall pass that he holds out to Jessica just as the sunlight catches on his cuff link, and I can't move.

My hand flies to the cut at my neck, the one from the knife's blade. I close my eyes, and I can see the way the streetlight reflected its surface onto the brick, and then, the smaller square of light just to its right.

I'm fixated on his wrist, the ring of irritated skin just beneath the cuff he keeps tugging down to cover it. I can taste that citrus and acetone tang again, covering my mouth with the thick winter glove, trying to block off my air, my screams.

I can see Wentville in the chemistry classroom that day, coming to collect whatever he'd ordered and didn't want the teacher to know about.

"Ms. Linden." He's holding out my pass, and I can't make myself take it. I've spent my lifetime learning to move my body the way I want, when I want, but right now it won't obey any of my commands.

It's impossible and obvious that this man held a knife to my throat, threatened to kill me. Threatened to kill Nora.

That's what does it—the thought that springs me from my chair and forces my hand to reach out to his. I even thank him for his magnanimity.

Jessica's waiting for me right outside the offices, spewing threats about what she'll do if I don't return her phone immediately.

I ignore every one of them. Nora isn't safe. She won't even sleep at home anymore.

Wentville tried to kill me.

He threatened my sister.

And I'm going to prove it.

CHAPTER THIRTY-SEVEN

NORA

It's not important to know what I told her. It's only important that you know she had full approval from her manager to show me the tapes from that night, and that they produced nothing but another lead.

I sat there for hours, my food forgotten on the table until a busboy whisked it away, scanning through video footage for anything that might help. I sat there, my breath held, my heart stuttering, waiting for the moment I'd see Adam or Garrett or Joseph Graham on the screen.

Instead, I got two relative imbeciles trying to perform skateboard tricks on a railing set twenty feet above the ocean.

Lance and Ryan were regulars, by which I mean they were regularly removed from the pier for doing exactly what they'd been caught on video doing the night Maddie disappeared.

The only positive part of this was the revelation that Lance and Ryan often videotaped their stunts for their adoring social media fans.

The drawback to this was Layla and me standing outside the club they were known to frequent, hoping our fake IDs would allow us in, so we could possibly track down Lance and Ryan, who would potentially have some snippet of video that would give the proof I needed.

The club was well outside the city, surrounded by swaths of woods and manufacturing buildings that may not even be open during daylight. Palms swayed lazily in the breeze, the ocean air too far to reach us here. I clamped my hand around my fake ID, let the edges cut into my palm. It wouldn't pass even a liquor store clerk's scrutiny, but here, I suspected the bouncer was more for appearances than utility.

Layla had a fake already. I, of course, did not. Which left us with several days of delay and two more assignments on behalf of Garrett. Also gave enough time for my mother to ambush me with yet another "I just don't know what to do with you" lecture.

Truthfully, I didn't know either. Soon enough, Brown would no longer be an option for reasons that had nothing to do with Garrett Packard stealing my paper.

Somewhere along the way, my life had begun to slip into nothingness, grains of sand dispersed in the ocean's currents.

I hugged my arms over my chest, feeling exposed in the thin dress Layla had put me in. "The outfit I had on was more than acceptable."

"Sure. For like, a chess tournament or—"

"I don't even play chess."

"You look hot."

"Shut up."

She laughed, that laugh of hers that had everyone staring, including the bouncer, who she winked at. "Can I ask a question?"

I did not like the tone of her voice, the one that suggested whatever my answer, it would not be suitable for the line of a club. "You will anyway."

"True. What will you do if you can't prove any of this and you don't get into Brown?"

We stepped forward, shuffling with the shrinking line, the club's music growing louder, harsher, the closer we advanced toward the door. "I hadn't really considered it."

"Of course not. Failure is never an option for Nora Linden, right?"

She wasn't wrong. She wasn't entirely correct either.

"I can't leave if Sophie isn't safe." The words burst from my mouth like they'd just been waiting to be set free, like I hadn't been able to admit them even to myself.

Layla blinked, so stunned she didn't move when the line advanced, leaving her scrambling to keep up. "You'd stay for her."

A question? A reproach? I held out my license to the bouncer. "Maybe I won't have to."

He took more than enough time studying them, and I'll admit I was disappointed he asked me no questions with intent to verify the information I'd memorized.

He waved us in, and I barely contained my shock, which earned me a sharp elbow from Layla. The floor vibrated beneath my feet, the steady thrum of bass like a heartbeat, the press of bodies making the air thick and hot, spice and floral melding with the sting of sweat.

Lights strobed overhead, splashing the room in a rainbow of colors as we forced our way through the crowd toward the bar. Layla ordered a drink. I did not. But then I remembered the cup pressed into my hand, I remembered Ainsley on the trampled grass, her eyes glossy, and I grabbed the glass from Layla, downing half in two large gulps that burned my mouth, my throat, sprung tears to my eyes, and burst warmth into my belly.

I pulled her close so I could yell into her ear. "Wait five minutes to drink. Keep it covered."

Why didn't I just insist she not drink? Or dump the entirety of it onto the floor? Those are questions I've asked myself every day since that night.

If perhaps I'd done that one thing differently, I may not be writing this confession at all.

It was nearly an hour before we spotted Lance and Ryan, an hour of alcohol settling into my skin, loosening my limbs, making the world go languid.

It was an hour of Layla pulling me to the dance floor, her body perfectly in sync with the music that seeped through every atom in the room.

I do not dance.

But that night, I did, forgetting everything for just a few stolen breaths when Layla's arms roped around my shoulders, pulling me close, surrounding me with hints of her jasmine-vanilla lotion and the sweetness of cranberries on her tongue.

Until reality slithered its cold claws back in, dragging me away from Layla's warmth and plunging me into wakefulness. There was no time for anything but discovering the truth.

I shoved through the throngs of patrons, pulling Layla behind me until we approached the table where Lance and Ryan sat, a crowd of girls surrounding them.

Layla may have been able to catch their interest, but I certainly lacked the wiles to entice the kind of men who spent their nights yelling into their GoPros.

Instead, I held out a stack of cash, waiting until their

attention had turned to the paper in my hand. "I have a proposition."

As it turned out, Lance and Ryan weren't fools after all.

Several hundreds of dollars—far too big a portion of my bank account—seemed enough motivation to offer a viewing of their raw footage from the night of Maddie's death.

They led us into a corner of the club, where just beyond it, a hallway stretched deeper into the building, only bare bulbs spread a dim haze of illumination. Waitstaff and bouncers hurried down the hall, carrying boxes or trays of food from the small kitchen, groups of girls skittering through the space in search of bathrooms. The bass still rumbled beneath my feet, but it no longer became necessary to shout.

The cool air chilled my fevered skin, my stomach still roiling from the alcohol I'd drunk on a stomach that still hadn't quite recovered from whatever landed Ainsley in a coma.

"So, uhh . . ." Lance said. "Big fans? You can catch behind-the-scenes vids if you support our Patreon."

Oh dear.

I did my best to smile. "I think you may have inadvertently caught something on video, during your . . . theatrics."

Lance frowned, and Layla said, "But we're actually huge fans!" and she pinched my side in what I could only assume meant I was to shut up. "I love your video where you broke into that old swimming pool!"

The guys responded with a string of "That was dope!" and "Yeah, man!" and I stood very still so I wouldn't roll my eyes, but in the end, they handed over their camera. They crowded around us, poking at buttons over my shoulder when we didn't follow directions fast enough.

Minutes rolled by in seconds, each of them more disappointing than the last. I didn't *want* to see Adam or Garrett on those videos. Certainly did not want to see Maddie. I *did* want answers.

I wanted this. All of it. To be over.

We shuffled out of the way for the fifth time while an enormous man heaved boxes down the hall, the bottles within them clinking with each step, but it was clear this wouldn't show us what we needed—not unless the culprit walked straight by both Lance and Ryan without them noticing. The camera was a fixed view, down the length of the pier—the only thing it disproved was that Maddie could've walked down it and jumped from the edge while they were filming.

I handed the camera to Ryan. Or maybe it was Lance. "What about other cameras?"

Layla rubbed my back as if to soothe me. "Yeah, you normally have helmet cams, right? That one where you showed that nollie flip noseslide from your cam was baller."

I had no earthly idea where or when she learned any of this—likely right before we came here, to annoy me with how well she had prepared when I had not. It was working, and judging from her smile, she knew it.

But then Ryan's phone got shoved into my hand, just as the music amplified, shaking the floor beneath me.

This footage was far harder to follow—shaky, with quick jerks and changes. The view flipped with each movement, lighting trails

298

following each spin, the world twisting upside down as the men did.

Sweat sprung from every pore, the alcohol and haphazard video joining forces against my recovering stomach, but I breathed through it, pushing on as the video played.

Another man approached, and we shuffled to the opposite side once again, still taking up far too much room, but then, a flash of dark shadow as Lance rode the rail of one of the pier's benches. I scrolled back, just a little too far, my finger jolted as Ryan bumped into me.

"What the fuck, man?" Ryan spun on the man who'd obviously run into him, and I'd turned my attention back to searching for the correct place on the video just as the man muttered a "sorry."

The universe reduced to that single word, his voice a needle in my vein, blurring my senses until I couldn't think straight. *Let it go, bitch.*

I pressed the phone into Layla's hand, instructing her to search the rest, saying that I had to run to the restroom, and I hurried down the hall.

I spotted the man just at the hallway's end, the red glow of the exit sign like a taunt and a warning as he swung the door open, slipping into the night.

I ran, shoving aside the same girls that had passed us earlier, nearly upending a tray of food and the waitress carrying it.

Following him at all was against every rule I'd set for myself. It was stupid and dangerous and impulsive, and those were not the decisions I made.

And yet, my muscles burned as I burst out the door, sucking in the chilled air, my feet slipping on the gravel lot. It crunched beneath me as I scanned in every direction, finding empty space instead.

The bladed palms rustled, their stretched trunks reaching toward the moon, their canopies blackening the woods just beyond their ranks. The branches of oak trees twisted from their heavy trunks, reaching toward each other and to the starry sky. Moss dripped from their arms, swaying languidly as the wind swirled.

My legs moved of their own volition, driven by something I couldn't name. Maybe it was the alcohol streaming through my system, maybe the sheer desperation of the questions I'd yet to answer.

But it was more than that. It was Maddie leaving her home and never returning; it was the empty, hollowed-out home her parents inhabited like ghosts; it was Ainsley, lying on the trodden ground, in the sterile hospital bed, her mind locked in a prison of her body. It was the tears in Monica's eyes, crushed beneath the blame for a crime she didn't commit.

It was all of it. All the victims, discarded and forgotten—if they'd ever been considered at all. It was all those men with more than they ever needed but still not enough, reducing people to tools, to objects to achieve a means they hadn't earned. It was my father, making a fool of my mother and walking away, still indignant, letting everyone they knew blame her for what he'd done.

It was the injustice. The heartlessness. The refusal of decency and the destruction of actual lives without even a hint of conscience.

And they'd paid for none of it. No one had even questioned their innocence. If I ignored this, went through the rest of my life in denial of what I knew, I'd be complicit.

So I ran into the woods, the wind cutting through the thinness of my clothes, the branches pulling at my arms as twigs cracked underfoot, my shoes slipping over rocks worn smooth by decades of elements.

He had to have gone this way. There wasn't enough time for any other option.

I pressed on, scanning each trunk, waiting for the moment he emerged from one to finish what he'd started on the beach. For him to do to me what he may have done to Maddie.

Maybe this was all connected after all. Maybe Garrett hadn't killed Maddie. Maybe Adam hadn't either. Maybe they just placed a request and the man who could be only inches away did what they couldn't.

I paused, my heart tripping over its own rhythm, and closed my eyes, listened to the whine of wind through the trees, straining for a single sound that felt out of place.

My feet left the forest floor, arms roped around mine, pinning them tight to my sides, and I didn't have the chance to scream before we crashed down down down to the branches and twigs and earth. The air fled my lungs, my ribs too caged to inhale, his weight too heavy to move from my back.

I clawed at the ground, mud jamming beneath my fingernails, roots scraping my stomach as I fought free.

He grunted above me, his hands everywhere, trying to regain control of my arms, until he flipped me to face him, my head cracking against the ground.

I expected recognition, some familiarity that would explain why he was here. Perhaps I expected to see Joseph Graham himself, all that anger he'd shrouded behind civility bursting from beneath his skin. But this man, he was a stranger.

His hands circled my neck, squeezing, crushing, my throat gagging beneath the force of his grip. He seethed, "I told you to let it go," like this, my death, was the punishment I deserved.

My heels dug into the ground, panic rising, shoving against my skin until I thought I might die from that alone. From the mud and blood and bits of his flesh I'd scraped free from his hands.

My vision tunneled, two pinpricks of his face as the last thing I'd see, and my name floated on the wind, drawing louder, closer.

Layla. Maybe even Lance and Ryan. But they'd find me dead. They'd find me like they'd found Maddie and Ainsley, lying prone on the ground. Just another soul lost.

And Sophie. She'd be alone.

I threw my arms wide, palms scraping the ground for anything that might mean salvation. Anything that might free the burning from my lungs, the unrelenting pressure from my neck.

My nails scraped over it—a rock, buried into the depth of the earth, and I raked at it, until my fingertips stung and bled.

It sprang free, just one sharp edge, and I palmed it, gripping as tightly as I could while this stranger's face loomed over me, my life ebbing from my eyes, all the things I'd left unfinished, the future I'd spent a lifetime sacrificing for, slipping into nothingness, a star dying, flaring to dark.

I swung the rock wide, connecting with his temple, and a sickening thud rent the air, a nauseating crack that would stay with me long after that night. Hot blood splattering my face, trickling past my lips to bloom copper on my tongue.

He toppled sideways, his head on my outstretched arm, hot, sticky blood seeping into the fibers of my dress. I wheezed in air, more painful now than when he'd held his hands tight, my lungs still burning and my throat raw.

I rolled, my entire body aching, and shoved his head from my arm. My finger slipped in the slickness of his blood, every heartbeat forcing a new gush from the jagged wound.

I stuttered to my knees, sinking into the clammy dirt, my hands outstretched, blood-soaked palms turned to the canopy of trees.

My entire body shook so hard I couldn't stand, didn't trust myself to try, and like time had stopped while I lay dying, it crashed back in with the sound of my name.

A beam of light splayed over me, casting my shadow over the body before me, bathing him in an even greater darkness.

Blood, black as night, trickled in a river down his cheek, dripping into the soil below. He wasn't moving, his mouth lolled open. I should check for a pulse, hold my hand to his chest and wait for a heartbeat, see if I'd ended it.

"Nora," Layla whispered, appearing from the trees like an apparition. "Oh my god, Nora."

One of the boys skidded to a stop to her left, a mumbled "Holy fuck" matching the abject horror on his face.

My mouth moved, but words failed me, all the thoughts in my head eclipsed by the blood on my hands, the rock only inches away.

Layla appeared at my side, the pads of her fingers gentle against my bruised neck. "Did he do this to you? Nora. Talk to me."

Ryan, I think, jogged up next, his eyes wide, his breath coming in quick puffs of air that twirled into nothing. "Let's get the fuck out of here."

"No." One simple syllable that scraped its way up my throat, all the pain worth it as I pointed to the phone in his hand.

He tiptoed forward, holding it as outstretched as he could, not willing to be any nearer to me than absolutely necessary, and Layla said, "We found this one part. It's not clear but—"

Her hand covered mine, holding us both steady, the warmth of her seeping into my skin, and blood streaked across the screen as I pressed play.

Two men, walking toward the pier on the night of Maddie's death.

It wasn't long, maybe twenty seconds. It was blurry, captured from too far a distance, but there are things you know about a person when you've been near them enough.

The slope of their shoulders, the way they run their hands through their hair, the way they stand and the way they walk.

The video played, each second confirming what I knew—Adam was at the pier that night. And so was Garrett.

CHAPTER THIRTY-EIGHT
SOPHIE

It's a good thing I've given up on the whole shaping-up-and-flying-right thing, because I don't think breaking into your principal's house would fit those requirements.

I had to wait until night fell, walking through the hallways at school, waiting for the moment Wentville would be there, his knife at my throat, glove over my mouth, acrid, thick wetness dripping past my lips and burning my gums.

And then I'd be gone. Gone like Garrett. Gone like Dad. Another empty place at the table. Another room where the dust grows thick without hands to disturb it, without breath to disrupt its rest. A faded memory, slipping from minds, even of those who try to hold it.

But as every hour passed, all that fear hardened inside me. All those times Garrett watched me struggle over a test or a paper I had due and he'd hit me with that patronizing fucking tone and useless directives to just *concentrate*, and he was walking around with the answers?

High and mighty Jessica acting like she was better than me for being in AP classes when she didn't deserve them either. I wonder if *she* told the police what she knew when Garrett left.

Hypocrites. Every fucking one of them. And then I get nearly murdered by Wilbur fucking G. Wentville? I'm gonna have PTSD from a second-rate hitman who tried to take me out using high school chemistry compounds and a *QVC Today's Special Value* carving knife?

I swear to Christ if he actually murdered me, I would haunt his ass forever.

Sitting here, waiting for him and the wifey to leave so I can ransack his house, I'm almost willing to let him murder me just so I *can* haunt him.

There's a basketball game tonight. They're going to be late.

Finally, they shuffle out of the house, smiling like he isn't a psychopath and she isn't married to one, and I hunch farther into my seat. It takes a minute, but soon their headlights dip over the road in front of me, and the car whooshes past.

I wait a full sixty Mississippis, and then another, before turning over the engine and easing a few houses closer. I don't want to have far to run if I need to.

The last time I tried to sneak around someone's house I nearly got killed—obviously Wentville again, when I was *with* Jude, which is pretty damned good evidence that he was *not* the person who attacked me yesterday. If that's even what Tickner brought him in for.

But that doesn't rule him out as Garrett's accomplice. Or even the person who caused the blood on that necklace in the first place.

I stroll up Wentville's driveway like I'm supposed to be there and pretend to knock on the door, just in case anyone is watching. It's locked. Sadly.

So I mosey around the side, checking for any window that might be open. There are none. Also sad.

The back door is locked too, but it has a glass pane and I'm beyond giving a fuck.

I grab the nearest hefty rock, making sure I have a good grip through my gloves (fingerprints—I'm not *that* stupid), and I channel all my rage into launching it into the glass.

It shatters instantly, a million slippery shards raining over my hand and tinkling on their way to the cement. Definitely gonna be a bitch to clean.

The lock flips easily, and I shove open the door, not bothering to close it behind me. I mean, who or what is it going to keep out at this point? I hope Wentville comes home to a hoard of angry squirrels.

My first stop is the kitchen. In search of Exhibit A.

He's an idiot. The knife block is sitting *right there*. I'm sure it's hard to explain to your wife why you have to throw out your entire knife collection when "Well, honey, I tried to murder a student" is your argument, but it's not like he couldn't lie.

It smells like spaghetti and garlic bread and the sheer normalcy of it—the idea of them sitting down to a happy meal when he traumatized me last night makes my fingers flex, begging to ravage the entire room.

Maybe on the way out.

I snap a picture, using Jessica's flip phone, and send it off to Detective Tickner. He might as well do something useful for me.

I grab one of the knives—just in case—and fling open cabinets, searching for something that looks like it came from a chemistry set. Or even the soaked gloves he wore.

There's nothing, so I go to the next most logical place: his office.

I creep through the living room, my footfalls soft on the hardwood, grandfather clock giving a reassuring cadence to every second as they pass. Shadows coat the room, bits and pieces of Wentville's life dotting the walls and shelves. All of it lies.

A principal. An upstanding citizen of the community. Just like Joseph Graham and his gorgeous house and dashing smile, all of it hiding the rot beneath.

I have no doubt Nora would've been infuriated to discover there was a massive cheating ring at our school. I can absolutely believe she'd dedicate herself to exposing every person involved in it. But this can't be all about cheating.

There's something Jessica is terrified I'll find out. There's something Joseph Graham knows and Amber Donahue has made herself sick over. There's something Wentville is willing to—no matter how ineptly—risk imprisonment to threaten me for, to tell me to stop looking. For *Nora* to stop looking.

Maddie Armstrong.

A bloody necklace.

The thought those things are related in some way makes my stomach churn, my breathing go shallow. Like maybe Wentville tried to threaten her too. Maybe she didn't have a ballet teacher to interrupt.

And somewhere, in the midst of all this, is Garrett. Is Adam. Is Jude.

There's something I'm missing. Something Nora knows. And whatever it is, it drove her into hiding.

My heart slams as I ease down the hall, a tiny night-light casting a pool of hazy illumination at my feet. To the left is the bathroom, guest bed on the right, master just a bit farther than that. I skip searching for the cuff links—somehow I doubt Tickner will consider a flash of light evidence.

I risk using my phone's flashlight once I'm in the office, sweeping it over his bookcases and desk. Shadows jump and scatter, and the illumination reflects back against the window, blinding me to the shift of dark trees outside.

The desktop is empty save for a planner and computer monitor. I flip through the planner, past months of Wentville's boring life, until I stumble upon a passwords section.

Seriously? So he's just absolutely incompetent, then? Cool. I'll just have a panic attack every time a steak knife comes near me because of someone who keeps all his passwords with a literal tab that reads "passwords."

I fire up his computer and log in (using his password) and sift through his files, looking for anything that reads "shit I would do a murder over," every cell in my body standing at attention from the window at my back. I could turn around and reassure myself there's no one there, but I'm too much of a coward to look.

After several failed plunges into useless folders, "Data" gives up the goods. It's sub-foldered by years. Six of them. The exact year Joseph Graham's oldest son would've started at Birmingdale. That *can't* be a coincidence.

It's password protected, but . . . for fuck's sake, I'm embarrassed *for* him.

I stifle a victory scream as the 2016 spreadsheet loads. Eric Graham is first on the list, along with a column for every single grade Wentville must've changed for him.

The list of other participants is small, many of them seemingly not signing on to the program until later in the year. But 2017's is longer. 2018 even more so.

And then. Then! There's another tab, and it shows how much Wentville is making off this sham.

That son of a bitch.

I'm scraping by, begging to just be able to go to a single intensive, and Wentville is funding his goddamn retirement.

I slam my finger on the print icon and the printer comes alive, doing all its buzzing and clicking while it prepares itself. But most recent is probably most important, so I send all his current data too. Then 2021. The spreadsheets are so wide each year is going to take ten years to print.

The smart thing would be to email them—log in to my Gmail and erase his entire history. And really, is a man with a page of his passwords going to know how to track my online movements? But then . . . Joseph Graham would. I'm basically asking Wentville to come finish the job. He may be inept and was clearly scared shitless given the amount his hand was shaking, but that doesn't mean he wouldn't do it.

But the alternative is one I can't deal with. Being constantly afraid of a threat that won't leave, that I can't predict. I thought I might die last night, and he can't be allowed to get away with that.

Neither of them can. Wentville is clearly no criminal mastermind. He didn't invent this scheme. Why should he go down while Joseph Graham and his shiny white teeth get to go on with life, reputation intact?

I log in to Wentville's email (guess how) and search for Joseph Graham.

Bless his heart.

Wentville seems to understand the power differential between him and old Joe Graham, and has gone to great pains to put every single email between them in a file for documentation, and fuck it. Let them know I did it.

I select and send as many as I can, fingers fumbling over the key thanks to my gloves. I tear them off because I'm in this thing now. I even snap a few screenshots and text them to Tickner. The printer whirs and new pages flutter to the floor, a patchwork quilt of all their lies, and I try not to think of how long I've been here, and how long I might have left.

I click faster, and my gaze catches on Garrett's name.

I have not been apprised of the Garrett Packard situation. If I'm considered a partner in this venture, I should have all the information.

My fingertips lift from the keyboard, my mouth gone dry. It's dated weeks before Garrett left. Only two days after Jessica's "you can't ignore me" text. Graham never bothered to respond.

Tears blur the screen because for the first time, I truly consider that Garrett might not just be traveling the country or even shacking up with some manic pixie dream girl in a converted loft apartment while he ponders the merits of veganism. There was a Garrett Packard situation long before he left.

Garrett's mom suddenly makes so much more sense. Like she knows. She knows he's gone. *Gone* gone.

I make it to the bathroom just in time to lose the dinner I barely ate, but it does nothing to calm the way my stomach rolls every time

I think about Garrett . . . lying in the woods somewhere? His body floating in the ocean? Secretly buried in some unmarked grave that only certain people know about?

Jessica's phone buzzes, and I jump so hard I land square on my ass. Tickner, asking who this is. Like I'm going to answer.

After I flush (I'm not a monster), I force myself to move, using the towel bar to drag my shaking legs from the tile.

"Hello?"

I freeze, afraid to move and afraid not to.

"Who's here?" It's Wentville, and I'm stuck in a bathroom with no exit.

His footsteps echo through the living room, and I grasp tight to the knife but it's slippery in my hands, palms covered in sweat.

I fling open the small closet, grabbing the first washcloth I see and wrapping it around the knife's handle, but just as I'm about to close the door, my gaze snags on a dark corner, and the small duffel inside it.

My shaking hands rip the zipper open as the footsteps draw nearer, moving slower, like Wentville's as terrified as me. The smell hits first—citrus and acetone—the bottle of chloroform nestled above gloves that have stiffened as they dried. Chloroform. Even *I* know it doesn't work like in the movies.

I grab the bag, slinging it over my shoulder, and peek out the door. Wentville's not in sight. Probably grabbing the cleaver from his knife block.

My stomach threatens to heave again, and I regrip the knife. I could run straight out the back, but my email is still open, and he'd be able to delete everything I sent myself in seconds. Garrett may not have been a great boyfriend or even a great person, but if they—

If they killed him, I can't just walk away.

I hold the knife out in front, feeling my way along the hallway, straining for the sound of footsteps over the rasp of my own breathing.

I'm nearly to the door, glow of the computer spilling into the hall, when I'm launched from my feet, heavy weight on my back slamming me forward.

The knife flings from my hand and slides across the floor, my elbows throbbing, every breath labored from the weight of him on my back.

I squirm, Wentville climbing higher over me to muffle my screams. His palm hits my mouth, and I bite down. Hard. The salt of his skin poisoning my tongue.

It's enough to throw him off-balance, enough for me to spin beneath him, dig in my heels, and shove. I land a kick to his face, blood spurting from his nose and splattering over the darkened wood planks. My fingertips graze the hilt of the knife, and I stretch farther, curling it against my palm just as Wentville lunges.

He stabs himself, landing right on the tip of the blade, and he screams as it pierces his shoulder.

I scramble to my feet, pulling myself into his office so I can shove a chair against the door handle.

He bangs against the door, each slam thundering louder than the last, calling out to me that he's calling the cops (ha! sure you are), that I'll spend my life in jail, then comes the inevitable calling me a bitch.

I log out of my email, erase his entire history, and cram as many pages as I can into the duffel. The window slips open easily, the screen not so much, but I don't even feel guilty as I slice through it.

The duffel lands with a thud, and I'm close behind, off and running to my car, sliding into the seat just as Wentville bursts from his front door.

If I spend the rest of my life in prison for killing Detective Tickner, it will be worth it.

I tried to give him the benefit of the doubt. I called him, agreed to meet in a parking lot so he couldn't force me into another room and interrogate me, and I showed him all my evidence.

I told him about the knife block and the rash or whatever around Wentville's wrist—obviously he was wearing latex gloves beneath his thick ones and the chloroform got above them. I told him about the chloroform in the duffel bag and, yes, even about the cuff link, which he nearly rolled his eyes at. I told him to check hospitals for a one-shoulder stabbee with a suspect story about how he obtained his injury.

And then I *showed* him the printouts and the screenshots I didn't have time to text him. I showed him the emails I forwarded to myself.

He asked me to send them and then launched into a lecture about breaking and entering and how committing a crime is not a way to solve a crime, and *then* he scolds me for grabbing the duffel because evidence procedures and chain of custody and a bunch of other shit that implied I had ruined his entire investigation even though I was the one who actually *investigated* his investigation.

Anyway, I threw the bag at him and took off, ignoring every single call he made to both mine and Jessica's cell phones.

And now I'm sitting across the street from my own home because I'm afraid once I go inside either Tickner or Wentville will come for me and at least in my car I can *see* them coming.

But maybe not hear them because my music is once again on the highest volume, drowning out all thoughts of Garrett and how he may or may not be actually *really* dead.

I bolt upright, slamming off the volume as my thoughts crash into each other.

I jam my hands into my back pocket where I've kept the note Nora gave me, hands shaking as I pull it out, her straight and even handwriting pressing deep into the paper.

Paper I've seen before.

I fling open my door, not bothering to close it as I sprint toward the pile of ashes from the fire Nora started.

My knees hit first, sliding into the rocks at the edge of the firepit, and I dive my hands into the ashes, covering my fingers, my palms, my wrists with blackened soot.

I feel my way through them, searching for remnants that escaped the flames, and I come across one, then another, but all of them blank.

I lose track of time, moon moving higher in the sky to hide behind thick branches, when I finally find it, just as Adam's light blinks on, his form watching as I smooth the soot from the page to reveal the design below.

Someone may have killed Garrett.

A girl named Maddie Armstrong is connected to whatever happened to him.

Nora knows about all of it.

And the paper she wrote Maddie's name on is the same mono-grammed stationery as Garrett's goodbye letter.

Wentville wouldn't have access to that.

And if Garrett is dead, someone else has been sending me those text messages.

Adam's light blinks off, and Nora's voice fills the empty night air.

The worst thing you can do to a man is force him to admit the things he's done.

CHAPTER THIRTY-NINE
SOPHIE

I tried to find Maddie Armstrong the easy way and call Nora, but I got sent straight to voice mail every time. Mom does not find this odd and "she's probably studying, Sophie," which she manages to say in a tone that makes it very clear how she feels about the fact that I am not. Right before she demands I come home immediately after dance and that Detective Tickner would like us to come by the station, and even though she sounds angry, I know she's more scared.

Well boo-hoo to her. Did she almost get murdered by her principal? Nope. She sure didn't. And she didn't want to listen when I tried to explain after that night at the station, so I'm not about to try again.

She already took away my intensive. Next it'll be my car, my phone, dance class. And then Wentville and Graham will go free and so will Jessica fucking Horton (for whatever evil thing she did).

I feel even less bad about running her over with my car now. For the record, she was standing at my bumper, accusing me of not loving Garrett because I wasn't looking for him, and then she said I was the reason he ran away, and I said, "I swear to fucking god, Jessica, if you don't get out of my way, I'm running you over," and she didn't, so I did.

She was fine. It wasn't my fault someone caught it on video and the whole school made memes of it.

I slept at Isa's last night. I'm crashing at Charla's tonight. Avoiding Mom is the bonus though. It's Adam I'm worried about.

Adam, who was in our house as often as his own. Who used to fall asleep between Nora and me, movie playing with the shadows in the dark room as we all drifted off, one by one. Adam, who taught me how to ride a bike and swim, and who threatened Kevin Wright when he made fun of my attempt at cutting bangs in fourth grade.

And now he's a suspect. There's this angry side to Adam that I didn't know existed. A side that will cause a scene in a gas station, stare out the window at Nora sitting below. He's always been in love with her. Everyone has always known. None of us stopped to think what he might do if, in the end, he couldn't have her.

Maybe he had the same suspicions as me—Nora and Garrett spending so much time together, the rumors they were together that night when he showed up at the gas station and lost his shit.

Then Garrett left.

No. Not left. Maybe not left. And if he didn't . . .

I don't know who besides Adam would have any chance of overpowering Garrett.

Maybe Jude could, but I still can't make that connection stick, no matter how much I worry I'm just not willing to.

And as much as it guts me to even think of Adam that way, I can't fathom what it's done to Nora.

Adam always belonged to Nora in a way he never would to me. They were destined from the moment they were born, two perfect pieces that fit together from the beginning—soft to hard edges, slopes to angles.

No matter how far apart their worlds seemed to be, this invisible connection kept them close, intertwined, until there were days the fire of jealousy burned so deeply I couldn't bear to be near them. I wanted what they had. That ease, the familiarity, the way he'd so easily slip past Nora's surface and into the parts of her she kept from the world.

But now it seemed she'd handed me the name that might sever their connection beyond repair. And if I'm being the most brutally honest version of myself, I'm afraid it'll be the thing that sets her free from this place. Lets her drift away until there's no trace left of her here.

I'm afraid I'm not enough to make her stay.

These are all the thoughts invading my brain space as I trudge up the driveway to Maddie Armstrong's little farmhouse, the heavy smoke of chimneys cloaking the air.

I know I'm in the right place because Amber Donahue told me where to find her. Not the exact address, but there are only so many Maddie Armstrongs in this state, and only one in Leeland, which is where Amber said she was from.

I didn't even have to convince her. After dance practice, Charla, Isa, and I waited in the school bleachers while Amber fumbled her way through cheer practice, her gaze snapping to mine when it should've been focused on the coach.

I lost track of how often her coach yelled at her to focus, pay attention, "get your head together, Amber, before someone gets hurt!"

Amber may as well have been me. I recognized way too much of my last few weeks in her, and I think she knew it.

She headed toward the locker room after practice but didn't even try to run, and she wasn't surprised when I called her name.

We stood just beneath the bleachers, where the gym's bright lights couldn't reach, the sound of shouts and giggles just down the hall but a lifetime away.

I pointed in the direction of the massacre that was their practice session. "I'm sure tomorrow will be better."

She gave a rueful sort of laugh. "Thanks. But I'm not so sure."

I sucked in a breath, part of me begging to not ask the question and walk away from all of this. Let Tickner figure it out. Or not. And Amber could go back to being an asshole but winning cheerleading competitions and I could go back to being Sophie Linden. The dancer. And nothing more. "Amber? Who is Maddie Armstrong?"

She crossed her arms over her middle, hugging herself tight, and whispered, "You should let this go, Sophie."

Except Nora is a ghost, Jude is under suspicion, and Wentville might be waiting for me in the hallway. "It's too late for that."

She nodded, more to herself than me. "Maddie Armstrong was my . . . tutor. She lived in Leeland. I didn't know. You have to believe me. Not until—" Tears flooded her eyes. "I have to go."

My hand raps against the Armstrongs' wood door, and a curtain to the left shifts just a fraction. Footsteps shuffle, like each movement is more difficult than the last. A lock clicks, the handle turns, and the hinges squeak as a face appears in the cracks.

A white woman, brown hair that used to get dyed to cover the grays, eyes red and permanent lines etched into her skin. She says, "Can I help you?" and even her voice sounds strained.

I'm struck by that feeling again, the one that says to go, to run far from here and back to the safety of the world I knew before.

I smile, my friendly, reassuring one. "Hi. My name is Sophie, and I'm a friend of your daughter? Maddie?"

"Oh." That's all she says, and the universe lies in that simple syllable.

That's when I know for sure that Maddie Armstrong is dead.

CHAPTER FORTY
SOPHIE

Amber's use of past tense wasn't a slip of the tongue.

The bloody necklace in my car wasn't an accident.

Jessica's panic wasn't just about being a cheater.

And Nora's words won't stop slicing through my thoughts, cutting deeper with every pass until I'd swear my heart was too battered to beat.

Adam killed Maddie. And Nora wants him to pay for it.

Unless she's wrong. Wentville tried to kill me. Three times by last count. Why not Maddie too?

It took fifteen minutes to get Mrs. Armstrong to stop crying. Fifteen minutes of holding her hand and taking in her grief, so palpable you can taste it, feel it on your skin, so thick it may never come clean.

It takes twenty more minutes to understand, to pull the full details from the portions of Maddie's life that she gives me.

Maddie was so smart, bound for college, the first in her family. She was worried about affording Columbia though, working so many hours as a tutor that her parents worried, told her to slow down. But she only pushed harder. Failure was not an option for a girl like Maddie, just like it wasn't for a girl like me.

Maybe her mother sees that in me. Maybe that's why she keeps talking. About how one day Maddie's soul seemed to break—the day the letter came, saying the university had received an anonymous report about academic dishonesty.

When was it? She's not sure, just shortly before.

Before, she says, without an end to the sentence. As if there isn't a need. For her, there is only before. And after.

It wasn't long after, and Maddie was gone.

I can't hide my shock, even as her mom crosses herself to ward off whatever evil she thinks accompanies what Maddie did. And maybe it's the shock—the confusion and relief and, yes, the anger too—that opens my lips to the words a polite girl wouldn't say. That a religion that would punish people for pain they never asked for would not be one I could ever accept.

It's a misstep. A break in the tenuous bundle of threads I've been weaving from the moment my foot crossed the threshold.

There's no more talk of Maddie's talents, her childhood anecdotes, or teenage accomplishments.

If Maddie did die by suicide, it wasn't Wentville. And Adam can't be guilty.

A heaviness releases from my chest, but it's back in the next breath. I know there's more than this seems. There are too many lies, too many people involved, too many secrets.

And after all of it, Maddie is still gone.

Her picture centers the mantel, perched above a fire that crackles and flares. The heat sears my skin, baking through my clothes while I reach for the likeness of her.

Her mom doesn't understand. That's what she says. She doesn't understand why. She was so happy. Had so much life ahead of her.

My gaze travels lower, past her wide smile, to the necklace at her throat. A music charm.

My hand shakes as I place it back, carefully, reverently, like I can show her memory the kindness she was owed while alive.

My fingers move numbly, plodding through photos until I find a photo of Garrett.

No. She's never seen him.

Next, one of Adam.

She sucks in a breath, her head nodding. Only once, on a night she and her husband came home early from church to rising voices in the backyard. Maddie's loudest, proclaiming that he didn't understand, *could* never understand, that he always chose *his* side.

Then the boy in the picture grabbed her arm tight, raising her to her tiptoes, and hissed something they couldn't hear, until they both turned at the feeling of being watched.

That's when Adam left, with barely a curt nod at Maddie's parents. She gave them even less, no matter how many questions they asked.

"We should've kept asking. Made her tell us." That's what Mrs. Armstrong says through her tears. But no. Some people can't be forced. Some people can only open in their own way, and only with the ones they trust.

I can't tell her all the things I know. That I held Maddie's necklace, caked in her blood, in my hand. I can't tell her that the *he* in that conversation was my ex-boyfriend and that the boy next door murdered their daughter.

I can't tell her because I can't prove it, and until I can, I won't add to her pain. I won't destroy what's left of her until I know for sure.

It hurts, being in this house, wading through an emptiness that pulls at you, threatens to drag you into its depths where it's quiet, where there's no pain but no joy either. I want to sink into it, let it consume me until everything I know disappears and all the things I can't face fade into darkness.

Instead, I flick to the last picture, grasping tight to Mrs. Armstrong's hand as I turn the image of Jessica to her.

I know the moment recognition strikes, her free hand flying to her lips. She came by. The night of.

She doesn't finish that either.

She claimed to be Maddie's friend, coming to pick up Maddie's portion of a group project. They let her in, let her search through their daughter's room and leave with a folder clutched to her chest.

It all makes the worst kind of sense. This. This is what Jessica is so afraid of. Of the role she played when a girl died.

When a girl was murdered.

She drove all the way to Leeland, putting her future at risk, and entered this house with intent to steal, based on a simple text. A single request. *I need your help.*

There's only one person Jessica would do that for. And it isn't Adam.

CHAPTER FORTY-ONE
NORA

This was where everything ended. When I got the answers I needed but did not want. Where suspicion gave way to brutal truth and tore through the life I'd planned for myself.

But first there was that night in the woods. I hadn't killed the man, but then I discovered that Ainsley had slipped quietly into death that same night and I wished I had.

Lance carried me, bundled me in his arms, and ran from the man's bleeding body to Layla's car, where we drove in silence, my hands still crimson, pale skin glowing through the cracks.

She insisted I come to her house. Then she insisted she stay at mine. I was not safe there, she thought. I thought I was not safe anywhere. Not just because they'd tried to kill me a third time, but because this time, I'd gone in search of it.

It was me who followed him down the hallway, me who ran into the woods. It was me who searched for him and me who found him. For so long, I'd prided myself on my calm, my measured responses. I'd clung to certainties and guarantees. It seemed I'd lost those, and I wasn't sure I could trust the part of me I'd ripped free from deep inside. I'd given her life, and now it was too late to see to her death.

I walked through the yard on bare feet, grass cold and wet against my soles, my shoes dangling from two crooked fingers at my side. My hair tickled my face, and I scraped it away, my hand snagging where strands had stuck to my skin, held fast by the blood of the man I'd nearly killed.

Adam and Garrett were at the pier the night Maddie died. No court of law would have accepted my evidence, but I was no longer concerned with such a metric. What did court matter when two girls were dead? What good was the law when it would fail them both?

And for Adam and Garrett, it had changed nothing in their lives.

But they were still a constant presence in mine. In Sophie's. And there was no world in which I could allow that.

I reached the middle of the backyard, tilted my head toward the procession of gray clouds that shielded the moon, closed my eyes, and dreamed of the stars and a time when my hands were clean, not caked in a man's blood. A time when just breathing didn't ravage my throat.

I wound the chain of Maddie's necklace around my fist—I'd taken to keeping it on my person, lest someone find it like I'd found it in Adam's room. But it was a reminder too. A talisman. My promise.

My shoes tumbled to the grass, the fabric of my dress stiff and smelling of pennies, the memory of hands around my throat stalling me where I stood.

I pulled out Maddie's phone and texted Garrett: *Bring it to the party*.

There would be a Halloween party at Del Mason's that weekend, and that was where I would need to make my stand. If Garrett brought the money Maddie planned to extort from him, it would be one more bit of evidence.

"Nora?"

I shuddered at the sound of Adam's voice, goose bumps rising on my skin, fear splintering from deep inside me.

I turned toward him, both of us hidden in the shadows, the stretch of ground between us the span of the ocean and a grain of sand all at once.

The clouds freed the moon from their grasp, and soft light bathed the yard. His expression flitted between so many I could hardly keep track, finally taking in the sight of me. Blood-spattered and bruised.

He stepped forward and I back, and he pulled up, whispering my name like he knew what I held in my hand before I showed it.

I held the necklace out to him, let it catch in the moon's rays, twisting in the breeze. I let it speak for me when I could not. Pulled forward his palm to drop the necklace into it.

His lips fell open, his chest rising and falling so quickly I had to stop myself from reaching out to feel his heart beat, slow and steady as it always did.

He whispered, "Nora, please."

"Please." It scraped through my throat, slices of a knife's blade. "Please *what*?"

It was me who should've begged. For him to tell me he didn't do what I thought. For him to explain everything, remove the pit of fear from my chest, fill it with assurances so I could reassemble my heart, piece it back together from the shards it lay in.

"Are you okay? Just . . . tell me you're okay." His voice broke at the end, and a better person may have taken pity.

I pulled back my hair, let him see the purpling bruises circling my neck, let him see the blood he couldn't be sure wasn't mine coating my skin. "Did you tell Joseph Graham about me?"

His silence was his answer.

"When? Immediately? The same night we called from the office? Did you even debate whether to betray me or—"

"Fuck, Nora, it wasn't like that! I did it to protect you! You can't *beat* a guy like Graham. He's got too much to lose. He was never supposed to hurt you. He was just supposed to get you to stop asking questions."

And that's it. His entire defense. That he knew what was best for me, and also best for him. He stood there with Maddie's necklace, and there was still no sign he cared.

I kissed him because I wanted to and now I wanted to take it back. I wanted to rewind our entire history, not for noble reasons, but to spare myself the pain. There was no part of my life that didn't include him, no part of my future that I could imagine without him. And in a blink, all of that became an agony so potent it threatened to bring me to my knees.

"Did you kill her, Adam?"

Tears slipped down his cheeks, his body strung tight like it took every bit of his willpower to stay where he stood. "No. God no. Nora, how could—"

"Who did?"

He sucked in a breath, and then he shook his head.

Every word ravaged my throat, my voice strained and scratchy as it rose. "Did you kill Maddie Armstrong? I saw you, at the pier—"

"It wasn't me!" He scrubbed his hand over his face, his every breath shuddering. "Please, Nora. I need you to believe me. You *know* me. You know I couldn't do something like that."

I swiped away my tears, my knuckles coming away smeared. "Prove it."

CHAPTER FORTY-TWO
SOPHIE

I show up on Jude's doorstep unannounced.

Because Del is a saint, they gave me his address with only a small amount of pleading and no fewer than three future favors owed.

Truth is, I'm only hoping I'll be around to fulfill them.

Maybe I'm an idiot. Silly little Sophie all caught up in her emotions because a cute boy with good hair and Oscar Isaac vibes smiled at her. Maybe Jude is guilty and caught up in this just as much as me.

But I don't think so. And for once, I'm trusting myself to get this all right.

The door swings open to tousled waves and nothing approaching a smile.

I stare over his shoulder. "I'm sorry. No. That's not right. I mean, it is. I'm sorry that you got pulled into all of this. But I'm not apologizing for me because this is not my fault. For once."

He nods once and pulls the door wider, motioning me through. My shoulder brushes his chest, and I try not to pause. To not stand there just a second and remember what it was like on that roof where there was only the moon, the stars, the breeze, and his calloused fingertips skimming my skin.

He mutters a grave "Sophie," because I am absolutely just paused halfway through his doorway.

"Right. I'm moving now." I ease into the dark room, the buttery smell of popcorn making my stomach rumble, the mess of blankets on the couch calling to me to snuggle up tight, stay here, to not do what I need to when I leave this house.

I spin to the only source of illumination in the room, a wide television mounted above a dormant fireplace. With an all-too-familiar scene of Baby and Johnny practicing lifts in the lake.

It short-circuits my entire brain, peeling away some of the heaviness from Maddie's house, and I point to it. "Are you—"

"No!" He sprints to the remote like the house is on fire and only turning off the TV can save us. "I was watching something else and then you knocked and—"

"It's literally paused."

He slams his finger on the power button, and the room goes dark. "Fine."

"Fine *what*?" I try to stop it, but a snicker escapes.

"Fine—I was watching *Dirty Dancing*. I *like Dirty Dancing*."

"I mean, who doesn't?" Even Nora used to watch it with me. One day I forced her to practice the lift with me, until I fell on top of her and nearly drowned her. She made Adam take her place.

"Do you"—I force down my laugh, mold my face into something resembling serious—"do you sing Johnny's parts? Like when 'She's Like the Wind' comes on?"

"Yes. And"—he grabs hold of my arm, yanking me forward until I'm twirling into him and then away, before his hand hits my back and I'm dipped over his knee, my head swirling—"I do his dance moves too. Nine years of ballroom dance lessons. My mom is Cuban."

He sets me upright and my entire body flushes, and for once in my life, I'm speechless. Nearly speechless. "They worked. The lessons I mean."

His smile fades, and his eyes drift from mine, like whatever refuge we forged just came crumbling down. He holds up a single finger and says, "Don't go," like I'm not the one who showed up here.

He disappears down the hall before rushing back out, holding out a pile of fabric in his hands. "You left this."

My sweatshirt. I kissed him and ran away and left it on the roof, and he kept it. It smells like lavender and dryer sheets. He *washed* it for me.

I pull it from his hands and blink away tears because apparently I'm all caught up in my feelings because a cute boy washed my clothes.

I whisper a "thank you," and he stares at the floor. "What did he tell you? Tickner? About me?"

That's why I'm here, and the truth of everything crashes into me, plunges me beneath the surface until I can hardly breathe.

I'm here so I can pass on the information I have, the things that will clear Jude's name, in case I don't come back to tell it myself. "He said you were involved in some girl . . . getting hurt."

He lowers onto the couch, only to stand again. "Did you believe him?"

"I think that was the conversation that ended with my mom pulling me from the interrogation room before I got myself arrested."

It almost draws a smile but not quite. "She died." His voice goes gravelly at the end, and he swallows hard. "It was a house party, all of us were drinking. They asked my band to play and he was a friend, so it was cool. I thought it was cool."

332

He sits again, running his hands over his jean-covered thighs. "This one girl, Liza, she got way too drunk. And if I'm being really fucking honest, I thought maybe—" Tears gloss over his eyes, and he blinks them away. "I thought maybe someone might've slipped her something, but I was in the middle of the song and I lost track of her in the crowd. She slipped at the edge of the pool."

I keep my voice gentle. "Jude, that is a tragedy, and I am so sorry that happened but—"

"They put the drugs in my guitar case. They were fucking sloppy about it. Left a partial print and just dropped it in the open case. Sober enough to realize they were all sorts of fucked, but not enough to do a decent frame job."

"Did the police charge you?"

He scrapes his hair back, and it immediately falls. "No. They threatened. But my dad had a military buddy who's a defense attorney now. Not such a great scapegoat after all. But once the cops know you, they don't forget."

I don't have words to make any of this better, or erase what happened, so I charge forward and hug him instead.

His body goes stiff, but only for a second, before his arms come around me and squeeze just as tight as mine. He trusted me, enough to tell me what happened. Enough to let me in on the thing he wanted to keep hidden the most. And neither of us are running away.

I let my cheek rest against his chest, his heart thrumming. I don't feel like I need to say the right thing or be the right person. I don't need to measure to some standard I'll never reach.

The decisions I make tonight are mine. And they may be stupid. They may be the wrong ones. But they're *mine*.

I'm Sophie Linden, the dancer, and nothing more, and it's enough.

I pull away, because as much as I'd like to stay here all night, there's too much out there that's left to do. I yank Jessica's phone from my pocket, and it's still hideous.

Even Jude agrees—I can tell from the way he says, "Wow."

"It's not mine."

"Sure it isn't."

I grab his wrist, pulling it up to place the phone in his palm. "This belongs to Jessica Horton. I need you to keep it for me. If it becomes necessary, you need to take it to Detective Tickner and tell him everything I'm going to tell you."

"Define necessary."

I pause. My choices. My decisions. "If I don't come back."

CHAPTER FORTY-THREE
NORA

Normally I wouldn't have cared in the least that it was Halloween. Any costumes I'd been forced into over the years generally ran similar to the year I carried a tiny flag with the word "ceiling" on it and called myself a ceiling fan.

But this year, All Hallows' Eve could not have come at a better time, nor had I ever needed a chance to disguise myself more.

Not only was I covered in bruises I'd had to develop a habit of scarf-wearing to hide from the passing brushes with my mother and Sophie, but I most certainly did not want to be seen or noticed at the party I'd be attending.

The party Garrett was sure to be attending too, thanks to Adam. He swore he didn't kill Maddie, but he was far from guilt-free. He was on the pier that night—he knew what happened to Maddie. He held me after that night on the beach when I thought I might die and he said sorry but not the reasons why.

If I gave myself even a moment to consider it, my heart would've splintered into shards so small they'd have blown away on the breeze. I'd have fallen to my knees, right there in the grass, Adam only a handful of feet away, and I'd have wept for everything I thought I knew, for the boy I thought he'd always been.

Instead, I'd wrapped it all tight, bound together by the force of will alone, and I'd placed it deep inside me, caged it, buried it beneath the weight of the ocean. I did not let the tears in my eyes fall. *Be strong, Nora.*

Some part of the Adam I knew must have broken free because he promised me one thing. That he'd make sure Garrett was at the party. He asked no questions, and I offered no answers.

I owed him no explanations. I refused to unburden him with assurances.

I would let him wonder, let his mind suffer through frenzied speculation, over what he'd agreed to. Somehow, I doubted it was worse than the sins he'd already committed.

Cars lined the street, their engines pinging and knocking as they cooled, streetlamps pouring illumination over their hoods. I stared into my hazy reflection as I passed the endless stream of windows.

Layla and Monica* had joined forces to dress me, my skin as white as the moon, my lips a crimson red, my eyes lined and rubbed with the color of ashes.

We didn't discuss which persona I was meant to represent. Perhaps I was death, come to bring clarity to those whom I sought.

Whispers of music swept through the trees as I drew closer, the thrum of bass reaching me first, plunging me into the club where I'd found Lance and Ryan. Where I'd bludgeoned a man with a rock and left with his blood on my hands.

But the party was nothing like that. The rooms were bright, the music loud, and the voices louder. Glitter sprinkled the floor, scraped from some girl's costume as she moved through the room. I recognized no one and hoped no one recognized me.

I kept to the walls, scanning for Garrett, for Sophie too. There were too many things I had to answer for, when I could answer for none.

It took well over twenty minutes before I found him. Another ten before he broke free of his fans long enough for me to catch his eye.

We didn't speak. Didn't have to. Everything I needed to say came in the form of a silver necklace stained red.

Some men may have sat silently when faced with their lives crumbling before them.

Not Garrett.

Garrett did not shut up.

There was no reflection. No reckoning with what he'd done. No hint that he felt the slightest guilt for taking Maddie from this earth.

That was when I knew he'd done it. The car ride to the beach, Garrett driving, me in the passenger seat, listening to him plead and threaten but never once—not even for a moment—showing a shred of remorse.

He'd followed me from the house, his fingers digging into my elbow, steering me in the directions he'd wanted, words seething from between flatlined lips. His anger beat against me, dark and sick the way it simmered beneath his skin.

I'd directed him to his own vehicle, pausing one last time before we entered to scan for witnesses, seeing only a flutter of curtains in the upstairs window.

He drove, following my directions for every turn, removing bits of his costume until he was very nearly himself, questioning our destination, our purpose, my plans, whether this was all about the ten grand, whether I was just like Maddie. His voice rose as we drew nearer, as if he knew exactly where we were headed.

Maddie's necklace, and the place not far from where her body was found. Her cell phone in my pocket—the one she used to call Garrett the night she died.

It was all the evidence I had, but it wasn't enough. Nothing short of a confession would be. So I'd borrowed a camera from Lance and Ryan, mounted it on a piling that held up the pier, and now it waited for me to deliver Garrett to its watchful eye.

The rain came when we were halfway there, dotting the windshield with fat droplets, slithering down the windows, rainbow reflections of streetlamps caught on their rounded sides. His driving got worse, a swerve through the adjoining lane, a delay in braking, until I became convinced Garrett was not completely sober.

His rage grew with every passing mile, with every minute of certainty that I knew. I knew what he'd done, and there were no excuses I might accept. For perhaps the first time, Garrett Packard might have to face consequences.

We pulled into a lot, quite possibly the same one he and Adam had entered the night Maddie died, and he slammed the car into park. "What the fuck are we doing here? You want the money? I'll give you the fucking money."

I left the car as a response, left Maddie's necklace where her blood couldn't be washed clean by the rain, letting the storm soak into my clothes, matting my hair to my face. The angry churn of the ocean was building in the distance. It wouldn't be long now, until we'd stand before the very pier they claimed Maddie jumped from.

Garrett followed because he couldn't not, his body coiled and bursting with rage. I led him down the small bridge, until my feet hit the sand, pockmarked and packed solid from the beat of fat droplets.

He grabbed my elbow again, this time undoubtedly hard enough to bruise, and spun me to face him. "Answer my—"

I shook him free, hurrying faster, my calves burning until I got him where he needed to be. Waves crashed against the piers, splitting the water to spray forth from the edges, and Garrett swiped the rain and ocean from his eyes. He blinked once, then again, as I held up Maddie's phone.

"Why did I bring you here, Garrett?" At his shrug, I said, "Do you recognize this?"

"Everyone gets one of those."

"You *know* why you're here. You and Adam, I saw you on video." I had to shout to be heard above the winds, and I risked a step closer to him so he wouldn't miss a word of what I'd said. "Who do you think called you from this phone Monday night? It was me, and I know everything."

I let it hang in the air between us, watched the color drain from his skin only for it to rise up again, red and angry. "You fucking bitch—"

"She blackmailed you, and you couldn't take it. Couldn't stand to answer for what you'd done, so you killed her. You—"

"I didn't kill her!"

"Liar!" I swiped at the rain coating my face, and my hand came away with smears of white and black makeup, until we were just Nora and Garrett, stripped clean, no mask to hide behind.

Lightning flashed, touching the horizon as white foam built on the tops of waves as they barreled toward shore, reaching higher with every moment until they soaked my shoes, splattered against my calves, working a cold numbness through my legs.

I flipped open the phone, and let the screen blare bright against the dark. "It's all in here, Garrett. You told her to come to you, and then she died."

339

"No."

"I have her necklace, covered in her blood."

"No!"

"What did you do, Garrett? Did you hit her? Choke her?" My own bruises throbbed, the memory of hands tight around my neck making my stomach turn. "And then you killed her, and you brought her here and *dumped* her like she meant *nothing*. Like she was—"

"It wasn't my fault!" He tunneled both hands through his hair, rain dripping from every bit of him. "She was going to fucking *ruin* me, Nora. And not just me—Adam too."

I did not stumble at his name, didn't fall to my knees like I wanted to. Adam made his choice. He protected a murderer at the expense of the murdered. He was not the boy I grew up with. Not the man I lay beside. Not the person I cried for, more times than I'll admit in any confession.

I swallowed, salt and seawater touching my tongue. "How did you do it? Did you lure her in? Did you—"

He stomped forward, long legs erasing the safety of distance until we stood only inches apart, the hatred in his eyes bright in the refraction of rain against the moonlight. "I didn't *kill* her! It was an accident! And Joseph—"

His lips snapped shut, like he'd realized he'd gone too far. Revealed too much.

"Joseph what?" I kept my voice low, soothing, like Sophie would've. "You can tell me."

It was an out. A justification he believed I might accept, and he wanted nothing more than absolution.

Tears mingled with the rain, forming rivulets down his cheeks.

"I told him that she was trying to blackmail me, and he just wouldn't stop saying I needed to shut her up. I needed to keep it quiet, make it go away. I couldn't be the person who ruined this for everyone. Fucking *everyone*, Nora. Adam. Sophie."

I stumbled in the shifting sand, waves clawing at my knees. Sophie would never. Sophie was smart, brilliant in her own way. She'd never had interest in being the highest or best, but she never needed to cheat. She would ask me for help if she needed it.

The rain battered my skin, every pinprick like an accusation. If she'd tried to come to me, would I have listened? All those times she reached out, only for me to pull back.

This, then, was my fault too. I'd done everything to be strong, sacrificed everything, and it left her standing alone.

Garrett moved closer, each step kicking up more of the ocean's swell. "You think she'll be able to dance in that intensive—in *any* intensive—if you out her as a cheater? You think they'll take her at that conservatory if she gets kicked out of high school? Her dance career will be over, Nora. And it'll be your fucking fault. First you took away her dad, and—"

"No." I blinked, and hot tears rolled. "He did that to himself. It was *his*—"

"That's not how Sophie sees it. And she'll see this the same way." His chest heaved, his shirt clinging to every inch of him. "You can hate me, Nora, but are you going to ruin Sophie's life? Would you do that to your own sister just so you can prove how fucking superior you are? How you're so goddamn noble and the rest of us are liars and cheaters?"

My chest felt heavy, the swelling in my throat too thick to swallow through, and no matter how many tears I scrubbed away, new ones rushed to replace them.

He was wrong. He *wasn't* wrong. That's how this had started. Me, determined to discover Garrett's secrets. Me, determined to make Garrett pay for his wrongs.

But that was when his wrongs were stolen tests and fraudulent papers. This was bigger now. This was about Maddie and Ainsley, and about Monica and Sophie and anyone else who became collateral damage while Garrett Packard rose above them. Impervious to consequence. Unashamedly lacking in remorse.

Sophie would never forgive me. But one day, perhaps she would understand. I was the sunflower, killing all the good things around it, my existence a deterrent to anyone and anything close. I'd spared her that. I tried to. It was the one venture at which I'd failed.

I squeezed tight to Maddie's phone, raising it so he had no choice but to look. "You *killed* someone, Garrett. Her name was Maddie Armstrong, and you—"

"She fucking fell!"

"You pushed her." That was right. I'd bet everything on it. Garrett was then as he was now. Scared, angry, Joseph's threats in his ear and his future on the most precarious of cliffs. This, as I was now, was exactly how Maddie died.

"She wanted to ruin my life, and Joseph wouldn't let me just pay. He said then everyone would do the same thing. I did what I had to."

And there it was. A confession. Made willingly.

He wasn't even sorry.

I screamed, my voice shaking and hoarse. "You and Adam. You

brought her here. You just . . . left her. Threw her away. Like she didn't matter!"

His hand circled my neck before I could react, thick fingers pressing into the swollen spaces that hadn't come close to healing. It was always there—the throat, the mouth, any way to silence, to cut off the ability to speak the truth.

His fist closed around mine, around Maddie's phone, trying to wrench it free, and my arm twisted, my grip failing as he pried my fingers free one by one. Maybe the evidence I had would be enough, but I couldn't risk it. Not after all this.

I barreled into him, shoulder slamming against the hard planes of his chest, but it was enough. He tumbled backward, his balance thrown off, and then we crashed into the water, my body weightless above Garrett's.

I had precious seconds before his head rose from the surface, and I took full use, throwing Maddie's phone deep into the beach. And then, when he scrubbed away the ocean from his eyes, he watched as I threw *my* phone into the waves, thinking it was Maddie's.

It felt like years, the seconds we stared, each of us daring the other to move. Even had it been Maddie's phone, we may never see it again, lost to the pull of the ocean, its components ruined beyond compare.

But like the shells that dotted the beach every morning, the ocean was known for giving as well as taking, and Garrett, he couldn't risk it. He'd killed for this. And if I ran, he would follow.

I plowed into the water, the waves pushing at my calves, then my thighs, until I dove in, tunneling beneath the waves as they rolled in, each bigger, more violent than the last.

I tasted salt and brine with every inhale, the water stinging my eyes and blurring my vision, my arms and legs burning with the effort of fighting against a force so strong it could upturn boats and topple cities.

The ocean always won.

This night was no different. The waves came faster, so close I could barely sip for air before the next descended, until I was too far out to stand, at the mercy of each wave.

And then, at the mercy of Garrett Packard as his hand closed around my arm, dragging me under, *holding* me under.

It was my greatest miscalculation, assuming Garrett wouldn't think to kill me. Assuming there was decency left in him, that my connection to Sophie would be enough.

I was a witness now. I knew everything. I could ruin him.

His other hand pushed against my shoulder, shoving me down down down while his legs pistoned to keep himself above the surface.

I pushed against his hand, scratching, pounding while my lungs begged for air, begged to scream into the quiet rippling of water around me.

They say drowning is the most peaceful way to die—your body adrift, soft water blocking the sounds of the world until you slipped into total quiet. A soft drifting into nothing, into the depths of darkness, body weightless, mind set free.

But tonight, *I* was death, and the waves saved me.

It slammed into us, breaking us apart, sending us both tumbling into its depths—up muddled with down and left with right. My body twisted, plunged deeper only to be raised to the surface, my lungs sucking in air only to pitch back into darkness.

My shoulder slammed into an immovable object, pain flaring so deep I cried out, sucking in salt water on my inhale. I coughed, throat so bruised I thought I may never breathe again, and my fingernails dug into the hard wood of the piling.

The next wave crashed, and I held on, splinters driving deep into my skin. My eyes watered, my breath thin and reedy, and I searched the swell for signs of Garrett.

I spotted him then, looking so small against the massive wave behind him, building, growing, churning faster, and there was only a moment when I could have yelled out. Warned him before it enveloped him.

I didn't.

I don't remember what happened next. Not truly.

I remember losing my grip on the piling, the wave tearing me from its safety, sending me rocketing toward shore. I remember floating to the surface on strong arms, Adam's face blinking into view. I remember the rumble of his chest as words I couldn't hear launched from his throat.

And I remember the spiral of crimson, snaking through the water, spreading to pink as raindrops dotted the surface.

I broke free and swam, letting the waves shuttle me to shore, until my knees scraped the sandy bottom, ripping open my flesh on rocks and shells brought with it. I stumbled to my feet, coughing, shaking, each step a victory.

I rushed to the piling, to the camera I needed most, the one that had captured Garrett's confession.

Some small part of me had hoped Adam might be redeemable. A bigger part of me, so desperate to reclaim some of the life I used to know, was desperate to believe he was. That he hadn't had a hand in throwing Maddie away, despite appearing on camera that night with Garrett. That he hadn't been following me, tracking me, the night of my flat tire.

I wanted, so badly, to believe I hadn't been wrong about him, this boy I'd loved so deeply, for so long.

But when I made it to that final piling, I knew the truth.

I found it empty.

CHAPTER FORTY-FOUR
SOPHIE

I sit behind the shrubs alongside our house, Nora's bedroom window a full floor above me, and swat at the swarms of mosquitos that threaten to leave me itching for days.

Binoculars dangle from my neck, ready to spy on Adam the second his shadow flickers behind his window.

I am being monumentally creepy, but if there's evidence of what happened between Garrett, Maddie, and Adam, it has to be in his room. Garrett's has been searched by the private investigator his parents hired, and Maddie's mom took me upstairs, to show me who her daughter was. When her back was turned, I went to the only book on the shelf that looked out of place, and flipped it open to a hollowed-out center. Someone took the only thing that mattered there. A flip phone like Jessica's would've fit. Maybe that's the thing she was sent to retrieve.

Adam moves again, the light in his bedroom flicking off, only to spring back to life again when he comes back for the backpack on his bed.

My breath catches.

He's been carrying that thing everywhere he goes, and right now he's going *somewhere*. Fast.

I beat him to his car by just enough to slip inside the back seat and for the lights to go dim again. He peels out of the driveway, his breathing hard and erratic, and every turn and bump threatens to throw me back into his view.

His backpack thumps onto the floor at my feet, but I don't dare reach for it. Not when the car is this quiet. There's no radio, not even the droll ramblings of sports talk that Garrett always insists on.

We drive for miles, until time blurs and all my doubts threaten to take over. I can't solve a murder. I gave up after ten minutes in the one and only escape room Garrett took me to. Even if I find the evidence I'm looking for, I'm now miles away from home. Miles from anything—we're surrounded by forest, an endless stream of treetops swirling by, the moon moving from left to right until it disappears completely.

Adam's phone rings, and I swallow a yelp, my shaking hands fumbling over the zipper as he answers.

It's just enough to make space for my hand, and I reach in blindly, feeling for anything but finding only air.

Adam says, "Five minutes," and the call is over, my hand frozen in his open backpack. I slide my arm just an inch deeper, stretching my fingers until the tips brush against something soft.

I scissor the cloth between them, gathering it up a handful at a time until enough is fisted in my hand to pull it toward the opening.

I expect a T-shirt, some old worn-through thing with Adam's numbers splayed across the back. Instead, it's soft florals, muted in the darkness until the colors are all shades of gray. It brings a Ziplock with it, like it had been sealed shut and slipped free. The shirt flutters over my wrist as I pull it closer, scented with subtle lavender and something else I can't quite place.

Adam makes a sharp left, and I slam my hand into the seat so I don't tumble into the middle, the shirt slipping from my hand and onto my bent knees.

It lies there, spread over my legs as the moonlight frames it, and I have to bite down on my hand to stop myself from screaming.

Blood cakes the front of it, dark and red and stiff, soaked into the fibers until it erases the pattern beneath it.

My stomach heaves, eyes filling with tears for the smiling girl on her parents' mantel. Whatever part of me may have hoped I'd gotten things all wrong fades away, leaving me gasping for air when I'm too afraid to breathe.

The car rolls to a stop, and I close my eyes, praying Adam leaves, goes anywhere, just far enough away that I can run.

But his footsteps stop after only a few seconds, until headlights sweep over the car, chasing the shadows that slip back into place only a moment later.

I jam my hand into the bag again, yanking out the GoPro with the footage he didn't want me to see.

I can't watch whatever's on this. Not because the light might give me away. Because I *can't*.

"You need to *handle* this, Adam." Jessica's voice travels through the closed-up car, and I want to jump from my hiding place and strangle her even if it gets me killed.

Adam mumbles a response, so low I nearly miss it. "I'm not the one who lost your phone."

"I didn't lose it!" She whispers then, beyond my hearing, and I can't spend another minute in this car.

I can't sit behind him, only inches away, holding the shirt Maddie died in.

Once it's sealed in the Ziplock, I shove it into the backpack, sliding the bag onto my shoulders, then flick the record button. If they say something damning, it might as well be on record.

Jessica seethes, "I *stole* for him. Her parents know what I look like. I'm not going to jail for stealing some stupid papers and spreadsheets."

Adam tells her no one's going to jail, and I sincerely think he's wrong about that. But it hits me, how careful Garrett was, how calculating. He'd just murdered a girl and still couldn't see past himself. He sent Jessica to gather whatever paperwork Maddie had kept about him, probably essays that would match the ones he turned it. She sat in Maddie's room unsupervised—she could've erased anything off her computer before anyone knew to look for it.

I tip forward, my hands walking me toward the other door while Adam and Jessica argue in tones too soft to hear. I'm flat on my stomach, lips nearly touching the remnants of dried leaves on the floor, when the smallest hint of silver glints from between the seats.

I reach for it, bending my arm at an impossible angle until my fingertips graze cold metal.

It's jammed in tight, stuck no matter how hard I pull.

The seats. They fold down.

I squeeze my eyes shut, trying to remember how to work Adam's stupid seats like he did when he helped transport the entire dance team's costumes for recital.

Webbing. A fabric strap at the back of the seat. I just need to climb up there and . . . pull it.

I shrug off the backpack and crawl over the seat bottom, contorting myself to its shape, then rise up, hand searching for the thick fabric.

Jessica yells something I'm too terrified to listen to, and I yank the lever just as she slams her car door. The seat shoves forward, pinning my legs, and I jam my hand between the cushions, not even caring how the metal gouges my fingers, until I can rip the object free.

It loops around my palm, so familiar it may as well be mine.

It doesn't matter that I'm sitting exposed, upright in the seat while Jessica's headlights wash over me. It doesn't matter that I'm surrounded by forest, not a single person to scream to for rescue.

All that matters is that Garrett's watch lies against my palm, the face cloudy with unreleased moisture, the second hand still keeping steady time, the *tick tick tick* as loud as a tsunami's wave.

This watch belonged to Garrett's dad. His grandfather before him.

There is only one way he'd be without it.

And that's how I know Garrett is dead.

CHAPTER FORTY-FIVE
NORA

Here is my real confession.

I remember everything.

CHAPTER FORTY-SIX

SOPHIE

It's the feeling of being watched that pulls me from my trance. The absolute certainty that there is no way for me to escape without being seen.

I don't even turn to look at him.

I jump into the front seat, slamming my foot against the brake and punching the start button.

Adam always leaves his key fob in the console.

The engine turns over, but then he's screaming for Jessica to go to the other side while he rushes toward me, slamming into the driver's door before I can shift into reverse.

There's a moment, a slow-motion flicker of time where seconds feel like minutes and Jessica flashes in the rearview mirror. I can't fight them both. I can't even fight Adam alone.

I hit the gas, and my body shudders as I run Jessica over. Again.

It's different this time—not just a simple tap that barely knocks her to the ground. This time it's a thud. Silence instead of screams. And maybe I'm no different than Garrett.

The door flings open, and I don't have time to slam the car back into park. I only have time to fly into the back seat and grab the backpack, Garrett's watch sliding loose over my wrist.

Adam grabs at my ankle, sending me crashing into the back seat, but then the car jerks as he hits the brakes to stop the car from rolling over Jessica, and maybe there's some good left in him.

I break free, scrambling out the back door, and flee for the cover of the woods. Thick trunks and leafy branches swallow me whole as I dive into them, Adam's footfalls cracking the twigs beneath him as he follows.

But I'm quieter than him, my feet lighter, and I flit through the woods like I'm one of the shadows.

Branches scratch at my face, catch on the backpack as it bounces against my ribs. My feet slip in the moist dirt, even the moonlight fading as the canopy thickens.

"Sophie!" Adam's voice echoes through the trees, startling a flock of birds that take to the sky. "I didn't do it!"

I skid to a stop, every cell in me desperate to believe him. My lungs heave, the backpack with Maddie's shirt pressed against the blackened trunk of a tall pine.

"Garrett killed Maddie." A twig snaps to my left, far enough it's clear he doesn't know where I am. "It was an accident. The shirt is just . . . insurance. You know how Garrett's dad is. I had to protect myself. He didn't hurt her on purpose. You know he could never do something like that."

Once, I'd have agreed, fully and without reservation. Once, I'd have apologized for daring to believe otherwise.

I let the bag slip down my arms and shove Garrett's watch inside. It's safer if I hide the backpack here, since I have no hope of hiding from Adam while wearing it.

The lowest branch is far overhead, so I hook the strap over my wrist and leap. My fingers catch on the branch, my body swaying beneath me as Adam calls, "I helped a friend when he needed me most. That's all I did!"

My stomach turns because I can't bear to know what help he provided that ended with Maddie's shirt in his bag.

I plant my feet, climbing higher, fingers sinking into soft moss, until I can hook the backpack's loop onto a pointed nub protruding from the trunk. I could stay here, surrounded by the clean scent of pine in the crisp night air, delicate needles pressing against my fingers. I could be who I always am and give up, give in, let it be someone else's problem. But no one else is coming for me and Maddie's shirt is here and I'm the only one who knows it. I'm the only one who can prove what happened to her.

My feet hit the ground softly—like a feather not a brick—and I strain for any sign he's heard.

"And Nora—fucking *Nora*! I know what she's trying to do. She's trying to pin this all on me. After I saved her from drowning! After I—"

His voice catches, and it stabs straight into my heart. This is *Adam*. The closest I will ever have to a brother. There hasn't been a single part of my life that hasn't included him. I don't know how it's ended here. I don't know how he became this person.

I press my back against the tree, bark cutting into my skin, hands fisted as tears track down my cheeks. There has to be some mistake. The words he's saying, the things he's done.

I'm just confused, misunderstanding. At the end of this, I'll be surrounded by people shaking their heads at Sophie just being Sophie again—blowing it out of proportion, getting it all wrong, letting her head run away with emotion rather than fact. For once I won't mind it.

"Soph? You know me. You *know* me."

His footsteps hedge closer, and it's Nora's voice in my head. *We're conditioned to sympathize with men, Sophie. It's why the worst male characters produce cult followings and a woman of the same personality is metaphorically burned off the page.*

I creep from the tree, weaving between them and keeping to the shadows, tiptoes only, barely disturbing the soil beneath me.

Outrunning Adam is impossible. He's faster than me. Stronger too. Even if I could lose him, I have nowhere to go.

I call out to him. "What was with the creepy texts from Garrett's phone, Adam?"

The second I finish, I race from my spot and to another, leading Adam away.

He disappears into a pocket of darkness, but his voice carries through the trees. "I didn't send those."

My nails scrape into the bark, heavy breaths forming clouds of white that float toward the forest's ceiling. There's a moment, where I let myself believe Garrett is still alive. Because if he is, it means his watch in Adam's trunk is just an accident too. It means I don't have to wonder, for even a minute longer, what happened to him after he left that party with Nora.

Nora.

"I'm not the enemy here, Soph. You need me. *Nora* needs me. I know you lied for her—you didn't tell the cops Garrett left with her that night. She'll go to prison, Soph. Or we can pretend this never happened."

I squeeze my eyes shut, letting the sick feeling wash over and leach into the ground below. Nora sent me those text messages. Nora has Garrett's phone because she was the last person to see him alive. Nora with Garrett's stationery and its monogrammed head-ers. Nora burning the scraps of paper she wrote Maddie's name on. The paper Garrett's note was written on. The paper she handed me so I could piece this all together.

She handed me her confession.

I step from the cover of my tree trunk, holding the GoPro in one hand behind it where he can't see. The wind gusts over me and I have to scrape my hair free, and in that moment, he moves closer.

I can barely stand to look at him, knowing what I know now. Knowing who he is. "Pretend it never happened? Maddie is *dead*."

I didn't know her. I've only known of her existence for a bundle of hours, but none of that matters when I think of her room—the photo board covered in snippets of her life. She was just a girl, dreaming of college like Nora, desperate to earn her place like me. But once she was gone, the world went on like she'd never been.

"It was an *accident*. And she brought it on *herself*." His face is streaked with tears, mottled red, and even through the muted light of the forest his eyes are wild. "She was blackmailing Garrett. Did you know that? The little angel you're willing to sacrifice your sister over? She threatened to expose your boyfriend if he didn't pay up."

"So she deserved to *die*? Is that what you both told yourselves?" Adam could kill me before I have the chance to scream and I *should* be terrified of that. If I were rational, calm, *smart* like Nora, I'd calm him down, talk sensibly so we both left here calmly and . . . not dead.

But I'm not Nora and never have been, and I am angry. It builds

357

inside me like the power of the ocean trapped deep in my stomach, pressing against the edges of my skin. "Did he call 911 after he accidentally killed her? *Did he?!*"

He doesn't respond because there is no response.

"Who did he call instead? Jessica, to go steal things from Maddie's house. Let me guess—his dad?"

It's true, I can see it in every inch of Adam's face. Mr. Packard knew, maybe even Garrett's mom. Garrett called them, and they fixed it all. Made it go away. Made *Maddie* go away. "Then, Adam, he called you. And you . . . what? Gathered up any trace of her? Tossed her into your car and drove to the pier, tossed her over it like trash. She had a *life*, Adam!"

"And so did Garrett!" He barrels forward, stopping just a few feet away, and his voice goes low. "She killed him. Nora killed Garrett. Do I need to spell that out for you? She killed him and you covered for her and so did I."

He scrubs the tears from his face, sadness gone, the Adam I've always known gone with it. "I dragged my best friend's body from the fucking ocean after she left. My *best* fucking friend. And I put him somewhere no one would find him. I did it for *her*. I did it to protect her just like I did for Garrett."

I whisper his name because I can't say anything else. I can't stop the barrage of images his words plant in my head, the horror of every act like something I can't unsee.

He steps closer, hand held out like a peace offering. "We can end this now, Soph. You and me. Nora—she thinks she's doing the right thing, pinning Garrett and Maddie on me, making me seem like the villain, but if the truth comes out—really comes out—she's gonna ruin her life, Sophie. Can you live with that? Can you live with being the reason your sister goes to prison?"

Tears pool in my eyes, and I blink them away, cold by the time they hit my cheeks. "I trust her, Adam, more than anyone in my life. And I know that—"

The forest spins, my heart too heavy to beat right. "Whatever she did, she won't run from it."

He sighs, like he used to do when I'd insist on one more piggy-back ride when I was six, when I'd wake him up at dawn to head to the beach when I was eleven, when just two weeks ago he kissed the top of my head and told me he'd miss me when he was at college.

But I don't recognize him when he closes the distance between us.

"Adam. Come with me. We *can* fix this. By telling the truth. All of it. We—"

"No."

"Adam, *please*." I'm begging. Not just for this, but for everything. For the person I need to believe he still is, and always has been.

I shouldn't trust him. I know I shouldn't. But I can't stop myself either. I can't bear for him to be the person he's showing me right now.

"Please." My voice cracks, tears blurring my vision. "I'll go with you. I'll tell Nora—"

"I need to know where that bag is." There's none of the Adam I know in his voice, and it breaks my heart.

I don't blink when I look him in the eye. "I don't know."

"Sophie."

I whisper, much more to myself than him. "The worst thing you can do to a man is make him admit the things he's done."

His hand darts out to close around my throat, pinning me to the tree behind me, even the slight pressure making it hard to talk, hard to swallow. "I don't want to do this, Sophie. You know I don't."

"Then stop."

He squeezes and my eyes water, my breath wheezing for the threat he's only implying, and he rips the camera away with his free hand. "Tell me. Tell me where—"

I mouth a "No!" because my voice won't work and stars pinprick my vision, gasping for air as my head spins and my limbs flail and some stupid Sophie part of my brain keeps telling me this is Adam. He won't hurt me. Even as he presses harder and my vision narrows I tell myself he'll stop, that he just doesn't know what he's doing.

But he does. He knows now and he knew with Maddie, and if I die here today, no one will ever know about her.

I drive my knee into his groin and he buckles, his grip loosening enough I can stumble free, sucking air through my ravaged throat.

My legs give out, knees thudding to the forest floor, and Adam's hand freezes just inches from mine.

Seconds pass where the world seems to stop, my muddled brain slowly putting the scene before me into place, and Nora says, "Help me move him against a tree."

I blink, everything still covered in spots that blot the forest from view, but then Nora appears, syringe in hand.

She tosses it to the ground to help Adam scoot himself against a tree, and his face mirrors mine. He whispers her name, his hand reaching to cover hers, confusion swimming in his eyes.

360

She crouches beside him, only a few inches apart. "I'm sorry."

Her eyes well with tears, spilling onto her cheeks a moment before her face turns to steel. "I didn't want to have to drug you, but then you nearly killed my sister, so maybe I'm not sorry at all."

I choke out a "Nora," and she stands, brushing the dirt from her palms, and helps pull me from the ground.

She turns back toward Adam, like she doesn't trust him enough to turn her back on him. "He won't be out long. I erred on the side of caution in my calculations."

"Your *calculations*?"

"I borrowed some tranquilizer from the vet clinic."

I press the heels of my hands to my eyes, taking in a full breath for the first time as Adam's eyelids droop. "I don't think you can *borrow* something you can't give back."

She gives a single-shouldered shrug. "I suppose not. I stole it then."

"You drugged him."

She points. "Clearly."

We stand in silence, watching Adam's eyes fall fully closed, until it's just the rush of wind, the chirp of crickets, and I can't take the silence anymore. "You could have just *told* me."

She knows what I mean. Told me everything.

It takes several moments, like she's weighing her words more carefully than she ever has. "Could I have?"

I know the answer, and it's not what I want it to be. *You never let anyone help you.* Not with dance, not with anything. If she'd come to me, I'd have pushed it all away, ignored the evidence because it would be too much to take in, too frightening to believe.

She says, "I'm sorry, Sophie, for so much of what happened," and I whisper back that I know.

She fishes Adam's keys from his pocket and holds them out to me. "Take the camera, the bag, give them to your Detective Tickner. He wouldn't have been my first choice to champion this case, but I suppose we work with what we've been given. He *did* work with the detective on Maddie's case to get it reopened."

Of course she knows that. When I had no clue. Maybe I shouldn't have screamed at him. No, he was an asshole to Jude. He deserved it.

I swallow the lump in my throat, and tears spring to my eyes. "They'll pay for it, right? What they did to her?"

She nods, resolute, like she won't accept any other outcome. "Thanks to you."

My voice barely makes a whisper. "And what about you?"

I lied to protect her. If she asked, I'd do it again. I'd erase all the parts of the video that mentioned her name. I'd look Tickner in the eyes, and I'd swear I never once considered that Nora could've harmed Garrett.

I don't know if that's right or not. If I'm a hypocrite, if I'm everything I hate about Adam and Garrett and Joseph Graham and Mr. Packard and all the evil men that knew a girl was taken from this earth and chose to look away.

I'd do it because I know she'd never ask, because I know there's no end to the things she'd do for me.

She turns to me and smiles, the sheen of tears making her eyes bright in the moonlight. She tucks my hair behind my ear. "I'll be okay."

Her hand drops, grasping tight to mine, so tight my fingers

throb, and I squeeze back, pouring all the words we haven't said into all the places our skin touches.

There's no barrier between us now. No unanswered questions, no lingering doubts. No resentments to splinter us.

In this moment, side by side in the silent woods, beneath the moon and stars bearing witness to the things we've done, we're The Linden Sisters again.

Until Adam stirs, his eyes sliding open, and Nora whispers, "Run."

CHAPTER FORTY-SEVEN
SOPHIE

They find Adam in the woods, tied to the tree I left him by.

They find Jessica, tied to the bumper of her own car.

They did not find Nora.

I stumble into my room, dawn inching over the horizon, a pink-and-red smudge growing wider in the sky, and close the door without a sound.

I gave Tickner the GoPro and Adam's bag. I kept Maddie's shirt. I kept Jessica's phone. I kept Garrett's watch too.

I stopped looking at my phone hours ago, when all the texts and messages got to be too much, when all the news began to spread like a tidal wave crashing against the shore.

My room feels different in a way I can't explain, until understanding crashes into my muddled brain.

The bed is made. Corners pulled tight, pillows carefully placed. I never leave mine anything short of a rumpled disaster.

I whisper, "Who's the creepy one now, Nora?" to the empty room and head to the pillow on the right that sits higher than the other.

It makes no sound when it falls to the floor, revealing a letter beneath it, set above a wide, low-profile box. Next to that, a phone that makes my breathing erratic.

My name sprawls over the front of the envelope in handwriting I've known for every day of my life. The box holds the gold embossed name of a local jeweler, though I doubt Nora has gifted me a necklace.

The lid slips off easily, and several hundred-dollar bills flutter to a stop against my comforter.

My hand shakes as I shift the remaining ones to reveal more, then smaller denominations, until I'm sure their value is in the thousands.

I stuff them all back, cramming the box and letter into a bag.

And then I head to the ocean, to sit on the sand and watch the sunrise, let the crash of waves remind me of the days Nora and I spent side by side, the other never out of reach, and I read Nora's story in the way she needed to tell it.

CHAPTER FORTY-EIGHT

My dearest Sophie,

I hope you can forgive me.

I hope that one day, you'll understand my actions.

I killed Garrett. Or perhaps I didn't stop the universe from doing so.

It may not have been by my hand, it may not have been me that delivered the final blow, but I haven't reconciled whether any of that matters.

In my waking hours, I can convince myself that it does. But at night, when surrounded by only the silence of my thoughts, all the distinctions become the same.

I wrote the letter he left. The pages I burned right outside our home were the ones that failed to adequately imitate Garrett's handwriting. All but one.

By now the police will have received my complete confession, along with supporting documentation including that page of practice. The confession is a detailed account of how and when I came to be involved in the events that led us here. It should not surprise you to know that it all began with a desire to protect you. It was an instinctual compulsion, a fear that overrode all others, that you were too close to something that might cause you harm.

But what Adam claimed is the truth—and my confession is only an approximation of it. You see, there are pieces I failed to include, parts I claimed to lack recollection of.

There is nothing about the moments leading up to this one that I do not remember with vivid, terrifying detail.

I remember the violence of the waves. The strength of their grasp, winding around me, pulling me from my feet until my body went weightless.

I remember the quiet.

My head beneath the surface, the water a cocoon that shielded me from the chaos above, the soft gurgle against my ears.

I remember the rain.

Dotting any surface not marred by the churn of the ocean, an army of droplets, rocketing from the sky to snake over my sodden body as the air greeted me, filling my lungs before the waves pulled me under again.

Until I tumbled onto the packed sand, my limbs heaving and dragging, my fingers curled into claws that dragged me from the depths.

I remember the pain.

Shards of rock and glass and shell and other nameless beings the ocean rejected onto its shores, all of them slicing deep beneath my skin. Flaying open my palms, my knees.

A sacrifice.

A penance.

I remember the moonlight.

Glowing against the night, a silent witness. Glinting from the grains of sand that coated my legs. The salt water that stung my open wounds as I collapsed onto the shore. As I coughed the ocean from my lungs, and with it, all the secrets I cast to the waves.

But before that, I remember manipulating Wentville to gain

access to his office, I remember puncturing my own tire and intentionally exceeding the speed limit in a known trap to create an indisputable record of my actions with Garrett that night. I remember calling Adam to bring him there, to create a greater divide between him and Garrett than their own actions already had. I remember stealing into a certain private investigator's house and waiting for him. (We came to an agreement. If he never came near us again, I wouldn't make use of the same Compound 1080 that he intended for me—that killed Ainsley—to unidentified food products in his home.)

I'm not proud of these things. I don't regret them either.

From the moment I discovered who Maddie was, from the instant I stepped into her room and knew it could have been someone else stepping into yours, I did the things I had to.

Maddie had no sisters, so I made her ours.

I fought for her as fiercely as I would you. I vowed to the memory of her that she would not be forgotten. That she would not be overlooked. We may not be able to give her life, but we can give her justice. Ainsley too. As much as this world allows.

It was never my intention to put you in any harm.

Wentville proved to be an adversary I hadn't anticipated, and for that, I may never forgive myself. I hope you know how hard I tried to always be near. And in my absence, a few friends—one who infiltrated the clan of a certain nemesis of yours, the other you know well but by a different name than you'll find in my confession.

I hope you know how immensely proud of you I am. How I only handed you this burden because I had no doubts you would succeed in ways I couldn't.

And you have, Sophie. In more ways than I could have hoped.

It's very likely you're wondering about the gift I left for you. It's more than enough to cover all necessary costs for your intensive this summer, as well as a portion of your University Arts Conservatory tuition.

In the event you're worried I stole it, I can assure you I did not. I sold something that was ours and nearly taken from us. I simply took it back when we needed it.

The ten thousand dollars that Garrett withdrew the week before his death has been left to the police. I considered giving it to Maddie's family, but it felt far too close to placing a value on her life, when so many others already had.

I'm going away for a bit. Leaving high school and even college behind. I'm not running. I'll atone for my actions and suffer the consequences, but there are several people who need to suffer for theirs first.

Adam did not lie this evening, when he said he killed neither Maddie nor Garrett, but the evidence—and my confession—imply otherwise.

Perhaps it's a miscarriage of justice to do what I've done. To position him as guilty for crimes he has not committed. I do so with no small amount of guilt.

But Adam will tell his story. I know him well enough to ensure it. And in so doing, he will be forced to tell the whole truth, leaving nothing shrouded in secrets, leaving no one who participated in Maddie's death unpunished.

That will take time, and I'm willing to let it. I suppose I've finally found the thing that matters more than the plan I constructed for my future.

You're safe now, free to be fully who you are. Never doubt that you were destined to be any less, that your value is anything short of immeasurable.

If you are asking yourself how I could do all these things. If I recognized the full impact of my actions. The full scope of what I'd be giving up. The answer is yes.

There was no decision I did not make with full understanding or willingness. No action undertaken that I did not perform without the weight of its consequence crushing upon me.

If you're asking just how much I'd be willing to give up for you, dear sister, the answer is simple.

Everything.

CHAPTER FORTY-NINE
EPILOGUE

February 17, 2023
Sophie Linden (simplysophie@umail.com)
To Nora.Linden@umail.com

My dearest Nora,

I don't know if you'll ever read this, or if you've decided to permanently disappear from the grid with Layla to live in a bunker somewhere, but you said you weren't running and I believe you.

That's actually why I'm risking sending you this email even though the cops are still very curious about whether I've talked to you. They seem to think you'll make an excellent witness.

They arrested the private investigator Graham hired, for what he did to you and Ainsley. They arrested Wentville. Jessica Horton too. They found her flip phone when they searched her room, the same as they found Garrett's watch and Maddie's shirt in Adam's. They questioned me on both, but no one really believes me capable of planting evidence. If someone did, clearly they understand the rules of police procedure and chain of custody.

The cheating ring has been exposed—grades, honors, and early admittances being retracted for so many students, and it feels like a victory but it's not the one that matters.

Adam confessed everything, just like you said. They're discussing a plea deal. Today was Garrett's memorial. I didn't go.

I know he paid for what he did to Maddie. I'm glad he did, and I don't know how to feel about that. I don't know how to feel about Adam in prison and Garrett in a grave, and mostly I don't know how to stop feeling like it will never be enough.

There are so many things I want to say, but I'll save them for a day on the beach, in between racing for the biggest shells. I'm not leaving—not for the intensive and not to the University Arts Conservatory—until that happens. Just so you know.

And because she'll never forgive me if I don't say it, Monica* says hi. And that you better be wearing your seat belt.

Come home, Nora. You're safe now too. And I'll be here waiting. A sunflower is nothing without its potato.

ACKNOWLEDGMENTS

I wasn't sure I was capable of writing this book. I knew what I wanted it to be. I knew what the story deserved to be. I just wasn't sure it was in me to do it right. Sibling relationships are messy and complicated and some of the most beautiful connections in existence, and I wanted to do them justice, even when I wasn't sure I could capture that magic on the page.

Despite all that doubt, there were so many people who encouraged me to keep going, who cheered for me even when I was sure this book and its messy timelines had broken my brain. And then there are all the people who helped make it the best version of itself, even after the last word was written. I owe thanks to them all.

To my agent, Chelsea Eberly. I firmly believe that sometimes the universe puts you exactly where you need to be. You are such a relentless advocate, and I am so thankful for the opportunity to work with you. I'm eternally grateful for your guidance and your knowledge of this eternally complicated industry, and I am so very blessed to have you on my side!

To Mallory Kass, editor extraordinaire, who didn't even blink when I sent this book alongside a note that it just might be a disaster. Two books later and I still love working with you just as much as on day one. You are such a source of support and enthusiasm, and I love knowing that my books are safe in your hands. Thank you for everything!

No acknowledgment for *Tell Me No Lies* could possibly be complete without a special thank-you to Maeve Norton, whose genius led to this gorgeous cover. And to everyone at the Scholastic team, who I am so grateful to, for all their hard work and enthusiasm.

To the best group chat. My forever friends. My sisters. Sonia Hartl, Annette Christie, Auriane Desombre, Kelsey Rodkey, Susan Lee, and Rachel Solomon. Would I survive publishing without all of you? Maybe. But let's never test that. Thank you for always being there, for sharing your lives, and for always being a part of mine.

Pitch Wars has been such a blessing, perhaps most importantly because it brought me Emily Thiede and Rajani LaRocca. You are both such a bright spot in my life, and I will cherish you always. I will gladly spend the rest of my existence celebrating all the joy and successes I know are in both your futures!

To Kylie Schachte and Anna Mercier for being some of the earliest and best friends! And to all of PW 17—always and forever the best class of Pitch Wars history.

Every once in a while you come across the rarest, most wonderful type of human, who is giving, selfless, and constant in their support. And that is definitely the amazing Elle Cosimano. I can't express how much your support means, and I am so grateful you're in my life.

To Kara Thomas, who has been so gracious and also happens to be the loveliest human. So honored to have your support!

Major thanks to Kit Frick, who is both a literary inspiration and so incredibly kind and supportive. Thank you for lending your name to all my books!

To my wonderful Pitch Wars mentees, LL Madrid, Elora Ditton, and Erinn Salge. I'm so grateful for the chance to know every one of you, and I will always be your biggest fans.

To Claribel Ortega, who's been there since the beginning. You were always destined for great things, and I've loved watching the world see what you've always been capable of.

Roselle Lim. Everyone deserves a person who understands their every reaction, because they think the exact same. You are my mind-meld person, and I couldn't be happier about it! Love you!

To all my readers and fans who've read and loved my books. I am so grateful for you all!

To all my friends and family for your constant enthusiasm and support.

And to Eva and Joei. If you ever wonder just how much I'd be willing to give up for you, dear daughters, the answer is simple.

Everything.

ABOUT THE AUTHOR

Andrea Contos is an award-winning mystery and thriller writer. She's the author of *Out of the Fire, Tell Me No Lies,* and *Throwaway Girls*. Andrea is the recipient of the International Thriller Writers Award for Best Young Adult Novel, and her debut was named a *Kirkus* Best Book of 2020. Andrea was born in Detroit and currently lives outside the city. Follow her at @Andrea_Contos on Twitter and at @andreaacontos on Instagram, or visit andreacontos.com